HE F
AMONG ARTISTS

STAN FREEDMAN

Stan Freedman was educated as a scientist at London University. He taught biology and environmental studies in schools and colleges in various parts of Britain and has published numerous educational texts for students from school to university level.

He is married with two sons and lives in Yorkshire.

Pam Watling is a graduate of the Royal College of Art. After extensive experience of teaching and lecturing, she has recently become a local councillor.

She is married with one son and lives in Kent.

Stan Freedman

HE FELL AMONG ARTISTS

Cover and illustrations by Pam Watling

"– and what is the use of a book," thought Alice "without pictures or conversations?"

Scaramouche Press

Published 1995
by the Scaramouche Press, 54 Bolton Avenue, Yorkshire, DL10 4BA.

Copyright © in text Stan Freedman.
Copyright © in illustrations Pam Watling 1995.

ISBN 0 9525297 O X

Except in the United States, this book is subject to the condition that it shall not by way of trade or otherwise, be sold, re-sold, hired out or otherwise circulated without the publisher's prior consent in any form of binding or cover other than that in which it is published and without a similar condition including the condition being imposed on the subsequent purchaser.

All rights reserved.

All characters, incidents and locations are fictitious. Any resemblances to real persons, incidents and locations are coincidental.

Printed and bound by Wensleydale Press, Hawes, Yorkshire.

TO PAT, PAUL and THOMAS. For laughing in all the right places.

Chapter One
Across The Great Divide

He knew the job was going to be something different from the way his new boss had worn mirror sunglasses throughout the day. It had been hard not to be affected by the strange distancing effect the glasses lent to the various interview sessions he had undergone. Although these had been with panels of assorted Councillors, Governors and Brindling Polytechnic big-wigs, always there were those enigmatic glasses, occasionally glinting and flashing with, even more disconcertingly, their curved lenses throwing back at him a distorted image of himself, swollen from what he knew to be his actual youthful slimness - skinniness if he was being honest with himself - to a caricature of a bloated Mr. Toad. As this shocking image impinged, he had made a determined resolution never, never to eat or drink excessively, no matter how well his fortunes might be restored should he get the job. He could understand why glasses like these were the favourite interrogation wear for third-world thugs. Whether his interlocutor, Noel de Vere, in charge of the Art and Design Department at Brindling Poly, wore them himself to test the candidates' nerve or because he had something to hide, Brian could not tell. But there was certainly something odd about his manner apart from the glasses; throughout the day he had seemed even more nervous than the applicants.

All the other candidates had complained bitterly amongst themselves about the glasses while they waited their turn in the reception rooms of the main Poly tower building but Brian had not joined in. In his desire to be successful in the interview, his first short-listing for months, he would not have let himself be completely put off even if de Vere had chosen to wear a paper bag over his head. And he had been successful: he was now Lecturer in charge of Information Technology in the Related Studies section of the Department of Art and Design!

Sitting now, at last, at the end of this nerve-stretching day in de Vere's office, tired and elated but still wary, he watched his new boss carefully. He was tall with abundant dark hair becoming grey at the temples, in his long sideburns and neat goatee beard. Brian guessed he had once been slim but his waist now showed a generous, middle-aged spread under his expensive leather jacket and his face was more florid than could be accounted for by the combined heat of the unaccustomed warmth of the late spring day and the central heating in the building. He had still not relaxed, nor had he told Brian any further details of the job. (The description in the job spec. sent to him had been so vague that had Brian not been so desperate he might not have applied at all.) They had come directly to de Vere's office in the old Art School building which housed the Department in the municipal park, and de Vere was now pacing round his desk and the chair in front of it in which Brian was sitting. Occasionally, he stopped and looked out of the window into the park. "Fucking joggers," he said, during one of these pauses, but nothing else.

Brian, from his experience of two years of interviews since his previous college had been closed, was thoroughly adept at recognising when undercurrents were surging below the surface of academic life, and de Vere's manner now and throughout the day, had all the signs of unease. He had noted this especially in the way he had placated and conciliated the other members of the panels no matter what scepticism they let show about his judgement. And they had had scepticism aplenty, not only about the candidates, but about de Vere's intentions as to how the new appointment was to operate. Brian had quickly picked up that de Vere needed an appointee like himself - for what reason he couldn't tell - but had no real idea of what he was to do with him. He sensed trouble brewing somewhere and, as he sat showing an apparent outward calm, he prayed that it would not include him, but he had a nasty feeling that it would. Abruptly, de Vere sat down behind his desk and hunched forward. He slapped a fist into the palm of his hand.

"Right! What we need in this department, Dr. Mather, is some real intellectual muscle. Ok? So from here on in that's you. Savvy? You've got to hit the ground running man, knock 'em dead. Show the Poly we've got some academic balls."

Brian presumed he was staring intently at him from behind the glasses. (The figures of speech de Vere employed were not surprising to him by this time. All day he had been sorting out meaning from the Americanisms with which de Vere peppered his statements. He had gathered that de Vere had spent some time on an exchange in the States about twenty years ago and this seemed to have put a permanent crimp in what Brian guessed was originally his public school English.) Mentally, Brian flexed his intellectual muscles and hefted his academic crotch. He supposed they might just about do: Dr. Brian Mather; first degree in environmental sciences; Ph.D. in numerical analysis of the architecture of Nicholas Hawksmoor; made redundant from a College of Education rationalised away by government fiat; some useful publications. All very fine but what did he really know about art or art students to apply for a job here in the first place? Of course: anything to get off the dole, then promotion, money, marriage, settling down, mortgage, children, pension, death. Smashing! Roll on!

His momentary day-dream that he had made the first step in his life plan was thoroughly unsettled as de Vere went on:

"Intellect-wise, this joint is not the greatest, Dr. Mather, I have to tell you. I mean - look, now we're going to be working together, can I call you Brian? The doctor handle's a bit too much, man. Artists aren't used to titles. It's first names here and with the students too. Ok?"

"Of course," said Brian. Here it comes, he thought, the bit they never tell you. "In what way precisely is this department lacking intellectually, Mr. de Vere?" he said, as innocently as he could muster beyond the alarm he felt at de Vere's surprising confidence to him.

"Noel."

"Er. Noel. I thought it was supposed to be a power-house from the description in the job spec."

"Oh, sure, it is, it is. Of art." Brian detected an ominous hollow ring to his enthusiasm. "Yes. Of art. Of course. No question. Great track record. But it is art and design, you see, that's the point. That's what the guys and gals here are about. Well, mostly Fine Art, actually. Thinking in words isn't their bag." Brian noticed his shoulders droop slightly. "In fact, to be frank, it's pretty dim material I'm stuck with here, Brian." His shoulders fell a few degrees more. "Not to say downright effing thickies!" From the bitter expression of his last words and the sudden total slackening of his posture, Brian guessed de Vere had all his time cut out to cope with the limitations of his staff. De Vere leaned across his desk conspiratorially. "To be honest with you, Brian, I'm the only guy who can cut it here, wordwise. Except maybe Dr. Spill... Never mind that. You see, this is a poly we're in now. In the past when we were on our own we did our own thing but now - well, painting, sculpture, printmaking, film, pots - to people like engineers and the other woodentops, it's all just jerking-off like hobbies their wives do - and we've plenty of them coming here to extra-mural classes. To get anywhere in a poly, you've got to have words. Words!" He hit his palm again. "And numbers, even. Jesus, do you have to have numbers!" He slumped back in his rather posh, executive swivel chair and ran his fingers though his thick, byronically-styled, dark hair. "And words," he finished.

It was obvious to Brian the 'bag' of words and numbers was not really his forte either. Brian was startled as de Vere suddenly lunged from his chair and came aggressively round the desk towards him. Brian flinched but he went straight past him to the filing cabinet near the door and flung open the bottom drawer. There was a crash of glass.

"Let's celebrate," he said. "You're on the team now." He took two tumblers and a bottle of Talisker from the drawer. "You do drink, don't you? Because if you don't, you'll be the forgotten man in this place."

"Yes, I drink," said Brian.

"Good," said de Vere. He poured out two large ones. "To art - whatever that may mean at Brindling Poly," he said, and downed a good half of the measure. Brian sipped his. He hadn't had pure malt for so long he was going to make it last.

"How exactly do you see my helping with words and numbers?" he asked carefully.

"You've got a doctorate in numbers, haven't you? You handled the woodentops on the panel ok. The others all had art back-grounds."

"And what will I be asked to write, exactly?"

"Don't worry. I'll let you know," said de Vere, looking at him appraisingly over his glass. There was knock at the door. "Christ!" said de Vere. "The bastards in this place can smell free drink through a six foot wall." Brian realised the whisky had begun to take the edge off his tension and also the politeness he had been forced into during the day. Brian jumped as he suddenly shouted: "Piss off, will you? I'm busy!"

An angry reply came from beyond the door. "Is that you in there, de Vere?" it said.

Brian was fascinated to see Noel de Vere's over-ruddy complexion drain to ashen white almost instantly as he bleated slightly. "Jesus, it's the Rector," he hissed. He threw the whisky bottle into the cabinet and his glass into a potted plant by the window then rushed to the door, slamming shut the filing cabinet drawer as he did so. Brian thought he detected the sound of breaking glass. Brian had quickly concealed his own glass so de Vere overlooked it in his haste to reach the door. Here he paused very slightly to take a deep breath and Brian sensed him retrieve the politeness he had discarded, "Rector," he said, opening the door, "I'm so sorry. Do come in. I thought it was a student."

"And that is how you speak to them, is it?" said the Rector contemptuously as he entered. "No wonder everybody says this department's a shambles." He crossed to the desk and slammed down a sheet of folded paper.

Brian had seen as much as he wanted of the Rector, Dr. Robson, during the interviews. His pugnacious questioning, especially on the topic of Brian's doctorate, clearly showed he thought Brian had soft-option written all over him. It was only Brian's digital imaging experience which gave him sufficient credibility with the Rector to allow him to approve reluctantly to his appointment at all, a fact he had made abundantly clear by his lukewarm congratulations at the end. These included also a short but pithy appraisal of the worth of art and design as a proper pursuit in Higher Education. He himself was a large, beefy, bouncing ball of a man. His egotism and ambition, Brian guessed, was that of a working-class lad made good through remarkable academic success. He had mentioned at least three times during the day, with considerable pride, that he had never passed the eleven plus but come up the hard way via night school at the Tech, which now formed the core of the Poly. Chatting with other panel members at lunch, they had told Brian - well out of earshot of Dr. Robson - that he had returned fairly recently to Brindling after a long spell as a fiery don in Applied Physics at Cambridge and Brian observed for himself how he relentlessly exploited the pecking-order superiority this gave him, especially with Noel de Vere. In fact, Brian was aware that with Noel - and some of the other panelists as well - his manner had shaded only a whisker away from outright contempt. Brian had made a strong mental note to himself that if he got the job, he would keep Dr. Geoffrey Robson at more than arm's length if he could. And yet, here he was, and not in a good mood apparently. Brian carefully slid his whisky glass out of sight.

"Because that's what they do say, you know," the Rector went on rudely. "A lot of so-called artists and idle students sitting about painting pictures of naked women. What do you think, Mather?" Brian shifted in his seat uncomfortably at this sudden question, forgetting his whisky glass. "From that glass you've got clutched in your fist, I'd say you'd fit into this department very well. Most of them are alcoholics as well as sex maniacs, so they tell me." Brian sensed he was being challenged to fall into his allotted place in the pecking order but before he could think of a suitable reply, de Vere cut in:

"Merely a celebratory slug of red eye, Rector," he laughed nervously. "Would you care to join us?" He opened the drawer of the cabinet, looked in and shut it quickly. Brian definitely heard the sound of broken glass this time.

"Oh. Ah," he said. "Er..."

"I don't need to get through the day with the support of alcohol like some people," said the Rector, with a dismissive gesture at Brian's glass. "There's a good deal too much drinking in this Polytechnic as it is. Every time we have an official function, the place is awash with sherry. And at our expense. Well, now we are a Higher Education Corporation we can do something about that and it's all going to stop. From next session, entertainment will come out of departmental budgets. That'll put a cork in their bottles." He said this with satisfied venom then sniffed with distaste. "This place reeks of whisky. How much have you had? Open a window, man."

De Vere hurried from the filing cabinet to the window leaving a trail of wet footmarks on the parquet floor. Brian saw he had been standing in a pool of Talisker seeping from the filing cabinet. "In any case, I didn't come here to see about the morality of your drinking habits, de Vere, which are no doubt beyond any intervention on my part by now. This is what I came about. This! This!" He banged the folded sheet of paper on the desk.

"What is it?" said de Vere, puzzled.

"Open it up and look, man. It's disgusting." The Rector folded his arms and smouldered. Brian took a surreptitious but deep draught of his whisky; he was very fond of single malt and needed it to steady his nerves. De Vere unfolded the paper and looked at it. After a few seconds he said: "Good Lord!" The image on the paper seemed to have shocked his accent back to its origins, Brian thought, and he was highly intrigued to see what had caused this effect. De Vere removed his sunglasses and looked at it with his head first on one side then the other. (Brian could see now why he had felt it necessary to wear the alienating shades: 'Pissholes in the snow' sprang into his mind as a fair description of Noel's eyes.) He took the paper to the window to get a better light. Brian noticed he avoided the Rector's eye with an embarrassed air. Finally de Vere said:

"It's rather well done, Rector, isn't it?"

Brian flinched as the smoulder burst into flame. "Well done? WELL DONE? What's that got to do with it? It's disgusting! You know what it is, I suppose?"

"Of course," said de Vere. He handed Brian the sheet and replaced his glasses. At first Brian had difficulty making out the object on the print. Then he realised that it was a large multi-coloured image of a female vibrator. About to be used!

"Good Lord!" he said, the shock producing an echo of de Vere.

"Well, what do you think of it?" said the Rector. Brian did not at first realise the Rector was addressing him as he stared fascinated at the image. "Well?" said the Rector. "You must have some opinion or has it struck you dumb? Come on, man, I'm interested to hear what you have to say."

Brian could think of no adequate reply nor why the Rector was showing them the poster, so he handed it back to him and said:

"Whatever turns you on, I suppose."

He realised from the Rector's reaction that this was not an acceptable reply.

"What the hell do you mean by that? By GOD! Are you implying that...?"

Noel de Vere cut in quickly, which Brian, leaning away from the Rector's pugnaciously thrust forward head and loud voice, thought was quite brave of him, with:

"I'm sorry Rector, but I don't understand why you're showing us this."

The fire became a cold one. "I shall tell you why, Mr. de Vere," he said, emphasising the 'mister' heavily, "because these have been appearing fly-posted all over town. On police stations, banks, council offices, solicitors' offices, the law courts, as well as this Polytechnic. Anything remotely official or even respectable. Like church wayside pulpit boards. And what is more damaging still, even " - his voice became very seriously menacing - "in the Town Council chambers. On the portraits of two former lady mayoresses, no less. You should have heard the Leader of the Council on the phone to me just now. And he is not the only one. All the complaints have been flooding in to my desk, de Vere, MY DESK! And it has got to stop, do you hear, it's - got - to - STOP!" He emphasised this last with a bang of his fist on the desk.

"But - But what has it got to do with us?" said de Vere.

Brian was sure he detected a slightly bogus quality in de Vere's bewilderment.

"Don't be a fool, man. It's obviously your art students that are doing it."

"Has anybody any proof of that?" De Vere moved behind his desk and sat down, Brian guessed for protection.

The Rector dismissed this objection with an impatient snort.

"Who else has the skills to produce such things?" he said. "The police say it's been taken from one of those dreadful magazines, blown up to this size and screen-printed. They're all done in different colours. They're even signed with some daft artist's name."

"Are they?" The Rector handed him the poster and he looked at the image closely. "Oh yes. 'Handy Whorehole'." He laughed. "Hey, that's really quite nifty."

At this, the Rector became almost incandescent with rage. He snatched the poster back again.

"I'm glad you can see the funny side of it, de Vere. My wife was confronted with one of these on the door of her bank in the High Street yesterday. She had to come home and lie down from the shock. The doctor says it's put back her treatment for nerves by weeks."

"Of course, I'm very sorry about that, Rector, but I really don't see what I can do without proof." De Vere leaned back in his chair and tried to defuse the Rector's anger. "I can make discreet enquiries, naturally, and I will..."

The Rector stretched right across the desk and put his face close to him.

"Look, de Vere, as you well know, Art and Design has got a quinquennial review coming up next term. If this sort of thing hits the newspapers, this department and its courses will be rubbished from here to kingdom come before the panel even gets to the door. And that will be that! Never mind what it will do to the good name of Brindling Polytechnic. About which, I may say, I am a sight more concerned than protecting you! After all, you hardly covered yourself with glory last time, did you? They're going to go through you with a fine tooth comb, in any case, never mind obscene flyposting to add to all the other charges."

As the Rector stood upright again, a small satisfied smirk about his mouth, Brian realised that de Vere's anxieties during the day were more substantially founded than mere nervousness at the opinions of the 'woodentops'. This was another little item he had omitted to mention.

"You may have realised by now, de Vere, that I am somewhat more tough-minded in my attitude to lame-duck courses than was my predecessor, nice enough chap though he might have been. The days of carrying dead wood are over - except to chuck it on the fire. And if the worst comes to the worst for you, that bunch of illiterate layabouts you call your staff will be out on the streets trying to peddle their pictures to make a living." He turned suddenly to Brian. "And you will be out there with them, young man!"

Brian had been taking another furtive sip of whisky as the Rector spoke to him; he swallowed it badly and began to cough. The Rector looked at him coldly. "Incidentally," he said, "you'll have to undergo a medical examination before we confirm the appointment. If that cough is anything to go by, you may be fortunate to be spared that long." He turned his attention once more to de Vere.

"Of course," he said, "if your staff were any good, they'd be doing that already instead of taking taxpayers' money to spend their time drinking and painting nude women - always assuming they're not producing pornography like this." He waved the poster about and shook his head despairingly. "It was a black day for this Polytechnic when we had to take you lot under our wing."

This last remark finally stung de Vere into retaliation.

"We didn't ask to be lumped in with a bunch of - mechanics, did we? The art college managed quite well for nearly a hundred years on its own."

Having achieved a reaction, Brian sensed the Rector moving in for the kill.

"I think, de Vere," he said, smoothly, "that it would be a good idea to get your staff together now so I can point out to them the seriousness of this poster business, personally. Especially if Polytechnic time and equipment has been used to produce it. Just think of the implications of that."

He folded up the poster calmly and watched Noel de Vere's almost panicky reaction.

"Do you have a problem with my suggestion, Mr. de Vere.?" he said, with his head on one side enquiringly.

"But...," said de Vere, "I mean...Well, it is four-thirty on Friday afternoon. I don't know how many..."

"What you are trying to say - correct me if I'm wrong - is that they've all gone, is that it?"

Brian thought how de Vere really must need those glasses.

"Well...They may be giving tutorials. I'll see if...."

The Rector snorted. "Tutorials! Hah! The working day, even on Fridays, does not end until five in this institution, Mr. de Vere. Five! I think you should do something about that. When I came up here, this building was like the 'Marie Celeste'. I think I'll take a walk around it now and count up many people are still on the premises and actually earning those vast salaries we pay them." He turned to the door. "Perhaps you need to control your people by clocking them in and out. And sort out this poster business. I'm not having the good name of the Polyte...Uhh. What the..." His triumphant exit was spoiled as his foot slipped on the Talisker, now liberally spreading itself from the filing cabinet. It splashed onto his shoes and trousers as he retrieved his balance. "And get this mess cleaned up. It's disgusting."

The door slammed behind him. Noel de Vere let out a long hiss of breath.

"Jesus H. Christ, how I loathe that guy! Pity he didn't break his effing neck. At least it'll cost him a cleaning bill to get the stink of whisky out of his suit."

He came round from the desk and rubbed his shoe thoughtfully in the whisky. Then he opened the drawer and took out the remnant of the bottle. He held it up and looked at it. "Ah, all is not lost." While he retrieved his glass from the potted plant, wiped off the soil and carefully poured in the remainder of the whisky, he continued:

"Of course, the trouble is that just because he's got a few brains and has come up from shit he thinks he's been blown out of God's backside. And he's a physicist as well. Most of those buggers wish they'd never been born as people. That's why they invented the bomb. Ah! That's it! Want another snort? There's a drop left above the glass bits." Brian shook his head. De Vere took a drink. "A bit earthy but passable. As would not anything be after that."

He resumed his seat behind the desk.

"No wonder his wife's going potty. Nice woman too. Much younger than him. Former student of his at Cambridge. Just imagine being shagged by that. She probably has to clock him in and out." He glanced at Brian who had become very thoughtful. "I expect you're wondering if you're wise to take this job, aren't you?"

"I can't deny it was crossing my mind."

"Have you any experience of the thought police?"

"The what?"

"The CN double A. Council for National Academic Awards. The CNAA. The mob who award our degrees and keep an eye on us."

"No, not really. The training college got its degrees validated by the local university. Very civilised arrangement. They took our word for most things and let us get on with it."

"What a nice cosy set-up for you. Edinburgh did the same with their art degrees. Well, CNAA are not like that. They're a very uncosy mob and can be right bastards if you get a panel with a lot of ambitious gits on the make. As you may have gathered we're due for a visit at the end of next term to see if we're still capable of teaching Art and Design." He stood up suddenly, looked out of the window and took an angry pull at his glass. "Christ, it really is a damned sauce. What the hell do they think we've been doing in this college for the last hundred years, teaching cookery? Bloody cheek! It's our centenary year, this year, if you didn't know that, by the way."

"Yes. It was on the information you sent out."

"That's where you come in."

"What?" said Brian. "I don't see...."

De Vere sat behind his desk again and put down his glass. He put both arms on the desk and hunched forward.

"Last time we were told we were - what was it? 'Not relevant to the needs of the times.' Do you know what that means?"

"No."

"Neither do I, and neither, I suspect, do they, except they thought we were old-fashioned, out of date, a bunch of fuddy-duddies because we produced a damned sight better results than most colleges in the traditional areas of the subject using tried and tested teaching. Ok?"

"I suppose so, but ..."

"But what we didn't have was a bunch of whizz-kids flashing their intellectual dicks and blinding everybody with science. Well, from now on, that's you."

"Oh," said Brian.

"Yes. You are now the Mr. Relevant of Brindling art school."

"Am I. I see," said Brian slowly. "That's a bit daunting. You didn't make that clear at the interview."

De Vere leaned back in his swivel chair and swung it from side to side.

"If you were still being interviewed," he said, "wouldn't you use the word 'challenging'?"

"Perhaps. But I do think this might have been made clearer before I accepted the job."

"If you had known it would you have taken it? Your application was right on the spot we need." He leaned forward again on the desk. "Look, I'll play fair with you - I'll give you the chance to back out now if you like. I can always tell the number two candidate the job's his if he wants it. What do you say? By the way, that crack to the Rector was neat. 'Whatever turns you on.' He laughed. "God, his face!"

"I couldn't think of anything else to say. I didn't know he'd take it seriously."

"Of course, it makes you a marked man from now on, you realise that. He's got a very long memory and a nasty mind." He paused and watched Brian's troubled face as he struggled with his thoughts. Not only was he going to be thrust into the limelight as a whizz-kid, which he certainly had never imagined himself to be, but within an hour of getting the job he had made an enemy of the supreme being in the Poly. The day was not turning out as he had expected. Already he could see a chasm opening up between himself and his modest life plan. He took a slow sip of his drink. But it couldn't be worse than the dole. Could it?

De Vere interrupted his thoughts.

"Well, are you in or out?"

"In," said Brian promptly. No, it couldn't, and there might be compensations. "Now I come to think of it, I've always wanted a job where someone actually pays you to consort with naked women and drunken layabouts," he said firmly. "I think it might be my kind of scene, man."

De Vere raised his glass and grinned. "Welcome to the team, then. Come on, down that. I'll show you round the place."

"What about the poster business?"

De Vere gathered up Brian's glass and put it in the filing cabinet, avoiding the now sticky pool of whisky.

"Storm in a piss pot, " he said. "I've got a pretty good idea who's the cookie responsible. I'll get it stopped. If I stamped out smoking grass in the basement, I can squash this quick enough. Get me a sheet of blotting paper from that plan chest will you. Louie won't mind my using his stuff."

"Who's Louie?" said Brian, opening the drawer.

"Course leader. Printmaker. Damned good one too. The students love him. Shares this office. Italian originally. You'll like him if you can follow his version of English."

He spread the cartridge-sized sheet Brian handed him over the whisky.

"So, it is one of your students, the poster?" said Brian.

"Of course. Yours too now. That should do it."

"Yes, I suppose so," said Brian. His heart sank a little when he thought how different they would be from those he was used to. Vibrators! What else? he wondered.

"Get another sheet will you, to make sure." Brian did so and de Vere went on cheerfully: "Not a bad effort, really." Brian could see that he approved of the whole thing. "It's good to see the spirit hasn't been knocked out of them entirely yet. I wonder how they got it into the Council chamber. Still the Rector's right about one thing, bad for our image with a quinquennial in the offing. This whisky is bloody difficult to soak up. Let's have another sheet. Charlie Huggett must have had a fit." He laughed. "Lady mayoresses."

"Who?"

"Leader of the Council, Chairman of the Governors and the local Mr. Big. He was on the interview panel this morning. You must remember him - the one who looked like one of the Kray twins gone bald. The one who was keen to find out why you weren't married."

"Oh, yes. I was wondering about that."

"Trying to find out if you were bent. Has a thing about gays. You're not bent, are you? Not that I give a toss whether you are or not but it's good to know where we stand."

"If you'll pardon the expression?" said Brian

"What?" De Vere looked puzzled. "Oh, yes, I see." He didn't laugh.

"No, I'm not," said Brian

"Good. At least that's one person you don't have to worry about. He wants them all locked up and the key thrown away. Of course, the students are after his blood with that sort of attitude - and all his cronies. Labour mafia, bank managers, police, whatever. They're all on the square as well, you know. Most of them are a bit cracked on religion too. Very odd sort of town, this. Huggett's dead against us, of course. Has us all marked down as nancy boys. Hence the poster. Wankers anonymous. Right. That should do it."

"So, it's political?"

"It's also quite funny. Come on."

Leaving the room, de Vere suddenly stopped and gripped the door frame.

"Christ!" he said.

"What is it?" said Brian, alarmed.

"I just hope nobody on the staff encouraged them. Christ, oh Christ!" He pulled himself together. "Sorry. I get these attacks of paranoia from time to time."

"Are you quite sure you're alright?" said Brian, genuinely concerned.

"Nothing for you to worry about. But I think they're getting worse. I'm getting them before the trouble starts now."

"Probably a reaction to the Rector."

"Probably. But some of them are dopey enough to... Never mind. My problem. Come on."

When they had crossed earlier to the college in the park from the main Poly buildings, Brian's design-historian's eye had taken in the college building and received an impression of its quality. The Victorian half, dedicated to 'The Improvement of the Arts and Crafts of Mankind' as Brian had read on its terra-cotta facade above the entrance, was airy and spacious with its high studios divided into individual work spaces. At one side of the entrance hall was a gallery with its doors and windows covered. De Vere told him a student was working in there on a ceiling painting commissioned for the centenary. Attached to this building was a standard Sixties glass and concrete box divided into four floors with workshops in a long new extension at the back. Looking now with de Vere in detail at his new home, Brian was impressed and felt himself becoming more and more excited about the place he had landed in.

Although, as he had suspected would be the case, there were few students - or staff - about to animate the place, the work in progress which he saw was impressive and, he was relieved to note, very varied; there didn't seem to be a house style which he knew was the bane of some art schools. Those students who were still on the premises greeted de Vere cheerfully with a "Hi, Noel." as he passed. De Vere himself also became more animated and it was obvious to Brian how proud he was of the whole set-up. In one of the cubicles he stopped to take a closer look at the work in progress. He spent some time examining a large charcoal drawing of a still-life of bottles and jars.

"She's been at the Morandi again," he said. (Brian did not know whether this was a liquor or an artist.) "Pretty neat. But that's the sort of thing CNAA hated last time. Well, I'm buggered if we're going to sacrifice that to please them. They can lump it and like it." To a female student in the space next door, he said:

"Is Connie Grey around?"

The student said she'd gone ages ago. De Vere asked her to tell her to see him first thing on Monday morning without fail. He also left a note.

He was thoughtful as they moved on and did not say anything until they were making their way along a corridor on the upper floor of the old building to the entrance hall. "She's the phantom bill sticker," he said at last. "Although I suppose she'll be cross I told anyone. At least, I'm pretty sure she is."

"A girl?" said Brian.

"Why not? Well, woman, I suppose. A bit older than the general run of our students. American. She's usually at the bottom of the political stuff. Shit-hot student, though. No doubt you'll meet her soon enough. She's quite intrigued about this job of yours. Especially the computer bit.

But..." he stopped and held Brian's arm.

"Yes?" said Brian, puzzled.

"Anything she asks you for, you clear it with me first. Ok?"

"Fine," said Brian. "Of course."

"And don't mention I told you about the posters."

They were descending the polished granite staircase back to the entrance hall when an agitated young woman's voice called to them from the landing above.

"Noel! Noel! Hold on. It's quite important."

She came rapidly down the stairs. As she did so her full summer dress billowed out, and Brian had a glimpse of a good pair of legs shod, he noticed, with sensible shoes. She was about his age with fair hair tied in a bun at the back, some of which had escaped to the side. She was of medium height and fresh-complexioned, pretty but slightly plump and gave an impression of scattiness but whether this was from her rushed descent which had flushed her face or was her general demeanour, Brian couldn't tell. Altogether she was attractive and Brian hoped she was one of the staff rather than a student.

"What is it, Hermione?" said de Vere wearily. "Can't it wait till Monday? I've had a hell of a day."

"No, I don't think it can, Noel. I've been searching the building for you. Oh, I'm quite puffed out! All those stairs." She took a deep breath and her words came out in an excited rush. "Did you know there's a strange man wandering round the building?"

"Oh shit!" said Noel. "Not another wino from the park. How do you know?"

"Well, I was sitting in the staff room when he came in and glared at me very angrily. I asked what he wanted but he just muttered something about "At least there's one them here and she's got some clothes on which makes a change." and went out. I was terrified, I can tell you. He must have been disgustingly drunk because he absolutely stank of whisky. Could he be a rapist, do you think? Anyway, you've no need to worry, I called the police straight away. They came about five minutes ago and started searching the building."

Noel de Vere sank slowly down on the steps. He took off his glasses, formed his hands deliberately into a cup and carefully placed them over this face. From behind his hands there was forced a strangled, rather high-pitched voice.

"Oh dear," it said, with a matter-of-fact expression. "Oh deary, deary me."

Hermione was alarmed. "Are you alright, Noel?" she asked him.

De Vere pulled himself together and rose. Suddenly, there came the sounds of a violent altercation from below. They looked over the balustrade. Into the hall came two policemen dragging the figure of a loudly protesting and struggling Rector, followed by a bunch of students cheering them on.

"That's him!" she said excitedly. "Gosh, isn't he an ugly brute? An alcoholic out of the park. He absolutely stank of the stuff. Well done!" she called out to the policemen.

De Vere pulled her back. "Stay there and keep out of sight, for Christ's sake," he said urgently, and dashed down the stairs.

"Hold on, hold on, constables. There's been a terrible mistake."

Hermione turned to Brian. "This sort of thing happens all the time, you know," she said. "They come in because the students are quite sympathetic. This part of the building is so old, there are lots of convenient cubby-holes for them to hide in. The caretaker's dogs usually flush them out, though." She held out her hand. "I'm Hermione James, by the way. I/c Art History for my sins." She had to shout this to get it over the noise from the hallway below. "You must be Brian Mather. I heard you got the job. Congratulations." They shook hands and she smiled at him warmly. Brian smiled back and shouted above the din:

"How do you do and thank you. You don't know who that is down there, then?"

"Good heavens, no! Why should I?"

"I hate to tell you this but it is actually the Rector of the Polytechnic."

"No! Oh dear, what have I done? I mean, I know I'm far too humble a member of staff ever to have been vouchsafed even a glimpse of the creature. In fact, I thought he never came out of that Eagle's Nest he hides in at the top of the Poly tower. But it was a natural mistake, after all. He really did reek of alcohol. The Rector, you say, well, well, well! And an alcoholic to boot. Perhaps this will teach him to get to know the hewers of wood and drawers of water on his staff a bit better in future." She grinned and seemed not at all put out by what she had done. "I say, what a lark!" She began to chuckle. Her chuckle was infectious and Brian began to grin broadly along with it. "What's going on, I wonder?" she said. They peered over the balustrade at the noisy group below. One of the policemen was waving the obscene poster. He was assuring Noel that: "We've got this bastard dead to rights, sir. The evidence was right here in his hand." The Rector was bellowing dire threats to all and sundry while the students chanted "'Ere we go. 'Ere we go. 'Ere we go." De Vere was trying to make the policemen hear above the din.

"Do you know," said Hermione, "I think it might be a good idea to slip out of the side door, don't you? Come on, before the beak spots us."

Hermione offered him a lift when they had got to the calm of the park outside but Brian declined. He wanted to sort out the events of the day in peace. She congratulated him again, said she would see him next term, got into her car and drove off. Brian stood for a moment reflecting on what a nice, normal woman she seemed and what a contrast to de Vere and the Rector. Between them, those two had created such an air of unreality in the last hour that he was finding it difficult to shake off the dream-like state into which his mind had fallen. Of course, the Talisker didn't help, either.

"I got the job," he said out loud to reassure himself. He was surprised to realise that such a mundane statement belonged to the rational world of interviews and careers and logical life plans he had come to Brindling with only that morning. Somehow, in the intervening time since then, he seemed to have crossed an invisible fault-line where those sorts of ideas were for another person entirely. 'Mr. Relevant' he now was, for good or ill. What the heck, he thought, did that mean? He blew out a loud breath and set off down the drive. Approaching the gates of the park in the late afternoon sunshine, he had to leap aside abruptly as a large limousine roared past him and screeched out to the road beyond. Brian caught a beetroot blur of the Rector's face behind the wheel. He had obviously not seen Brian at all. A few moments later, the patrol car exited similarly. Brian noted that both cars had the obscene poster stuck to their rear ends. Glancing back to the college, he saw that Noel de Vere was sitting on the front steps, his face once more carefully covered by his cupped hands. Yes, he thought, it was definitely going to be a different sort of a job.

Chapter Two
A Deeper Chasm

"I'm sorry I haven't been to your course before, Dr. Mather. I've just had VD."

Brian picked up the notes for his just-completed lecture from the lectern in front of him, shuffled through them distractedly and switched off the projector as he tried to seek inspiration for a reply. The girl, a pretty brunette, incongruously but attractively dressed in a merchant navy officer's uniform, smiled at him with wide-eyed innocence. Oh God, thought Brian, not another one.

Since the start of the summer term, four weeks previously, the women students had been deliberately setting him challenges like this, testing out his instinctive reflexes. It had begun almost immediately when he had made the mistake of titling his first year course 'Landscape and Man'. He cursed himself afterwards but during the time he had been out of Higher Education, he had not realised how deep the virus of feminism had gone. In his previous college, the title had provoked no response at all; most of the students were too concerned only to get through the next day's battle with schoolchildren to worry whether his course title was sexist or not. In Brindling art school, on the other hand, he now knew the title was an immediate challenge and within a few hours his notice announcing his course had been decorated with a variety of visual and verbal obscene feminist interpretations. One of these had stuck to it as a nickname and it became, to Brian's considerable chagrin, known to everybody - staff included - as 'Rocks and Cocks', despite an overnight change of title to 'Landscape and People.'

As he tidied his notes, Brian realised it would be quite hopeless to try and match the particular challenge still being smiled up at him. He noticed also that her friends were taking an unusually long time to leave the lecture theatre and wondered if she genuinely had had VD. Not improbable, he thought, given the uniform.

"Er. Well, don't let it happen again," he said, stowing his papers and snapping his briefcase shut. "And make sure you catch up with the notes."

He pushed open the door of the lecture room and gritted his teeth at the peal of feminine laughter which followed him. However, he sensed it was good-natured on the whole. In spite of the baiting he was receiving from the women, he knew his courses were quite popular. He had been waiting for years for a chance to spread his radical ideas to an audience willing to listen in Brindling he had at last found one. He knew they were interested because they actually bothered to attend his lectures. His colleagues assured him that, had they not found them interesting, they would have simply voted with their feet - and that would have been that. Art students were not like other students, they told him; it was what they did with their hands that counted and failure in theoretical subjects held no terrors whatsoever for them. So, even to get them to attend at all was an accolade, especially this late in the working day. Brian wondered, after what the Rector had said about timekeeping, whether de Vere had deliberately timetabled him for the most awkward spot in the day as a sort of test.

He made his way to the now empty staff room, glanced into his pigeon-hole and groaned as he picked yet another all-too-increasingly familiar blue memo form. That meant it was from Noel de Vere. As part of his managerial efficiency drive, de Vere had had all memos colour-coded: from him blue, from the secretary pink, and from the staff to anybody the sort of beige which, to Brian, recalled the unbleached lavatory paper he'd come across on a trip to eastern Europe a decade ago. Since the beginning of term, the memos from Noel de Vere - known to the staff as 'blue meanies' - had rapidly developed from a trickle to a torrent. The incipient paranoia which had been evident on Brian's interview day had been fanned by the vibrator incident and its aftermath into a raging complex. Brian had never seen such a traumatic change in a man; de Vere seemed almost another person entirely from the man he had met at his interview. Brian found that studying a dramatic personality change like this at close quarters was both fascinating and frightening. But in a new job he could well have done without it.

On his first day in his new job, Brian discovered that the poster-making had indeed been helped by a member of staff, although the man had innocently assumed it was a satirical student project on Warhol's 'Monroe' series and the Department's screen-printing facilities had churned them out. Whether the particular woman student de Vere had identified as the perpetrator of the fly-posting campaign was actually so, he could not discover. In fact, the college gossip was completely tight-lipped on the subject, an almost unprecedented occurrence in Brindling art school, apparently. Whatever the details, even though no more posters had appeared, the effect on de Vere had been devastating. Everything now threatened disaster. Nothing could be left to chance for the validation visit at the end of term. Although all the staff were being subjected to mental cruelty by memo form - Louie had told Brian that de Vere even sent them across to him sitting at the very next desk in their shared room - Brian knew, as Mr. Relevant, the new straight man of the art school, that he was a particular target. The mis-titling of his course had been fuel to the flames of Noel de Vere's fears and he was watching Brian's every move.

This memo was not specifically directed to him for once but a general one announcing a meeting. It was couched in the usual polyspeak which Brian guessed de Vere had adopted the better to demonstrate his dynamic managerial approach. It was peppered with 'outwith's', 'ongoing's', 'valid's', 'pertinent's' and similar left-over jargon of the Seventies, so much favoured, Brian noted, by almost everybody in Brindling Polytechnic that it was almost a house-style. What the memo actually said was that there would be a meeting of the Course Board to discuss arrangements for the CNAA visit, two days hence at 2 p.m. (or '1400 hrs' as it was put).

Brian picked up the internal telephone and dialled de Vere's secretary.

"Myra, have a look in de Vere's diary will you, please, and find out when this meeting is on Thursday afternoon."

"It's at four o'clock, Dr. Mather."

"Thanks," said Brian. He corrected the memo with a bright red felt pen and stuck it on the notice board. He then wrote out a memo of his own to Noel de Vere in large red letters, which he was disappointed to observe lost something on the brown background - he could see now why Noel had chosen that colour - pointing out the error and put it in the internal mail box.

Brian had taken to spending most evenings in the college library to save his heating and lighting bills, but, as he was due to give a lecture that evening to the extra-mural students, he settled down to go through his notes and take a nap. After about an hour he had dozed off but awoke with a start when a door in the corner of the room which he had not really registered before, assuming it was a cupboard, opened suddenly. Around it was cautiously poked the head of a man, tall, thin, and balding with spectacles. Brian had never seen him before. He registered Brian's presence with surprise and pulled the door as if to close it again but decided against it. There was a pause while he looked Brian over carefully. Brian returned his stare.

"Ah," he said eventually. Then he came out and closed the door behind him. He was wearing a suit - which meant to Brian he was not one of the artists - and carrying a mackintosh and briefcase. He cleared his throat officiously as he made smartly for the open door of the staff room.

"Hold on," said Brian, "can I help you?"

"Tick, tock. Tick, tock," said the man, and left the room.

Brian stood up and followed him out. He was moving quickly down the corridor.

"Look here, who are you?" Brian called after him.

The man did not answer but increased his pace. Nor did he slacken it as he reached the stairs. Brian had a sudden apprehension that he might fall and there would be nothing he could do for him, but he slipped down the polished granite with such expertise that Brian was immediately convinced he must have done it many times before. In a moment he was across the hall and through the front doors. As Brian descended the staircase more cautiously after him - the treads were notoriously tricky - he noticed Ridley, the caretaker, sweeping the floor at the side of the hall. As usual, he was muttering to himself and, as usual, he was accompanied by his two savage black labrador dogs. Brian had been warned by the staff to give both Ridley and the dogs a wide berth and especially not to come into the college late at night as Ridley loosed them into the corridors. Brian descended; the dogs rose and began to growl. He decided to go no further and called to Ridley from half-way down.

"Did you see that man?"

"Bloody students. Muck and crap. Eh? What?" said Ridley. "Belt up you stupid — sods. You speaking to me?"

"Did you see him. That man?"

"What man?"

"The man who just went out." Ridley paused, stuck his tongue in his cheek and rearranged his cap as he thought. Finally, he said:

"No. I never seen — nobody."

Brian had also been told of the peculiar way Ridley's speech impediment left odd gaps in his sentences.

"But you must have seen him. You were in the hall when he went out of the front doors. Tall, thin bloke in a suit. Brief-case and glasses. You must have seen him. Or at least heard him behind..." It dawned on Brian that the man had made almost no sound as he moved.

Ridley shook his head. "Couldn't have been nobody, else the - dogs would have - sounded off, wouldn't they?" he said triumphantly. He stared at Brian defying him to insist further. Brian knew from his manner that he had seen or at least been aware of the man but why hadn't the dogs gone for him? Whether Ridley was denying it from sheer cussedness or some other more obscure or even sinister reason, he didn't know.

He descended the rest of the stairs keeping a wary eye on the dogs who watched him longingly, and went out of the front door but there was no sign of the mysterious stranger. When he returned, Ridley and the dogs had gone. He made his way slowly for the stairs again, completely foxed, but a female voice halted him with:

"I saw him."

She was standing by the rack of student pigeon-holes tucked under the staircase. She moved into the better light of the hallway and Brian felt an electric jolt of adrenaline trigger a faster pace to his pulse. She was petite and very pretty with a style all her own but older than the normal run of students. Probably about twenty-three or four, Brian thought, and her clothes struck him as a real breath of fresh air after the off-putting protective colouration of hand-me-down Oxfam drab, which poverty and the molesting tendencies of the local hooligans forced most of the female students in the college to wear. In contrast, she was strikingly dressed in a blue sari, its shade almost exactly matching the colour of her eyes, which were artfully made-up. Brian wondered briefly whether the sari was a demonstration of ethnic solidarity, ironic comment, or simply to show off the ivory slimness of her bare waistline. Whatever the reason, its unexpected effect in juxtaposition with her blonde, curly hair and her lightly tanned skin was striking. In the theatre of costume Brian gave her a standing ovation. He also registered that she was an American.

"Thank goodness," he said. "I was beginning to think I was seeing things. Who was he, do you know?"

"I think he might be the one the students call 'The Invisible Lecturer'," she said. Brian noted the way she had separated herself slightly from the other students in her answer. "Hi, by the way. I'm Connie Grey." She held out her hand.

"Hello," said Brian taking it. It was warm and dry with the hint of a squeeze. He swallowed and his voice caught slightly as he replied. "You're - er - you're doing the ceiling in the gallery, aren't you? I'm...Excuse me." He coughed again loudly to clear his throat. This was embarrassing.

"Dr. Brian Mather," she said, and smiled her amusement at his stumble. "Yes, I know. All the women here know that. I've been meaning to come and see you. I need your help badly."

Brian felt his adrenals rev up again. Her voice was soft and her accent was not one of the standard ones familiar to him from movies but much rarer with musical and beautifully modulated vowel sounds. He vaguely thought it might owe a lot to a very expensive education. New England, perhaps? Whatever its origins, he guessed that, with the male psyche as its target, and reinforced by those quizzical and amused electric-blue eyes, its effect would have to be explosive. At least, that's how it felt to him.

"I'll be pleased to give you any help I can." Brian felt his face flushing slightly. Damn, he thought.

"Great. Know anything about computer graphics? You know, digital imaging and stuff?"

"A bit. Look, what was that you said about an invisible lecturer?"

"Well, there's a guy on the staff here no students ever see. I forget his name. He gives his lectures as tape-and-slide shows on aesthetics. The technician puts them on. And you just hand in your essays and they come back in your pigeon-hole marked."

"Good Lord," said Brian. "It couldn't be Spiller, his name, could it?"

"That's it, yes."

Since the beginning of term Brian had been trying to contact Dr. Oswald Spiller, to whom, as head of his section, he was ostensibly responsible, completely without success. Notes sent in the internal mail produced no response; he didn't seem to have a room of his own or a telephone extension and whenever Brian enquired about him, his colleagues became extremely vague, not to say downright shifty. Even Myra Tomlinson, the secretary, whose efficiency and helpfulness were legendary, could not - or would not - tell him anything about Spiller except that he was, like herself, one of the 'old stagers' from those halcyon days when the art school was run directly by the local authority. And all he got from Noel de Vere on the subject was a cryptic: "Let sleeping crosses lie, man. It is not pertinent to our ongoing plans at this moment in time." Which helped him not one bit.

"Look," she said, "could I come and see you in a few days? I'll know better what I need then."

"Fine," said Brian. "You say this Spiller gives his lectures on tape?"

"Yes." Brian noted absently from her responses that the oddities of Dr. Spiller seemed not to interest her.

"Say two o'clock on Friday. Will that be ok?"

"Er. Fine, fine," said Brian, still pre-occupied.

Connie spoke again and Brian realised she was trying to force his attention deliberately back to herself.

"By the way, they tell me you used to be an actor."

How on earth did she find that out, he wondered. He always played down on his CV the three years he'd had trying to make a break into theatre after his first degree. He was still unsure of how the intelligence grapevine worked in the Department. From the gossip he had picked up already, he guessed nobody would be able to keep anything secret for very long - except Dr. Oswald Spiller, apparently. And the phantom fly-poster, of course. Could it really be this super young woman, as de Vere had suspected?

"Well, for a short spell, yes."

She smiled broadly at him. "Did you blush like that on stage when you had to kiss the leading lady?"

Damn! Damn! And double damn! he thought. "I'm a bit rusty."

"Oh, I wouldn't say that."

"And the only time I got to kiss anybody on stage was on the cheek of the fat one of the Ugly Sisters. I was the thin one."

She laughed, and Brian was about to follow up this, to him, delightful turn in the conversation, when it was interrupted by the opening of the front door behind him. Connie looked past him and moved to give a warm greeting to the young woman who entered and for whom she had evidently been waiting.

"Hi!" she said.

"Sorry I'm late, Connie," said the woman. "Oh!" She became suddenly confused and uncertain as she saw Brian. In her arms she was holding a baby and quickly pulled the white lace shawl it was wrapped in over its head as if to shield it from Brian's inspection.

"It's alright. He's not one of the artists," Connie said, which Brian thought was odd. "See you on Friday about two? If that's ok, Brian?"

"Great, yes." He was aware that by the casual familiarity of the way she said this she had signalled that he might be of more interest to her than simply a source of expertise about computer graphics. Or was that how all Americans talked? It would be interesting to find out, he hoped. She and the woman went over to the door of the gallery and Connie unlocked it, talking in much lowered tones. Brian wondered who the woman was and why seeing him had so upset her. She was older than Connie, dark-haired and attractive. She looked very intelligent and her voice was cultivated standard English, with no trace of Brindling about it. Certainly she was not another student he concluded from the smart green two-piece she was wearing, never mind the baby. He moved to the staircase and began to climb it, aware that both women were waiting at the door of the gallery for him to leave before they went in. He knew that the security on the ceiling painting was total; even de Vere was not allowed to view it. As Connie was the apple of his eye, he let her get on with it. Brian wondered idly why she was so careful: another mystery - but nothing to rival that of Oswald Spiller, 'The Invisible Lecturer'.

One of the aspects of Brindling's art department which long predated the formation of the Polytechnic, Brian found on taking up his post, was its flourishing extra-mural section. It had become a tradition that any new member of staff should present his credentials to the community of evening students in a seminar or lecture, even though they might never see the evening students formally again. Brian was not going to be an exception to this rule, de Vere insisted. So, with the time fast approaching for his lecture, although he carefully examined the locked door in the staff room from which Spiller had emerged, he had no opportunity that evening to investigate further what might lie behind it.

Noel de Vere had told Brian that he had ambitious plans to develop extra-mural studies beyond the leisure art and design function it had fulfilled for many years. The courses were already always heavily oversubscribed and many of the students had considerable talent so the potential was there. As de Vere expressed it to Brian, the plan was to: "enhance the ongoing community pertinence of the Department". Brian reflected that polyspeak was beginning to corrode de Vere's speech patterns as well as his memo-writing.

The lecture he gave that evening was on 'The Concept of Value in Traditional Chinese Art'. He had mugged it up from notes he had made during his extensive reading whilst on the dole and it was enhanced by slides from the Department's collection, which, he had been stunned to find, was quite enormous. (He had also noted that many of the slides in sections dealing with non-western cultures had been acquired to service Oswald Spiller's aesthetics courses. He made a note to himself while giving his lecture to borrow some of the tapes Connie had mentioned and listen to them himself.) He was aware that a significant number of the extra-mural students in his audience were highly educated wives of Polytechnic staff so he had given what he thought was a humdinger of a lecture, not sparing any rigour he could get into it for the sake of the less academic members of extra-mural. Not that this seemed to have put anybody off. He had not noticed any shuffling or yawning and judged that the talk had gone down well with the audience as a whole. Questions and discussion followed. Here, for the first time he began to taste the pungent flavour of the local community.

De Vere had warned him not to be too controversial and, in uncorroded terms, had told him to: "for Christ's sake, keep off politics"; in Bindling it always led to trouble, apparently. He had thought while preparing the lecture that the function of jade, pots and paper sculpture in Chinese village society and their relation to Taoist beliefs in remote times would be sufficiently removed from everyday Brindling to fulfil de Vere's strictures. But, as the discussion developed, he soon realised his optimism in this respect had been misplaced; it seemed that in Brindling a talent for polemics ensured that almost anything could be made over politically. Within a few minutes, local polemics had displaced civilised discussion and the audience polarised into left and right. Brian also realised that the students had seated themselves that way before he had even begun his lecture.

Brian leaned on the lectern, tapping it, and coughing and making other ineffectual attempts to call them to order. He could see that most of his audience was utterly uninterested in order - or compromise.

On the right were those who were convinced that only an elite could properly appreciate and commission art works of quality. This group was led by a large, vivacious woman - in her late thirties, Brian guessed - with a lot of unruly dark hair and a commanding voice whom everybody addressed as Audrey. She pointed out that Brian had shown - looking at him with a big smile as she said it - that in Chinese villages, the community elite circulated the works amongst themselves by auction and used the surplus to fund rice for the poor. Without this wealth and enterprise of the rich there simply would be no surpluses. Hadn't Maggie clearly shown that in her brilliant exposition of the significance of the parable about the Good Samaritan? she said triumphantly. She concluded by dismissing the arguments of the opposition with the statement that: "Anyway, there's never any point putting pearls before swine - especially not the ones in this town." It took no guessing on Brian's part as to whom she regarded as the swine in Brindling.

On the left were the supporters of the communal function of art. They believed that valuable artifacts should exist only for the benefit of the community and the true art of a society, like the communal paper sculptures the Chinese villagers made and burned every year, lay in its collective efforts. In their definition, the precious objects should belong to or be used by everybody and, today, that meant large cars, houses, antiques and anything else owned by the rich, whom they accused of all being in the "bloody forty thieves" and nicking them by exploiting the workers, anyway. Brian did not understand the 'forty thieves' reference but from Audrey's hot rejoinder about the "bloody unions" it obviously stung her.

Brian perceived that this polarisation had very little to do with art, Chinese or otherwise, but represented a fundamental division in Brindling society. From the acrimony and fist-waving it began to generate, he thought it would be a good idea to avoid Brindling as a community as much as he could. In his previous post, he had worked as an unpaid adviser on listed buildings and their conservation to the Council of the rather sleepy southern market town in which his college was situated, but this evening alone had given him sufficient warning not to try the same here. He was rather obliged to the students, in spite of their noisy shouting match which was giving him a headache, for the insight.

Although the apparent political division he discerned in the room seemed obvious, he was nevertheless very surprised as the discussion became more personal, to discover that Audrey was, in fact, the wife of a very prominent Labour Councillor. He had already sensed there was more to Brindling's politics than met the eye.

He had been checking the back numbers of the local newspaper to familiarise himself with the town and had discovered that the press was so far to the right in its politics, that when a Lib-Dem candidate won a by-election from a Tory, the headline was invariably '----- Lost!'. He had also discovered that the Council was dominated by a Labour group of almost monumental indifference to public opinion. (Another fact he had dug up from his researches was that no public criticism was tolerated from members of the Polytechnic of any aspect of the Town Council's activities on pain of dismissal even. He found this extraordinary, but it had actually been agreed to by the staff of the old Tech in a vote many years ago and applied now to the Polytechnic. What sort of people were his colleagues, he wondered?) He did not yet know who were the gainers and losers in the town but his instincts told him that Brindling had the whiff about it of the classic rotten borough - late twentieth century style.

Sitting on the fence in the discussion were the Poly wives, whose expressions told Brian they were quite used to this split and found it very boring. They also appealed to him by their expressions to finish it as soon as he could. He tried this by harder tapping, looking significantly at the clock, packing up his notes and moving from the lectern, but the two sides were in full flow and would not be thwarted so easily. Both left and right claimed him as an ally but he took good care to be non-committal and it was only when it had all degenerated into the inevitable and tedious 'Maggie in!', 'Maggie out!' phase that he was able to stop them.

Audrey gave him a vote of thanks for the lively evening he had provided by his fascinating lecture and hoped they would have many more from him, especially now that extra-mural was to become much more integrated into the Department's development plans, a prospect Brian found particularly daunting. During her short speech, she managed to mention twice, her eyes shining with the excitement of battle and her broad smile beamed at Brian, that she was the Course Board rep. for extramural. Brian smiled back wanly and tried to look pleased for her. He thought of one small compensation as she spoke: at least they'd obviously listened to the lecture (even if they had managed to miss entirely the significance of the Tao in Chinese art) which in any teacher's life was a bonus to discover.

He began to sort his slides in the projection booth at the rear of the lecture theatre, together with those he had forgotten a few hours previously in his haste to escape from the baiting by the women students. Audrey came in to join him. The rest had gone off to the life class, still arguing amongst themselves.

"I hope all that hasn't put you off us?" she said, laughing. Her face was still flushed as she pushed her hair into place.

Brian laughed too, a stage laugh he was practised in. "Not at all," he said. "Spice of life to a teacher." Like the headache he was now nursing.

"That Labour lot will say black's white if it suits them."

"But..." he said.

"Yes?"

"I thought your husband was a Labour Councillor."

"He is. But that's not real politics, is it?"

"Isn't it?"

"No. That's just the Council. He never tells me what he votes in general elections. Could be Tory for all I know. Or care, frankly."

"I see." Brian mentally hoisted a warning flag at the "Or care, frankly" and the way it was said.

"I'm Audrey Reaper, by the way," she said, extending her hand. Brian shook it. It was large with a strong grip and felt housewifely roughened. She leaned against the wall and watched him as he boxed the slides.

"I gather you're the Course Board rep." he said.

"That's right, although I rarely get to meetings as they're during the day and I'm at work." Thank God for that, he thought. "But Noel and I work closely together."

She said de Vere's name with proprietorial pride. In her voice he detected a local accent concealed by heavily massaged vowel sounds. During the shouting match the disguise had begun to slip but was now firmly under control again. She wore a good deal of make up and - he registered this close to - quite a dousing of perfume which filled the small booth with its heady scent. 'California Poppy' he guessed, which was a particular bane of his and made him feel slightly nauseous on top of his headache. He hadn't thought they made it any more. There was also something else mixed in as well. Sherry! That was it. Was she masking the smell of the drink with the perfume? He tried to look as busy as possible with the slides but was aware she had moved along the wall closer to him. Like most of the female students in the evening class she was dressed in a voluminous wrap-around with many paint stains on it and the sleeves rolled up. But he could see nevertheless that her figure within it amply matched her height.

"You know," she said, folding her bare, muscular arms and looking at him with her head on one side, "this close to, you remind me of someone."

"Oh, do I? Somebody nice, I hope?"

"I'm not sure."

Brian was nonplussed by this. Candour was clearly another trait she had cultivated as well as the accent.

"Well, somebody interesting then?"

"Oh yes, definitely interesting. And very thin, like you."

"Oh, good," he said drily.

"Were you always thin?"

"Quite thin, yes." He was not about to tell her how two years of the dole had trimmed off even the little natural fat he had had.

"Now, how do you like it here?"

"It's fine. Just fine," he said.

"Where are you living?"

Brian named the street. Audrey was horrified. "Oh, you poor man," she said, and stood away from the wall. She reached out her hand involuntarily to touch his shoulder in a gesture of sympathy but hesitated and withdrew it. "It's awful," she said, and subsided against the wall once more. "Sorry, I shouldn't have said that."

Brian thought, then said: "Not at all. It is awful."

"Surely, you could have affor... I'm sorry, I know it's none of my business, but I hate to think of anybody living round there."

"It's handy and I can walk to work."

"You've not got a car, then?"

"No."

"Not that the wheels would stay on it for five minutes in that street. Of course, there are worse places in this town, like the 'Tofts', for instance. Look, could I give you some advice?"

"Of course."

"Just watch the ceilings," she said.

"The ceilings?" said Brian, puzzled.

"Yes, they go along the lofts and come down through the ceilings. There's a lot of petty burglaries in this town and that area's one of the worst. Brindling has the highest rate of petty crime in the country for its size, you know." She said this last almost with pride, Brian thought.

"Thanks for the tip," he said, although he had no idea how to stop anybody busting in through a ceiling. Did they come in like the SAS, he wondered, with stun grenades and smoke bombs? They'd find thin pickings in his flat for their trouble. A few old underpants and dirty socks, if they were lucky.

"You're welcome," she said. "You're around the college a lot in the evenings, aren't you?" she said. "I often see you in the library."

"Yes. I've got a lot of reading to catch up on." And a large overdraft to clear, he thought.

"Good. Perhaps I could come along and have a chat about art sometimes."

He'd have to find somewhere else to spend his evenings now. Damn! He put the last of the slides in their place and closed the box.

"Well, I'll say goodnight, then," he said, and tried to move past her to the door of the projection booth. In the cramped confines of the booth he had to move very close to her. As he did so, she stood quickly away from the wall and squeezed her bosom up against him.

"Oh. Sorry," he said.

She smiled at him. "That's quite alright," she said.

They walked down the steps of the lecture theatre to the door. Audrey stayed very close to him. When they reached it, she said:

"We could have a get-together in your room some evening maybe and discuss the plans for extra-mural. Or at my place. I've a little studio in one of the older parts of the town that I use for my own work. Gordon won't have my stuff in the house. He says he's allergic." She let this sink in but Brian did not respond. "Yes, Noel has told me you'll have an important part to play in the development of extra-mural soon." More than he'd told him, thought Brian, with a sinking feeling. What other little surprises had he in store? From what she had just said he began to think Noel was more devious than he'd even suspected from his duplicity at his interview. "We'll have some wine maybe."

"Er... I really don't think that would be a good idea," said Brian, after a longish pause during which he tried to avoid her eye without giving offence.

"Don't worry, Brian, I'll bring the bottle." Her sympathetic gesture was completed this time and she gave his arm a reassuring squeeze.

"I'm probably going to be very busy. New job and all that."

He was trying to be as gentle as he could be in putting her off. Her face, which lent itself to a frank display of her internal emotional state, showed Brian that she was not taking his backing off very well.

"I see," she said. She removed her hand from his arm. The movement was almost tragic as she did so. "Well, I'll say good night then."

"Ah. Good night," said Brian. He moved off quickly along the corridor in a direction he didn't want to go but which he knew led away from both the library and the life room. He was aware of her watching him until he turned a corner. He leant against the wall for a moment before taking a circuitous route to the entrance stairs, which he descended with a speed and expertise almost to the standard of the elusive Dr. Spiller.

The next evening he was able to stay on late in the library as there were no evening classes and therefore no chance of meeting Audrey Reaper. He had been studying some original plans of the old college he had obtained in his quest to solve the mystery of the locked room when Mike Brierley, the lecturer in charge of the life room came in. Brian knew Mike often stayed on in the evening, not only to teach the extra-mural life class but also to do his own work. He looked worried but Brian saw this look change to one of relief as he came over to him.

"We've got a problem, Brian," he said, leaning on the desk.

"Oh, have we?" said Brian cautiously.

"Yes," he whispered, glancing round to check the librarian. "It's Audrey Reaper."

Brian sighed inwardly. "What about her?"

"Look, we can't talk here. Come out into the corridor."

Reluctantly, Brian picked up his briefcase and followed him.

"What's it about?" said Brian, outside.

Mike quickly filled him in. Apparently, last night she'd gone in to her studio place in town and the neighbours hadn't seen her all day although the radio was playing full blast. They'd knocked on the door to get her to turn it down but got no response at first. They knew she was in there because the radio had eventually been turned down. They'd tried to ring her husband but couldn't get hold of him, and had gone round again a short while ago to find a note had been shoved through the door from the inside with the college number on it. They still couldn't get a peep out of her and were getting worried. "They could have called the police" said Mike, "but decided to ring the college first to see if we could do something about it, what with her husband being a Councillor. I'm going to stop that damned switchboard girl plugging the outside line in to me at night. What do you think we should do?"

"We? What do you mean, we?" said Brian. "Let them call the police."

"Look, I know she's only an extra-mural student but de Vere thinks the sun shines out of her for some reason. Local talent he's discovered. Great PR. Actually she's a lousy painter but not bad at 3D design. Anyway, never mind that. If we refuse to help and anything happens, there'll be all hell to pay. Her husband's one of Huggett's mafia. We can at least show willing. Come down there with me now and we'll see what we can do."

Reluctantly, Brian agreed. He could see that Mike was very anxious not to incur any of de Vere's displeasure; their Head of Department had become fond lately of loading onto his staff degrading menial tasks if they upset him. Brian got his coat and they set off in Mike's car for Audrey's 'studio' - actually a terrace house owned by the Council wouldn't you guess, Mike told him bitterly as he drove fast through the maze of old terraces which made up the inner part of Brindling.

The night was heavily clouded, ominously stormy and very dark with a nithering westerly gale blowing in from the sea. They got out of the car in the terraced street, and Brian's thin coat, which doubled as an extra blanket at night, proved quite useless at keeping the wind out. He shivered deeply and cursed inwardly. They tried knocking at the doors and windows of the darkened house and calling through the letter box. There was an acrid smell of coal smoke too which the wind gusted down to street level. It made Brian cough; it was a smell Brian had not yet got used to, coming so recently from the pristine air of southern England. The neighbour who had phoned, a middle-aged lady in slippers and her hair in curlers, joined them.

"It's terrible when she gets like this," she shouted over the wind's roar. "She's always doing it but it's never been this bad."

"Doing what?" shouted Brian.

"Going on a bender. She's awful for the drink, is Audrey, but a nice lass otherwise. Kindness itself when you want owt. Nay, I can't stand out 'ere. I'll catch me death. Oh, I phoned the poliss just in case."

"What? Jesus!" said Mike, as the woman hurried indoors. "Look, I'll just go and phone my wife from a box. She gets dead worried if I'm late. You hold on here and I'll be back soon."

Without waiting for Brian's reply he got into his car and drove off. Well, I'll be damned, thought Brian, he's chicken! He knew he was right when it suddenly dawned on him that Mike had kept his engine running all the time. He gave a last bang on the door and called Audrey's name through the letter box again. He stood up preparatory to moving off and saw that all along the street chinks of light had appeared at the windows. He turned to go but a police car with a warning light flashing came round the corner. It screeched to a halt outside the house. There were two of them in it, one uniformed, the other not. The uniformed one got out.

"Who are you? " he shouted at Brian, pugnaciously.

Brian explained as best he could against the wind who he was and the situation. The neighbour came out, added her details, and went back in again. While she was doing so, Brian observed the other man in the car watching him carefully. He had on a trilby hat pulled well down but Brian could see a grey moustache turned orange in the light from the streetlamps. The young policeman, who was large and heavy, hammered on the door with a force which made his own and Mike's efforts seem feeble. He bent down and shouted her name through the letter box. He used her first name as though he was already familiar with it.

"Come on, you," he said to Brian. "We'll try round the back."

The house was on the corner of one of the terraces so an alley ran at its side to join the rear alleyway. The policeman tried the side door to the back yard. It was locked.

"Right then," he said. "It's over the wall, sunshine. Come on. I'll give you a leg up."

"Me?" said Brian.

"Yes, you look wiry enough and you're a lot lighter than me. I'll look after the briefcase." He took it out of his hand before Brian could object. "Come on, don't mess about or we'll be here all night. Anyway, I'm getting married Saturday and I want to be perfect on my wedding day, not scratched up to the eyeballs winkling out lushes like her. If her husband wasn't Councillor Reaper and so thick with the Chiefy, I'd break the damned window and be done with it. And probably her blooming neck as well. Here, put your foot in there."

He cupped his huge hands and Brian reluctantly did as he was told. He found himself lying on the top of the wall so suddenly that he nearly went right over and had to cling on tightly to the rough brick to stop himself tumbling into the dark well of the back yard. He felt hands and wrists taking scratches from the wall top and saw the policeman's point. He also knew that he would now have to spend a few hours trying to restore his only suit before college tomorrow and wondered if he had any antiseptic in the flat.

"Go on, then, man. Get down and try the back door," ordered the policeman.

He carefully dropped down from the wall, but landed with a clatter on the dustbin top. His foot went down into its near-capacity contents as the lid slipped sideways and both he, it, and the bin's contents rolled onto the gritty surface of the yard. Oh God, why did he get involved with this idiotic woman? Christ knows what state his suit would be in now. The stink from the dustbin's contents suggested it would be a long night getting it cleaned up. He just hoped Audrey kept a clean yard; at least that might not add too much to the damage. He had been told that some of the local houseproud types even hoovered the back yard but somehow he didn't think Audrey would be one of those. Once upright inside the yard, the walls shielded out the light and he had to grope his way to the back door. It was unlocked. He went in and felt round for a light switch but could not locate it. "Audrey?" he called quietly, moving to the kitchen door. "Mrs. Reaper? Are you ok? It's alright. It's me, Brian Mather from the college." There was no reply but there was a pervasive smell of sherry. He opened the door to the passage to the front door. Suddenly, a powerful pair of arms grasped him round the neck.

"Erk!" he squawked.

"Oh, Brian, I'm so glad it was you," Audrey hissed into his ear.

"Erk!" squawked Brian again.

She was a strong woman and had got a good grip. She kissed him fulsomely on his cheek. "I knew you were sympatico really, last night," she said. "I've been so lonely down here all day. It was wonderful of you to come for me."

At last, Brian managed to loosen her grip sufficiently to breathe. He was immediately overwhelmed by the smell of hot sherry breath and California Poppy, neither of which mixed at all well with the smell of domestic refuse from the dustbin.

"You...erk," he tried again hoarsely. "You've got to open the door. The police are outside."

She laid her head on his shoulder. Her hair covered his face and tickled his nose. He sneezed, but Audrey had tightened her grip again and the air stayed inside his head. He felt his sinuses balloon and dancing bright spots appear in front of his eyes. He thought, panicking, that he might pass out.

"Please don't bully me," she said. "I couldn't stand that. When you were so cruel to me last night I just didn't know what to do. I just had to forget. I know it's only because you're so poor." He managed to unlock her grip again.

Christ, this is just pure soapy fantasy, he thought. "Please Audrey. Come outside. For my sake," he pleaded. Her response was to seize him again. They struggled fiercely for control of his wind-pipe.

"Stay with me, Brian. We could be so good together."

"Erk. Erk."

Audrey was gaining the upper hand. He was pushed against a door which suddenly opened to the front living-room. His legs gave way and he fell with Audrey following him, still keeping her stranglehold, onto something soft. Audrey squashed Brian and Brian squashed whatever it was beneath them. It gave out a loud braying 'hee-haw, hee-haw' directly into his ear. In a beam of light through the curtains, Brian found himself staring into the mournful face of what seemed to be a flower-decked donkey. He fleetingly thought that Audrey was so cutting his circulation to the brain that he'd begun to hallucinate. His panic increased.

"What the 'ell's going on in there, sunshine?" the policeman shouted, and hammered the door. "What was that noise? Have you found her?"

Brian made a supreme effort, surprising himself briefly at his own strength, and pulled her arm from his throat. He forced the words out. "She's - erk - fine."

"Then get the silly bitch out here quick."

"Please, Audrey," he croaked. "Please." At last he felt her relax and accept the inevitable. They rose and, although Brian felt very wobbly, he took her hand and made his way carefully to the front door, stretching his neck and trying to swallow. He led her through after him. When she reached the street, the policeman immediately grabbed her shoulders roughly and spun her round towards him. He wagged his finger in her face and spoke to her as if she'd been a naughty little girl. Audrey tried a half-hearted rude gesture to him.

"Look, Audrey," he said, "this is the third time I've had to come down here and sort you out. Next time I'll run you in, Councillor Reaper or no Councillor Reaper. Understand? And bugger the Chief Constable and his community bloody policing."

"Look Audrey, this is the third time I've had to come down here and sort you out. Next time I'll run you in, Councillor Reaper or no Councillor Reaper."

She didn't reply. Her defiance evaporated and was replaced with a manner so forlorn and woebegone that Brian felt almost sorry for her, but his sympathy evaporated as he went into a fit of coughing.

"Well?" demanded the policeman to Audrey.

"I'm sorry to cause so much trouble for you, officer."

"Never mind about that. I'm paid for this. This fella isn't. So just think on. And it'll be the press as well, if there's any more of it. Right? Right?"

He turned to Brian and calmed down.

"It's alright, she'll be ok now but if I was you I'd find myself another playmate."

"What?" Brian rasped out, startled. The policeman tapped his cheek. Brian touched his own cheek and felt the lipstick. He took out a handkerchief and wiped it. The policeman gave him back his briefcase.

"She goes off like a firecracker when she's had some, does Audrey, but she usually doesn't remember much. And if I was you I'd get a good bath when you get home. You'll probably smell like the bottom of a hooer's handbag. I had a hell of situation with my fiancee last time this happened." Brian could see now why the cop wanted him to get her out.

The policeman leaned into the window of the car and spoke to the man inside, while Audrey turned away and rested her head on the door jamb. She had on a dressing-gown which she pulled round tightly, more to distance herself than for warmth - or modesty, Brian thought; she was probably much too drunk to feel the cold but he was alarmed she might keel over now she was in the open air, she looked so seedy. The policeman stood up again with a sheet of paper in one hand and a torch in the other. He shone it onto the paper, trying to hold it steady against the wind.

"Have you ever seen one of these before, sir?"

It was the picture of the vibrator.

"Yes."

"And where would that be?"

"At college."

"Oh, was it now?"

"Yes, the Rector showed it me. I believe he got it from Mr. Huggett."

The policeman pursed his lips. "And what about you?" he said to Audrey. "Hey! You. Fanny Ann. I'm talking to you." She glanced at the poster without moving her head from the door post.

"No thank you, not today," she said. "I have no need for one of those things. Not with men like Brian around." She looked up at Brian and he caught a smouldering smile in the light from the torch. What sort of drunken fantasy was she lost in now, for God's sake? But it also struck him she hadn't answered the question.

The policeman leaned into the car again. "She's still away with the mixer," Brian heard him say. He opened the door. "Right, sir," he said to Brian, "I'll leave you to it then." Brian had once more become a respectable citizen, he noticed.

"Hold on," said Brian. "You're not leaving me here with her like this are you? You couldn't give me a lift?"

"Sorry, sir. Another urgent call. Carry on, you're doing great. Just shove her back in but make sure you don't go in after her. She'll have you for supper." He looked with pity at Brian's thin figure shivering in its inadequate coat. "And thanks for your help. My fiancee'll be grateful." He laughed as he got into the car and drove off. Brian saw the hatted man watching him through the back window. When it had turned the corner, Audrey suddenly pushed herself away from the wall and came unsteadily to him.

"You wouldn't like to come in, would you?" she said shyly. "I think there's some sherry left."

"No," said Brian.

She shook her head at him and smiled ruefully. "Rejecting me again, Brian." She threw her head back and arms wide from her sides. Her dressing gown swung open and with a shock Brian saw that she had on underneath only a suspender belt, tiny pants and a plunging bra all in black. He began to panic as he sure she was going to howl so he would have to grab her to shove her back in, and if she got that grip on him again, then what? But a voice next to him stopped her abruptly and she coughed instead.

"Hi, Brian. Having trouble? Hi, Audrey." It was Connie.

Brian blew out a breath. "Thank God for the US cavalry. What are you doing down here?"

"I live along that way." She gestured a direction. Brian was puzzled. As far as he knew, that way there were only warehouses beyond this street and the river beyond that.

"What's going on?" she said. Brian explained the situation while Audrey clumsily rearranged her dressing-gown.

"I think you'd better leave her to me," she said. "Come on, Audrey." She took hold of her arm. Audrey suddenly looked up.

"They wanted to know about that poster. They're always asking questions about that, Gordon says. They're going to catch the ones who did it eventually," she said. Brian caught a cunning look cross her face. "I didn't tell them anything. But don't think I don't know who did it. What a pity they missed you, Connie. They could have asked you about it, couldn't they? I always know everything going on in the college, Brian. Remember that. Noel tells me everything."

"Of course you do," said Connie. "Come on, now, let's go in. You'll be getting a cold. And there's a real funny smell out here as well. Good night, Brian."

She led her in and closed the door. Neither woman looked back at Brian or spoke to him again. After a short interval the lights came on. Brian was left with the wind whipping his coat against his legs. He pulled up his collar and set off on the long walk home. Passing along the street, he noticed the chinks of light disappear one by one. He wondered to himself whether all this really was better than the dole. Was being rolled in the contents of a dustbin and strangled by a woman in her underwear truly a necessary part of Mr. Relevant's "ongoing community pertinence"? The old signing-on queue seemed invitingly restful at this distance. It began to rain, the wind driving it hard into his face and making him long for his lost life in southern England. He knew it was a fantasy but, at this moment, it seemed to be always brilliantly sunlit in retrospect - even at night. How could people stand living in this dump, year upon year? No surprise really that northern England was falling apart; anybody with the nous got out years ago, and good luck to them. Taking no comfort at all from these black thoughts, Brian pulled his collar up further and pondered gloomily whether there might possibly be another convenient cubby-hole somewhere in the Brindling Polytechnic Faculty of Art and Design in which an extra invisible lecturer could be handily accommodated.

Chapter Three
Accepting the Challenge of the Nineties

By the time of the Course Board meeting on Thursday, Brian was not very much further forward in his quest to solve the mystery of his invisible colleague. Nobody seemed to have a key to the locked door in the staff room nor did anybody profess to know what lay behind it except, he was told vaguely by Ridley, some old storage cupboards. Ridley's attitude was, in any case, that what lay beyond the door was "None of your – business". Nevertheless, from his own observations - and the plans he had obtained from the Poly buildings' office on the pretext of his interest as an architectural historian - he had managed to glean some idea.

From the outside of the building, he could see that there were two small windows in a position adjacent to the staff room coincident with the locked storage space. On the original plans of the building dating from 1890, he was astonished to find that these matched, rather than a few storage cupboards, two rooms, a larger one and a smaller, the latter containing wash-basin and lavatory. They were marked on the plans in neat, copperplate script as 'Model's Withdrawing and Robing Room with Lavatory.' The adjacent current staff room was marked as: 'Studio for Drawing from the Life'. He began to see what Hermione had meant about cubby holes. Whilst the staff room was empty he had listened at the door and thought he detected some movement behind it but could not be sure. He had knocked on it as hard as he had seen the policeman bang on Audrey's door but any sounds he thought he might have detected beforehand ceased entirely. He determined that, after the Course Board meeting that afternoon, he would wait in the staff room for as long as it took and see if Spiller emerged from his lair once more.

The meeting of the Department's senior staff was the first chance Brian had had to see his colleagues as a group. He had soon discovered on joining the college that most of them rarely used the staff room, preferring to keep on the move, all the better, he reckoned, to dodge the attentions of an increasingly anxious Noel de Vere. Also, novel to Brian, was the tradition of 'studio days' - often referred to by staff less careful of the covering euphemism, as 'days off' - when theoretically they were pursuing their own work elsewhere. Noel de Vere had made it clear to Brian in the first week that, as a non-artist, he was not entitled to this privilege. How many of these days the artists themselves were entitled to and when they were, seemed to Brian to be a very grey area and only de Vere, Louie and Myra knew the closely-guarded details.

At lunch-times when they were 'in college' and often well into the afternoon, staff were usually to be found with several of their students, holding 'tutorials' in one or other of the seedier pubs far from college. Brian was beginning to map out the secret geography of these locations where there was little chance of encountering either Noel de Vere, who preferred, he understood, watering holes more suited to his status, or other staff from the more respectable departments of the Polytechnic. He soon learned that keeping to themselves the details of their attendance, movements and exact location at any particular time, had been honed over the years by his colleagues to a finesse that would have done justice to the best agents of the KGB.

He could see that the current master in all this subterfuge had to be Dr. Oswald Spiller, his missing head of section. By checking records in the files, Brian had discovered that in every set of minutes for the last four years his existence had been registered only under the heading 'Apologies for Absence'.

When he had tackled Louie Bonetti on the subject, he merely said "'E's a ver' sick-a man, that-a fella Oswald," and had then gone on with great gusto to regale Brian with the story of a former member of staff who had been so good at the great game of keeping his timing and whereabouts hidden, that he had managed to be appointed 'full-time' as a member of department of another art college at the opposite end of the country. He had finally been unmasked when a visiting lecturer had recognised him as the same man who introduced him to the students at Brindling the previous week. It was only the man's impaired vision - which accounted also for the peculiar but much-praised perspective of his paintings - and alcohol-sodden memory that had led him into the error of introducing the same man twice. The whole matter had been hushed up - another talent Brindling art school was adept at, Brian gathered - and he had gone on with a glowing testimonial to become a draughtsman of ancient artefacts at the British Museum. Louie banged the desk and laughed uproariously as he topped off this story with the fact that there had already been one conference held to settle all the cultural confusions caused by the embellished details which the published drawings had acquired by way of his poor eyesight. "'E's as blind as a fooking-a bat, Brian," he said.

Of course, all that was in the bad old days before the Polytechnic took in the art school, Brian was given to understand. "Iss-a not 'appen now, Brian," Louie told him. (From the sigh and the regretful shake of his head, Brian guessed that Louie was not completely happy about this.) But from Brian's perspective of trying to track down Spiller, he was not so sure; four years without attending either a single meeting or giving a single lecture was not a bad effort in his book, Polytechnic notwithstanding.

Brian thought that a large part of the successful elusiveness of his colleagues must be due to their mode of dress. He looked around the long table in the staff room at which they were gathered, and realised that his was the only suit present. However shabby its assault on Audrey's back yard had left it, it stood out against the dress of the senior studio staff, with one exception, all male. Nearly all were dressed in similar second or third-hand mode to their students and nearly all had beards, ranging from the bushy-unkempt of Peter Orrd, the distinguished Head of Sculpture, to the neatly-trimmed of Laurie Willoughby, the Head of Media Studies. The latter was the only staff member with anything remotely 'arty' in his dress but the flamboyant, frilly, red shirt, tight, white jeans and black boot-lace tie bespoke, in addition, a sartorial mode diametric to Brian's straight-man suiting. The lone woman artist, Zoe Tremaine, a ceramicist - or "potter", as she had corrected Brian severely - was dressed in well-worn dungarees and a leather jacket. This outfit went well with her close-cropped, iron-grey hair.

Most of the staff puffed furiously at Dartmoor-calibre roll-ups, which, as a non-smoker, – another trait which had been commented on by some of his colleagues as an obvious straight-man characteristic - Brian found hard to take. Few were talking because many of them, Brian guessed, had come directly from their 'tutorials' in the local pubs. Most sat staring straight ahead, looking bad-tempered. Sitting next to him, Peter Orrd, his head sunk deep in his beard pushed up round the lower part of his face by his thick sweater, and with an unlit roll-up protruding from its grey-brown shagginess, seemed, in contrast, to be studying the papers carefully. However, after a while, as they waited, Brian noticed Peter was not turning any pages. When he unobtrusively took a closer look at him, he realised that, behind his thick pebble lenses and hidden by his long hair which had fallen forward, Peter's eyes were tightly closed and he was sound asleep. Breathing easily and propped against the stout desk by his ample stomach, Brian imagined Peter would be able to maintain this pose indefinitely. He wondered whether he actually ever snored in this position.

Brian felt dispirited as he recognised that, set within the context of the studio staff, he could not escape the flavour of his role as Mr. Relevant, the new straight man of the Faculty. He had already realised that his artist colleagues seemed to have a grip on some aspect of life he would dearly love to have himself. He had felt it nearly within his grasp in his acting days before the 'resting' drove him back to academe. What was it, he wondered? The creative spirit? A complete freedom? Some sort of... His thoughts were interrupted by Hermione James smiling across the table at him.

"Thank you for altering that memo," she said. "I can never work out these twenty-four hour times myself."

"That's ok," he smiled back. He glanced at the wall clock. "This is a bit unusual, isn't it? He's late."

"Yes, and if he doesn't appear soon," said Zoe, indignantly crushing her roll-up hard into the ash tray, "I, for one, am going to piss off. He's always accusing us of never being on time."

In his lately paranoid state, Noel de Vere had taken to turning up to meetings ten minutes early and accusing everyone who arrived on time of being late. Peter had already told Brian that, on this occasion, the staff had all agreed to turn up ten minutes early themselves.

"Hey," said Wladimir Ostrowski, a performance artist with an international reputation and a skilled practical joker, "let's just do that and leave old Pete to face the music. Shhh." He indicated Peter Orrd's peaceful figure. "Pop to the door, Zoe, and see if he's coming." The staff grinned their assent as Zoe went to the door. "Just a sec." He took his chair and climbed onto the seat to alter the wall clock to ten minutes fast. "We can nip round the corner of the corridor and all come back in together when he's arrived. Come on. Don't wake him.".

"Is he alive still, even, one wonders?" said Laurie, raising his eyebrow at Peter.

"Who can tell?" said Wladimir, making for the door. "Come on, Brian. You too. Bring your papers."

"The only man you can film in slow motion without altering the camera speed," Laurie said wonderingly, glancing back at Peter as they crowded out of the door.

Wladimir's inclusion of himself in this daft game gave Brian's spirits a considerable lift. Since starting the term he had been slightly anxious about how the artist tutors regarded him. Especially when he found that his post was a replacement for a man who had left the painting department. They had been polite but many of them had not been particularly forthcoming in their welcomes. By this invitation, which was echoed in the expressions of the others, he felt that they seemed to look upon him as one of them. Or at least not somebody to be treated differently. He could see, on the other hand, as he joined them round the corner of the corridor, that by participating he would lay himself open to de Vere's victimising tendencies.

Once all had gathered around the corner, they whispered and tried to suppress their giggles, no doubt, Brian thought, engendered by the results of their lunch-time 'tutorials'. Mike Brierly came up to him. Brian had not spoken to him since the events of the previous night.

"Sorry about last night, Brian," he said, avoiding his eye. "Just couldn't find a phone not vandalised. I came round later but there seemed to be nobody about. Everything go ok, did it?"

"I got by," said Brian, coolly. He unconsciously rubbed his throat which was still sore. Mike waited but Brian did not elaborate.

"Oh. Good," said Mike. He moved away quickly, still without looking directly at Brian.

Brian was wondering whether to follow him and tell him the details; it was silly to hold a grudge against a man for running out on somebody like Audrey, especially as he had a family to think of. But Zoe Tremaine approached him before he moved.

"Keep your hands off Connie Grey," she hissed.

"What?" said Brian, startled.

"I said keep..."

"Shhh. He's coming." said Wladimir.

The sounds of voices were heard in the corridor. Zoe Tremaine gave him a last venomous look and moved away. Well, he thought, there were at least two colleagues who were not ecstatically happy with him, and Zoe's obvious interest in Connie Grey was also a considerable disappointment to him. Did Connid play for both sides? he wondered.

Before Brian had time to ponder Zoe's outburst properly, Wladimir, who was peeping round the corner, pulled back and whispered:

"He's got somebody with him."

"It'll be Louie," said Mike.

"No. Somebody else as well. A guy,".

"I hope it isn't the Rector," said Hermione, mildly.

This remark eliminated any further giggles. Like Hermione James, Brian gathered that none of the staff knew much about the Rector. Some of them had asked Brian, who had been party to the incident of his mistaken arrest the previous term, what he was like. He had told the story well and although they found it funny, Brian's estimate that the Rector seemed to detest art, artists and themselves in particular, had left them all very uneasy. They held their breath and waited for de Vere's group to enter the staff room. De Vere's voice rang out wildly to them.

"What's this! Where the fuck is everybody?"

They heaved a collective sigh of relief. Noel's language told them that it could not possibly be the Rector.

From the staff room following de Vere's outburst, Brian heard a strange barely human rumbling. He recognised it as Peter Orrd trying to collect his thoughts and reply. Peter had told Brian that, as a young student, he had been immensely impressed by Augustus John, whom he had contacted briefly when he had visited his college. Not by his art, which Peter thought, in any case, inferior to that of his sister, Gwen, but by his mode of speech, dress, hirsuteness, movement and relations to women - he had had a reputation for screwing any woman who came near him and was not above rape, apparently. Peter had decided at that early age to adopt these characteristics - apart from the rape - as the perfect mode for a budding art college teacher and, at this late stage of his lengthy career, as an ideal camouflage for dealing with jerks like Noel de Vere. After all, as he said, John got away without expressing a coherent thought or intelligible sentence for three generations without anybody noticing much.

"Well, where have they gone, for fuck's sake?" shouted Noel de Vere.

"Rumble, rumble, rumble," came the reply.

"Come on," said Wladimir.

The staff hurried back to the meeting room.

"Where the hell have you lot been?" snarled de Vere, as they entered and found their places.

"We all just nipped out for a spit and a draw while we were waiting," said Wladimir, glancing significantly at the clock.

Noel de Vere followed his glance and started as he registered the false time. He looked quickly at his watch and shook his wrist.

"In fact," said Zoe loudly, "some of us were here at two o'clock. That memo you sent..."

"Well let's get on, let's get on, now we are here," said Noel, testily smothering any further reference to timekeeping. He took his place at the head of the table, and Brian noticed that he surreptitiously tried to adjust his designer watch as he took it from his wrist and placed it in front of him.

"Rumble, rumble, playing silly buggers," said Peter to his colleagues as they settled down.

Noel de Vere looked round fiercely - he had abandoned his mirror glasses for this meeting, Brian guessed in deference to his visitor, who must therefore be important - and tapped the table very hard with a ball pen for order. The pen broke.

"Shit!" he said vehemently. "Er. Sorry about that," he apologised to the visitor, although whether for the broken pen or the word, was not clear. The staff were all attention now as they could see how nervous Noel was. Although new to meetings of the Board, Brian sensed the anticipation in the air. He saw that even Peter Orrd had not yet relapsed completely into his former comatose state. "Let me first introduce our guest. Or would you prefer to introduce yourself?" he said, turning to the very elegantly dressed figure next to him.

The staff looked at the man. Brian took in his details quickly. He was about his own height, in his forties probably, with dark hair carefully groomed, but more heavily built than Brian and dressed in a white shirt and expensive grey suit, which looked both incongruous and exotic in the art school. His tie was collegiate, Brian noticed, and he had on what looked like a gold wrist watch. Since joining the art department, Brian had almost forgotten there were people who dressed like this for work. His watchful face was handsome and had a healthy glow. From squash-playing, or he was into gulping down vitamin C, Brian thought. Altogether, his carefully groomed and polished exterior, whatever it conveyed to the rest of the staff, served only to thoroughly alarm Brian; he had seen that sort of face before topping the same kind of gear - at his last college when men like this had given it the bullet.

"Please, carry on, Mr. de Vere," said the man, smoothly. His voice was standard English, definitely public school, Brian thought. He noticed a small scar above his right eyebrow. Probably from his past as a dashing fly-half or some such.

"Thank you." said de Vere. "This is Dr. Marshall, Pro-Rector in charge of Academic Planning for the Polytechnic. He's ...".

"Po Rector?" said Laurie Willoughby, quickly.

"Pro-Rector," said de Vere, suppressing his anger. "In other words, Deputy Rector to you."

"Oh, my dear," said Laurie, adopting his camp mode, "if I'd known we were having company for tea, I'd have put on my best frock."

"Cut that crap now," said Noel de Vere angrily through the laughter.

Willoughby, sitting at the end of the table near to de Vere, Marshall, Louie and Myra Tomlinson, turned his face towards the staff so that it could not be seen by de Vere and the others. He raised his eyebrows archly and mouthed something. Brian saw that everybody was trying not to laugh again. He looked enquiringly at Hermione, whom he just noticed had sat down next to him on the other side from Peter when they had returned from the corridor. She wrote on the pad in front of her: 'Bona lallies.' He had no idea what this meant.

The meeting opened formally with apologies for absence. At this all the staff in chorus sang out "Oswald Spiller" and laughed. It was evidently a standing joke. Noel de Vere's face reddened with anger which he did not try to suppress. Brian guessed he was as much angry with himself for forgetting this usual reaction to the particular agenda item and thus exposing a glaring anomaly before his important visitor.

"That's enough, dammit," he called out, and banged the table with the flat of his hand.

Dr. Marshall intervened.

"May I be permitted to ask a question, Mr. de Vere?" he said. Without waiting for Noel's opened mouth to issue a reply he went on: "I've been going through the minutes of this Board in preparation for this meeting, and it would seem - please do correct if I'm mistaken here, Chairman - that Dr. Spiller has not attended one of these meetings for the last four years. And yet, am I not right in thinking that he is, in fact, head of the section titled Related Studies in this Department?" A single raised eyebrow remained at the end of this speech directed in mild, polite enquiry towards Noel de Vere. Brian was impressed, in spite of his unease about him, at Marshall's smooth academic apparatchik tone and timing. Watch your backs everybody, he thought, there's a stiletto concealed in those immaculate shirt cuffs.

The staff were all attention now, watching de Vere's evident embarrassment as he shifted in his chair trying to think of a reply. Brian wondered if the sleeping cross was about to rear up and smite him at last.

Finally, Noel shrugged. He opened his mouth to speak but shut it again abruptly as the mysterious door in the corner of the room was flung open with a crash as it hit the wall.

"Rumble, eh, what the hell?" said Peter, waking with a start.

Dr. Oswald Spiller entered.

"I apologise for my lateness, Mr. Chairman," he said, hurrying to the foot of the table and sitting down near to Brian and Hermione, "I had some essay marking to finish." He quickly opened the briefcase he was carrying and began busily to take out and arrange a huge sheaf of papers.

Laurie Willoughby broke the spell which had fallen. "My dear, it's so good to see you looking so well after all this time."

Spiller ignored this. "Shall we get on? Tick, tock. Tick, tock," he said, looking up from his papers. "That clock is showing the wrong time," he said severely, setting his huge watch in front of him. It seemed to Brian almost a miniature version of Big Ben with lots of extra little dials on its face and knobs around the case.

Brian could see that the papers which Spiller now began to arrange ostentatiously around himself were sheafs of Course Board minutes, all copiously annotated in different coloured inks. He looked at the head of the table again to see that de Vere, Louie and Myra were still transfixed by Spiller's actual presence. Marshall had been sufficiently nonplussed by this dramatic answer to his question as to replace his quizzical expression by one which involved a pursed-lips thoughtfulness. A gold propelling pencil had also appeared and was busily, but casually, making notes on a pad in front of him. Brian would have loved to have had a glimpse of them.

"Tick, tock. Tick, tock," said Spiller in a reprimanding tone, tapping the table with his pen.

The meeting began properly at last. If Spiller's entrance had provided a startling preliminary, Brian felt it was only a curtain raiser to the drama which followed. From the first item on the agenda, timekeeping, it became clear to him that de Vere had prepared a number of bombshells to spring on the staff. Whether these were to impress Dr. Marshall or to stamp his authority on his staff Brian couldn't tell, but what was clear was that de Vere's paranoia was now raging untrammelled.

"The timekeeping in this place has got beyond a joke," he began angrily, "so from next week, I've decided that all of you - without exception - " he added, looking at each member of staff in turn with a fierce expression, "will sign in with Myra by nine o'clock every day. In addition, you will all sign in for the afternoon session as well by one-thirty. And that will include you, Peter," he said loudly.

Peter Orrd raised his head slightly and grunted as he heard his name.

The silence which followed was broken by Zoe.

"You mean to say we have to fucking clock-in like fucking factory workers twice a day?" she said. (Brian saw Marshall make a quick note on his pad.)

"Exactly," said de Vere with satisfaction.

"It's fucking degrading," said Zoe.

"You shouldn't mind, darling, you're a militant union man, aren't you?" said de Vere cuttingly. "It's a chance for you to show some solidarity with the workers and earn those dungarees. The lists will be withdrawn at nine o'clock and one-thirty promptly and woe betide any of you if your names are not on it. I hope I make myself clear?"

Suddenly Oswald Spiller spoke up.

"An excellent idea, Chairman, if I may say so. But we must have all the clocks corrected by then. Could this be seen to forthwith? An incorrect clock is the thief of time, you know."

The staff looked at Spiller with hatred and Brian guessed they all heartily wished him back in his cupboard. Marshall, he noticed, was watching their reactions with a very beady eye.

Having winded his staff with this pronouncement, Noel de Vere pressed his advantage with further edicts. The next concerned studio days. In the run-up to the quinquennial, all these were cancelled. The staff protested loudly, especially those with upcoming exhibitions but to no avail. As an addendum to this, in agreement with the Rector, all staff practice was now to be called 'Research' and come under the new financial arrangements which the Governors were to consider at their next meeting for sharing the proceeds from sales or commissions with the Polytechnic, half and half.

"Any objections?" said de Vere, looking round the table.

"My accountant might," said Willoughby.

"Just let him try," said de Vere.

Laurie Willoughby subsided.

Strictures concerning student timekeeping, record-keeping and course units all followed in quick succession. The staff sank further into their seats, their heads bowed by the sheer comprehensiveness of the new regime, and Brian could see that Noel de Vere was becoming more and more elated as he enjoyed the sense of his own power. To Brian, he almost seemed to be making up some of the edicts as he went along and certainly did not refer to any notes or papers. His eyes assumed a glazed stare as they poured out. Brian guessed they had been festering for years but until now he had no idea of how to apply them and still maintain good relations with his staff. It was only now in his panic about the visit that he had the excuse to do this, his paranoia fully protecting him from any awkward personal consequences. Brian also guessed that someone - probably the Rector or his henchman, Marshall - had opened the sluice gates to release this pent-up flood.

One after another, the various sections of the Department - painting, graphics, printmaking, media, performance, ceramics - were swept aside by the deluge. Brian was dismayed at the feebleness of any resistance offered by his colleagues. Only when it came to the turn of the last studio section, sculpture, was the flow halted. Here was the only section run by an artist of truly major critical note. Peter Orrd emerged from his beard and, roused at last from his usual Course Board torpor, spoke up in a voice pared of any residual Augustus John mumbling. This close to him, Brian could see him shaking with anger.

"Are you damn well trying to tell me how to run a sculpture department, de Vere?" he said, with a forceful challenge in his voice.

"No," said de Vere, not reacting to it.

"I should bloody well hope not," said Peter. "Anyway, you were supposed to be a painter at one time, weren't you?"

Brian saw that Noel's face flush with anger at this. Even Brian, who was new to the college, was aware that this was a very piercing jibe. He had been told by Mike Brierly that Noel de Vere had once seemed, in his days as a young artist at the Slade, to be the 'white hope' of post-war British painting but had settled to nil output some time in his late thirties when the gallery fashions had swung towards the Americans. It was even rumoured he had been approached by Huw Wheldon at one time to appear on 'Monitor', but the programme never came off when the idea had been sabotaged by a young editor whom de Vere may or may not have treated badly in an affair as a student. By the time the abstract expressionists and pop artists had run their course, younger, more fashionable figures like Hockney had become the darlings of the art-hype industry and de Vere's moment had passed.

The staff leaned forward in anticipation of a show-down but before de Vere could respond, Peter fuelled his ire with a further thrust.

"If it wasn't for the sculpture section, this course would never have any damned firsts at all. There aren't any painters, are there?" he said contemptuously, "And you've only got to look at the number of post-grad. students we produce. Half the sculpture M.A.'s in the country are ours."

This twin challenge was even more damaging than his first one. Before taking up his appointment, Brian had gone carefully through the degree results for the last few years and it was obvious that the section which showed up consistently well was sculpture. Whether this was due to the quality of the teaching or Peter Orrd's reputation attracting the best students, there was no way of knowing. But the rivalry between the two senior sections, painting and sculpture, was something which Brian had picked up in the first few days he had been at Brindling. Brian could see why de Vere thought so much of Connie Grey, as she was clearly a first and headed for great things.

Along with the rest of the staff, Brian was surprised by de Vere's reaction. He sat back in his chair, linked his hands behind his head, and looked up at the ceiling. Gradually, his normal colour returned.

"I would not pretend to tell you your job as a sculptor," he said, unexpectedly calm in the face of the challenge, "but..."

Peter snorted. "That doesn't stop you trying to rubbish my students at finals time," he said.

"But," de Vere went on, ignoring this, "I do know what the panel will want to see when they come." He leaned forward suddenly and put both elbows on the table as he pointed a finger aggressively at Peter. (Brian was surprised to see how thick and darkly hairy de Vere's finger was, and also the hand and wrist to which it was attached; this unexpectedly simian aspect to Noel was something he had not had occasion to notice before. Its primitive quality lent an almost dangerous emphasis to de Vere's hostility and Brian was glad it wasn't directed at him.) "And what they won't see from your section are any records of student progress that don't look as if they've lined the bottom of a dog kennel," he said, the menace in his voice matching the threat from his hairy finger. "I asked Myra here a few days ago to collect up all student records for checking so the panel would be assured that our management of the course and student feedback systems were working fairly." At this point he turned to Myra and held out his hand. She handed him a sheaf of tatty- looking bits of paper. De Vere threw these violently across the table to Peter. "This crap is what your section passed in. Would you like to comment on them?"

Brian could see from his position next to Peter, that the state of the papers alone, some coffee and beer-glass stained, some with cigarette burns, knocked a fairly gaping hole in the credibility of Peter's defence. He gamely tried to play down their significance.

"Bits of paper. What the hell has that got to do with getting students to realise their ideas? You can't put that sort of thing on paper."

De Vere followed up his advantage quickly. "No, perhaps not, but you can try to put onto 'bits of paper', as you call them, some reasonable estimate of what a student is doing. When I read them through, I came across would-be witty comments like 'This man couldn't piss in a bucket.' as a summary of a term's work or 'Cack-handed junk' as a judgement of someone's work." Brian knew that Peter liked to cultivate this image of the curmudgeonly hairy sculptor and his comments were written as much for the students' amusement as a true estimate of their worth. Brian also knew that de Vere must be well aware of this - after all he was ultimately responsible - but was now more concerned to turn them here to his own advantage in a public confrontation in front of the Deputy Rector. De Vere leaned back once more in his chair, placed his hands on the table and looked round the staff, many of them with their heads bowed staring dumbly down at its surface, appalled at the overthrow, Brian guessed, of the only possible champion of the free spirit of art teaching on the staff.

"You know who's on the panel, don't you?" said de Vere.

"You know damned well we don't," said Peter harshly. "You only got to know yourself this morning."

"Ivor Evans," said de Vere, ignoring Peter's attempt to disconcert him.

The staff groaned.

"Oh God," said Mike Brierley, "He's a right bastard."

"Bastard?" said de Vere. "Make no mistake, kiddo, he is the original Father of Lies, the Prince of fucking Darkness. Look what he did to that course at Ipswich. Finito. And they weren't that bad because I was on their previous panel. What do you think he's going to make of shit like this?"

"Paper artists," said Peter dismissively. "He's a wanker."

"Look, Orrd, you may be God's gift to sculpture," said de Vere rudely, (Brian could see he was now fully confident that he had triumphed over him and was taking the chance to kick him when he was down, especially after his crack about his painting career.) "but it's about time you learned that this sort of junk isn't good enough any more. There's such a thing called admin. and it's about running an efficient ship - not just for art but so the students and everybody else can see they're being dealt a square deal. The days of spot-the-artist and fly-by-wire intuition in art colleges are out. Where've you been for the last fifteen years, for Christ sake? We're part of a Polytechnic. Haven't you heard? Nobody in these places gives a fuck about ideas and art. If it can't be put on paper it doesn't exist. Ok? We're in the nineteen nineties now. Savvy? Even Michelangelo would have been kicked out on his backside from a place like this."

"Oh, my dear, I'm sure he would have positively relished the prospect," said Laurie Willoughby, looking round for the laugh. His spirits were recovering but not his judgement of the mood of the meeting, thought Brian. He saw his face fall as nobody grinned back at him.

"Jesus H. Christ!" shouted de Vere, exasperated. "Give me strength. Can't I get it through your thick skulls that this is the last chance saloon we're at? Any major cock-ups with this one and that's it! We join Ipswich and history. And your own records are no great shakes either, Willoughby, and that goes for the rest of you as well. You'd all better be sure there are some decent records for the panel to see by the time of the visit - " he paused significantly and hissed: "because all of your jobs may depend on it. You tell them, Dr. Marshall. See if you can get through. They're plugged in to another line here."

"I think you've been doing it very well, Mr. de Vere," said Marshall calmly. Noel de Vere squared his shoulders and drew a deep breath at this praise. "But perhaps I may be allowed to put how we in senior management see the situation. As you know, ladies and gen...."

Before he could make his point the door to the staff room was flung open and a student named Ronnie Oliver walked straight in. He looked round as all eyes turned towards him.

"Hey, Vlad," he said to Wladimir Ostrowski, in a thick scouse accent, "'ave you seen that 'and drill I was using the other day, wack?"

"Not now, Ronnie," said Wladimir, embarrassed.

"Oh, are you busy, like? I'll see if Ghandi 'as it then."

('Ghandi' was a workshop technician, Brian knew.) He went out whistling. They heard him singing "'Ere we go. 'Ere we go. 'Ere we go." down the corridor. Hermione got up and closed the door quietly.

Brian was amazed that none of the staff seemed to find this interruption in any way surprising or disconcerting. All that is except Noel de Vere, who, when they turned their attention back to the head of the table, was seen to have lowered his head onto it and to be slowly banging it gently on the wood. Dr. Marshall watched him without expression.

"Can't you stop him doing that?" he said to Wladimir when he finally looked up.

Ostrowski shrugged. "Well, he's stabilized at the moment and the specialist says not to hassle him too much."

"Sorry about that," said Noel to Dr. Marshall. "He's a bit of a sad case - touch of the m and d's - but his work is ok when he's up like this so there's not a lot we can do. 'Care in the Community' you know - and his parents are very grateful. With any luck he'll be off our hands this summer when he graduates."

"Oh," said Marshall, making a note. "But to continue. As you know - or possibly don't know - " he said doubtfully, looking round at the staff, "the

Polytechnic Higher Education Corporations have been asked by central government to look for rather extensive cuts in our budgets for next session and possibly beyond that. This means we are having to look particularly closely at our courses - all courses I might add, not just this one, naturally," he said, with a smile of reassurance, "and any we find are outwith the quality control criteria set by CNAA and ourselves will be graded accordingly when it comes to the annual allocation of what are, after all, the scarce resources taxpayers contribute to fund Higher Education. As taxpayers yourselves, I suppose you would not expect us do otherwise than get our ongoing management strategy efficiently streamlined to fit the parameters of financial constraints which are likely to be strict for a considerable part of the current decade. The prospect is not a happy one for any of us, I assure you. Nobody likes to think that education should be starved of funds or that the valuable experience of staff might be lost but these are the times we live in and it behoves us to make eminently rational decisions so that we should, in future, have no cause to regret that such decisions as we make were not pertinent to a coherent and proper analysis, taking all the factors into account at the particular moment in time." He turned to Noel de Vere and smiled. "I don't think I could state it more plainly than that, Chairman," he said.

Looking about him it was obvious to Brian that its plainness to most of the staff, whose attention span to any speech unseasoned by expletives was limited, was entirely obscure. Even de Vere was frowning as he backtracked the speech; Brian had seen his eyes glaze over around the "parameters" stage.

"What you really mean is that you'll chop our courses, if we don't get a conditional discharge by the thought police," said Peter Orrd harshly. Brian guessed his early training with John had given him a better handle on digging out meaning from obscure English than the others.

"I'm sorry?" said Marshall, whose turn it was to be confused.

"The bloody CNAA, man." said Peter. "The thought police."

"Er - yes," said Dr. Marshall guardedly, his urbane manner slipping a little at Peter's forthrightness. And Dr. Marshall was a smooth man, but Peter Orrd was an hairy bloody sculptor, thought Brian.

"So that's where it's at!" said de Vere, cutting off any further polyspeak from Marshall. "Got it? So now you know what you're up against. Now Art History."

Next to him, Brian felt Hermione jump. Although de Vere did praise the record-keeping in Hermione's section, he came to the point he had to make quite brutally. Where were the completed dissertations to send to the external assessor? Why were they always late every year? Hermione pleaded that it was extremely difficult to get art students to put pen to paper. Some of them were barely literate after all and even dyslexic, for goodness' sake. But Noel de Vere would have none of this and implied softness and lack of sinew in the section. The eventual result of his badgering was a tearful exit by Hermione. Brian thought that de Vere had really gone far over the top by this time to bully someone who was so obviously as hard-working and well-meaning as Hermione.

"Fucking women," said de Vere. "Every time the waterworks. I exempt you from both charges, Zoe."

It was now Zoe's turn to walk out but not in tears.

"You used to be quite a nice guy, de Vere," she said, as she stood up, "but these Poly bastards have taken over your soul. Judas is the name that comes to mind. I just wonder what the thirty pieces of silver are," she said, and slammed the door behind her.

Noel de Vere did not react to this at all. "Now then, Related Studies," he went on.

While the drama of de Vere's attack on all sections of the course had been going on, Brian's mind had shifted quickly into overdrive. He knew from his reading of students' files that the section couldn't be faulted on records - Spiller was apparently as obsessive about words on paper as he was about clocks - but there was the little matter of his head of section not addressing the students for four years and hiding in a cupboard. Not easily explained to a man like Marshall - or anybody else for that matter. He had also noticed that Spiller, with de Vere's spotlight swinging nearer and nearer to Related studies, had become increasingly agitated. He was making furious notes and constantly checking his watch and probably deeply regretting coming out in the open. Brian knew, with the tension increasing in his solar plexus, that it was going to be up to him to ride shotgun for the section. Marshall's little burst of polyspeak had not fooled him for an instant, nor his deprecating little smile. He had seen a whole college go under with cartloads of wreathed regretful smiles like that cast on the waters after it from Marshall's sort. It was how they got up the ladder to their Rectorial positions, large salaries and delightful perks - Department of Education pit bulls with pussy-cat purrs. Well, two could play at that game. Now, without deviation, hesitation or repetition:

"Perhaps I might, as a newcomer to the section be allowed to give my impressions of where Dr. Spiller and myself see the future course of management of our responsibilities." He saw that his inclusion of Spiller had startled the staff, not least Noel de Vere. "We had a short meeting on Tuesday evening, by the way, but our discussion was perforce brief." (Tick, tock.)

No objection was forthcoming to his speaking for the section from Noel who sat open-mouthed, nor from Spiller who was still staring at his watch. The rest of the staff looked at him, bemused. Brian could see how his announcement of contact with Spiller must have grabbed them; they had not set eyes on him for four years.

"I am sure the visiting panel will be interested in any ongoing plans we have for future benchmarking of the aims of the section, as no doubt will this Course Board," he went on. "I regret that I have not been able to prepare any papers for your attention prior to this but, as you will understand, in the few weeks I have been here, there has been insufficient time. However, these are ongoing (Damn! I've used that twice. Always a danger when ad-libbing. Time for 'outwith'.) and will be with you shortly (A quickie written overnight should do it.) which will not, I hope, be at all outwith the sense of where the course should be looking for future growth. I am sure you will agree that growth to satisfy perceived future educational demand, always within the constraining parameters (Thank you, Dr. Marshall.) of current and future national and overall Polytechnic financial resources, of course, will be the essence of a dynamic (Good old word, that!) approach to Higher Education from now on. (Quick, think of something. A bit of philosophical reflection now to gain time.) Since taking up my appointment, I have been very struck that the ethos (Another golden oldie!) in the Department is very heartening at this moment in time. A strong sense of fulfilment of the current, (Emphasise that!) traditional (Prepare the ground for something new. What? What?) overall aims and objectives of the course seems to animate both students and staff. Staff/student relations seem excellent (Especially, in the legover relations of the randier male staff and the female students, I understand.) and the results speak for themselves. Thus the Department, to my mind at least, (A bit of modesty here to temper the ego.) although there has not been time to discuss this with Mr. de Vere, is well poised to accept the challenge of the Nineties. (Come on right brain, cough up something, this is the crunch.) Therefore, we would like to propose (Hurry up then, damn you!) that we develop a course at the interface (Spot-on buzzword; old hat but still useful here.) of new developments in the field of information technology and the environmental applications of the skills and talents of artists and designers." (God knows what it all means; sort that out later.) He sat back to enjoy the stunned silence round the table. It was finally broken by Peter:

"Holy shit," he said.

"Er, yes," said Noel, coming to. "Splendid. Yes. Er. You'll let us have something on paper then telling us what the f – er – what it is you've been rabbit – er – what these ideas are. Splendid. Yes."

"Of course," said Brian. "Within the next week. With a full numerical analysis of SSR and resource implications etc. Dr. Spiller and I will work on it together." That gets Spiller, who was still staring at his watch, off the hook at least. Brian just hoped he didn't disappear into the woodwork again.

From the corner of his eye, he could see Marshall watching him. During his speech he had seen his pencil cease its note-taking and an increasingly thoughtful expression come into his face. The meeting broke up and Marshall approached him. He looked at Brian steadily.

"Bien joué, old man," he said. Brian was surprised by his friendly manner. "It will be interesting to see if you can cut it from here. Working in an art school will be a new experience for me as well as for you, I imagine." He grinned. "I'm quite looking forward to it. Interesting lot, aren't they? By the way, do you play squash?" Bingo, thought Brian.

"Yes," he said.

"Good. We might have a game some time. You could join the Polytechnic ladder."

"Sound idea," said Brian. Marshall did not appear to register the slightly over-the-top manner in which he said it. Don't push your luck, son, he told himself.

Brian watched him as he went to join de Vere who had invited him for a drink. He suddenly felt the need of a stiffy himself and a deep warm bath. He looked round for Spiller and saw him making quickly for the door in the corner of the room. Before he could reach it, Noel de Vere moved even more quickly and confronted him. There was a short, whispered and, Brian guessed from de Vere's manner, pithy conversation between them and he saw Spiller hand over a key to Noel. He looked back to Marshall and saw he was trying to keep his face straight as he watched the two men as well. He grinned broadly at Brian. Noel de Vere joined him again and Spiller went out of the room by the normal exit, looking longingly at the door in the corner. Brian knew that both he and Marshall were quite aware that neither of them had fooled anybody but a bunch of artists. So be it. It's words and numbers that count, kiddo. And if you can't paint, wear a big hat.

Chapter Four
Femme Fatale

The morning following the traumatic staff meeting saw Brian present in the Art and Design building very early. De Vere had said to sign in by nine o'clock. Brian, whose habit was to be on the premises by eight fifteen, was determined he was not going to do that; he agreed wholeheartedly with Zoe Tremaine. To make sure de Vere could not fault him he had anticipated the effect on de Vere himself of his own edict.

He had noticed that his Head of Department always arrived about eight twenty and Brian's greeting to him when he met him in the corridor was always returned grudgingly. Brian guessed that de Vere was slightly miffed that Brian always preceded him. So Brian ensured he got himself into the building that morning by eight o'clock and waited for him. He was gratified to see that he had surmised correctly when de Vere arrived earlier than usual at eight ten. Brian waved his briefcase at him in the entrance hall as he entered.

"Good morning, Noel," he said cheerfully, mounting the stairs to climb to the tiny room (formerly broom cupboard) he had been assigned as an office on the top floor of the new building. "Feels like summer might be on the way at last, doesn't it?"

"Don't give me that shit," snarled de Vere balefully. "And don't forget to sign in," he shouted up the staircase after Brian, who was quickly leaving him behind as he took the stairs three at a time.

"Sorry, old boy, can't be done," called Brian. "Myra's not there until eight forty-five and I've an appointment in another building at nine. you've seen me now, haven't you?"

While most of the staff disguised their movements using the local pubs as cover, Brian had decided to keep his own comings and goings vague by moving round the various buildings of the Polytechnic scattered across the town. (He had learned quite early in his days at the College of Education, that, unlike the theatre, if you want to survive in academia, it does not do to be available too easily.) Brian guessed that none of the Art and Design staff, even Noel de Vere, knew anything much about the rest of the institution which employed them. To them the place was infested with troglodytes like scientists and engineers. Even Humanities dealt in words with which he knew they were uneasy as well. Thus, if he left a note with Myra as to his whereabouts, to the rest of the staff he knew he might just as well have said he was on the moon.

Brian had used his peregrinations to make many potentially useful contacts amongst the staff of the various departments he had visited. He knew he was welcomed in most of them because he was quite good at dealing with new people and had many amusing stories about his current colleagues and the students he dealt with, which he told well, (although he made sure that he gave away nothing damaging to the Department itself, like the two-salary man, its invisible lecturer, extra-mural females with rapacious tendencies, or the interest of the constabulary in vibrator flyposters.)

In spite of his desire to be accepted fully by his artist colleagues, he had nevertheless found these expeditions across the fault-line a relief, R and R after the anxiety and hysteria in the Art Department. He blessed his ability to get on with people and tell a good tale and occasionally hankered for the possibility some time in the future, of a free transfer to the real world of academic life from what he was beginning to think of as its virtual reality version in Art and Design. (The feeling was especially acute this particular morning after the Course Board coming so soon as it had on top of the incident with Audrey Reaper.)

His major disappointment in his tours of the Poly was to find how few women there were on the staff, all of them either married or, if not, too old for him. That left Connie Grey as far as he was concerned. She was the most exciting girl he had met in a long time and it was to set up her session in the computer facilities of the Poly that he was bound at nine o'clock. But first to his room to copy up the paper he had written overnight on his proposal for a potential new course. He whistled as he went along to the new block.

In roughing out the draft, he had become convinced that what he had started as a diversion probably had some mileage in it as a course proposal. Not couched in the jargonese he had used at the meeting but straight, as a genuine proposition to get students out of the studio-bound, ivory tower traditionalism on which a lot of the Department's teaching was based. He didn't feel there was anything wrong with this approach per se; after all it was thoroughly tried and tested. But he was sure it led to many students feeling that both they themselves and what they did were irrelevant. And in Brian's book, that was bad. (He had begun to see what the previous panel had meant. Also, he had learned from talking to staff that the problem of 'relevance' was not peculiar to Brindling; many other departments around the country were wondering how to adapt to contemporary demands.) His course would force students at least to confront the present-day cultural landscape of shifting sand in which their artistic ambitions were being fashioned. It might help them to ride the tiger of restless change which had been the essence of western society since the Renaissance. (His Ph.D. work on his own idol, Hawksmoor, an architect consciously revolutionary in his work, had shown him that.)

To do this and help them contribute their own ideas about environmental change at a level more sophisticated than their command of traditional skills allowed, would have to involve computing, and especially the command of computer graphical skills. He was fully aware that the ability to use information technology was the sine qua non for intellectual respectability with the trogs. In writing the proposal, he knew that the course would be - could be - only led by himself and although ambition played a part in his proposal, he genuinely believed the course could be exciting, both to teach and study if it ever came off and, at the very least, it might help to throw some grit in the eyes of the 'Prince of fucking Darkness' and the rest of the thought police.

Where all this left Spiller, on the other hand, he had not really thought about. Sufficient to the day etc. Brian had obtained one of his tape and slide lectures the previous day after the meeting and had played it through in the lecture theatre on his own. Intellectually, he judged that

Spiller's thought was perfectly respectable, if a little old-fashioned in content. Brian wondered whether he had made the tape before or after he became alienated.

Brian ran up the whole of the flights of stairs to the top floor of the new building, a habit which substituted for jogging to which many of the staff in the rest of the Polytechnic, but not a soul in the art college, seemed addicted. He could see a group of them from the top corridor window even now, doggedly completing their morning circuits of the park. Amongst them he was interested to notice the Rector and Dr. Marshall. He had been told by Myra that the former already had at least one heart attack. He wondered whose idea it was to jog, Marshall's or the Rector's. Brian was still suspicious of Marshall, in spite of his recognition of Brian as a possible brother under the skin. He speculated idly that if Marshall could only get the Rector to play squash as well, there'd be a large pair of empty shoes waiting to be filled.

Brian pushed at the door of his office. It opened part-way then sprang back and hit him on the forehead. Brian cried out, rubbed his head and pushed again. Again, the door bounced back. Brian gave it a strong shove with his shoulder to it and squeezed through into his room.

"What the...?" he said aloud when he saw the cause of the obstruction.

The floor of the tiny office was almost completely filled by a bivouac tent, the kind with inflatable ribs and a tunnel entrance. From inside came the muffled but recognisable voice of Oswald Spiller.

"Good morning. Is that you, Dr. Mather?" it said. "What time is it?"

"Spiller?" said Brian furiously. "What the devil do you think you're playing at? What is all this?"

"I hope you don't mind, Dr. Mather. I'm afraid Mr. de Vere has banned me from my own office. He's even having the lock changed. He said as we are part of the same section I should share your room until he assigns me another one. I thought I'd keep out of your way with my little tent, a sort of office within an office, as it were. I came in earlier and set it up so I wouldn't disturb you doing it after you arrived. Just ignore it and carry on as usual, what? By the way, what is the time now? It's rather difficult to see in here I must get some new batteries for this torch."

"Jesus wept," said Brian, "you can't stay here like this. It's a nonsense."

"But surely you can get to your desk, if you squeeze past? It's very flexible," said Spiller. He shook the tent from the inside.

"Look, Spiller, I see students in this room all the time."

"I'll be very quiet," said Spiller. "They won't even know I'm here."

"And what do I tell them? That I've got an invisible friend living with me in a tent? They'll think I'm as crazy as you are." He wondered if he had gone too far.

There was a pause.

"I know the staff in this place think that. I know it all too well. But I'm not in the least 'crazy' as you call it. I have very sound reasons for my behaviour. Would you like to hear my side of it?"

"Dear God!" said Brian. "No. Come on out of..."

Spiller ploughed on unheeding. "Four years ago the students in this place instituted a boycott of all theoretical lectures as they had decided -

The floor of the office was almost completely filled by a bivouac tent, the kind with inflatable ribs and a tunnel entrance.

they decided, mind you - that artists did not need any theoretical understanding of the subject. Aesthetics was a waste of time, the gesture was all, and, of course, de Vere, to whom the student is the ultimate sacred cow because he's mortally afraid of seeming old-hat to them, refused to support me and force them to attend. So, there and then, I decided I would give them tit for tat and institute my own boycott in return. And unlike them, I have stuck to my principles ever since. Is that so crazy?"

You betcha life it is, thought Brian. Aloud he said:

"I don't care what happened four years ago, Spiller, I want this tent out of this room now." In spite of himself, Brian was intrigued as to how Spiller had kept his invisible status for four years. It must constitute some sort of record almost on a par with the two-salary man. "Incidentally, what have you been doing for the last four years, Spiller? You couldn't have been just sitting in that cupboard downstairs every day, surely. You'd have gone..." He avoided saying it again as it was clear the man was crazy already.

"What I have been doing is my business. I have many private interests connected with my wife's work as a...Never mind what I've been doing," he said testily, "but I assure you I have not been idle, dear me no!"

Brian was about to remonstrate further with Spiller when there was a knock on the door. "Come in," he called out, forgetting that to enter was almost impossible. The door went through its bouncing routine and smote the potential entrant.

"Wassa matter wid this-a fooking-a door?" said Louie Bonetti from the other side. In spite of his anger about Spiller, Brian had to laugh aloud. Louie's version of English reminded him irresistibly of Chico Marx.

"Hold on," Brian called out, forcing the door open and holding it against the ribs of the tent.

"Good-a God!" said Louie, when he finally entered and saw the tent. "You join-a the Boy Scoutas or sometink, Brian?"

"It's Spiller, Louie. He's inside there and I want him out. Maybe you can shift him," said Brian.

Louie called into the tunnel of the tent: "Hey, Spiller, wadda you do 'ere, man, eh?"

"There's no need to shout," said Spiller. "I can hear you very well, thank you. Please carry on with your business and imagine I'm not here. If Mr. de Vere says Dr. Mather and I are to share this office temporarily, then that is what we will do. I have a perfect right to be here, therefore. I have been assigned to this room by the Head of Department."

Louie shook his head at Brian. "This-a guy's off-a the wall," he said. He took from one of the many pockets of the capacious Italian hunting jacket he wore, an etching tool sheathed with the cap of a ball pen. He uncapped it, and, winking broadly at Brian, neatly punctured the ribs of the tent one by one.

"That's outrageous. How dare you!" came the cry from inside, increasingly muffled as the tent sank quickly down on its occupant. "This is damage to personal property. I shall report - report - I can't breathe in here. Oh! Oh!" Louie gestured to Brian to come outside and they left Spiller struggling to find the tunnel exit from the now flattened canvas.

In the corridor, Louie handed Brian a large stiff envelope.

"It's a invite to my new show-a next-a mont'."

"Thank you very much," said Brian. He was delighted and flattered that Louie had bothered to come up to the top floor to hand it to him personally when he could have sent it in the internal mail. He was a bulky man and Brian could see on the only small part of his face left exposed by the mass of unkempt grey beard and wild hair, that the climb had cost him some sweat. Brian slipped the invitation into his briefcase.

"Iss ok," said Louie with a deprecating gesture. "I tink-a you like-a my prints. Iss a nice galeria, the Arts-a Centre. An' will be plenty good-a food an' vino, an' all. My wife, Elizabet', she make a cracker pizza. My ol' mamma in Bologna teach 'er. Er..." Louie hesitated as though he was looking for words.

"Yes?" prompted Brian.

"Yesserday. The meeting-k. All-a that shit-a you talk. You mean all that?" It was obvious that this was the real reason for Louie's visit.

Brian thought for a moment. Louie, he guessed, was worried about his ability to handle the challenge of the upcoming visit. In the report of the last quinquennial, Brian had read that Louie, as Course Leader, had come in for the bulk of the flack as to the prevailing 'traditional' emphasis of the course. His position as Course Leader long pre-dated the Polytechnic when the Art and Design College needed someone with artistic charisma to lead its courses. Louie certainly had that; Hermione had spoken to Brian of his flair and passionate dedication to art, artists and art students and it was this unbounded enthusiasm and exotic Italian background that had got him the job. In those days, words on paper and 'managerial efficiency' came well down on the list of priorities. The students, even the most bolshie amongst them, were as devoted to Louie as he was to them and none of the staff had a bad word to say about him. But inside a Polytechnic? Who needs passion? Who needs charisma? It's words and numbers that count, kiddo, as de Vere had said. And Louie spoke like Chico Marx - and probably counted like Harpo.

"It's what's expected, Louie," said Brian finally. "Whether it has to mean something is another matter."

"Well, I tell-a you this for nothin-k, Brian, it mean-a fook all to me," said Louie with a sniff. "Mebbe I should take-a the early retire, eh? Go and live in Italia, drink vino and poke-a my wife. This-a game's beyon' me, now. I don' know-a what-a anybody's talk about any more. Iss nowt to do wid art, I know-a that. And that-a guy, Marshall, 'e's-a sometink else. 'E give-a me the creepses. 'E 'olds onna 'is balls alla time, you know what I mean?"

"It's 'ow - er - how he was trained at school," said Brian.

"You-a don' do that, do you Brian? The way-a you talk, yesserday, I tink mebbe you do. An' dat Marshall guy, e' talk to you after like 'e was your long los' brother." He looked at him with a strong hint of suspicion.

Brian was disconcerted at Louie's perspicacity. But, after all, he thought, Louie doesn't know me very well. He might be regretting telling him the story of the two-salary man, for instance, a story Louie would certainly never tell a man like Marshall; he was trusting but not naive.

"No," said Brian firmly. "Absolutely not. If you ever see me do that it's because I need a pee. OK?"

"Ok, ok," said Louie, holding up his hand. "Ah. Fooking-a Englishmen. Who unnerstan' any of 'em. They alla crazy. Look-a Spiller. Jesus!"

Louie shook his head and suddenly pushed his face towards Brian and looked him straight in the eye. He was about Brian's height and Brian detected that Louie might have had a goodly helping of garlic sausage for breakfast which caused him to flinch back from him, but Louie gripped his shoulders tightly.

"Issa big crunch comin', Brian. You gonna 'ave to take-a sides. Mebbe we all-a lose-a our jobs, eh? But watta the 'ell, we gotta put up a fight. Cos we stand for sometink, Brian. Art. Tousands-a years of it. These Poly bastards don' know from shit. No bloody culture, none o' dem. Dat Rector. Jesus! Wadda you say?"

"That's a bit dramatic, isn't it, Louie?" said Brian.

"You tink-a so?" said Louie, maintaining his grip. "You wait an' see." He let go abruptly, turned and went to the stairs. Brian followed him. Louie turned again to him as he was about to descend. Brian kept beyond his reach. "Remember, Brian, you gotta pick-a your side. You sell out to dem, you mebbe get on, like-a Marshall. You stick wid us, you got some honour left. We Italians, mebbe's we's talk-a comical but we's know about honour."

He turned abruptly and went down the stairs.

Brian had little time to reflect on Louie's outburst as he heard him speak to Noel de Vere who was obviously on his way up, but he was impressed nevertheless. Damn, thought Brian. He glanced at his cheap digital and saw that it was now quarter to nine. He might just slip away down the second fire escape staircase, but it was too late; de Vere had reached the last turn in the stairs and saw him.

"Ah, there you are," he said, puffing. "Hold on a minute, Mather. That - that paper. Have you got it?"

This was typical of de Vere in his current state, thought Brian. Everything had to be done yesterday or the sky would fall in; it was why he had roughed it out overnight. He took it from his case and handed it to de Vere as he stepped onto the top corridor.

"I'm afraid it's only in rough," he said. "I was about..."

Noel de Vere interrupted him with clawing movements of his hairy right fist directed towards him. As he did so, he bared his teeth at Brian. "Ssss! Ssss!." he hissed. He grabbed the paper without thanking him for it and did not seem in the least surprised that it should have been prepared so promptly. Brian reflected that de Vere was beginning to acquire some very odd habits; he had noticed the gesture of the 'hissing claw', as the staff had dubbed it, was becoming increasingly frequent. He was quite sure de Vere was unaware of its effect or even that he was doing it. He went straight on to another topic.

"Connie Grey!" he said, staring intently at Brian and pushing his face close. Brian flinched but thought that at least he doesn't eat garlic sausage for breakfast - just a normal halitosis this time. Nobody in this place seemed able to talk to you without their face a few inches from your nose.

"What about her?" he said carefully.

"You tell me, kiddo." said de Vere, in his best hard-boiled style. "What are you up to with her?"

"I'm not up to anything," said Brian mildly, moving sideways from him slightly. He wondered briefly if Zoe had been talking to him. "She asked for help with computer graphics and I'm arranging it."

"You didn't clear it with me, though, did you, did you? Her tutor," said de Vere, following him and wildly jabbing his finger towards him. Again, Brian registered the extra hostility lent by its dark, furry covering, and moved back instinctively towards the edge of the stairs to avoid its jab into his chest. "What does she want with computer graphics, anyway? She's a painter. The best we've had for five years." His voice began to rise even more emotionally. "I won't have it, do you hear. I won't have any of your computer shit spoiling that. Savvy?" He lunged forward again. Brian sidestepped neatly and de Vere shot down a few stairs and had to hold on to the rail to stop himself falling.

"Stand still, for fuck's sake, while I'm talking to you," he said climbing back up again.

"I supposed as a third year student in her last term that she could ask for help without consulting 'sir' first," said Brian pleasantly. "In any case, I naturally assumed she would have done so. I see now I was mistaken. I obviously misread the situation. My mistake. However, I'll tell her when I see her this afternoon that you don't want her to have anything more to do with me, shall I?" he suggested, looking evenly at de Vere.

"Yes and tell her - ' His vehement answer was cut short and a look of panic came into his face. "No, no, don't do that."

Brian reflected that Spiller was right about one thing at least: Noel de Vere's mortal fear of being seen by students as a fuddy-duddy.

"No, no. Just keep me informed. Yes, that's it. Just keep me informed." He glanced down at the paper in his hand. "This is it, then?"

"Yes." said Brian. "I think you might find it an interesting read. I've calculated its effect on staff contact hours and..."

De Vere made his curious grimace and hissing sound again.

"Ssss! Save it for the next Board meeting. I haven't got time to stand here all day chatting, for Christ' sake. We've got a visit in a few weeks time." He turned towards the stairs then quickly spun round again. "In writing, mind."

"What?" said Brian, bewildered.

"Connie Grey. I want everything in writing." He spun round once more but went too far and set off along the corridor past Brian and towards the emergency stairs. Brian watched him hurry away and saw him stop, look round with a slightly puzzled air, then set off once more, making the odd hissing sound as he went. Brian descended the main staircase thoughtfully. If Noel went on at this rate, he reflected, he'd soon be joining Spiller in his little tent.

Brian had just finished loading the programme he thought suitable for Connie's project when she came into the computer lab in which he'd arranged to meet her.

"Hi Brian!," she said,

He saw the computer students, all of whom were male, look up from their VDU's at this surprise addition to their Friday afternoon session. He felt quite pleased with himself as they stared at her crossing the room towards him. Brian reflected that she might have had dance training she moved so well. The sway of her hips and bra-less bosom was perfectly set off by the simple, loose, sleeveless print dress with plunging neck-line she was wearing. Its thin shoulder straps left most of her shoulders and upper chest exposed. She had on no make-up, but her excellent skin and a beautiful pair of ceramic shell ear-rings in an aquamarine blue glaze, too good a match for her eyes not to have been made specially for her, rendered make-up superfluous. With alarm, Brian guessed he knew their maker and hoped it didn't mean what it could mean. In the ration of a few days of early summer sunshine which was all, Brian guessed, that Brindling was allowed at this time of the year - bring back the south, all is forgiven - she had nevertheless managed to achieve a light tan which glowed tantalisingly deep into her cleavage. There were no lighter strap marks on her shoulders. Brian's pulse once again assumed the beat it had when he first met her. He wondered whereabouts in Brindling she had found the privacy to sunbathe at least topless if not fully nude. And how he wished he knew where it was.

"Connie, hello," said Brian, trying to control his grin of pleasure. "Great. How nice you're so prompt. I've set up a progra..."

"Hello, introduce me, Brian. I'm Dr. Bill Johnson, by the way, in charge here."

Bill Johnson had emerged quickly from his office at the rear of the lab at Connie's appearance. He stuck out a large hand. Brian had told him that Connie would be in the computer section that afternoon and Bill had been hovering around pestering him with questions about the art department and especially its female students, since lunch-time.

With his approach to Connie, Brian was suddenly made aware of the big contrast between Bill and himself. Bill's clothes were designer-dashing and his brilliantly white casual shirt, open at the collar to expose an expanse of hairy chest, was monogrammed. (Brian made a mental bet his underwear was monogrammed too.) His fair hair was wavy and expensively floppy whereas Brian's was a cheap, barber-shop quickie. He was also taller, and much more muscular-looking than Brian. Brian's only consolations in his comparison were that Bill had the beginnings of a paunch which his expensive clothes could not quite disguise, and his tan, unlike Connie's, obviously could not have been acquired without artifice. But as compensations went, he did not feel these were particularly encouraging.

When they had first met on one of his early Polytechnic explorations, Bill had been fascinated to learn that Brian worked in Art and Design. Did he have access to the life-painting studio? he wondered. He'd heard the model was a cracker. Whenever he wanted which was never, Brian told him. (In fact, he'd had no reason to enter the place since coming to the college.) Perhaps he could come along some time and visit Brian in the art department? He wouldn't mind trying his hand at a dab of life-painting himself. He had an 'O'level in art and used to be pretty good. Brian did not have to be very sensitive to pick up the aridity of Bill's life amidst the aseptic glow of the VDU-packed computer labs and their almost all-male inhabitants. With a sharp sense of annoyance that he'd ever mentioned Connie to Bill Johnson, Brian introduced her.

Connie smiled at Bill in her open, American way.

"Hi, I'm Brian's student." They shook hands. Brian noticed, his annoyance increasing, that Bill held on to her hand beyond the conventional interval. He was also uncharacteristically bent forward, the better to ogle her cleavage, Brian thought, the creep.

"Brian's told me you're after help with computer graphics. Right?"

Connie nodded. "That's right. Can you help me as well, Dr. Johnson?"

"Bill, please. Can I help? Can a duck swim? I can make these babies jump through hoops," he said, waving his hand at the rows of screens. "Anything you need, just tell me."

"That's really great," said Connie, giving him a broad smile. Bill swelled visibly. "Is that ok with you, Brian?" She looked at Brian who was trying to keep his annoyance hidden.

"Of course," said Brian, tight-lipped.

Connie picked up his true feelings quickly. She smiled at him.

"My, my," she said, "aren't I the lucky girl, though? Two big strong experts all to myself."

In spite of how he felt, Brian was amused by Connie's irony. His irritation evaporated and he smiled back at her. Brian saw that Bill was too busy flexing himself to notice he was being sent up.

"Now what have you got in mind, Connie?" Bill patted the swivel chair in front of the largest console in the room, not the one Brian had selected. "This one isn't allowed to students - unless they're very privileged, of course. And you certainly come into that category." He grinned at her and took another chair for himself from the next work station. "You sit here and tell your Uncle Bill all about it."

She outlined her idea, which was to use the computer to alter a videotape in which the original images of the Madonna and Child from various famous paintings were to be replaced by an image drawn from her own work. Brian could see that Bill was only paying half attention to what she was saying. The other half was busy drinking in her looks.

"Yes, well, ok. I'll give you a quick run through and show you how the programme can help. I think there might be a better choice than the one Brian loaded. That's ok for student work, but not for something like this. I loaded this one in here this morning when Brian told me you were coming." The cunning sod! thought Brian. "Ok with you, Brian?" He smiled at him indulgently. Brian held his fury in check.

"You're the expert," he said, grinding his teeth. He saw Connie smile to herself, which increased his annoyance.

"Your idea poses quite a problem but I think this baby can crack it. It's state of the art. Here, let me show you what it can do." They both leaned forward as Brian got himself a stool. There was no way he could sit without being marginalised behind them. The display flashed dazzling arrays of colour on the screen as Bill put it through its paces, handling the console with the aplomb of a man driving a Ferrari. Brian was reduced to taking notes and admiring the fine blonde hairs at the back of Connie's neck. Bill encouraged her to try the mouse, keeping his hand on hers to guide it and leaning far forward. Brian's chagrin became almost unbearable. If he stares any further down her dress, he thought, his eyeballs'll be bouncing off her knee caps. He found he was not alone in his ire at Bill's behaviour, however.

"Hey, hinny!" A loud Geordie voice made all three of them jump as it called suddenly from behind them. "D'yer think if I 'ad your knickers instead of my knackers I could gerra bit of attention, an arl?"

"I think the natives are getting restless," said Brian. Connie turned. "Bill, I think I've taken up enough..."

"Take no notice of them," said Bill. "Bunch of peasants." He winked at Brian.

As Connie had turned, Brian noticed two tiny spots of red tingeing her cheeks. Brian decided that Dr. Bill Johnson had had quite enough of a good thing for one afternoon.

"Oh, by the way, Bill," he said lightly. "Connie's tutor, Noel de Vere, wants to be kept informed in writing of all she does with her project. Is that ok by you if you're going to help her? It's for her finals, you see. In case the externals want to check on her work." He spoke to Connie. "I presume this is going to be part of your final show?"

"Oh, surely," she said.

"A couple of thousand words should do it," he said. "And as technical as possible, please. Always a good idea to blind 'em with science, don't you agree?"

It was now Bill's turn to be annoyed. Brian knew very well that Bill would feel out of his depth with the idea of writing for something as abstruse as an art project, especially one which might be examined closely.

"That's ridiculous. To hell with that," he said, dismissing the idea.

Brian shrugged. "Well, that's what he wants. And if he doesn't get it, he'll be dancing up and down to Rector, CNAA examiners and anybody else who'll listen. All about lack of co-operation from the computer section and how they mucked up his student. Connie here is his star, you know. You don't mind my saying that do you, Connie?"

"Not in the least," she said, watching Bill struggle with his dilemma.

"And if anything does go wrong for her there'll be merry hell to pay for both of us. He can get really stroppy about causing trouble for people these days as you probably know. Appeals committee, the lot." Brian was well aware of Noel de Vere's increasing reputation all over the Polytechnic for irrational reactions to even the slightest provocation.

"You could write it," Bill said impatiently.

"Oh, I'll be writing my bit, naturally," said Brian, "but I can't speak for the parts of the project you'll be responsible for, can I?"

Brian could see Bill's enthusiasm waning. He knew very well the project was laborious and one Bill could not possibly have the time for.

"I want to thank you a lot for this, Bill," said Connie, firmly bringing the session to an end. "It's going to be really useful," she said, smiling at him. "By the way, perhaps you'd like to come to my birthday party this evening? If you're not engaged elsewhere, of course," she said, unexpectedly. And what about me? thought Brian. I'm the guy you came in with, after all. "Please bring anyone with you - wife? girlfriend?"

"I'd love to," said Bill, cheering up. "Thanks. And I'll be on my own." He leered at her significantly.

"That's just great. It's at 'BoZo'Z', the night club. Do you know it?"

"I'll find it," he said.

"From nine, ok?"

"Fine. Look forward to it."

At last he took his leave, accompanied by an "Aboot bloody time, an' arl," from the Geordie. He leered confidently at Brian before turning his attention to the student.

"God, you're a pest, Brandon. What is it now?" He went into his office with the Geordie.

"That was slick," said Connie. "Putting him off like that."

Brian shrugged. "He was going on a bit."

Connie looked at him levelly. "I can take care of myself, you know. I'm quite a big girl now. But thanks all the same."

"I'll remember," he said. "And many happy returns."

"Thank you. Did you follow all that?"

"Oh, yes. I've got all we need down in note form. We can get to work next week if you like." After I've been to your party and got to know you better, he thought. Where's my invitation?

"Good. Would Tuesday week before your lecture be ok?"

Still no invite but at least she's sussed out when my first year lecture is. "Yes," he said, "that'll be fine. Shall we meet here about one-thirty?"

"Great," said Connie, rising. "A week on Tuesday, then."

It's not possible. No! She's going. Come on, come on. Yes, I'd love to come to your party. I'll wash up, sing comic songs, bake the effing cake, anything.

"I hope you don't mind if I rush off?" she said. "I've got to prepare a few things before this evening. Bye."

In a moment she had gone. Brian sat stunned. He turned slowly to the computer, and, before closing it down, put into the programme a beautifully designed and coloured virus.

'BILL JOHNSON IS AN EGOTISTICAL FATHEAD!' it said.

By nine o'clock that evening, Brian could stand it no longer. He tried to read, listen to the radio, work on his new course idea, copy up notes from the afternoon, eat, clean the flat, anything to keep at bay the depressing thought that he had been deliberately omitted from the party. Nor did the wallpaper in his tiny bedroom help. A previous occupant with an odd taste in exotica had chosen one with a black background on which pink flamingoes disported themselves. Oscar's Wilde's reputed final words that "Either this wallpaper goes or I do." seemed quite believable if he'd had to put up with anything like this. Finally, he bathed for the second time that evening, shaved, also for the second time, and assembled an outfit as jolly as he could muster from the straitened wardrobe to which his spell of unemployment had reduced him. He went out with the intention of crashing the party anyway.

The bus driver seemed surprised he was even contemplating walking to 'BoZo'Z!' at that time of night and reluctantly gave him directions. By the time he got near the club it was after ten and had started to rain. He was wearing only a light sweater and slacks so he began to hurry.

The area in which the club was situated was not one anybody would choose to walk in late at night, as the driver had warned him. It was an ill-lit clutter of old mills and warehouses with neglected streets and broken pavements. He was passing one of the empty buildings when an old female drunk, reeking of 'bo', damp wool and cheap sherry, and rattling a plastic bag of empty bottles, lurched from an alcove and grabbed his arm tightly.

"Hey, chaw," she said. "Give a lady a fag, will yer?"

"Get off," said Brian, trying to disentangle himself. "I don't smoke."

"Then I'll tell you summat for nowt, then. Them pakki fellas is a damn sight more sexier than what you h'Englishmen are."

"Yes," he said, freeing himself, "and if you're speaking from personal experience, madame, they surely must be."

He increased his pace to get away as she digested this.

"Cheeky bugger!" she called after him. "All you middle class bastards are the same. Yer don't give a monkey's for a poor old working woman when yer meet one."

As Brian kept up a faster pace, he was less able to pay full attention to where he was walking in the poor light. A few yards on, one of the many broken paving stones snared his feet and down he went. He heard the screech of laughter from the old woman. He picked himself up, his one set of clothes suitable to a party in need of a complete clean. He was mortified as he heard the drunk cackling and calling out:

"Hey, do that again, chaw! It were better than the telly. Arse over tip. Serves yer bloomin' well right, yer rotten sod!"

Brian went on, cursing Brindling, its Borough Council, Bill Johnson, Noel de Vere, Zoe Temaine, the Polytechnic and above all himself for letting Connie Grey get so much under his skin. After an early student romance with a glamorous French girl he had chased round half Europe, to the detriment of his health, bank balance and psyche, he had made sure all his subsequent liaisons were light-hearted. To be stuck, humiliatingly filthy and soaked, in the back streets of Brindling for the sake of a woman he had only just met, reminded him forcefully of the back street in Prague when Natasha had finally told him that he bored her and left him penniless to find his own way home. It had been raining then too, he remembered. Perhaps this sort of thing was the proper fate for the romantic he knew himself in his heart to be: a ludicrous figure of fun to be laughed at by tramps. Still, when she wasn't being bored, she had been worth it - probably.

He tried ineffectually to wipe himself down with his handkerchief. It made little difference and he was now getting very wet. He was about to abandon the idea of the party altogether but the thought of Bill Johnson drove him on. At least his wet clothes wouldn't show the dirt so much, he thought. He turned a corner and 'BoZo'Z' lit up the street in front of him. With its flashing pink neon sign reflecting in the puddles and from the roofs of the parked cars in front, it was like a bizarre oasis in the desert of discarded junk. Behind the sign he could see the still grimy walls of the old warehouse from which it had been converted.

"Hey, Brian! 'Old on, wack."

He was startled to be addressed by name from an alcove like the one from which the drunken woman had emerged.

"Who's that?" he said suspiciously, peering into the dark.

"It's me, wack." Ronnie Oliver emerged into the light. "Hey, 'ave you come to watch the fun, then, eh?"

"What fun?" said Brian. "I was going to Connie Grey's party."

"Did she invite you, then?"

"Well, no," said Brian. He moved nearer the alcove to get out of the rain slightly.

"Then she must like you. You'd best stay 'ere wi' me, wack, 'cos the real party's about to start."

Brian was completely foxed by this speech. In spite of his lurking in an alcove in a derelict back street, there seemed no hint of oddness in Ronnie's manner. In fact, he seemed to be completely in charge of himself now. And what did he mean by Connie's showing she liked him - his heart had given a jump at this - by not inviting him to her party? Ronnie moved back to merge completely into the shadow once more.

"Come on, wack, man. You don't want anybody to clock yer," said Ronnie urgently.

Brian moved into the shadow with him but kept his distance nevertheless.

"What's going on?" he said. "What fun? What party?"

"You'll see," said Ronnie. He could hardly suppress the glee in his voice.

"This is ridiculous," said Brian, deciding he had been mistaken and Ronnie was unstable, after all. He moved back into the street but Ronnie grabbed him and pulled him back.

"Look at that! The Old Bill's spot on time for once. The fartistas strike again!" He began to chatter the theme of the 'William Tell' overture. "Hi-oh Silver, yer bugger! Go get the sods, Tonto." He seemed beside himself with excitement at the sight of a line of police vehicles with blue lights flashing and wailing sirens which had erupted round the corner at the far end of the street. They came to a noisy halt in front of 'BoZo'Z' and, like a Hollywood cop movie, squads of policemen, some in riot gear and some with dogs, poured from them. There were not only car and van-loads of them but police buses as well. In a moment they had entered the club and a pandemonium of shouting and barking could be heard even at this distance from inside. Very soon they had thrown cordons across the road and shortly afterwards began escorting the club's revellers out and into the vans and buses. Brian had not noticed but, in the meanwhile, Ronnie Oliver had collapsed beside him, shaking, against the walls of the alcove. With some alarm, Brian finally registered this.

"Are you ok, Ronnie?" he asked him urgently.

"Smashing, wack," came a strangled reply. Brian realised that Ronnie was, in fact, doubled up with silent laughter.

In a very short time at the cordon's edge, a small crowd of spectators had gathered. Brian wondered where they could possibly have come from in his district but nothing was beginning to surprise him about Brindling. Silhouetted amongst them, he made out the drunk from the alcove. She cheered and catcalled each group as it came out and was loaded. Very quickly she found herself frogmarched into one of the vans along with them. The police seemed not too bothered about the other spectators so Brian decided to take a closer look. Ronnie called to him to stay but he took no notice.

He joined the crowd at the back. Some of the groups were still in a hilarious mood and waved the bottles and glasses they carried at the crowd before they were taken away from them. The crowd responded in kind. Others protested loudly. In one of these groups, and protesting the loudest of all, Brian spotted a red-faced Bill Johnson. He ducked behind the back of the man next to him until Bill had been bundled into a van and the door slammed shut. He resumed his watch but started at the sound of a woman's voice with a soft American accent speaking from beside him.

"Exciting, isn't it?" said Connie. "And not a gun in sight. It always amazes me how they can do that in this country."

"What the...How did you get out?"

"Out of where?" she asked in a matter-of-fact voice. "Did you see Bill? He looked quite put out, didn't you think, poor guy?" She slipped her arm through his. This sudden intimacy made him start. She held onto his arm firmly. He could still feel the grip of the drunk's fingers as well as Ronnie's under the soft pressure of her raincoated arm. "And poor old Betty Flynn.

She should have kept quiet."

"Who?" said Brian.

"The old bag they popped in with the others."

"The drunk? You know her?"

"Oh yes. She's very useful to us. They'll clean her up, give her a free meal and let her out with a caution."

Brian was suddenly aware that his mouth had fallen open with astonishment.

"Look, just what the hell is going on?" he said.

"Drugs bust," she said simply.

"How do you know?" he asked. She didn't answer.

"What about your party?"

"What party?" she said. "Gosh, poor you, you're all wet and filthy. What have you been doing?"

"It's nothing," he said, but the now familiar racing of his heart began as she said: "You must come back to my place and get cleaned up. Were you trying to crash my party?"

"Something of the sort," he said.

"Wouldn't you have been the disappointed one, though," she said ironically. "Still, it is quite flattering and all."

"Well, what did happen to the part..?"

She gripped his arm tightly to steady herself as she went on her toes to see over the man in front.

"Oh look, here come the main event. The Godfather and his capos."

Escorted by a dense phalanx of police and their dogs came a group of older men. Unlike the other groups, who were now loaded and some of whom were singing loudly inside the buses, these men were silent. Central to the small knot of sober-suited figures, Brian made out four faces familiar to him. The first was the editor of the local newspaper he had met while researching local politics. The second he recognised from his interview to be Charlie Huggett, Chairman of the Council. Another was the moustachioed and hatted policeman from the patrol car who was tightly holding onto Huggett's arm, to his obvious resentment. The last was also holding tightly onto an arm but it was his own arm which he was stretching up to peer earnestly at the watch face on its wrist in the light from the cars and vans, oblivious of his surroundings.

"Hey," said Connie, "isn't that the guy we saw the other day, the Invis..."

"It is." said Brian. "It's Dr. Oswald flaming Spiller."

Chapter Five
Femme Fartista

Connie led Brian away from 'BoZo'Z', now dark and silent after the raid, through a maze of streets and alleyways towards the dockland district. He quickened his pace slightly when he traversed the only part he recognised: the end of the street where Audrey had thrown her bender. Like the parent mill for 'BoZo'Z', the old warehouses and yards had largely fallen into disuse so that the atmosphere became even more gloomy the nearer they got to the river, even though the rain had ceased. Connie offered no explanations to enlighten Brian further as to what she was doing or what had happened at the nightclub, and, in any case, the unlikely sight of Oswald Spiller being led off by the police had so confused Brian that he was quite incapable of thinking of any sort of rational questions. Also, the company who had now joined them in their walk, which included Ronnie, precluded any conversation. To Brian's disappointment when the first of their companions, a student named Bernie Rodenstein, had joined them, Connie released the easy hold she had had on his arm and walked briskly at his side maintaining a friendly rather than intimate distance between them.

In the light of the occasional street lamp, Brian glanced at the faces of their companions and recognised them as the elite of year three of the college. They were students who had been pointed out to him in his first few weeks by Peter Orrd as some of those most likely to do well in finals. Apart from Connie herself and Ronnie Oliver, who, Brian gathered, had had frequent breakdowns requiring postponement of his course so that he had been at Brindling long enough to try almost every discipline in the college, the other three men and four women were sculptors. Walking beside Connie, he could feel their suspicious glances probing his presence. None of them spoke to Connie, although Brian sensed she was the central figure in the group. Nor did they talk to each other so that, apart from the slap of 'Doc Marten's' and the distant police sirens still excitably wailing in the vicinity of 'BoZo'Z', the only sound accompanying them was a muttered "'Ere we go. 'Ere we go. 'Ere we go," from Ronnie Oliver. There was, however, also a delicious smell which wafted along with them, masking the occasional assault of broken drains, which came from a very large pizza-case carried by one of them. Finally, they arrived at a pair of tall dock gates. Connie took a set of keys from her raincoat pocket and opened the three locks in a door set into them. All the group filed through. Entering the yard, the silence was shattered by a couple of large, mongrely-looking guard dogs which bounded towards them in the darkness, barking savagely.

"Good God!" said Brian, preparing to flee.

"It's ok," Connie said. "You're with us." She and the rest of the group began to fuss the dogs and call them by name.

With the door safely locked behind them and the animals pacified, the students broke into frenzied hilarity, hugging and congratulating each other on what Brian was only now beginning to have his suspicions about. Connie told them to be quiet. They complied immediately. Brian was reminded of her effect on the dogs. Their hilarity subsided and they formed a circle round Brian. Nobody spoke to him but in the pale moonlight which had broken through the thinning rainclouds, Brian could see seven pairs of hostile eyes examining him carefully, as the dogs familiarised themselves with the smell of his soaked trousers. Connie, busy testing a small torch, was not amongst them. Nor was Ronnie, who had taken the giant pizza box and was now sniffing loudly inside it. He was soon joined by the expectant dogs.

"Err," said Ronnie breaking the silence. "Another bloomin' veggie pizza. I 'ate them things. Far too many bloomin' veggies in this group," he said. "'Ere, you greedy sods." He tore off some pieces and gave them to the dogs. "But you're not 'brown-ricers' either, are you?"

The others ignored Ronnie. Finally, one of the girls in the circle, Julia Lee, who was originally from Hong Kong, broached the question that Brian knew was in all of their minds and his too. "What he doing here, bloody hell?" she said pugnaciously. They all moved closer to him.

"I asked him to come," said Connie, stepping into the circle to stand beside Brian. This seemed sufficient explanation for the moment and they broke away slightly. "Come on, let's go. I'm starving," she said, making a move.

"Yeah and I'm bustin'," said Patience Richardson, a black girl from London.

The others laughed and set off after Connie who lighted their way with the torch. The dogs trotted along with them close to Ronnie.

"Leave off giving them that pizza, man. There'll be naff all left," from one of the men was all that Brian heard as they moved through the yard.

They went beyond some enormous heaps of scrap iron, about the only trade of any note left in Brindling port, to the edge of a smaller dock basin. Brian stumbled occasionally but the others obviously knew where the pitfalls were. Connie disappeared over the side of the dock down some stone steps. Brian and the rest followed her. The dogs watched them descend and stayed put. Brian's light, smooth-soled shoes, which he had imagined would have suited the dance floor of 'BoZo'Z', nearly betrayed him again and almost tipped him into the oil-filmed water of the dock as they slithered uneasily on the greasy, worn steps. At the bottom, Connie stepped onto the gently rocking deck of a boat and quickly disappeared. Brian could only make out that it might once have been a fishing boat. As he awkwardly mounted onto the deck over the rail and groped his way after her, there was a sudden flood of light from the wheelhouse and companion-way. He went below into the now brightly lit interior. The others followed, closing the hatch behind them.

Brian gasped at the sight of the boat's converted interior. He was sufficiently aware of interior design to see that little expense had been spared to fit it out. There were well-upholstered benches, good wood panelling and quality fittings. From behind a door in a panelled section at the opposite end to the companionway entrance to the main cabin, came the sound of a phone ringing. Connie quickly exited through the door and Brian had a glimpse of a small cabin with a neatly made bed within it. Stacked against the panels and on one of the benches in the main cabin were lots of paintings and drawings. Brian assumed that this beautiful, neat boat was Connie's home. On top of one of the piles of artwork, he recognised the still-life of bottles he had seen on his interview day. He wondered where the money had come from for the boat. Did she own it or was it rented? It certainly beat the cold-water bedsits most of the students could hardly even afford on their grants; chez Connie smelled of real money somewhere.

On the top of the fitted cabinet at the end of one of the side benches he noticed some family photographs. Prominent amongst them was one of a much younger Connie standing with an older, tall, bearded man, who was also featured in some of the other pictures. Her father?

Patience disappeared into a compartment at the rear as the others draped themselves on the bench to one side which was unencumbered by artistic clutter, and removed their coats. None of them was as wet as Brian, he noticed.

"Don't be too long in there," called out Alex Uruski, whom Brian knew to be Patience's boy friend.

Brian removed some paintings from the other side bench and sat on his own opposite the students. Ronnie put the pizza onto the long table in the middle of the cabin and collected some plates from a cupboard. Bernie Rodenstein opened a small fridge near the stove at the rear of the cabin and took out some cans. Only Shaheen Nazmir, an Asian girl from Birmingham, refused one. Before handing one to Brian, Bernie hesitated, but another student, Bridget Ryan nodded and mouthed a "Yeah, go ahead." and Brian was handed a can.

They settled down and began to drink, watching Brian warily and speaking to each other in undertones so that he could not hear. Working with Peter Orrd, they had evidently picked up his useful habit of mumbled communication, thought Brian. He felt like a patient with some interesting condition brought before a medical class for examination. Some of the students brought out tobacco tins and took out roll-up paper. Alex reached down, pulled up the edge of the carpet and began to lift a concealed panel in the floor boards. Another student, Gerry Hodgson, grimaced and poked him with his foot as he did so. Alex lowered the panel and replaced the carpet. Brian was fairly certain he knew what the floor panel concealed. Ronnie cut up and shared out the pizza; Brian was included. He was aware of his own very grubby hands as he took his portion, from which most of the dogs' tit-bits had come, he noticed.

Patience re-appeared. "God, it's a real pleasure to use a decent loo, for a change," she said, shaking out her dreadlocks and patting them dry with a towel.

Alex followed her into the washroom and came out again. Still nobody spoke directly to Brian, and he could think of nothing to say to them. By the time Alex had returned he was becoming very uncomfortable, not only from his wet and dishevelled clothing, and was ready to leave. He stood up and put down his half-emptied can and plate as Connie emerged from the bedroom cabin.

"Connie, I think I'll be on my way. It's getting..." he began to say.

"Oh," said Connie. "Look, why don't you go and get cleaned up first in the washroom?" she said. "You'd probably get arrested looking like that in this neighbourhood. Here." She handed him a large sweater she'd brought into the cabin with her.

Although his curiosity would have changed his mind easily, the sight of her now in jeans and a tie-dyed baseball shirt, her figure moving loosely beneath it, banished any further thought of his leaving. Also, she seemed to want him to stay, but whether from her personal preference or some other reason, he couldn't tell.

"Was that our friend on the phone, Connie?" said Shaheen.

Connie shook her head warningly at Shaheen and frowned. The boy sitting with his arm around her shoulders, Gerry Hodgson, shook her slightly to be quiet.

Brian closed the door of the washroom behind him and heard the group break into animated conversation. He cleaned up as best he could and tried to make out what was being said but, apart from the occasional loud "No, that's not on." from Gerry, he could make out nothing really coherent through the well-crafted panelling. By the time he re-entered the cabin, feeling a little more kempt, the conversation had ended and from the expectant air of the faces turned towards him, he imagined some decision about his presence had been resolved.

"Have a seat," said Connie. "Put some coffee on, somebody."

Alex rose and began filling up the percolator by the stove. Patience joined him and rubbed his back.

"Ah, domestic bliss," said Bernie.

"You're only jealous because it's something you'll never have," said Alex.

"Don't be too sure," said Bernie. "Even we of deviant proclivities can live in hope."

"I expect you've got a few questions, haven't you?" said Connie to Brian. Brian had so many he was uncertain where to begin.

"I gather you knew all that business at the club was going to happen," he said. "Am I right?"

"Yes," said Connie, without adding any further explanation.

"And there never was any party, was there?"

"No," she said.

"And you asked Bill Johnson deliberately to get him caught up in that raid."

"Yes." This was like pulling teeth, he thought.

"Why?"

"It seemed appropriate."

Ronnie giggled and rolled round the bench. "Christ, did you see his face? I wish I could get that sort of colour in my prints."

The others stayed serious.

"Leave it out, Ronnie," said Gerry, and Ronnie subsided.

"What do you mean, appropriate?" said Brian.

She shrugged. "It's a knocking shop. He'd love that sort of thing. You saw him this afternoon. He's notorious for putting it across female students. We've had a lot of complaints about him. Students are scared he won't help them if they complain formally. He's such a hot-shot expert on the latest programmes, they're dependent on him. But, let me tell you, if you're a female, you've got to go into that computer section like John Wayne fighting off a giant squid."

"I see," said Brian. Something she said struck him. "We've had a lot of complaints? Who's we?"

"Us," said Bridget Ryan.

Brian knew the answer to the next question was crucial.

"And who are us?"

"The..." Shaheen began, but Gerry nudged her quite hard and she stopped.

Nobody else volunteered to answer his question.

"You knew the raid was going to happen, then?"

"Oh yes," said Connie. "As a matter of fact we arranged it."

"Connie! What the hell are you doing?" said Gerry hotly.

Connie did not respond but her admission that they had more to do with it than he even suspected left him both confused and impressed.

"You arranged it, but - I mean, how?"

"That's enough questions for now," said Connie. "Now it's our turn. Is that coffee ready?"

"Coming," said Alex.

Nobody said anything as Alex and Patience passed out the coffee. All took it black and unsweetened.

Connie began when they had drunk a little. "Do you actually believe in what you say in your lectures?" she asked.

"Yes," said Brian bewildered. "But none of you have ever been..."

"Because some of the things you've said about attitudes sound quite interesting to us. Isn't that right?" Most of the group nodded.

"I really think this is a bad idea," said Gerry.

"Oh, Gerry," said Shaheen.

"I think Gerry right," said Julia Lee.

"Look, we can't go back over it all again, now," said Connie sharply. "We took a vote." This was the first time Brian had seen Connie lose her cool even slightly and reveal the steel beneath the velvety exterior. He knew once again his romantic - masochistic? - instincts had led him to another Natasha. But as he looked at her now, he could feel his caution rapidly diminishing.

Gerry and Julia subsided.

"What sort of things?" said Brian warily.

"Well, like how the instinct for freedom's diverted by the Establishment because it's dangerous and how the system works to reward playing safe at the expense of any originality - pallettised thinking you called it - and how art becomes marginalised and tamed and how imagination is strangled down in the education system so we have thousands of experts to run things who've never had an original thought in their lives. So they get things wrong again and again. You said in one lecture, for example, you felt the main trouble with this country is not lack of experts who know all there is to know about something, it's the lack of imagination to know what to do with it. It's too upsetting for the complacent bastards who run the system to change their comfortable pay-offs. Well, that's what we feel. And all the examples you gave where you can see this, like planning and armaments, and mass housing and energy policy and roads and science policy and Parliamen...."

"Hold on, hold on, hold on!" said Brian, shocked as his words came back to confront him in this odd context. "How do you know all this? You none of you come to my lectures."

"Somebody tapes them."

"Good Lord," said Brian. He had a sudden frisson as to how subversive his words might sound outside the context of the lecture theatre.

"Well, we agree with you so what we want to know before we go any further is, are you prepared to put your money where your mouth is?"

They looked at him critically.

"Of course," she went on coolly, "you may be just saying all this stuff because it's only a bunch of art students you're putting it to and they don't count, so you won't get any come-backs saying it. Maybe we're just on one of the - what did you call them - 'intellectual branch lines'? - shunted off to entertain the power brokers on the express as they go past, like opera and ballet and arty novelists."

Brian suddenly felt very uncomfortable in the face of her insight to what he was beginning to feel himself might be an essential lack of seriousness in what he did and said. Perhaps he was just a lightweight, after all; their obvious earnestness was definitely beginning to erode his self-confidence.

"We don't think we are like that, by the way," she said, reading the uncertainty in his face.

"What Connie's saying, Brian, is are you just all mouth and trousers?" said Bridget cynically. "Another middle-class, 'Guardian' wanking lecturer."

Brian was shocked as to how much to heart his casual radicalism had been taken by these students. Even though he knew he had enough evidence from his researches to justify what he said in his lectures, he had never thought of himself as other than on the branch line with his audience. These students seemed to be out to derail the express.

"I believe what I say, yes," said Brian finally. Did he? Yes, he did.

"Yeah, but are you prepared to do anything about it?" said Bernie. "That's the pointy point, darling."

"Like what, for example?" he asked, still cautious.

"Like hacking into the Civic Centre data bank and finding out what they're up to," said Connie.

"Jesus Christ!" said Brian, swallowing his coffee awkwardly and spluttering. He was suddenly fearful that this little group really meant very serious business indeed. "You can go to gaol for that," he said, coughing.

"We can all finish up in court for what we've done already," said Bernie. "Like that poster business and tonight's little caper. And poor Bridget here is in and out of the cop shop like a yo-yo because of her brother. Anyway, Ronnie here has kindly volunteered to take the rap for all our little peccadilloes, haven't you, Ronnie dear?"

"No problem, wack," said Ronnie crisply. "I'm barking you see. Everybody knows that. Call for a shrink's report, then it'd just be another spell in the cuckoo nest for yours truly. Lots of time to get on with your own work. Jolly good therapy, what? - like, they really think it's aces in there, drawing and performance and video and stuff, and my tutor, Vlad the Impaler, to see me every week. I tell you, it beats trying to live on your grant. It's been a godsend to me these last five years. I'm really going to miss it. Any time I get stuck for cash I go voluntary and the scran's not bad either and there's some cracking nurses about, except some of the male ones. Some of them are right out of the 'SS'. They love giving you injections and a bit of ECT. Like, that really turns some of them bastards on, I can tell you. And the chat can get a bit weird sometimes, especially with the shrinks, but you get some good laughs. Good as a holiday camp, wack, really. Hey, I couldn't half go a jam buttie though. Is there any bread about?"

He rose and began rummaging in a cupboard.

"Look," said Brian, calling a halt, "just what is this all about? What do you think you're doing, anyway?"

"We are trying, in our own small way, to strike a few blows where it's at," said Connie.

"Where what's at?" said Brian.

"Shit," said Connie simply.

Brian looked round the expectant group and was very aware of how much of a spot they were placing him in. If he refused to help them he was just another wanker as Bridget suspected and it was down the tubes with his credibility in the college. He knew he would be just another 'teacher', pissing in the wind, no matter how true the things he might have to say. And that would be the end of any interest Connie might have. But, if he did agree to help, he was really putting himself on the line. For what? Well, Connie might come across for one but was that enough? He looked at now her across the table: cool, ironic, intelligent. beautiful, exciting, definitely going places, but an enigma. What was she, an American, doing stuck in Brindling, anyway, if she was that good? Brian longed to know more. But criminal charges - and gaol yet! He rather hankered for the familiar ghastliness of his flamingoes at this moment. Oh God, he thought, looking at her again, I can't help myself.

"I've got to know a good deal more before I can see my way forward," he said carefully.

"Christ, I knew he'd come up with something really boring like that," said Gerry. "He's a jerk-off like the rest of them, I told you so."

Brian did not respond but the contempt stung him.

"Well?" he said, looking round the group. They all looked to Connie, except Gerry.

"I think that's fair enough. If we ask a lot, we've got to give a lot," she said.

"I'm against it," said Gerry.

"We know that so don't go on about it. That's quite boring too," she said in a matter-of-fact tone. Gerry looked angry but said no more. "What do you want to know?"

"Well, for a start," said Brian, "what shit exactly? I mean, the world's full of it. Which particular brand of turd are you kicking into the gutter?"

As Patience Richardson suddenly spoke, he realised his own ironic tone had stung her - and probably from their expressions the others as well.

"I'll tell you one for a start, Dr. bloody Mather," she burst out at him. "The kind me and Alex have to put up with in this town. The insults and catcalls and abuse we get from all kinds of people. Not just the dead-head yobs in the pubs and the football ground, you expect shit from them, but the little old ladies with the perms and the posh clothes and the people serving you in shops. They don't insult you direct but they let you know they'd run you out of town if they could. And the Old Bill. They're all shit in my book." Alex put his arms round her shoulders. "They deserved that poster because that's what they are, wankers and shit." Brian could see that her anger and frustration was making her near to tears. "Why can't they just leave us alone? It's right out of order."

"And that goes for me too," said Shaheen. "I've had that sort of stuff all my life and I'm sick of it. One of those awful women told me the other day we Asians didn't like work because all we were interested in was selling stuff in the markets. Silly cow. My dad's a hospital consultant and he works damn hard."

"And try being gay," said Bernie, "and just see what you get. When the Chairman of the Governors of this Poly insults you that's supposed to be on your side and that damned Rector as well does fuck-all to defend you, what sort of place is it? All of them deserve what they get."

"And try being a chink with slitty eyes." said Julia, pulling at the side of her eyes to exaggerate their shape. "Like the man said."

"And try the interview room at the police station and see how you're tret if you're Irish and it's your own brother they're after. And how they treat your things, never mind yourself. They buggered up all my last year's work for spite, so they did. And this Poly does zilch for you 'cos they don't give a toss."

"And maybe just try being young and poor and an art student and see how often you get stopped and turned over for drugs," said Gerry. "And..."

Connie cut in. "Ok, guys, that's enough. I guess Brian's got the message by now." She looked at him with an eyebrow raised. "Well?" she said.

The vehemence of the students' statements had driven Brian back against the panel behind the bench. He moved slowly forward and rested his arms on the table again. He looked round the group. Their grim, tightly set faces demanded a response in kind from him; even Ronnie looked serious for once. Brian glanced at Connie: she was cool but her eyebrow was still raised, quizzing him challengingly.

"And what about you?" he said to her. "You're an American. I mean, I don't mean to be insulting or anything but what has Brindling to do with..."

"Just try being a woman, Brian. Anywhere," she cut in.

"I dressed up as a woman once, for a bit of a lark," said Ronnie suddenly cheerful and scattering crumbs from a mouthful of his huge jam buttie as he spoke. "Remember, Connie, in your first year. You lent me the gear. Just to find out what it was really like, like. Do you know some twat tried to rape me. He was only about this high, an' all. He got a hell of a shock when he found I wasn't. So I tried to rape him. He thought I was a trannie. I told him what a lovely bum he had. He nearly shit a brick, I don't reckon he stopped running for a week." The tense atmosphere dissolved as they all joined in with his spluttering laughter. "Mind you, it was a right 'mare being a woman, I can tell you," he said feelingly. "Of course, that was long before we started the fartistas and got serious."

The laughter was suddenly halted.

"Oops. Sorry, like," he said. He hid his face behind his jam buttie.

They turned to Brian.

"Perhaps there's something else you'd like to tell me," Brian said. "Who or what exactly are the fartistas?"

Once again they looked to Connie for a lead.

"We are the fartistas," said Connie. "And I think you know by now what we stand for."

"I thought we had an agreement," said Gerry angrily. "We took a vote. Remember?" he said, throwing her own words back at her.

"If he's going to work with us he has a right to know," said Connie.

"He hasn't said he is, yet," said Gerry.

"Oh, to hell with it, man," said Alex. "We've come this far. We've got to go the whole hog. Agreed?" He looked round the group. They nodded and shrugged.

"Yeah, go on," said Julia. "He keep his trap shut. Yeah?" She looked to Brian for confirmation. Brian nodded.

"Ok," said Connie. "Ask away."

"Why the name? Is it just a joke?"

"Partly," she said. "It's short for 'Fine Art Radical Terrorists'. That's us. The Fartistas."

"Wicked, eh?" said Ronnie. "I thought of that. See, if we get caught, they'll just think it's some sort of crappy student joke, like. A sort of jolly rag, dontcha know, what? And they won't even want it published in the papers or the courts 'cos they'll get laughed at."

"So most of it has to be a kind of send-up. Like the vibrator thing," said Connie.

"What about tonight?" said Brian. "Making fools of the police and getting innocent people arrested is a bit more than a send-up, isn't it?"

"Yeah, but look who they were," said Alex. "The local mafia."

"How on earth did you arrange it?" said Brian, his curiosity driven on by his reluctant admiration of their achievement.

"It wasn't particularly difficult," said Connie. "You saw old Betty Flynn get arrested, didn't you?"

"Yes," said Brian.

"Well, she's a bit of a grass. So we fed her with stories of how we all get our drugs at the club. At least Ronnie here did. Ronnie knows everybody. We know when that sonofabitch Huggett's there so we told Betty there was going to be big acid drop in the club tonight, and she told us it was going to be busted. I expect the Chief Constable will cop a real earful at the next lodge meeting. By the way, don't develop those pictures at the college. You'd better give them to me and I'll get them done myself."

Bernie, Alex and Julia took out professional-looking cameras from their coat pockets and began to extract films with a whirr of precision motors.

"You took pictures as well?" said Brian. "I didn't see any flashes."

"There was plenty of light from the vans," said Alex, with an air of expertise. "As the man said; "My dear, if there's even the teensiest chinkie of light, you can take a picture." Brian recognized Laurie Willoughby's tones. "I think I got a couple of real beauties. I had the camera right over the crowd." He was the tallest of the group.

"I saw you doing that," said Gerry aggressively. "That was a hell of risk, man. You could have been clocked and pulled in. This isn't about art, you know. Nobody gives a damn about good pictures provided you get the information."

"Ah, what the hell," said Alex. "I'd have slipped Patience the camera."

"Gerry's right," said Connie. "There's no need to take any risks."

"There's some private stuff on this film I need for my dip. show," said Bernie. "I think I'll hang on to mine." He slipped it into his pocket.

The others looked at each other.

"It's not what you think," said Bernie. "At least - anyway, never mind."

"Suit yourself," said Connie. "But keep it out of sight."

"Don't worry," said Bernie. "These shots tonight would be the least of my worries. I've got a friend with a dark room. I'll develop them myself."

"What will you do with the pictures?" said Brian. "You could sell them to the press."

The students received this with withering contempt. Brian realised he had damaged his credibility a little by suggesting something so crassly commercial; after all, they were Fine Art students.

"Jesus," said Julia, "he from another planet, man. He talk just like my father."

"And mine," said Shaheen.

"What we do with them is our business," said Connie, taking the films and putting them into the pocket of her jeans. To do this she stretched up and leaned sideways so that her breasts pushed out the baseball shirt. Brian sighed inwardly. "Now what about the Civic Centre data bank?" she said, abruptly bringing him back to reality.

"Look, what on earth do you think you'll get from hacking into the town data bank that could possibly be worth the risk? Even if it could be done. It's not that easy to do, you know. I mean, Ronnie here won't be able to take the blame for that, will he? And I'd be stuck out on a limb. It would hardly be a jolly student rag dontcha know, if I got caught, now would it? I'll be risking my whole career. And you've got to know what you're looking for, anyway."

Connie glanced round the whole group before going on. They all nodded assent.

"Have you ever looked at how much it costs to put up a new building for this Poly?" she asked him.

"No," said Brian. "Not in detail. It depends on the kind of building and what it's for. You're usually talking in hundreds of thousands for anything substantial. Maybe a million plus, I suppose. Why?"

"Right. But just suppose you already had a building. Large, impressive-looking with plenty of character and set in a nice park. Just the sort of building Poly managers like to see themselves poncing - really terrific word, that - poncing about in, especially if they've got the idea of transforming themselves into a university. Wouldn't it be much cheaper as well as more convenient to convert that building? And wouldn't it be so much easier for everybody if the current tenants could be evicted by being terminated permanently?"

"Good heavens!" said Brian, shocked. "Is that what you think? But do you know this for sure? I mean, how?"

"Never mind how. We know," said Connie. "There's a small group been discussing it for at least a year. We do know that. Very secret. I mean real clammed-up. Huggett's one of them. Of course, nobody knows exactly what they're planning although the university thing is common knowledge."

"It's the first I've heard of it," said Brian.

"That's about par for the course," said Bridget. "Don't the muppets live in a world of their own all the time? Aren't they the last to hear anything?"

"Muppets?" said Brian.

"The art college staff," said Shaheen. Brian thought of all their wild hairiness and was glad he had decided long ago that a beard didn't suit him.

A thought struck him. "Look," he said, "do the mupp...er... college staff know about you lot?"

"No," said Connie. "Nor do the students really, although they know we stick together and they tell us things. They're just glad somebody's doing something without wanting to get involved themselves. We've kept pretty schtum. Even Ronnie."

"I'm not as daft as I look, wack," said Ronnie, who was sucking his fingers after finishing his jam buttie. Brian was beginning to suspect he was not daft at all.

"We think Noel de Vere might have an idea about us but he's better off letting sleeping dogs lie," Connie continued. Like the case of Oswald Spiller, Brian thought. "Obviously, he knows all about the university thing but not about the plans to kiss off Art and Design and take over the building."

"Well, why don't you tell him?"

"We need proper proof to confront them with or they'll just talk their way out of it like they always do. And that's in the plans somewhere and knowing the way these guys work, those'll be in the data bank because they live by computers and so on. What we need you to do is get hold of them. We do know the Poly computer system accesses the same data bank so it shouldn't be too difficult for you. Do you know who does all that sort of building work for this Poly, by the way?"

"No. Direct works, I suppose. Why?"

"No. It's all put out to tender like Maggie says it should be. All by the book but..."

Connie hesitated and looked at Alex.

"Yeah, go on. Show him them," said Alex.

Connie got up and bent down at a locker under the benches as the students shifted out of the way for her. From the locker she took some large photographic envelopes and brought them back to the table. She spilled out their contents of big, black and white prints in front of him. He knew enough of photography to see that they were very professionally finished. All of them showed building sites at various stages of their construction. Almost all were intensive studies of craftsmen exercising their skills: chippies, brickies, sparks, plumbers and so on. The pictures caught the concentration on their faces and their native intelligence beautifully.

"These yours?" he asked Alex, who nodded. Alex produced a magnifying glass and handed it to him. Brian was bewildered.

"Well?" he said.

"Look at the faces of the guys working," he said.

The students watched him intently as he went through the photographs one by one. He began to recognise individuals from print to print.

"I still don't get it. They're the same set of guys, right?"

"Right," said Alex triumphantly. "I've been doing a photo doc. of the Poly buildings from first year. All of these are from different years. Each packet is a different job. And if you look at the name boards on the site, it's a different builder. But it's always the same architects and the same site workers. Even the JCB's and stuff are always the same. The penny didn't drop there might be something funny going on until last term. Nobody ever really looks at the faces of these guys, you know. They're just part of the brickwork or something. They're really interesting." He began to study the pictures himself. "You can see how a brickie's expression is different from a chi..."

"This isn't a seminar, man," said Gerry impatiently.

"Yeah. Right. Well, about three months ago I got the hard word from the site foreman - he's always on these jobs as well. That's him," he said, picking out a picture of a burly man in a battered trilby and donkey jacket waving his arms threateningly. The picture had much less clarity than the others. "I had to take that with a concealed camera. Bernie's a hot-shot doing that and showed me how. But this guy is really camera-shy."

"Not much of the worthy artisan about him," said Brian.

"No, he's a real nazi," said Alex. "The guys are scared stiff of him. He told me how building sites were very dangerous places and how accidents happened to people who wander onto them uninvited. The message was pretty clear. I appealed about it to Noel because I'm making all these the centrepiece of my installation for finals. He took it up with the Rector but the word was lay off. The word came from the Chairman of the Poly Governors, no less."

"Your pal and mine, Charlie Huggett," said Connie. "And you know what friend Huggett's line of business is, don't you?"

"I'm ahead of you," said Brian. "Buildings, right? But he couldn't get the contracts, it'd be far too obvious. Even in Brindling they'd be onto that like a shot."

"Of course, but you must have heard of shell companies. And if you're on the inside, how easy it must be to get your tender to the right price. And the conversion of the art college would be a very nice little earner, wouldn't it? Maybe half a million plus contingencies? Very difficult to cost control any sort of conversion. You don't have to tell me from this outfit," she said feelingly, waving her hand at the cabin. Again, Brian wondered where the money came from.

"So you think Huggett's bent?"

"We know he is."

"How?"

"That's our business."

"Well, he's hardly likely to keep his accounts in the Civic Centre data bank, is he?" said Brian.

"No, but there might be other ways of getting that."

Brian rubbed his face and speculated what those other ways might be for a moment. They obviously had some source of information he knew nothing about. He noticed the increasing air of conspiracy in the cabin was beginning to make him breathe more tightly, as was the smoke. The smokers were all pulling hard on their roll-ups as they waited for his commitment. He began to cough.

"For Christ's sake, open a hatch somebody," said Ronnie. "All these veggies and smoking themselves to death. Some health jag that is."

Shaheen climbed onto a bench and opened a hatch.

"We are vegetarians for the sake of the animals and the planet, not just our health," she said primly.

"Yeah, well you ought to think of somebody else's health for a change, never mind a few fucking cows," said Ronnie.

"I don't smoke," she said.

"No, but you other veggies do. Bleeding roll-ups, they're coffin nails them things. They do my head in."

While Shaheen and Ronnie bickered, the others' attention did not waver from Brian.

"Supposing I get these plans for you. What would you do with them?" he said.

"Huggett's boss of the Labour mafia, isn't he?" said Connie, her eyes beginning to shine with excitement. "But the press in this town is somewhere to the right of Adolf Hitler. What do you think they'd make of it?"

"Not a lot," said Brian.

"What do you mean?"

"I recognized the editor being wheeled out of the club with Huggett's group. I met him the other week. They're as thick as thieves, I'll bet."

He saw her face fall at this. "Well," she said, "there's always 'Private Eye'. That's if we need to use it at all. It may not even be necessary. And we could always organise an occupation with the art students when they find out they're trying to chop their Department. That's if we get at it before the summer recess begins. Of course, the Rector's hoping that the CNAA will do it legit. for him."

Brian realised that his initial scepticism that all this was merely the overheated imaginings of a bunch of students hopped up on their own cleverness and high on the excitement of conspiracy, had now almost vanished. Her mention of how the CNAA could act as nemesis for Art and Design was all too plausible.

"And suppose they traced the source back to me?"

"They won't," she said with certainty.

"How can you be so sure?"

"Because we'll be doing it together, Brian." She smiled at him across the table.

The careful placing of his name, used for the first time that evening, and in the context of their working together, did not escape him. Connie was obviously destined for higher things. Like selling double glazing, he thought.

"Computer graphics will be all you know about. I'll take the rap if there's any come-back. The most they can do is deport me, probably. If it came to that, which I doubt it would." She watched him challengingly.

Brian said quietly after an interval: "Oh gosh." He saw that Connie had boxed him in almost completely, answering any doubts before he even thought of them.

"Look," he said, trying the expertise ploy to divert them, "the kind of information you want will be very difficult to access. You need special codes and passwords to get at it if it's guarded, which it very probably is. And information like that won't be in any data handbook will it? Otherwise hacking means hours and hours of trial and error and I don't have that sort of time - and neither do you, I imagine, with your final shows to prepare."

Brian thought the last point might make them think again.

"That's no problem," said Connie, dismissing his objections with a wave of her hand, "we've got the codes and passwords already, we think."

"What? I mean...How? Where? But..." If this was true, his last escape hatch except outright refusal was closed. Connie rose and went into the bedroom compartment.

"Your mouth open, man," said Julia, grinning. "Catchee flyee, as we slitties are supposed to say."

He came to his senses and was aware of all their grins. Connie returned with a sheet of paper. She handed it across to him. Scrawled on it were numbers and phrases. The hand which had written them appeared to have done so in haste. The number and password codes, which were certainly what they looked like to Brian, were scattered almost at random over the page.

"What do you think?" said Connie. He was aware of the intensity of the students' attention. He shrugged.

"They look like passwords. But if you've got these, you could do it yourselves. You don't need me."

"None of us has a clue how to use them," said Alex. "You do."

Brian looked around their eager faces again. He realised the evening had made him feel very much older. He suddenly longed for the shell-shocked docility of the trainee teachers. They'd never even give a thought to who was screwing what graft from which taxpayers. If he had ever doubted it, he knew now how different art students were from other students. They breathed in that same oxygen of freedom without which art suffocated and died. It came with the territory and it was dangerous stuff. No wonder the first thing dictators did was shoot the artists. He knew also that if he took up their challenge and did as they asked he might, at last, be granted some of that same freedom himself and which he suddenly realised he longed for: what else was in it for him, after all? It was obvious that his desires for Connie's favours were entirely to one side of where he was at this moment. That kind of carnality seemed almost as paltry as Bill Johnson's, although the chase might still be worth it as he looked into her coolly challenging eyes. He thought he saw a hint of amusement there as well. Just what was she really after? Could he be just a figure of fun to her? But the corollary of agreement was risk, in spite of Connie's confident assurances. And a big risk at that; the boundary from student prank to criminality was barbed with razor wire. Was it worth it? Perhaps art demanded its practitioners should have the zest of illegitimacy if they were going to be any good. And students had to feel it in their mentors or it simply degenerated into jerk-offs anonymous. That smooth life plan of his slow, steady progress to a serene retirement he had thought was his destiny now seemed a forlorn remote dream. And also boring. God save us from the young and idealistic.

"Ok, I'll do it," he said. He stood up and felt the weight of at least a few years slip from his shoulders.

Chapter Six
A Spur to Action

On the Monday following his meeting with the Fartistas, Brian continued his campaign to precede Noel de Vere by arriving at half past seven. This proved to be another correct guess but closely run: he arrived on the front steps only a minute and half before Noel's car drew up. Brian was already calculating next day's arrival by the time he gave Noel his usual wave and chirpy "Good morning," This time, instead of a snarl, Brian was greeted with an even more unexpected response. Noel called his name sharply to stop him entering the building. Brian halted and turned back to him. Noel's face prefigured the revelation of some sort of neurosis boiling up inside him.

"There's been a nasty outbreak of conceptualist minimalism in year one!" he said, thumping his fist into his hand.

"Good God!" said Brian, flinging his hand in a mock gesture of dismay to his brow. "Get Rentokil to burn the lot of them."

De Vere looked at him witheringly. "I'm glad you can find it amusing," he said. He moved up a few steps to stand above Brian so he could look down at him. Brian was quite aware that Noel de Vere's paranoia had by this stage of the term completely displaced his sense of humour.

"It's got to be stamped out before it catches on," de Vere continued, hitting his fist into his palm again and tightening his jaw grimly. "That stuff can spread like wildfire. Look what happened at Goldsmiths' - students picking lint out of their navels for three years and a wigwam in a whitewashed room to show for it at the end."

"I thought that sort of thing went out with the Seventies?" said Brian.

"It never goes away quite. It creeps back every time the Tate brings out that shitpile of bricks. Students see it and think they needn't do anything either to prove they're artists. All they have to do is think it. They must be smoking more in year one or dropping acid or something, dammit. They think it turns them on but all it does is to fool them into believing they're some sort of genius with nothing to prove. Anyway, we've got to do something about it now. Ivor Evans will smell that crap a mile off and the Poly will never understand - try explaining a pile of old bricks to the Rector - even if it was on for undergraduates, which I don't believe it is. Don't you agree?"

"Er..." said Brian, who was only vaguely familiar with the subject of de Vere's outburst. "Where's it coming from? None of the staff are that way inclined, are they?"

"It's that bitch in the first year who wears the sailor gear and the 'I've had VD' button. She's a real troublemaker that one. Anything to avoid a bit of honest effort. And she can talk the hind leg off a donkey. God save us from gabby students. And the others listen to her - Christ knows why. Anyway, she'll need a bloody good story come assessment time to convince me or she's out. I've drawn a bead on that young lady," he said with stern relish. "Of course, she's got her tutor lapping up every damned syllable she utters, wouldn't you know. You ought to read her reports -

brilliant, wonderful, the girl's a genius. Genius my left arsehole."

"Who's her tutor?" said Brian.

"That dopey dyke, Tremaine. It's probably the uniform and the leather knickers that does it."

"How do you know?" said Brian, intrigued.

"Common knowledge," said de Vere dismissively. "Red lined too."

Brian was aware by the sniff which accompanied this statement and the slightly patronising look he gave, that Noel de Vere still prided himself on being more in touch than someone like Brian who was theoretically nearer the wellsprings of student gossip than himself. Brian was still not clear as to how gossip leaked between students and staff but realised what a really disciplined group the Fartistas must be to keep their sort of activities as watertight as they did. He was mightily relieved about this when he thought of the agreement he had made with them, especially when the group contained somebody as erratic as Ronnie Oliver.

"But I thought Zoe was keen on Connie Grey?" said Brian.

"Old hat," said de Vere crisply. "Connie's too straight for her. Anyway, it's got to be stamped out, do you hear, and quick. That's your job."

"Eh?" said Brian, startled. "What do I know about lesbians? That's ridiculous."

"Not that, you fool," said Noel, impatiently giving him a quick hissing claw. "This minimalism nonsense."

"Oh," said Brian. "But how? I'm not a studio tutor."

"That's the whole point," said de Vere. "I've read that stuff of yours and it's just the job. You can start putting it about straight away with year one. Get the buggers out of the studio and into the real world. Make the sods look at where they are. This town has its shirt tail sticking out of its pants' back-side. Alright then, make them see it. Rub their noses in the shit that people have to live with round here. Especially that VD joker. See Peter Orrd and work with him. He's always on about site-specific sculpture commissions. Take him with you. He could do with the exercise anyway. I'll give the bastards minimalism. Bloody sculptors," he said fiercely. "What time is it? My watch has been up the creek since that meeting for some reason."

Brian glanced at his watch. "Half past seven," he said. "I love these early summer mornings, don't you?" he said, drawing a deep breath. "The air's so fresh."

Noel de Vere snorted. "Time's getting on," he said, shortly, and went up the rest of the steps and into the front door. As Brian watched his retreating figure, he thought that Noel had the most indignant backside of any man he knew. At no time since Brian had begun his game to arrive first had Noel allowed him to see he was competing or even that there was anything unusual about the time he arrived. However, Brian was amused to notice that Noel's eyes were almost permanently covered now by his mirror glasses. Louis Bonetti had told him that he had caught Noel asleep behind his desk on more than one occasion, not slumped over it but propped up, his shades hiding his closed eyes. Because only Noel and Brian knew about the time-keeping game, rumours were soon circulating amongst the staff that de Vere's overtired state was due to some new female he was knocking off. Brian knew that sexual activity was - often correctly - the normal explanation for almost any change of behaviour amongst his colleagues; from their experience the key to most art history was sex or alcohol or both. Brian had had this rumour from Louis, who informed Brian that Noel cut quite a swathe amongst the female students soon after he had arrived at Brindling. Maybe he was reverting to type and "poking-a somebody" under stress.

Tomorrow, thought Brian, quarter to seven should do it. He knew that de Vere lived over fifty miles way in a small country village and would have to start out practically at dawn to beat him. In any case, it meant less time with the flamingoes. He really would have to do something about them, he thought; as he had fallen asleep the last few nights, he had imagined them beginning to feed and splash about. Perhaps this was his kind of response to sleep and sex starvation.

He stood for a few moments more on the steps and enjoyed the early morning sunlight as it brought alive the vivid splashes of colour of the flower beds in the park. Noel's ready adoption of his idea for field visits cheered him enormously. It would be a great relief legitimately to cross the fault-line and spend a day in the real world and not have to circulate round the Polytechnic. A group of early morning joggers were passing the front steps by now.

"Good morning!" he called loudly and waved his briefcase at them. Startled, they swerved and bumped into each other. "Bloody fool!" one of them wheezed out. "Have a really nice day!" Brian replied enthusiastically, his euphoria undimmed by the display of bad temper.

He reflected how sensible it was of the town's worthies to have sited the college in the park. In those days, they knew what art was for - beauty, truth and goodness. At least they could buy it even if grinding the faces of the poor couldn't earn it for them. He could certainly see why the Rector was after it. How agreeable it would be to spend one's days in this beautiful Grade II listed Arts and Crafts gem of a building in this well-ordered landscape instead of the wind-swept eyrie of the Poly tower, especially as its lifts and one's blood pressure were notoriously uncertain: not much beauty, truth and goodness there. He wondered, as he had for long hours over the weekend, about the wisdom of getting involved with Connie's schemes. In the sober light of early morning, without her exciting presence, the thoughts he had had of its potential for liberating him from the inhibitions of his boring bourgeois sensibilities, just seemed dangerously crack-brained. Labour mafia, fraudulent contractors, bent Councillors - he couldn't get interested or worked-up about any of them. But he could see that in the light of youthful idealism, the students would instinctively recognise in such people the ingrained, careless malice and prejudice they saw as the enemies of human progress. It struck him suddenly that they might all still believe in that - had he once believed too? Or had he been born one of life's sceptics? If coal strikes or cruise missile sites or police brutality or Nelson Mandela or US imperialism or green politics or any of the myriad exciting causes which passed on with the Eighties were now unavailable for the lively-minded, right-on student to get worked up about in a place like Brindling, with only a few pathetic, practically brain-dead neo-Fascists to wave the Union Jack, then you had to make do with what you could find: good, old-fashioned swindling.

Apart from the sexual tang of being involved with Connie, the only thing which really did intrigue him about the affair was how Oswald Spiller might tie into it. To see him trooping into the arms of the constabulary along with the local Mr. Big, was one of the most unexpected sights he had ever experienced. He had bought the local paper the next day to see a report of the raid but it was quite silent on the subject. As the editor had been swept up as well, this was not entirely surprising. He was beginning to realise that Brindling was very tightly sewn up as a town. Still, he thought, turning to follow de Vere into the college, he could always say the codes and passwords were wrong or had been altered or something: there was bound to be an out somehow. But his heart leaped, nevertheless, as he went through the doors to recall the way Connie had looked at him when he finally said he would help.

During the next two days, Brian efficiently organised groups and schedules of field visits for the next several weeks. He stood on a few staff toes cutting through tutorial times and so on but Noel de Vere backed him up and firmly quelled any squawks. Peter Orrd grumbled at first and was highly suspicious of why he was being asked to participate - Brian could see that he imagined de Vere might be doing it to get him out of the way so that he could swing something behind his back - but Brian's enthusiasm swept him along and he agreed to contribute. He did confide in Brian at this point that he was, in truth, like Noel de Vere, deeply worried that the conceptualist virus might infect his section and was glad that, for once, he and Noel could agree on something.

By the time of his first outing on Wednesday morning, the weather had changed to a gale with squally showers. Brian had arrived at college kitted out in his weatherproof site-visit gear at six-fifteen. As he suspected he would, de Vere had arrived the previous day just before seven to be greeted once more by Brian at the entrance. Brian had calculated that six-thirty should beat him this morning but at last de Vere seemed to have got his measure. His car, a scrofulous-looking Skoda - few of the staff, Brian had noted, seemed to take any account of cars at all, and certainly not to clean them - was drawn up at the side of the front steps. He must definitely have started before dawn, Brian thought. Good! Serve him right!

He pushed open the front door, slightly disappointed at not preceding de Vere but relieved that he could now safely abandon his campaign; it had probably served its purpose and was becoming very tedious. He did not imagine Noel would make any fuss about his signing in again. As the door moved inwards, there was a violent, savage barking and snarling from the other side as a hundred and twenty pounds of muscular black labrador crashed into it. Brian leaped back. Of course, Ridley's dogs were still on night patrol. He cautiously peered through the elegant, patterned glass panels of the entrance doors. The animals, making out his vague shape in the glass, redoubled their furious noise and jumped up against it. Between glimpses of their jaws and wild eyes as they bounced up and down, he saw that the entrance hall was clear. He supposed he would have to hang about for Ridley to come on duty and call them off guard. He would try the side entrance but imagined if Ridley was not yet on duty that it would be locked. He wondered briefly why this entrance was open.

He was turning away from the doors when he thought he heard a faint voice call his name above the sound of the wind and the racket the dogs were making. He peered through the glass again closely. The voice was now distinct enough to recognise as Noel de Vere's but oddly strained. It called his name again but he could still see nobody in the hall. He moved his head from side to side so that he could get angled glimpses via the facets of the cut glass of the sides and recesses of the hall between the dogs' heads as they now frantically tried to bite their way through the panels. He pushed carefully at the door so that he could call through the crack. The dogs began to fight each other for the privilege of taking his leg off.

"Noel?" he called loudly above the noise. "Where are you?"

"Over here," came the voice, still strained.

The dogs having settled their argument, hurled themselves at the crack. Brian closed it off hastily. He cupped his hands over his eyes and peered through the glass again. De Vere's voice had been sufficiently distinct for him to locate its direction. At the side of the entrance hall was a large, white alabaster sculpture on a tall plinth which had been created by the first principal of the college as a demonstration of the quality of the artistic endeavour to which his stewardship would be dedicated. It consisted of two larger-than-life, classical female figures, one representing ART, the other COMMERCE. The former, upright and haughty, was handing to the supplicant and grateful latter, the charter of enlightenment. It was from this direction that Noel's voice had come. Although the light in that part of the hall was not good, Brian could make out that this tableau appeared to have acquired a third figure. Cradled across the charter and the arms holding it and with his own arms round the neck of ART and his legs round the neck of COMMERCE, was Noel de Vere.

"For Christ's sake, get Ridley, will you?," Brian heard above the racket.

"How?" said Brian. "I can't get in."

"Phone him! Phone him!" shouted Noel frantically.

"What's the number?" Brian shouted.

"What?" shouted Noel.

"The number. What's the..."

"Good morning," said a voice behind him. "Is there some problem?"

Brian whirled round to be confronted by the thin, ascetic face of Oswald Spiller.

"Er." said Brian, confused. "It's the dogs, you see."

"Excuse me," said Spiller. He moved to insert a key into the lock.

"It's not locked," said Brian. "You're not going in, are you?"

"Unusual," said Spiller, ignoring Brian's warning. He pushed the door. Brian prepared to flee. The dogs prepared for their feast. "Down, Bruno. Down, Tyson," said Spiller firmly, stepping inside. Immediately calm was established. Brian cautiously went into the hallway after Spiller. The two dogs had now rolled over on their backs and Spiller scratched their bellies.

"It's quite safe. Because you're good dogs, aren't you?" The dogs wagged their tails furiously. They rose and came over to Brian to smell his trousers, their claws clattering on the tiled floor.

"I've known them since they were puppies," said Spiller.

"Do you come in at this time every morning?" Brian asked.

"Oh yes," said Spiller. Brian suddenly saw how it was that Spiller had remained invisible for so long.

"When you have quite finished your conversation, perhaps you wouldn't mind helping me down?" said Noel de Vere from his refuge.

"Good heavens!" said Spiller, noticing him for the first time. "What on earth are you doing up there, Mr. de Vere?"

"Waiting for inspiration," said Noel. "What the fuck do you think I'm doing? Give me a hand, I've got cramp."

Brian climbed up onto the plinth and helped him painfully down. Close to, he saw that the dogs had left their mark on both legs of his trousers, which were shredded from ankle to knee, and on the seat which had a few square inches of cloth missing.

"Did they clip your flesh?" said Brian. "You should have a tetanus jab if they did."

"No," said de Vere shortly.

He reached the floor level and the dogs came over to have a satisfying sniff at their morning's guard work. De Vere backed away slowly. Tyson cocked his leg to mark the site of his triumph. Noel leaped back with a cry of disgust.

"I'll kill that bugger, Ridley!" he shouted hysterically.

"Somebody call me?" said Ridley's voice from the landing above.

They looked up. The unshaven face of Ridley was peering down at them. He had on loudly striped pyjamas and a tatty bathrobe.

"Ridley, come down here!" shouted de Vere.

"Don't you fucking shout at me, de Vere," said Ridley truculently. "I'm not one of your fucking lecturers. I'll have the fucking union on to you for abuse. Anyway, I'm not on duty till fucking seven-thirty. I'm going back to bed."

"Look what your damned dogs have done to my trousers," said de Vere. "What are you going to do about it?"

"Nowt," said Ridley. "You shouldn't come sneaking in at this time of the fucking morning. Stands to reason the dog's'd go for you. What the fuck are you doing here at this time of the day anyway? Morning, Dr. Spiller," he said, and with that he disappeared. It struck Brian that not once had Ridley shown his peculiar speech impediment; he realised suddenly what the gaps in his sentences concealed. When he was not on duty he clearly felt quite free to fill them in.

"Er. Yes," said Spiller. He moved smoothly towards the exit doors from the hallway. "Well, time's getting on. Tick, tock. Tick, tock. I've got essays to mark," he said importantly.

"Hold on, you," said de Vere. "I want a word with you."

"See me after nine when I've signed in. Until then I do not believe I'm required to speak to anybody. Tick, tock. Tick, tock," said Spiller, and in a moment he had slipped through the swing doors.

"What the...Come back here, Spiller. Ouch!" Cramp made de Vere double up as he tried to follow Spiller. He hobbled awkwardly to the swing doors and pushed them open.

"You...What? Where?" he said, spluttering.

Brian joined him. "Good Lord! He's gone!" he said. As they stood looking down the corridor which led to the new building, they heard a door slam in the distance. The dogs registered the noise and barked. Stimulated by this, they remembered they were still on duty and, with their friend gone, snarled with enthusiasm and turned their attention once more to the early morning intruders.

Brian and Noel pulled the doors closed behind them as the dogs leaped towards them. While de Vere held them closed, Brian got a couple of wedges from a bracket on the wall nearby and secured them against the dogs.

"Come up to my room, I want to talk to you. We'll have to go the long way round now, dammit." said Noel.

He became gloomily thoughtful as they passed into the new building. Brian decided it was too early in the day for de Vere to indulge in idle conversation and kept quiet, but he was aware from the way Noel was moving that his silence was not solely a result of the early hour; whatever was preoccupying his thoughts seemed to be weighing increasingly heavily on him. He did not speak again until they were in his office. He handed Brian a percolator. "Here, go and fill this from the washroom next door."

When Brian returned, Noel was slumped in one of the two easy chairs in the room. His legs were stuck out in front of him, hairy white shanks protruding from the strips of his torn trousers. He had removed his sunglasses and Brian saw that his face was tired and drawn. Altogether, he seemed to Brian to be a man near the end of his tether. He almost regretted involving Noel in the early-bird game; it must have put an extra strain on him. Still, he didn't have to play it and he had rolled over for the Rector.

"The coffee's in that tin. Put it on, will you?" said Noel. "I tried to get rid of that bugger, you know, when he fled into his cupboard," said Noel bitterly.

"Oh." said Brian. A little item friend Spiller had omitted to mention, he thought.

"Yes." said Noel. "Some hopes in this town. Do you know, he went into a disciplinary hearing with the Governors and came out promoted to PL in charge of Related Studies."

"How come?" said Brian.

"He's one of the mafia, isn't he? That's how they all got their jobs in the old Tech. Most of them. And if you weren't in the Labour Party, the forty thieves'd do it for you."

Brian was startled at this reference. "The what?"

"The lads with the funny handshakes. That's what everybody calls them round here."

"Oh."

"Yes. Bare your left tit and you were away in this town. Maybe I should have joined up myself. It might help now."

Brian was intrigued; Noel had said this with considerable meaning. But he couldn't see how it would help a CNAA visit.

"Why now particularly? Is Evans one?"

"No, but the damned Rector is. He's just offered me early retirement."

The coffee fell off the spoon as Brian reacted to this.

"Oh," was all he said, in as matter-of-fact a voice as he could muster in face of this bombshell.

"Careful with that coffee, it costs a fortune. Incidentally, I've been meaning to mark that jar. I think somebody's helping themselves to it. It's not you, is it, in the evenings?"

"No," said Brian. Shades of the 'Caine Mutiny', he thought. De Vere will be playing with ball-bearings next.

"Yes, Marshall brought it up the other day," continued Noel. "From the Rector, of course. You know what that means, don't you? It's a polite way of saying we don't want to lose you but we think you ought to go. Incidentally, don't tell anyone else about this."

Brian wondered why Noel was telling him in the first place, although he was not especially surprised that he had done so. All his life, Brian had found that people insisted on thrusting their unwanted confidences onto him, even though he was never sufficiently convinced of the strength of his own personality to offer them much in return. Perhaps that's why they did it – simply to use him as a sort of emotional dustbin. From when he was quite small, his mother, and even his father, had told him all the ins and outs of their disastrous relationship. This, and the shards which fell to him from many another shattered relationship amongst his friends and colleagues, had kept him wary of displaying any very strong emotional commitments for himself. When he had done so, they had all ended badly. He had come to the conclusion that he must have been born with the sort of blank face people found it necessary to decorate with their own emotions.

One of his former girl friends - as emotionally retarded as himself - had likened his face to that of Montgomery Clift, glimpsed through the grill of the confessional-box in Hitchcock's 'I Confess.' Brian had deeply resented the comparison, particularly with the priestly aspect, at the time. (He later found the girl used the clerical ploy with all her men to make them sexier to disprove the slur.) But it was true, he knew, that his face - narrow and finely-formed - and dark hair did resemble those of the actor. It was this resemblance that had got him the odd juvenile audition in his short acting career. But, whereas Clift's face was all intense feeling, Brian knew his to be a wary mask. Perhaps this was why he had never got the parts.

As if in answer to his unspoken question, Noel went on:

"I'm telling you this because you can be more neutral about it. You've been redundant once, and you can probably keep your trap shut. If I told any of the old hands on the staff, they'd panic. And I can't afford that with CNAA on the horizon. What do you think? Should I take it? How did people feel in your old college about it?"

Brian felt the desperate appeal in Noel's voice for some kind of reaction to help him. After all de Vere's efforts over many years to make Brindling art college one of the national top, first-choice colleges outside London, to be simply dismissed as not wanted on the voyage had obviously devastated him. Noel had not been paying sufficient attention to what had happened in the Eighties, thought Brian; he had found out too late that loyalty works only one way in market-force Britain.

"Well?" said Noel.

Brian was carefully non-committal in his reply. It was very uncomfortable to be chucked into the role of counsellor to his boss as to whether he should let himself be fired - especially around seven o'clock in the morning.

"Did they give you any reasons why they think you ought to go?"

"Just some cock and bull story that it was going to be their policy from now on to offer early retirement to everybody senior who reaches my age. So not to read too much into it, old chap, at this stage, eh. Merely routine policy, you know."

Brian recognised Dr. Marshall's smooth delivery of a message like that in Noel's bitter parody; nothing was ever routine with people like Marshall.

"Perhaps it is," he said, nevertheless.

"Well, there's plenty in this Poly in that bracket including the effing Rector but I've not heard of him firing himself - huh, that'll be the day - so I'm not swallowing that for one single instant. Catch him passing up the gravy boat."

"What age is that, if you don't mind my asking?"

"Fifty-six," said Noel. "I've only got four years to go and it's an attractive package. Difficult to refuse. Enhanced to pensionable age with a notional terminal salary. They pointed out the difference between my current salary and what I'll have with pension and lump sum interest would only be about seventy quid a week. And therefore that's what I'm actually working for now. I'm useless at figures myself but my accountant thinks that's just about the case." He paused. "My wife's dead keen. She thinks this place is killing me." He glanced at Brian meaningfully. "And, of course, she's complaining that she sees less and less of me these days."

Brian did not react. "And is it? Killing you, I mean."

"They're not doing it out of kindness, you know," he said sharply. "Poor old de Vere's knackered, let's turn the decrepit old sod out to grass. If they get shot of me, they can more easily get shot of Art and Design. Because that's what they're really after, you know."

"I know," said Brian, simply. So the penny had finally dropped with Noel.

"Who've you been talking to?" asked Noel quickly. "The staff? I didn't think any of them had wind of it."

"No, the students."

"Which students?"

"Some of the third year."

"I bet I can guess which." Brian saw that the fact he had been talking this over with the cream of the college had impressed Noel. "And did they tell you about the university idea?" Brian nodded. Noel's paranoia began to reassert itself. "We could have real trouble on our hands if that third year lot decide to get the troops out over this, you know. Sit-ins and I don't know what not. I can see the CNAA visit turning into a real confrontation. Of course, that would just suit these Poly bastards down to the ground. Fighting on the barricades? Wow! No place for that sort of thing in our posh new university, what, what? We settled all that sort of thing in the Eighties, old chap. And that destructive bugger, Evans, would have a real field day. Does he love drama! I've had some run-ins with him before. What else did they tell you?"

Brian decided to keep the rest of the Fartistas' suspicions to himself. Everything Noel had said had increased his alarm over the potential trouble he could be involved in.

"Not a lot," he said, switching off the percolator jug.

"There's some milk and sugar in that cardboard box next to you on the window sill. The milk should be ok." Noel lit up a first cigarette of the day and inhaled deeply. He took the cup Brian handed him and visibly relaxed. "Have you ever smoked?" he asked.

"No," said Brian. "Except passively, of course." He waved a cloud of smoke from Noel's deep lungful away from his face.

"What else don't you do?" said de Vere, blowing more smoke towards Brian. "You never swear much either, do you? Tcha! All you non-smokers are the same. Self-righteous bastards."

"It seems to be common knowledge about the university thing amongst the students," Brian went on, changing to a less embarrassing subject, "but not about the idea of getting Art and Design out. At least not as far as I know. To most students, the quinquennial means just another long word they don't understand."

Noel drank his coffee abstractedly.

"What the hell am I going to do about these strides?" he said contemplating his exposed shanks. "Stupid animals. Of course, Ridley's Labour mafia as well, wouldn't you just guess."

"Go and buy a new pair when the shops open. Or send Myra for some," said Brian.

"Everybody would see it as the rat leaving the sinking ship, early retirement, wouldn't they?" Noel went on, ignoring Brian. "Especially the students." Brian realised that this, to Noel, would perhaps be a greater betrayal than leaving his staff in the lurch. "And what would happen to the rest of the staff? Redundant, I suppose. But I don't have to tell you about that, do I? The older ones might not do too badly but the younger staff would be left high and dry. And they're a good lot. Real dynamos. Terrific track records some of them and not just in this country. Up and coming artists. The real McCoy. You won't have had much chance to see them at close quarters yet, probably, but they're a damned sight more distinguished in their own way than some of the time-servers in departments like Engineering and Education. Try and find a research paper from some of that lot. But they've not got the polyspeak to defend themselves. You have. And the Ph.D. So I'm asking you now to run with the hounds on our behalf."

"How do you mean?" said Brian suspiciously.

"I don't know whether you are aware of it, but there's a research committee in this Poly. It has quite a lot of money each year for staff research purposes. I want you to join that committee and put a case for projects here. It's too late for this year's bulk cash but there's always a reserve fund. We've never asked for any before and I want something in the pipeline by the time CNAA get here. It's got to be genuine, mind you, and well-presented. You must know the sort of thing they'll be looking for. Get it organised with Peter Orrd. And try Laurie Willoughby for some ideas. And try the regional arts fund, you might get them to match up with us. Yes, and it would look better if we had more than one project. Make them substantial. We need the credibility. And get that new course off the stocks properly while you're at it. And get something written up for the Poly research report. Circulate the staff and get updates on their CV's. I want to forward copies of both of them to the visiting panel."

"And shall I be cleaning the chimbleys in my spare time, your honour, sir?" said Brian, tugging his forelock.

"Silly bugger," said Noel.

"You're losing your sense of humour, Noel," said Brian.

"It wasn't funny."

"Not a lot is at this time of the day," said Brian, yawning.

"You should stay in bed longer, then," said Noel balefully.

"Is it a good idea, to send the panel this course proposal beforehand, do you think?" Brian said. "Why not wait till they get here and present it to them? Throw them off balance so they have to discuss something new. Say you'd like their opinions. Flatter them a bit. In my experience it doesn't do to hand over too many hostages to fortune too early."

Noel's look changed from baleful to thoughtful. "You've been here before, haven't you?"

"That I have, squire, that I have," said Brian feelingly, recalling all the variety of dodges they had tried in his last college to stave off closure.

"Well, if you can think up any more good wheezes to put them off the scent - not that we've got anything to be ashamed of, mind you - let me know." Noel clicked his tongue and looked thoughtful. "Seventy quid a week," he said.

Brian decided to push him harder on his personal plans.

"Do I take it you're not abandoning ship just yet in spite of the package, which I must admit does sound pretty attractive? The chance of a lifetime if it's true that that's all you're actually working for. You could soon make that up with the time to do your own work. The rest of us should be so lucky," he said.

Brian's reference to Noel's own work, now notoriously long in abeyance, he realised was a mistake. He could feel Noel draw away from him as a confidant, although he had had no intention of offending him. In fact, although Noel's news was worrying, Brian had been enjoying the unexpected friendliness the early hour and shared dog attack had brought him.

"I haven't decided yet," said de Vere shortly. "There are a lot of things to think about." He rose abruptly. Brian could see the stiffening mantle of his super-efficient personna fall on him once more. It squared up his shoulders and set his neck at the slight angle it habitually assumed these days. He donned his sun glasses. "I need a crap," he said in a sharp executive tone, put down his mug and left the room briskly, his shredded strides flapping around his ankles. Brian reflected that if he had not been so slick shinning up ART and COMMERCE, there'd be no need to take his pants down.

It was with a sinking feeling that Brian followed him out of the room and made his way to the top corridor. If Noel took the offer made to him they could all for sure kiss goodbye to art education at Brindling. He knew it was going to be essential now that he dig into the data bank. Damn! There might be nothing there, of course, but if there did chance to be any skeletons as the Fartistas seemed to think - where did they get their information? - then rattling their bones might keep the polycrats at arm's length for a bit. Oh God! he thought, the things one does for sex and survival. And Art? Get to the back of the queue, man.

In his room he sat down at his desk and rested his head on his hands as he tried to think things through. Soon he was fast asleep. The joyful distant barking of Ridley's dogs as they located Noel once more was not anything like as disturbing as the secret rustling and splashing of the pink flamingoes haunting his dreams.

Chapter Seven
Mind Where You Step

"Dr. Mather. Brian. I wonder if you could help me, please? There's something awfully peculiar going on in my office."

The voice which had halted Brian's descent of the main staircase to meet his first year field party two hours later, was that of Hermione James. Brian turned to look back at her and realised she looked both puzzled and genuinely upset. The expression of, for her, a very unusual state of mind removed for the first time in Brian's experience of her, the habitual pleasant vagueness which gave Hermione's features such lack of definition. He realised that she had actually got very good skin and features. Although her chin - with a hint of doubling - and her cheeks were rather unmodernly rounded, her grey-blue eyes were large, bright and well-shaped and her lips were full and soft. Also, this morning she had her hair let down. It was shoulder length, fair and shiny, reflecting the glowing light of the entrance hall. And she was wearing a light yellow, flower-print dress which was not far from see-through. Brian noted the lacy outline of her bra. She also had the beginnings of a tan which reminded him of Connie's. He wondered briefly if it was as extensive.

"Of course," he said. "What is it?"

"Perhaps you'd better come and see."

She led the way to her office on the second floor of the old building saying only that she had arrived to find this "thing" in the middle of the floor. When they reached the office she threw open the door.

"There," she said.

Brian's heart sank as he saw the now too-familiar shape of Oswald Spiller's newly-patched tent occupying the space between the wall and one side of Hermione's desk. Her office was much larger than Brian's with easy chairs for student tutorials so the tent was not so crowding but it was nevertheless completely incongruous.

"What do you make of it?" she said. "Is it a student joke, do you think? Oh dear, I hope they're not going to send me up with practical jokes. I should absolutely hate that - too much like what happened at school. I was always far too trusting. Well, naive really, I suppose. What does it mean do you think?" She flapped her hands helplessly.

"Don't worry," said Brian. "It's nothing so sensible as that. I presume you haven't heard what happened last week over this?"

"No," she said. "I don't get to talk to many of the studio staff. What did happen?"

Brian walked into the office and shook the tent.

"Spiller, come out of there, you silly man," he said sternly.

"Dr. Spiller? Good heavens," said Hermione. "Is this his? Is he inside? I mean, what is he doing? Has he gone quite insane finally? Oh dear, he won't be violent, will he?"

"Calm down, calm down," said Brian. He listened with his head against the canvas. "I don't think he's inside. Hang on, I'll have a look." He crawled into the tunnel entrance. Inside were some cushions, a very low folding table with Spiller's bulging briefcase, a large battery lantern torch, a clock and a packet of sandwiches on it. To one side stood what looked like a small chemical toilet. Altogether, Spiller seemed set for a life of cosy isolation in the calm of Hermione's office.

"No, he's not here," he said, and stood up again. At this moment an agitated Oswald Spiller bustled into the office.

"Oh. Ah," he said. "There you are," he added irrelevantly. "Good morning, Miss James. I was hoping I might have preceded you and got out of your way before you came in but this signing-in business..." His voice trailed off and Brian and Hermione stared at him coldly.

"Ah well, tick, tock," he said, and made a sudden dive for the tent. His form quickly disappeared into the tunnel, and Brian was reminded of the expression 'a rat up a drainpipe'. He had to move equally quickly to grab Spiller's feet.

"Oh no you don't," he said.

"Let me go!" shouted a muffled Spiller indignantly. "How dare you!"

"Come on out of it," said Brian pulling him back.

Spiller's tones became even more a parody of dignity affronted as he grabbed desperately at the smooth canvas.

"I would remind you Dr. Mather - oh, oh - that I am head of your section in this department and - oof, ah - therefore your superior. Will - you - please - let go - of my - legs? Get off. It is quite unseemly for you to be - oh God! - doing this to me."

"Come out, you daft idiot," said Brian, gritting his teeth and pulling hard so that Spiller and the tent with him slid across the floor. Brian backed out into the corridor and the tent jammed in the doorway. With a final yank, Brian broke his grip on the canvas and he popped out of the tunnel, depositing Brian on the floor of the corridor. A small cheer arose from a group of second year students who had been passing.

"Great stuff, Brian. Can anybody have a go?" said one whom Brian recognised attended his lectures. "Who's this, then? A burglar or what?"

"No, no, nothing so interesting," said Brian.

"Are you alright?" asked Hermione, who had got out of her room just ahead of him.

"Fine. Just fine. No problem. Just another one of the little quirks that make life in this place such superjolly fun," said Brian, suppressing his anger. He picked himself up and dusted his trousers. Spiller had already done this and was backed up, dishevelled, against the wall. He was trying to sidle once more to the tent. The students inspected him with interest. Brian realised that to them he was a total stranger even though he had been marking their essays for the last two years.

"Shall we grab him, Brian?" said the student.

"Leave it be, Alan. I'll see to it."

"Ok. If you're sure."

"Yes. It's ok. It's a private affair. An architectural experiment - er - temporary accommodation for the homeless eviction test. Research, you see. Why don't you go along now?"

Brian waited while the students reluctantly moved off, then, when he was about to remonstrate with Spiller, a sudden snort from Hermione stopped him. He saw that she was grinning widely at both himself and Spiller.

"That was absolutely priceless, you know," she giggled. "What a wonderful idea. Homeless eviction test. And the way he just came out - pop - just like that. Pop!" Her giggles turned to loud laughter. Her laughter was unexpected to Brian, loud and hearty, far removed from the meek impression she gave normally. Brian felt himself swept along by it and began to laugh openly himself.

Spiller, who had turned his face to the wall to avoid the students' inspection, suddenly spoke:

"Please don't laugh. Please don't." He was obviously quite distressed.

Their laughter subsided slowly and Spiller turned round to face them again, although he still would not look at them. It struck Brian that, from the small wriggling movements he was making against the wall, Spiller was acutely uncomfortable. Not from any injury that Brian might have caused him but from the mere fact of his being out in the open like this. He was, Brian thought, rather like a hermit crab when it has to find a new shell, vulnerable and, yes, frightened. He wondered what had happened to reduce him to this state. It was clearly pathological: just one step away from gibbering. It was only at this point that the grotesque nature of what had just occurred struck him. Good Lord, he thought, I've only been here a few weeks and already I don't even notice the sheer lunacy of my own behaviour: manhandling my own head of section out of a tent at nine in the morning. Somehow the time of day made the whole thing even more bizarre. Mornings were when the world's work got done, after all. In a world of lunatics like this perhaps only the sane were mad. Were all art colleges like this? From some of the stories his colleagues had told him he suspected they might be. In fact, Brindling could even be one of the more coherent ones. It just had to be something to do with the subject; somehow a lot of people all working with the right sides of their brains set up a sort of paranormal field in which all the usual thought processes began to curl away from reality. Well, as a working hypothesis it would do to be going on with - there was something very odd, that's for sure. Perhaps it was this atmosphere which had caused Spiller to sink gradually into his own particular tar-pit of nuttiness without even noticing what was happening to him. He may have been - presumably had been - perfectly normal once. The thought struck him that perhaps he would be well advised to seek out that free transfer for himself fairly soon.

"Look, Spiller, get that silly tent dismantled and out of Hermione's office pronto," he said sternly. He turned to Hermione. "I presume you don't want a lodger in your room?"

"Certainly not," she said, shaking her head firmly.

"But..." said Spiller.

"Yes?" said Brian.

"You see, there's nowhere to go," Spiller almost wailed. "I haven't got a room any more and Mr. de Vere won't give me one. And this college is so crowded now. Every space is used for something. Please can I not share with you, Dr. Mather? Just until I've got myself somewhere? I'll pop out at any time you need it for a tutorial. And of course -" he paused as a look of deep resignation crossed his face, "there won't be any students to see me. I used to have lots once in. I was quite good, you know."

Although he had been in the 'education industry' for a number of years, Brian had resisted the creeping hardening of the emotional arteries which afflicted lots of teachers he knew. He had observed that forcing their students to try and win life's prizes with the ever-narrowing rings on the academic hoop-la stall often seemed to produce a parallel shrinking of the soul. Suddenly, he felt very sorry indeed for Spiller.

"Ok," he said. "I'm probably going to regret this but only provided you're quite clear that it's strictly temporary. And I don't ever want to see that idiotic tent again. Understood?"

Spiller was pathetically grateful in his thanks.

"I'll just get my things out," he said. "If I could hand them to you?"

Hermione looked at Brian with respect as he bent down to receive the contents of the tent. "That was really kind," she said.

"I just hope I'm not being conned, that's all," said Brian.

"No matter what the outcome, your best instincts should never be a cause for regret," she said seriously. "At least, that's what I believe,"

Her sincerity was patent and Brian was impressed.

"Perhaps I'll just have to look on it as charity to the afflicted then," he said. "You never know, it might shorten my time in purgatory. After a few weeks with Spiller they might even let me off altogether."

Spiller removed his belongings quickly and Brian put them against the wall of the corridor. He was emerging once more from the tent, when a first year student bustled up to them.

"Oh, Dr. Spiller, I'm so glad I've found you," she cried, and moved in on him quickly before he could attempt evasion. "I'm Dorothea Mulholland. I'm doing your course. Could I have a word with you about my essay marks? I don't understand them quite, or the comments you've written. I am right, aren't I? You are Dr. Spiller? Myra described you to me."

Brian was astonished: this woman must have more than usual visual discrimination and persistence. This was confirmed when she added:

"I've been looking for you for two terms."

At her use of his name, Spiller had leapt and whirled round. He looked desperately at the now-subsiding tent and then grasped his left wrist tightly and riveted his gaze fiercely onto his wrist watch as if both were about to escape from his arm. Brian was reminded of his similar reaction as he was led from 'BoZo'Z' surrounded by policemen. Dorothea, his temporary captor now, was a large girl, more mature than the majority of students. She eyed him closely and Brian thought he detected in her stare an almost professional scrutiny being exercised. Spiller shifted but Dorothea moved closer to him, almost pinning him against the wall with a bosom formidable enough to trap him and leave no sideways escape route. She'll go far, that one, thought Brian. He could see gallery owners desperately agreeing to Bond Street shows just to get her out of their hair, and critics relentlessly pinned to the wall, as Spiller was now, at the resulting private views, being given the themes for their reviews. He wondered how much success in contemporary art was due more to this ability to stick at it and hustle than to sheer native talent. After all, the country was stuffed with talent but only a few ever really made it.

"Er. Time, time, time. Tick, tock," said Spiller. He sounded terrified. "I'm afraid I won't be able to see you today. No. No. Er." Inspiration came to him suddenly as he looked at Brian. "I'm going on a field visit with Dr. Mather," he said in a rush. "Isn't that right, Dr. Mather?"

He looked directly at Brian and his eyes appealed to him to confirm his statement.

Brian sighed. "I suppose so," he said reluctantly, and was reminded of how Sinbad the Sailor acquired the old man on his back.

"Oh good," she said, "I'm going too. We can have a jolly good chat on the way."

Spiller bleated slightly at this. "But, but..."

"Perhaps I can give you a hand with all your things?" She gathered all the bits and pieces to her as if picking up small toys dropped by an untidy child, and handed Spiller the toilet to carry. "There you go. Be careful, it could have been 'used' as it were," she said. "Now then, where shall we put them all? Don't you want to fold up your tent thingummy?" Because mummy/ matron/teacher will be cross about the nasty patches it makes on the carpet/ward/classroom floor, thought Brian. He was certain from her tone she'd been a nurse, or teacher, or some such before landing up in Brindling art school.

"Put them in my office. I'll get the tent," said Brian.

"We're meeting in the canteen, aren't we?" she said to him.

"That's right."

"Good. Come along then, we'll take these upstairs, shall we?" she said briskly.

Spiller was mesmerised as a rabbit by a stoat. He could utter only a final feeble "Tick." before being swept along towards the staircase, clutching his chemical toilet.

When Brian first walked round the inner parts of Brindling, he realised with great excitement that, within walking distance of the college, the streets contained examples of almost every kind of domestic architecture from the Middle Ages (an old manor house and church) to the present. Brindling's bourgeoisie had, for four hundred years, built themselves substantial homes on the many profitable industries which had developed in the town. Because many of the industries required well-paid skills, during the last one hundred and fifty years lots of the workers' terraces had been built for sale, not renting, and had survived, with revitalisation, to the present day, and would presumably survive well into the next century. In researching the recent history of the built environment of Brindling, it had struck Brian that the numerous, well-kept terraces like these in the older industrial towns of Britain were the only lasting legacy of the otherwise little-lamented Heath government which had promoted their modernisation. (He had already begun a paper saying as much.) History was probably on Ted's side; they might well outlast the Canary Wharfs of the destructive Eighties. Indeed, many of the more interesting terraces had already become Grade III listed. To somebody like Brian, therefore, Brindling was proving an eclectic cabinet of gems, a gift from the gods for teaching his subject. At weekends he had explored the nearby districts and researched in the reference library and Civic Centre archives as well as taking numerous slides. Already, these were being used to illustrate his lectures and were transforming his students' appreciation of the previously unregarded drab background to their three years of colour and excitement in college.

However, not all of Brindling was sweetness and light. As the older industries had died, slowly at first from the end of the war to the whirlwind of destruction in the first Thatcher-Howe years, swathes of the town had been left in dereliction. Only now at the start of the new decade was some attention being given to these areas. Brian and Peter Orrd had discussed the potential for sculpture to play a part in the regeneration. Not so much as pieces of 'art' stuck on plinths but work springing from and involving the community. However, neither of them had much idea of how this might be done or where, but it was to one such area that Brian, Peter, and Laurie Willoughby, who had joined the field visit to reach those parts of the town he had always been far too nervous to explore on his own, were leading the students to assess its potential.

Brian had been surprised when he had joined the group in the canteen to find that all of the Fartistas had decided to come along as well. They hoped he didn't mind. When he had asked why, Connie had said in a languid American drawl that they thought they needed the exercise and might possibly get the odd interesting picture or two. They all had their cameras slung round their necks and the floor around them was littered with heavy metallised cases of extra equipment, tripods, a portable lighting rig, various back-packs and the college's high quality video recorder. No way would this quantity of equipment have been allowed to them, Brian knew, without Laurie's permission, especially the recorder of which he was particularly vigilant.

"We are taking in the 'Tofts' estate, aren't we?" Connie had asked.

"That's right."

"Mm, that's really great."

He had wondered what their interest could possibly be in that most notorious of Brindling's many areas of distressed housing but had decided to enquire no further, nor to give vent to the considerable annoyance he felt with Laurie Willoughby, who seemed to be mounting a major photo safari to the Himalayas; the prospect of having Connie along as a companion for the day had mollified him considerably. She was looking very attractive this morning, with a shaped, brown, dog-tooth check, hacking jacket and lemon-coloured, tight, riding breeches tucked into knee-length, shiny, brown boots. She had on a man's flat, tweed cap at a jaunty angle and a bright Hermes scarf. She could rob a scarecrow and still look stunning, Brian had thought. But he had said:

"Are you intending to ride or walk?"

"Pardon me?" she'd replied, puzzled.

Brian had said coolly:

"Well, if your horse bolts at the sight of Peter Orrd, don't expect me to catch it." He had given her no time to reply and went off to round up the first year students. Doing this, he had watched her reaction from the corner of his eye. She had looked annoyed. The other students had grinned at her. Brian knew she would not be used to having her carefully-composed outfit sent up by someone she had felt might be interested in her. But she shouldn't have used that languid American drawl on him.

"Hey, have a look at old Spiller," said Peter Orrd, grinning.

Brian reluctantly abandoned the bantering conversation he was indulging in with Connie and through which he reckoned he was making excellent progress and turned to look. Unlike Peter, Brian was not tall enough to see Spiller at the end of the straggling bunch of students. He hopped up onto a segment of broken brick wall, which had once enclosed the rubble-strewn, cobbled back-alley they were picking their way along.

"Mind where you step," he called out to the group as he looked over their heads towards Spiller. "There's masses of broken glass. We don't want any accidents. And watch the dog shit. It's the one product this town still leads the world in."

The students filed past him and Spiller approached. Brian shook his head in wonder at the sight. He was walking as a man in a trance. His mouth was slightly open and his head was held stiffly as he stared straight ahead. From his manner he could have been blind. He certainly didn't appear to notice Brian standing above him and seemed almost completely under the guidance of the firm grip Dorothea Mulholland had clamped onto his left arm with both her hands while she talked and talked, possibly about her essays but much more likely about herself, Brian thought. Whatever the subject of her discourse, its relentless exposition had obviously reduced Spiller's will power to that of a zombie.

Brian jumped down and rejoined Peter at the head of the group.

"Is Spiller married?" he asked Peter.

"Yes. Local woman."

"Oh yes, he did mention her once, I seem to remember."

"No kids, though. She's a big cheese in the town. Councillor for some slum or other. Round here, I believe. She's never at home. Rules Spiller with a rod of iron. That's why he's like he is. Real ball-breaker. She's Charlie Huggett's sister."

"What?" said Brian, startled. Before he had time to digest this information, Connie came alongside him again.

"My God, I knew Brindling was bad but not this bad. How do you know all these places? You've only just gotten here."

Over the previous two hours Brian had walked his party of students over a carefully chosen route through the most choice of Brindling's varied menu of dereliction. He intended to keep the more pleasantly architectural parts for the afternoon. By this time most of the students seemed to have got the message that the college studio - however wretched the rooms some of them were forced to live in - represented the proverbial ivory tower and that Brian's attitude to it might not be so approving as his colleagues'. Also, he knew the fact that the great Peter Orrd - whom they were aware normally stirred himself only to move in stately progress from sculpture studio to the public bar (never the despised lounge, Brian had noticed) and back - had come along and continually nodded assent and even added an approving mumble or two, had tremendously impressed them. To his relief, Brian had the distinct feeling from their reactions to what he told them and to his questions, that they had been waiting for something like this to happen: he felt that they might be facing up to the vague feeling of privileged guilt which the study of Art and Design in this context engendered. Brian had noticed that, unlike with normal student gatherings, their early lively chatter had gradually become subdued as the extent of the town's wretchedness sank in.

"Leg work," he said simply, in reply to Connie's question.

"It reminds me of the south Bronx," she said.

"Not big enough. No gunfire."

"True." She stopped. "Sweet Jesus, will you look at that?"

Emerging from the alleyway onto a stretch of waste ground which the Council had left as a sort of cordon sanitaire, the party was confronted by the 'Tofts' estate, which Brian decided would form the climax - or nadir - of the morning's walk. To most of the students, he knew that this set of soot-blackened, monumental, three-storey blocks of flats was known only by its reputation, which was uniformly unsavoury. Very few, even those students who originated from Brindling itself he imagined, had been this close to them. He was aware that students, however desperate they might be for cheap accommodation, could not be persuaded to take a room in these forbidding blocks, in spite of the constant attempts of the Accommodations Officer to tempt them. He had even been offered a flat here himself, with two bedrooms when he sought out his own accommodation but a quick perusal of the student union guide warned him off immediately. He knew the Polytechnic was under constant pressure from the Council to try and sweep students into them to alleviate the chronic rent famine resulting from the estate's largely unemployed and frequently feckless tenants.

Brian knew that when they had been built in the mid-Thirties, the idealistic municipal architects and councillors of the time like their counterparts in many other towns in the north, had looked to the workers' housing of socialist Vienna for their model. Unlike the Austrian blocks, named uncompromisingly after left-wing heroes, in Brindling, discretion as to their socialist ethos was maintained by harking back to a mythical rurality in the name 'Tofts' and even further removed by naming each block after an English poet - Keats, Byron, Shelley, through two more classic writers to 'Thomas Watkins Toft'. This last had puzzled Brian but he had finally tagged him via the reference library as a nineteenth century, local man, once popular for his bawdy verses extolling the sterling qualities of the local women and the local ale, and the iron men of Brindling who consumed both in such fearsome quantities. It seemed to Brian the only name at all appropriate to the setting.

The famous Viennese blocks which had inspired the 'Tofts' had been heroically defended against, and ultimately destroyed by, the artillery of the fascist Austrian army in the revolutionary conditions of the time, stirring the left-wing intelligentsia around Europe. Brian had written a research paper on the effects of these events and even identified that they were the probable inspiration for the young Kim Philby to become a Soviet spy. However, in Brindling nobody was inspired by anything which happened in the 'Tofts', except nowadays how best to get rid of them. Brian gathered from chatting to the planners in the Civic Centre that they could not demolish them as Brindling was now too poor to provide any kind of alternative. Brian speculated that if he was to make them aware of the Austrian solution, they might even be tempted to try a bit of right-wing explosive themselves, so despairingly had the planners spoken of them. Meanwhile, their condition inexorably declined further towards total decrepitude and they had truly begun to crumble. Only the previous week, Brian had noted an item in the local press reporting how some poor chap had been hospitalized after being hit on the head by a falling tile. And yet, as Brian had found, they still had a life within them.

On his weekend explorations, Brian's desire to get good pictures had obliterated any personal qualms he might have had about the wisdom of exploring the estate on his own. He knew the reputation the area had for daylight muggings as casual as buying fish and chips. The local inhabitants had eyed him suspiciously on these ventures into the labyrinth of the 'Tofts' but had left him alone. Even the ubiquitous packs of dogs, which roamed the estate untramelled, avoided him. He had the feeling that there was something about him that protected him but he could not work out quite what.

On one of these excursions he had gone into one of the four pubs which served the estate. The bar, which was crowded with Sunday lunchtime drinkers, fell silent as he entered. A sort of whispered clicking began and the bar started to empty almost as soon as he reached the counter. By the time he had been served by a cold-eyed landlord, the men had all gone. Only a few women remained. When the men had slipped smoothly through the four or five exit doors from the bar, they had continued to make the odd clicking sound to each other which sounded to Brian like "teck-teck-teck-teck". Brian had sunk his half quickly and left and, as he passed the frosted windows of the bar, he could hear but not see that it had filled with noisy customers once more. He was at a complete loss to understand what it was about him that could have had such an effect.

A sort of whispered clicking began and the bar started to empty almost as soon as he reached the counter.

He led his group across the rank grass, its surface alive with wind-blown paper and plastic, towards 'Thomas Watkins Toft', and felt rather like some young resistance hero in occupied Warsaw leading his irregulars against a Nazi strong point. He could feel the apprehension of the students as they followed him. The bright sunlight which had followed the showers did nothing to alleviate their unease.

The blocks were built round square, concreted courtyards with one, large, arched entrance and minor ones with staircases, at each corner. Brian led the party through one of these narrow, tatty corner passages into the central square. The women at home had hung out their washing across the corners of the upper balconies onto which the flats opened. (Most of the ground-floor flats were boarded up.) The sudden impact of colour and energetically flapping washing in the breezy sunshine gave a liveliness to the otherwise drab court. From the expressions on the faces of some of the more nervous women students, Brian could see they were reassured that perhaps normal life might exist here, after all.

Brian filled in the background to the flats and their difficulties and also who Mr. Thomas Watkins had been. He knew the last would grab their imaginations and had copied out one of his comic songs about a timid man becoming a lion under the influence of the local ale and seeing off the bailiffs to be satisfyingly reconciled with his formerly despising wife. He regaled the students with this song with gusto and got them laughingly to join in the chorus: 'He didn't give a fig for a judge in a wig. Or a rum bum, rum bum, bailie'.

After the last chorus had finished, the group was suddenly startled by a deep bass voice from the rear singing it once more. They turned to see Spiller, with Dorothea at his side looking up at him admiringly. Spiller went through the chorus emphatically, slowly descending the bass octaves to a very low note for the final 'bum bailie'. Delighted, the students applauded: Brian and Peter were too astonished to join in. Spiller looked suitably modest and sheepish.

"I remember how my grandfather used to sing it. It's how he heard it sung in the music halls of his day," he said.

Spiller went on to give a quick résumé of the history of the music hall in Brindling and its significance for the cultural heritage of the working class. At the end of his little talk, he suddenly stopped, drew in his breath and relaxed. He tried a slight grin. "I hope you don't mind my butting in like that, Dr. Mather? I've done a fair bit of research into it in the last few years. I was thinking of producing a small monograph on the subject."

"Not at all. Do go on, please," said Brian.

Spiller declined. He looked flushed and excited as well he might, thought Brian; it was the first words he had directed at students for four years. Dorothea grabbed his arm again and congratulated him effusively. Brian and Peter looked at each other; Peter winked significantly.

"Whatever turns you on," he said.

While Brian was congratulating himself that he, Spiller and Thomas Watkins had really got hold of the students' interest, he had not noticed particularly what Laurie Willoughby and his students were up to but the noise from them had gradually got louder and finally impinged so strongly that Peter had to abandon his discussion with students as to how an artist might relate to the flats and the people who were forced to live in them. The students' attention was now thoroughly distracted by Willoughby's group and its antics. Peter, the students and Brian, joined Laurie Willoughby who was directing events with a loudhailer. He stood by a small frame tent which the group had set up on the only tiny patch of grassed surface in the courtyard.

"What's going on?" Brian asked Willoughby, trying to control the irritation in his voice.

"It's a sort of cod fashion-shoot," said Laurie, impervious to any distraction his activities might have caused to the rest of the party. "I've got a show coming up soon and this is ideal for a satirical sequence in a video I've got in mind. The semiotics of fashion photography sort of thing. I've got 'Arena' interested. Good for the students too, this kind of location experience, you never know what they might be asked to do sometime. This place is absolutely ideal for what I want. Thanks awfully for bringing us here. I'd never dare to myself. So magnificently grungy, isn't it. Quite the pits. But the light's super this morning, now, isn't it. Wonderful shadows. Are you ready, loves?" he called out, his camp tones bouncing incongruously off the walls of the square.

He was answered by the third year students, scattered round the court area and from inside the tent came the muffled assent of Patience and Connie. Ronnie was handling the video camera and Bernie the sound boom. Shaheen, Bridget and Julia Lee followed Ronnie closely with a portable flood-lighting set, battery case and white umbrella reflector, the last giving a lot of difficulty in the gusty wind. All the male photographers had on excessively-padded, brightly-coloured jackets with baseball caps and were festooned with light meters and extra lenses. They all busied themselves consulting their equipment and waving and calling to each other in voices as camp as that of Laurie himself, while Ronnie, Bernie and the three women rushed round recording them with the video and sound equipment. The first year students - and Brian and Peter in spite of themselves - watched fascinated. Spiller was much too deep in conversation with Dorothea to notice anything.

"Right, quiet everybody. Ok, loves, you can come out now. We're ready for you," shouted Laurie, when the video group had returned to the tent.

From the tent emerged first Patience and then Connie. There was a gasp from the students at the boldness of their outfits. Each was dressed in a costume strikingly incongruous to the location. Patience had on an all-enveloping, West African-style robe in bold, deep blue and white patterns. Over her dreadlocks she had on an enormous turban head-dress and was hung with metal costume jewellery. She looked marvellously barbaric and haughty, a true daughter of Benin, crying out for tropical sunlight. Connie, on the other hand, was a complete contrast: her outfit was Thirties-style beach pyjamas in bold art deco black and white zig-zags with a large, picture-hat in cream straw. She had on huge dark glasses. As she moved, she reminded Brian of Norma Desmond enjoying the fresh air on her Atlantic liner crossing to 'Yurrup' for the premiere of her new picture. He had to admire the way both women handled their outfits in the gusty wind, which was giving them lots of opportunities to pose and preen in exaggerated gestures as they moved around the square while Laurie and the photographers zapped them with shot after shot, all the while keeping up a stream of campy jargon to encourage them.

"Ok, loves. Hold it a sec," called Laurie, eventually. "I think we've done the supermodel against draggy background here. What we need now is people contrast. Local flavour."

This was dramatically provided almost immediately.

Whilst the 'fashion shoot' and the students had been moving around, on the balconies above, unnoticed, the local female inhabitants of 'Thomas Watkins Toft', plus infants and the day's quota of truants, had been gathering and watching. When Connie and Patience approached the side of the courtyard, pirouetting on broken concrete as on a West End catwalk, there was a sudden crash of a large chunk of broken tile beside them. A raucous female voice bellowed out:

"Piss off back where yer came from, yer bangled 'arpies," it said.

The girls froze and began a slow sidle out of range.

"Oh dear," said Laurie quietly, looking round for the nearest exit.

"And you, yer puffy bastards!" said another voice, as a second tile was accurately skimmed across the court from above towards the photographers. There was a ragged cheer from the balconies as the missile was dodged.

"Hey, dead good shot, our mam!" said a child's voice. "That was nearly as good as the one you got our dad with last week. Can I 'ave a go?" A less expertly skimmed tile fell and broke in the yard.

A second tile was accurately skimmed across the court towards the photographers.

There was the sound of a slap.

"Shurrup you or I'll send yer back to school."

Brian thought he had better do something as this expedition was still ostensibly his idea. He moved forward but before he had thought of what to say, Ronnie's voice called up to the balcony.

"Is that you, Renee love?"

"Who's that?" The woman who had thrown the tile looked over the balcony to Ronnie directly beneath. "Oh. Is that you, Ronnie, son? What are you doin' with this lot?"

"I'm making a film. Would you like to be in it? It's going to be on the telly."

"Eeh, I dunno, like. A fillum? Eeh, well - what would I 'ave to do, like?"

"Can I be in it, our mam.? Can I? Can I be on the telly?"

Her child's pleading was taken up by a noisy clamour of other children.

Ronnie took over the shoot completely.

"Look, why don't you all come down here and you can all be in it?"

"What, looking like this?"

"It's perfect. Exactly what we want for local colour. Isn't that right, Laurie?"

"Oh, er, definitely. Excellent idea. Yes, indeed, quite so," said Laurie in a gruff manly voice, all trace of camp carefully eliminated. "How on earth does he know all these ghastly people?" he whispered to Brian.

"God knows," said Brian.

"He's a big favourite at the battered wives' refuge," said Connie, who, along with Patience, had discreetly joined the staff for protection. "People from here are always dodging their men in there. He shares his tranquillisers with them and chats them and slips them a bit of the other occasionally as well, so he says. And he's not picky about appearances either. Some of them have never been touched by their husbands for years. He reckons they come out of there new women. He's a sort of unlicensed social worker and sex therapist rolled into one. The authorities turn a blind eye because he keeps the women cheerful and stops them fighting among themselves. He says they've offered him a permanent job after finals."

"I see," said Brian. "Stunning outfits, by the way," he said to the girls.

"No joking this time?" said Connie.

"No joking."

"Gee, thanks awfully, kind sir," said Connie, lightly sending up Brian's faintly patronising tone.

"Your own designs?"

"Yes," said Patience.

"Terrific. I can see the African outfit would stand out here but why the Thirties? I know these blocks were put up then but I'd have thought you'd be against retro-style."

"Even though this may remind you of your youth, Dr. Mather, it isn't meant to be nostalgic," said Connie. "It's actually an outfit for the twenty first century."

"Huh? How come?" said Brian.

"Well, guys like you are always telling us how hot it's going to be what with global warming and all, and that we're going to have lots of leisure so I thought, when was the last time like that? and I thought, sure, the rich in the Thirties at the coast - so it's ahead of its time, you see. This is what Mrs. Tofts will be wearing to visit the bridge club by AD 2010."

Brian looked at the 'Mrs. Tofts' now assembling with much giggling in the courtyard and thought that the sky would have to set on fire to make that much difference to the Tofters.

"Ok. Can we have the models please?" called Ronnie, coming up to them. The girls moved off. "Oh. Laurie, I think I'd better have the shouter. Looks better."

Laurie handed over the loudhailer without demur.

"I always thought he was supposed to be a bit - you know - a bit doolally," said Laurie to Brian, as Ronnie began to direct the crowd with crisp efficiency.

"With some people it's difficult to tell either way," said Peter, giving a nod over his shoulder. Brian turned, and saw that Spiller had moved away to a nearby wall under a balcony and was leaning against it with Dorothea pressed close and his arm round her waist.

"Thank God for art," said Peter fervently. "At least it keeps the buggers off the streets and us in clean underpants."

"Dr. Mather, can I ask you something?" It was the girl in the sailor gear now minus the VD sticker, he noticed.

"Of course," he said, congratulating himself that the seriousness of her tone suggested a minor triumph for his educational methods.

"Are there any public bogs round here? I'm bustin'."

The shoot had finished and the party was ready to move off, when the woman called Renee and her child came up to Brian.

"I seen you in the pub the other Sunday, didn't I?" she said.

"That's right," said Brian, startled and impressed that she had remembered him.

"We thought you was the Old Bill, like. A 'tec." Brian wondered what it was about him that gave that impression. "Ronnie tells me you're some sort of housing expert or summat, is that right, like?"

"Sort of. On buildings," said Brian.

"And that you'd be willing to help us."

"If I can," said Brian. An advisory role on design to a local community might be an asset on his CV, he thought.

"Well, there's summat going on in these buildings you ought to 'ave a look at. We've got a residents' committee 'ere, like, and we could do with a bit of experting on our side just now. The bastards are trying to get us out. You just come wi' me and I'll show yer. Leave off picking yer nose, will yer," she said to the small boy with her. "You do that too much and yer 'ead'll cave in."

Brian and the other staff and the students together with a fair smattering of the residents followed Renee out of 'Thomas Watkins Toft'. Brian judged her to have some sort of leadership role. She was thin and small with a sharp-featured face and dressed in jeans and a sweater, but the most striking thing about her appearance was her hair. Her head was shaved close, apart from a fringe of mousey hair which stood up like a halo round her face and she'd left two tufts with small ribbons in them over her ears. Ronnie had enjoyed placing her with her aggressive angularity as a strong contrast to the height and haughtiness of Patience and the soft femininity of Connie and Brian had noticed that Laurie had been discreetly shooting her as well. Now, striding determinedly beside him, her fists clenched and her sharp features set in a stubborn expression, she looked a good deal more formidable than simply a photographic prop. He wondered what Ronnie had let him in for. She didn't look as though she'd be somebody to cross.He also remembered her skill with a skimmed tile.

"There!" said Renee. "What do yer think of that?"

They turned the corner of the street to which Renee had led them, and were startled by the abrupt assault of the noise from the scene which confronted them. The street was in the heart of the 'Tofts' between 'Shelley' and 'Keats' and was cordoned off with the walls of the flats encased in scaffolding. On this, and down at street level, men were working, bashing out windows and brickwork and throwing debris down, digging huge holes with JCB's and filling skips.

"They call it revitalisation," said Renee, "but I call it rebollockisation, 'cos all they're doing is buggering them up and getting the tenants out so's they can board them up. We think they're going to knock the whole lot down and sell it off for a development site. And they're getting our own lads to do it for them, the twerps."

So that's where all the men had got to, thought Brian. He'd wondered why they were not present at the fashion shoot; he knew that virtually all the men hereabouts were unemployed.

"What about your Councillor? Can't he do something?"

"It's a her, the useless cow! She's thick with those buggers in the mafia and does what she's told. And the stupid prats round 'ere go on votin' for 'er. Those that bother to vote, that is. And they mostly work for the Council anyway and wouldn't say boo to a goose, they're that scared of losing their jobs."

Brian had a sudden insight into how 'democracy' worked in a town like Brindling.

"Well, I'm not sure what I can do but I'll see if I can find out anything and let you know."

Renee sniffed and looked at Brian sceptically. Her reaction reminded him of Gerry Hodgson's similar expression before he agreed to help the Fartistas. Damn Ronnie Oliver! This was a far cry from a bit of expertise on the design of windows and doors. He also reminded himself of the penalties Polytechnic staff might be liable to for criticising the activities of the Council.

"I'll just get a picture for the record," he said, as much to escape that look as take an interest in photography.

He ducked under the cordon to climb the largest of the nearby heaps of clay. This action produced a subtle change in the scene in front of him, which he registered only subconsciously while he adjusted his camera. The men responded to his sudden appearance climbing the clay heap by an almost imperceptible slowing of the pace of their activities. They began to move with a subtle wariness, alerting each other through their body language of imminent danger, like a herd of animals with a predator nearby. Brian raised the camera to his eye and was astonished as he saw the scene change dramatically through the lens. Suddenly, men were running everywhere. Some of them, along the scaffolding, dived through gaping window apertures, some jumped into holes in the road, some leapt behind site huts or heaps of clay, some ran with their shovels or their caps covering their faces. As the men hid themselves, they fell and cursed but all of them cried to each other the universal alarm call of the British working class after the nineteen-Eighties: "It's the Social! It's the Social!" In a few moments the site was deserted.

Brian rejoined the others at the barrier.

"What happened?" he said.

"It's the hat, man," said Renee.

"The hat? What hat?"

"Yours," she said simply. Puzzled, Brian took off his hat and looked at it. He was very fond of it and had worn it for field work ever since his student days. Also, it enabled students to keep an eye on him from the rear.

"What's wrong with it?" he said.

"It's a effin' trilby, innit, man, like," she said, as if explaining the obvious to a dense child.

"So?"

"Look, chaw, anybody who comes sniffin' round 'ere in one of them things is either a 'tec, or the Social, or a bailiff, or the boss. And if you start taking pitchers, you're definitely the Social."

"I see."

"Hey, you, what the 'ell do you think you're playin' at?"

The figure from which this bellow issued had emerged from the largest of the portakabins. He was huge, heavily muscled, red-faced, ugly and very angry. He was also wearing a trilby hat and, with his clay-crusted wellies and donkey jacket, nobody could mistake him for anything other than a hard-case, site-gang boss.

"Bloody hell," said Peter. "What's that?"

"Good Lord," said Laurie. "He looks like something out of a Daumier. Wouldn't he just photograph well, though."

"Just watch 'im," said Renee. "That's Terry Degnan, the ganger. 'E's a real nasty bastard."

It was this remark which triggered Brian's memory. When he saw him he knew immediately there was something familiar about him. Of course, it was the man in Alex's picture. Confirming it, Alex said:

"Oh Christ, the nazi. Not again."

"I suppose I'd better go and have a word with him," said Brian reluctantly.

"Pity you haven't got a spare bone to throw him," said Peter. "Hey, why don't you offer to take a splinter out of his paw," he called after a Brian entirely unappreciative of his humour.

"I'd go but he's not my type, darling," said Laurie. "Get a few shots of him, Alex, will you, my camera's out of film." Alex ducked under the cordon and followed Brian. Ronnie joined him and began videoing the scene.

"Stay back," Brian called to them. "We don't want to provoke him needlessly."

"Oh, so it's you again, is it, you young bugger!" roared Degnan, recognising Alex as an old adversary. "I told you before about coming onto my sites with that fucking camera. I'll see you remember it this time."

He bent down and picked up a heavy baton of wood and made for Alex. Brian knew he had to intervene.

"Look, just hold it there," he called, and went towards him.

"You're another fucking twat photographer, are you?" said Degnan, turning his wrath on Brian. "You want some, an' all, do yer, yer cunt?" He lumbered quickly towards Brian brandishing the baton.

Never later could Brian recall exactly what happened next, even though he saw it on Ronnie's videotape afterwards. He moved back quickly from his attacker but his foot slipped on what he later imagined was either a particularly sloppy lump of clay or, more likely, one of the estate's abundant dog turds. His left foot went forward and he rocked back just as Degnan was raising his weapon to thump Brian with it. Brian's unexpected backward and downward movement caused Degnan to over-balance and lunge forward and, as he did so, Brian's arms, stretched out to defend himself, caught against his chest. Brian went down to the road surface, but the equilibrium between Degnan's forward lunge and Brian's backward subsidence must have been perfectly balanced to account for the exquisitely timed throw which caught a surprised and helpless Degnan. Still supported by Brian's arms and legs, the foreman took off and made a graceful arc over his head. Brian caught a whiff of a lion breath as he grunted above him and the next thing he knew was that he was on his back in the road and the foreman had disappeared. He heard a dull thump as the man landed.

He quickly picked himself up and looked round. The party of staff, students and residents by the cordon was staring at him open-mouthed. He looked behind him ready to defend himself again but Degnan was nowhere to be seen. He looked back to the cordon. Peter pointed behind where Brian stood to a large hole in the road. Brian approached it and the rest of the party joined him and looked in. Degnan was lying at the bottom of the hole, immobile. From behind some nearby heaps, the men of the estate emerged and pushed to the front to look in the hole as well. Nobody seemed to be in any hurry to help Degnan.

"Is he dead?" said one of the men.

"I fuckin 'ope so," said another.

They looked at Brian with wonder.

"That was karate, that, eh. Karate. Did you see it?" They agreed amongst themselves that it was indeed karate that had floored the awesome Terry Degnan.

"Let me through," said an impatient female voice. It was Dorothea. "Help me down," she ordered. "I'm a trained nurse."

Brian absently noted his correct surmise as he lowered her into the hole. She examined the unstirring Degnan expertly.

"Don't try and give 'im the kiss of life, missus," called one of the men. "'Ave yer smelt 'is breath. Christ, you'd be dead before 'e even came round. Hey chaw," he said to Brian, "we've got our shovels 'ere. Just say the word and we'll fill 'er in."

"What?" said Brian, puzzled.

"The 'ole, man. Nobody'll miss 'im and we'll say nowt."

"Or we can do it with the JCB," said another man. "It'd be quicker."

"Thanks, no," said Brian.

"Suit yourself but if 'e does come round, I'd make myself scarce, if I were you."

"'E can always use the karate on 'im again," said the second man. "Bloody 'ell, did you see 'im fly? Whee, whacko the diddley-o, yer bugger. That fettled 'im."

"Yeah, I suppose so." But he looked at Brian's thin frame with a similar scepticism to Renee's.

"It's alright," said Dorothea, straightening up. "He's just been knocked out and winded a bit. The bigger they come, the harder they fall. I don't think any bones are broken. But," she said, as Brian pulled her from the hole, "you'll just have to control that karate of yours in future, Brian - oh, it is mucky down there - it's too dangerous to let loose like that. I prefer aikido, myself. Much more controllable." Brian realised Dorothea was playing up to his supposed prowess; no doubt her experience of weekend casualty had shown her the importance of gaining a psychological advantage.

Julia Lee grinned at Brian. "He the Bruce Lee of Brindling Poly!" she said. The others laughed as their tension relaxed.

At this point, around the corner into the demolition site came a smart black Jaguar.

"Christ, it's 'imself," said one of the workmen. They began to scurry away.

Out of the limousine stepped Charlie Huggett.

"What the 'ell's going on 'ere?" he said angrily, as he approached the group. "Where's Degnan?"

Renee jumped in front of him.

"'E's where 'e belongs," she said. "Down in the shit."

"Get out of my way, woman," said Huggett, pushing her aside.

"Don't you shove me about, yer bum. We know what your game is 'ere," she said. Huggett ignored her and elbowed the students aside to look into the hole.

"What happened? Has he had an accident?"

"Naw," said Renee, who had followed him close behind. "It was this fella 'ere. 'E thought 'e looked tired so 'e gave 'im a touch of karate so 'e could 'ave a bit of a rest."

"Can I learn karate, our mam, can I?" said her little boy. "Hey mister, will yer teach me to karate?" he said, pulling eagerly at Brian's jacket sleeve. "Then I can bash this fella about for yer an' all, mam."

"Aw, that's a really nice thought, chuck. Would you do that for your mam?" said Renee, stroking his face.

"Just a minute," said Huggett, looking closely at Brian. "Don't I know you? You're at the Poly." He looked round the group. "In fact, you're all at the Poly. What the 'ell are you doing 'ere? 'Ang on, 'ang on, what's all this!" He shoved his way through the group towards Spiller, who was trying to hide behind some of the taller students.

"Oswald! What the 'ell are you doing 'ere? I thought I told you never to come onto one of these sites."

"Well, it's a sort of field trip and I came along with my colleagues. I didn't know we'd be coming here. Part of my teaching, you see."

"What teaching? You stupid sod, coming here. You'll ruin everything. Come on out of it now with me." He began to pull Spiller with him towards the car. Suddenly, Spiller asserted himself. Brian guessed the sudden attention shown to him by Dorothea must have done something drastic to him.

"Get off me," he said, pulling away. "Leave me alone! I'm sick of the whole sordid business."

Huggett lost his temper. "Don't you get funny with me, sonny Jim. You'll bloody well do what you're told." He made a lunge for Oswald.

Dorothea jumped between them. "You leave him be," she said. "How dare you!"

"Get out of my way, you stupid bitch," said Huggett, trying to push her aside.

He got no further than laying his hands on her arm. With a swift and expert movement, Dorothea sent him flying into the same hole where, unnoticed by the crowd, Degnan had been painfully climbing out. Huggett landed on top of him and they went to the bottom together.

As everyone moved quickly to the hole again to look at the prone forms of Huggett and Degnan, groaning and clasped in each other's arms, Connie stood beside Brian and said:

"It might be quite a good idea to get on finding what's in that data bank, don't you think? You're probably going to need it when all this gets out." With a heavy heart, Brian realised she was right.

Chapter Eight
In the Steps of the Old Masters

"It's her skin, you see. That's the challenge. Look at the way the light seems to come from inside her flesh. Do you see? From the inside! Especially round the tits, her bum and across the lower belly." (The sun shines out of it, thought Brian irrelevantly, trying to keep his demeanour suitably academic by not staring too closely.) "And the texture's so fine and the shape's so subtle. None of the others has skin like it. Degas would have given his right - well, left - arm for her. Or was he left-handed anyway? No matter - he could always have used his penis like old Renoir did." It almost wasn't a joke; Mike Brierley rarely took the name of any artist he admired lightly. "He did that, you know," he said seriously, "when his arthritis became too painful to hold the brush, poor old lad."

"Oh," said Brian, wondering about the nice people with the poor old lad's prints in their living rooms.

"I tell you, I've painted her dozens of times," Mike continued, "and I can still find new things. There's nothing like life-painting to develop the eye, you know."

"Or the penis," said Brian quickly but Mike was in too full a flow.

"That's why every artist needs to do it if they're going to call themselves a painter. It's still the real ultimate test. Students these days just don't understand that. It's a way of measuring themselves against the masters, but will they see it? I mean, just look at her. Doesn't she just cry out to be got down on canvas?"

Oh, yes indeedy, Brian thought.

Mike Brierley shook his head in open admiration of the artist for the naked woman leaning on a lyre-back, antique chair on the small raised dais in the middle of his life class. This was the first time Brian had had occasion to enter the life room while it was in operation and had not acquired that casualness of the professional attitude which set the sudden impact of naked flesh into a morning's round of mundane hackwork. He had almost withdrawn when he opened the door to the room not expecting somehow at this time of the day to be confronted by something so sensual. He moved his head and coughed so that, as he turned and raised his hand, he could inspect the model more closely but without seeming to be staring at her. He was nonplussed when, without seeming to move herself or give any other overt signal, she managed to convey to him that she had registered his interest and was amused. As an actor, he was intrigued as to how she did this but the full impact of her beauty was so impressive it diverted any thought of analysing it. Gosh! he thought.

She was in her thirties, Brian guessed, but probably older than him, tall, blue-eyed and her dark hair was lightly permed in a fashionable style. Like a fashion model, she had broad, square shoulders but they were well covered and again, unlike such models, the rest of her body was very well fleshed, with an emphatic bust - 38D Brian reckoned - firm stomach muscles and well proportioned buttocks. Her skin was, as Mike enthused, pearly translucent. Even at this distance, Brian thought he could see the delicate, faint blue veins.

"Pretty too," he said.

"Is she?" said Mike, momentarily puzzled by the expression. "Yes, I suppose she might be."

Brian was amused to note that Mike had to look a little longer at her before he agreed she was pretty; for him she had long ago lost any interest apart from the artistic challenge of capturing the play of light on that wonderful skin.

"At least, that bastard Huggett thinks so," Mike continued. "She's his bit of side-salad, you know."

Before Brian could digest this startling and unlikely congruence of beauty and the beast, a peeved but familiar female voice amongst the students gathered round the dais interrupted his thoughts.

"She moved," it said.

With a quick flash of annoyance, he identified it as originating once more from the girl with the sailor suit.

"She's a right one, that," said Mike balefully, under his breath. (Brian was glad there were others on the staff who were finding her trouble.) "No she did not, " he said aloud, very firmly. "You're just not concentrating to maintain your viewpoint. You should be as vigilant as the model. Rita never moves. She's not an amateur." ("Unlike some students I could name," he said, again sotto voce.) "Anyway, take a break, now. Back in fifteen minutes."

Rita got her wrap and descended from the dais while the students stood up and stretched.

"And no smoking while I'm out," said Mike. "What did you want to see me about?" he said to Brian. "Can it wait? I've just got to slip to the office - I won't be long. See they don't smoke, will you?" He hurried out.

From the hubbub of student discussion the same female voice, even more peeved at being rebuked, rose above the noise.

"Why can't we have a male model? It's just sexist this bloody set up here. I know a guy who'll come and model for us any time. It's about time we women got a thrill out of this life-painting stuff as well." She paused and said in tones of awe: "And he's got a dong on him like - like - an elephant's trunk, this guy."

Perhaps, Brian thought, Mike might have been slightly less than successful in getting his point across to this particular student about the challenge of the old masters in the life room. But he was nevertheless fully aware that the life class, as in most art colleges, the final bastion of the traditional, was a problematic part of the last CNAA visit and likely to be even more so during the forthcoming quinquennial. And this student was unwittingly tapping into one of the most critical points about it.

From what Noel de Vere had told him, Brian had gathered that, like all young people who think they invented the subject, some of the students resented being forced into what they saw as a stale historical exercise, the girl with the sailor's uniform being presumably one example. (Brindling insisted on life-painting as a compulsory part of the course so it could be a real irritant - even to very good students.) At the previous CNAA validation, Brian had read in the report that some of the panel agreed with them and had not been impressed by the intellectual justification offered by Mike for the emphasis on life-painting in the late twentieth century. Brian was reminded of de Vere's despair at his colleagues' lack of 'words'. The students themselves were certainly aware that, at many other colleges, their contemporaries had long ago abandoned the 'sterility' of the life room. However, there were still sufficient at Brindling who found that the practice of life-painting did provide that challenge to the estimate of their own artistic worth which Mike believed it should. Brian could see that it was to Mike's considerable credit that he had been able to hold out against the tide of painting fashion and carry a goodly number of these students with him.

To the students who did relate to him, the feminist critique of the sexism of life-painting seemed pointless. In talking to them, Brian was impressed with the way that Mike Brierley's enthusiasm for his teaching and inexhaustible knowledge of the subject came through. Mike could not only locate their efforts in relation to the total canon, great and minor, of European life-painting from the Renaissance onwards, but also, more practically, his unerring eye for faults in their work, and his suggestions as to how they might be corrected, they found invaluable. In other words, he was a crackerjack teacher of painting. And if Brian could persuade him to mount the small research exercise he had in mind, that quality would probably spike any potentially hostile criticisms the visiting party might have.

However, Brian was also fully aware of the fact that the lack of a male model in the life room these days was definitely a minus and rendered the course vulnerable to the dangerous charge of sexism. Especially was this so as he knew now that the art historian who was earmarked for the visiting party was a right-on, militant feminist whose extensive revisionist art historical publications had concentrated particularly on the nude. Brian was not anti-feminist himself; it was simply that he abhorred any kind of ideological squint which could subvert common sense. Having read some of these publications, however, Brian was sure that her anti-male bias was actually very formidably buttressed by an incisive intellect. His heart sank when he thought that she was ostensibly responsible for the scrutiny of Related Studies as well. It was partly on this delicate subject of gender bias that Brian had come to see Mike Brierley that morning.

In his haste to produce some sort of novel rabbit out of the hat to convince CNAA that the course had 'relevance', de Vere had given Brian the task of rooting out and making look respectable any activity of the staff which could be remotely construed as 'research'. It was then up to Brian to devise some suitable verbal context in which to dissolve the everyday practice of his colleagues' art. The whole was to be written up as the Department's contribution to the annual Polytechnic research report, a publication in Brian's opinion inaptly named 'Brindling Blue Skies' following the advice of the Poly's PR agency. According to Noel, this publication was the Rector's pride and joy, and little expense was spared to put out a de-luxe job.

So far, in its ten year life, Brian noted, the Department of Art and Design had featured not at all in the report, not even in the cover design, which the Rector had pointedly given to an expensive agency, the better to display his opinion of the talents of the Department. As part of a strategy of crashing into the pages of 'Blue Skies', it was Brian's intention to get Mike to employ a male model for a while at least, carry out a questionnaire survey he would devise on student attitudes to life room gender and how they thought it affected their work, and write up a quick paper (with Mike as joint author) for the Journal of Art Education: good for a couple of thousand words, Brian reckoned.

While he waited for Mike to return so that he could put his proposal to him, he wandered into Mike's small office at he rear of the studio, its windows overlooking the life room. Rita was sitting on an office chair looking very relaxed with her legs crossed under her all-enveloping, pink satin wrap with her expensive-looking gold mules hanging casually from her painted toes. Looking at her feet, it dawned on Brian that never, with any of the women he had known, had he paid much attention to the quality of their feet; he realised that he may have been missing something. Rita was reading a magazine and smoking.

"Oh, hello," he said, "I'm Doct..."

"I know who you are," she said, without looking up from her magazine. Her voice was surprisingly deep and oddly accented. It was local but had been cultivated and Brian thought he could detect the theatre somewhere in its edge of refinement. "You're famous."

This statement puzzled Brian.

"How do you mean?"

"Well, you're Brindling Poly's answer to Bruce Lee, aren't you?" She looked up at him suddenly with an ironic grin. Brian breathed slightly deeper as the quality of her good looks close to struck him.

"Er," he said, confused by both her appearance and her statement.

"I've seen that video."

"Oh Christ!" he said. "Sorry. I mean, where?" Since the episode at the 'Tofts' there had been a blessed - or ominous - silence.

"It's even got a title now. 'The Man Who Floored Dirty Degnan.'" She looked up at him and inspected him shrewdly. "Like in the movie, wasn't it? An accident. You don't know the first thing about karate, do you?"

"No." He saw no reason to prevaricate.

She nodded. "Well, I feel I ought to tell you that the word's gone out on you. I was going to drop you a note, anyway. Nobody has ever floored Terry Degnan - and lived to tell the tale, that is - and he doubles as Charlie Huggett's minder so he's got his reputation to think about. If I was you I'd stay off dark streets in future. It's baseball-bat time. In fact, why don't you move out of town altogether? They can be a very nasty bunch when they're roused. And you've definitely stirred them up."

Brian was almost speechless. "But...I mean, how on earth do you know all this?"

She shrugged. "It's all over the club. They're quite looking forward to it. They like a bit of excitement, the lads."

"Which club? What lads?" he said, with more than a hint of panic in his voice.

"'BoZo'Z'. I do a turn there as a stripper nights and Charlie Huggett and I are on - well- more than nodding terms, you might say."

"But where did you see the video? I've not heard a thing about it since that day."

"Con...er..Some of the students showed it me the other day."

"Did they?" Rita's hesitation was revealing. Brian looked at her speculatively. She returned quickly to her magazine to avoid his gaze. "You wouldn't be in with Connie's bunch, would you, the so-called Fartistas?"

She drew on her cigarette and didn't answer.

"That's where all those numbers and codes came from didn't they," he said. "And their information. You're a sort of spy for them. Did you get those from Huggett?"

Still no reply.

"Why do you do it?"

"That's my business. And don't you dare tell anybody or it'll be me and my little baseball bat you'll have to watch out for as well." She suddenly grinned and began to laugh, rocking backwards and forwards slightly. "God, you should see your face after that throw - what a picture - shock, horror. Oh Lordy! And that dame who bounced Charlie. Now, she really does know her stuff. I wouldn't mind a few lessons from her - come in handy at the club." She clapped her hands as she laughed and her wrap fell open from her knees to her crotch: Brian gulped, caught his breath and began to cough. He had forgotten she was still naked underneath it. "Oops!" she said and replaced it; like most life models and strippers she drew a clear line between on- and off-duty nakedness.

"You know, you're not bad-looking," she said. "Weren't you some sort of actor once?"

Brian confirmed this absently as he tried to calm down after the sudden shock, first of the thought of his head as a target for Terry Degnan's batting practice and secondly, the sight of Rita's upper thighs. He fleetingly thought in relation to the latter, that it was the covering up that made for the erotic charge. After all, he should not have been bothered as he had just had a full view of all of Rita's ample charms anyway. Also, the fact that Rita had noted what he looked like was fairly disturbing. It was the first time a woman had shown him some direct personal attention for months; Connie's attitude was still too ambiguous for him to be sure of any real sexual interest. But a target for heavies! Or, in Rita's case, middle- weights! She interrupted his thoughts.

"Have you still got any contacts in the theatre or telly or whatever?" she said suddenly.

"What? Yes, some," he replied. "Why?"

"You wouldn't know anybody who could give a girl a job, would you? I can sing and dance. I've got my Equity card and my passport says actress - and I'm not bad-looking."

"You're certainly that, alright, er, I mean to say, an actress. And the other as well, of course, I meant," he added hastily.

She smiled at his confusion. "That's rather sweet of you," she said.

"I mean it, about the acting, I mean as well as...I mean, I don't know quite how you got that message over to me when I looked at you just after I came in but it was a pretty nifty piece of body language. The camera would certainly like that. But, I don't know. A job. Yes. I suppose I could contact one or two people I used to know who've got independent production companies now, if you like. And I know somebody in casting for 'The Bill' - they're always looking for beautiful victims. But what for?

Why haven't you tried before? If you don't mind my saying so, it's leaving it a bit late to try and break in now, isn't it? And the money won't be very good to start off with, you know. Especially as you can't expect big parts."

"I've got no problems with money. You'd be surprised." She smiled to herself as she thought some private thought. Then she looked up at him more seriously and seemed to make a decision to tell him some more. "You're the sympathetic type, you know. Has anybody ever told you that?"

"Often," said Brian. "It can be a bit difficult at times."

"I can imagine," she said. "People telling you their life stories at the drop of a hat."

"Yes."

"Especially women, I'll bet." She drew hard on her cigarette. "Like me." She looked at him with her head first on one side then the other. "You do remind me of somebody, you know."

"Oh," said Brian. He hoped Rita found whoever it was 'nice' rather than just 'interesting' as Audrey Reaper had done

"I'll get it eventually. No, the reason I want to get out of Brindling is - well - tied up with being here all my life and how I started out. I mean, I was far too poor as a kid not to see money as very, very precious. I mean really valuable. I'm a really terrible tightwad, you know." She grinned at him challengingly. "Everybody says so. Even Charlie. And that's saying something, I can tell you," she said feelingly. "I tell you, I wouldn't give duff penny to a dying nun. And Oxfam and that lot - they can go jump. I've always saved every red cent I can lay my hands on. Maybe you wouldn't think it now but back in the Sixties when I was a little kid we were on the bread- line, our lot - we lived in your favourite buildings, the 'Tofts' so you can guess. It always amuses me when people rabbit on about the Sixties and how great they were. It was in the Sixties that this town really began to fall apart. Got it, Montgomery Clift!" She clapped her hands together triumphantly but more carefully this time, to Brian's disappointment. She waited for a reaction. "But you know that, don't you?" she said, when none was forthcoming.

"Yes."

"It's that same haunted look."

"If Terry Degnan was after you with a baseball bat, you'd look a bit spooked as well."

"Don't worry too much, a lot of it's just talk."

"He didn't look like a man of too many words to me," said Brian.

"Yes, I see what you mean," she said thoughtfully, but she was obviously much more interested in letting Brian know why she wanted out, than to worry about the future of his head, however like that of Montgomery Clift it might be.

"Anyway, as I said we were dead poor and we never went anywhere. You cannot imagine what it was like stuck in the 'Tofts' all the time for a kid like me. I was pretty bright, you know - I passed the eleven plus - there still was one then - but I never got to grammar school - when my dad saw what it would cost that was it. Even the sec. mod. was better than nowt, though. I loved school. I really did. I tell you, it was free school meals that made me what I am today. Christ knows what I'd look like if I'd had to rely on our mam. There was never money for owt but bread and chips. Like, for instance, I was always promised we would go to Scarborough for our holidays then. So about April, I used to start packing my bag and marking off the days on the calendar. I'd pack and re-pack it, trying to decide what doll to take depending on which was my favourite at the time. But we never did get to Scarborough - there was always something stopped us, maybe my dad lost his job - he was always doing that or one of the other kids was ill or my mam - or the money went on a bender - always something, and then it just got too late. Well, that's the story of my life all over. I'm still waiting to go to bloody Scarborough, still packing and re-packing the same damned bag see, and if I wait any longer for Charlie Huggett to take me - I suppose you know about Charlie and me - Connie'll tell you - anyway, I'll be past it. I'll be forty in - well, a few years - and that's your lot!" She threw the magazine onto the desk in disgust. Brian had noticed, during the course of what she had said, that her accent was reverting quickly to type. She must be confident of his sympathy to let her guard down to him so openly. It was that face of his, it would do it every time, he thought. She puffed hard again on her cigarette and blew out the smoke angrily.

"He used to be a fun sort of guy but since he fell in love with his money and became the town's big shot...Anyway, to hell with him. He's had the best years of my life so far but the rest are strictly for me."

She threw the cigarette onto the floor and twisted it hard with one of her beautiful slippers.

Brian was surprised by the strength of her vehemence when she spoke of Huggett.

"How do you mean - go to Scarborough?"

"Charlie Huggett has a wife, hasn't he? But will he divorce her? Will he buggery. And for why? Because he's got her name on everything, both her's and that dopey brother-in-law of his as well, for tax fiddles and I don't know what not dodgy schemes. So, though they've hardly spoken for years, they're stuck together like Tweedledum and Tweedledee. Well, I've had enough, not that he couldn't divorce her if he really wanted to, the rott..."

Brian interrupted her before she could launch her tirade as he remembered something.

"Hold on, did you say his brother-in-law. That wouldn't be Oswald Spiller, would it?"

"That's right. That stupid, ba'dy-headed pillock who works here." She stopped suddenly. "Oh oh, don't look now - here comes droopy drawers for his daily eyeful."

Rita had looked out of the office window past Brian who was leaning on Mike's untidy desk with his back towards it. Brian turned his head and saw that 'droopy drawers' was none other than the Deputy Rector, Dr. Marshall.

"He's in here nearly every day with some excuse or other." she said. "But all he's doing it for is to clock my assets, the dirty sod. I've been a stripper long enough to know when I'm getting the leery eyeball. Well, that's all the damn balling he's going to get, I can tell you. He may have a nice suit on but to me it might as well be a dirty old mac - they're all the same underneath, them types."

"That's very interesting," said Brian, wondering whether and how this information might come in handy in future.

"In fact, Mike's getting really pissed off with him. He's already spoken to Noel about it."

"Has he?"

"Yeah, but Noel seems scared stiff of him."

"Oh, I don't know. Perhaps, he just thinks that you're very beautiful. And who can blame him for that?" said Brian quietly. "It's not easy to ignore you, you know."

"Then he can come down to 'BoZo"Z' and pay like all the other dirty old men," she said, but without quite all her former vehemence.

As they watched him, Marshall turned to go, Rita not being on display. He saw Brian and raised a hand to acknowledge him. Brian was doing the same when Rita suddenly hunched forward on her chair.

"Let's give him summat to think about," she said gleefully.

"What?" said Brian, turning his head towards her. Before he could do anything about it, Rita had launched herself at him, pushed herself against him and planted a big smacking kiss on his lips. Brian, bent back against the desk suddenly, reached out both arms to hold her and prevent them both from toppling. As he did so, Rita's wrap came open and he found his hands holding not a piece of satin but a material much more interesting: that warm, smooth skin Mike so admired and covering an extremely intimate part of her. He knew immediately why Mike found it so fascinating; it felt even better than it looked. Before he had time really to enjoy the sensation fully, Rita pulled away, closing her wrap. She grinned at him.

"Nice," she said. She looked past him. "Cor, now look at old droopy-drawers. I bet he won't be in here again in a hurry."

Brian, confused and shocked, was reluctant to move, not knowing what kind of reaction there might be from both Marshall and those students who might have seen Rita's sudden impulsive move. He blew out a breath noisily and rubbed his hand round his collar: it had suddenly become very warm. When he finally did turn, Marshall was looking at him, his jaw tightly clamped. Brian raised his hand, completing the gesture he had begun before Rita had attacked him. Marshall did not acknowledge it. Brian looked at the students. He registered that perhaps only one of them had seen the incident. He cursed inwardly as he saw the marine uniform she wore. She was busily regaling the others with what she had seen and they were looking excitedly at Brian and Rita in the office. Brian smiled sheepishly at them. He felt very foolish and also apprehensive as to what the consequences of Rita's impulsive gesture might be. Rita seemed to have no qualms at all. She grinned at him.

"We must do that again some time," she said, moving out into the studio. She went straight over to the dais, nonchalantly casting off her wrap and stepping out of her mules.

"Time's up," she said crisply. "Let's get on."

She re-arranged her pose to match exactly its previous position. Brian could not help but register, in spite of his confusion, that she was conveying to Marshall, whose eyes, Brian noticed, followed her every movement, the unembarrassed boldness her nudity gave her. She really was very good at body language. Marshall turned abruptly and left. The students seemed completely galvanised and went back to their easels with a will; the life room had come alive at last.

Chapter Nine
In the Steps of the New Masters

"Bingo!" said Brian. "Possibly."

"Christ, don't say you've got something at last? I mean, you've said that heaps of times in the last two days," said Connie.

"I know, but could be this time we've struck gold. Keep your fingers crossed," said Brian. "Let's just go through it slowly. Nip to the door will you and see if you're still as repellent to Bill Johnson as you were, while I go deeper into this lot."

Connie rose from her seat next to Brian in front of the console, went to the door and looked out into the main computer lab.

"Can't see him," she said.

Since the incident at 'BoZo'Z', Bill had maintained a safe distance from Connie. He had told Brian that it had been a somewhat strained interview with his wife, Peggy, that night, after she collected him from the main police station. He had managed to convince her that his was merely a courtesy visit to a student thrash which had got out of hand. Although he thought she had believed him, she had, nevertheless, since taken to dropping casually and unexpectedly into the labs. These visits became more frequent and to Bill quite unnerving, after Connie, who was now there quite often herself, had, on the second occasion, given her a big friendly smile and a breezy "hello" as from one woman to another sharing something in common. A neatly positive result of this fly in Bill's domestic ointment was that Brian and Connie could hack away for long sessions on the mainframe computer with little chance of disturbance. So far, however, they had had no joy whatsoever in making sense of why the codes which Rita had supplied were so important.

"Right, here we go again," said Brian, when Connie had rejoined him. He began to tap in more passwords.

"I hope you're right!" said Connie. "I'm getting really pissed off with this. It really sucks."

"I know, I know. I'm getting RSI from it, myself. I told you it was going to be long-winded, remember. But I think we might be getting there. Just be patient a little longer."

Because of the jumbling of word and number codes when Rita had hastily scribbled them down - Connie said Rita had got them following some intimate moment when Huggett had carelessly left his Filofax along with his trousers dropped on the floor while he slept, an image which made Brian think how truly desperate she must be to 'get to Scarborough' - the only way Brian could input to the Civic Centre data bank had to be through laborious random combinations. Most of these were fruitless but some, usually incorporating the name FRED from the convenient keyboard position of those letters - Brindling was not very original with its security codes - had indeed accessed sets of data. So far these had seemed innocuous, and of a tediousness that only municipalities like Brindling with enormously swollen bureaucracies and delusions of future grandeur could devise. Brian and Connie had now chewed over numerous plans for relief roads, by-passes, new tramways, sewage improvement schemes, water pollution controls, industrial developments, wind farms, recycling, land reclamation, energy from household waste and assorted other modishly green environmental initiatives, without, until now, getting a whiff of the really spicy meat of civic expenditure not on the approved menu. There was no way they could see these items as being important enough to warrant their being guarded by security codes anyway. They had become thoroughly disgruntled with the task and, in Connie's case, with Brian as well.

All of the information they had looked at so far originated in one department, the Programme Development Unit. This section of the civic empire, Brian gathered from the dates and number codes on the material, must have been set up sometime in the mid-Seventies on that zenith of jobs for the NALGO hegemony during the Wilson era. Its function seemed to be to produce programmes of development for the town forward into the far future, even into the next century - and possibly beyond in its wilder 'Star Treking' brainstorms - and to submit these to a small subcommittee of the Environmental Resources Committee for discussion. From the variety of names appended to the massive number of documents this department had generated and from the way the initiatives followed the latest urban planning fad, Brian guessed that it was the base camp for many a young tyro planner beginning his or her climb to peaks of municipalities or consultancies with wider horizons for their talents than Brindling.

To Brian's experienced eye, most of the plans generated by the unit reeked of what his old tutor would have called "a load of shit from China" i.e. they were far-fetched. Virtually all of them required investment of monies which, even in the good times of the last Labour government, the town simply did not have. However, it was also Brian's instinct that it would be amongst the products of this unit - which he had gathered from contacts he had made in the Civic Centre was much-loved and cherished by friend Huggett - that they were likely to unearth whatever illegal slices might have been carved from the municipal suckling pig.

The codes which Rita had ripped off were one clue - why else would Huggett have them carefully written down? - but the other spoor which made him doubly certain was the appointment in the early Eighties to the chair of the controlling unit's sub-committee of the newly elected Councillor, Mrs. Mavis Jean Spiller, Huggett's sister. She appeared to have been there ever since, although the membership (wholly Labour of course) of the sub-committee was constantly and frequently changing; a classic ploy for keeping your feet in the trough and other prying noses out, and one honed to perfection in the north-eastern counties of England in the nineteen-sixties. Brian was thoroughly au fait with this sort of dodge. His degree course had even had a special section devoted to the scandal; it had, after all, produced lots of new buildings. Really, thought Brian, it was like meeting an old friend once more to see a scam so blatantly modelled on the old master crooks of municipal corruption alive and well and fiddling merrily away in Brindling. To Brian, the question had become not simply whether the Huggetts - and who else? Oswald Spiller? - were working the system but how they were doing it? With what he had on the screen now, he thought he might have the answer.

"Do you see this?" he said to Connie.

"What is it? We've seen all this before, haven't we? It's as boring as the rest of the junk."

"Right, but we've looked at it so long we've not been able to see the wood for the trees. Look, this is the list of proposals submitted to the sub-committee for its meeting of 28 March, 1982."

"Oh God! So?"

"Now look at this." He ignored Connie's flounce of irritation and fed in another code. A summary agenda appeared on the screen. "This is the list of proposals submitted from that sub-committee to the main Environmental Services Committee on 6th April. Look at that item there."

"What about it?"

Brian returned the previous list to the screen.

"Notice anything unusual?"

Connie checked the list for a few moments. "It's not there," she said, a faint interest, to Brian's intense relief, at last detectable in her speech.

Over the two days they had been working together, any appeal Brian might have had for Connie he had felt being eroded to dust, not only as a result of the de-sexing effect of the Environmental Resources sub-committee minutes, which would be enough to emasculate even Casanova, but also some other more obscure factor. He had no idea what it was or what he had done but he was sensitive enough to realise that she had been cool even before they started the trawl. Now he was on to something, perhaps he might see a revival of her usual high spirits and possibly even an interest in himself. Of course, it could be just the time of the month he told himself, but he doubted it. In Brian's experience, a woman who was interested in a guy usually covered that; it was only husbands, live-ins or bosses who got zapped with the hormones.

"Right first time," he said. "Give the lady her fluffy doll. It's the old three card trick. Now you see it, now you don't. The same with the planner in the Programme Development Unit who submitted the list in the first place. See, by the next meeting, he's moved on somewhere so when the sub-committee reports he's not around to spot the extra item. And if we backtrack over the other things we've looked at, a pound to a penny the same thing will happen. Every time the personnel in the Unit changes, an extra item will appear on the list. Eureka! I always knew it was possible to win at find-the-lady."

Over the next half hour, Brian and Connie hardly spoke as they confirmed Brian's suspicion to a racing certainty. Now they had found where to look, Rita's purloined codes opened up the trail to a steady stream of 'extras' right through the decade. Some years there were none, but in some, as when the Tory crunch on local government really began to bite and staff turnover increased, there could be two or even three items. And they all had one thing in common. Unlike most of the Unit's proposals, which were largely designed for discussion, the extras were real proposals for expenditure: not large amounts at first but growing more and more significant as, presumably, they got bolder through the decade. One example they unearthed which typified this, was a proposal put forward in the mid-Eighties for developing the town's - "For God's sake!" as Connie put it - 'heritage potential'. Central to this was to be a town 'Heritage Trail'.

As an item for discussion ludicrous perhaps but perfectly innocuous. However, the extra here was the proposal to ready one of the old textile mills in anticipation by immediate - and quite expensive - conservation of its fabric. Like most of the other extras, the money was earmarked from the nationally funded urban programme. Brian was giving a cursory final glance at this proposal when something about it struck him.

"Just a minute, just a minute."

"What?"

"You know where that is, don't you?"

"No."

"It's 'BoZo'Z'. The bent old devil. Some heritage trail: 'Ye Olde Casino and Strip Club'. Very traditional"

He fed in another code. "And just lookee here!" said Brian.

The information which the codes had now revealed was that in the minutes of the Environmental Resources Committee meeting for July '81, the decision as to the choice of tender for the extras would be left to the Programme Unit sub-committee, final approval resting with the parent Environmental Resources Committee: chairman - who else - Councillor Charles Huggett. It did not take a lot of imagination to guess where the taxpayers' money ended up.

"No wonder he wants these guarded with security codes," said Brian. "I wonder how much all this adds up to over the decade. Let's get some of this printed out." He fed in the appropriate instructions. "We can't do the lot but the heritage thing will be enough to be going on with now we've got the codes and know where the bodies are buried. In any case that heritage rubbish gives me an idea."

"What?" asked Connie.

"Just something for the Poly Research Committee. We can cover our tracks with it."

"How?"

"I'll work that out later. Whew!" Brian stood up, stretched and walked round the small office as the printer began to spew out spreadsheet.

"You're quite slick at this kind of stuff, aren't you? " said Connie, leaning back and swivelling on her chair.

"Handling a computer? Ah, well, not bad, I suppose. Not up to dear old Uncle Bill's standard, of course." Was this estimate of his computer skills a sign of reawakened interest, he wondered.

"Is working with computers a turn-on, do you think?" she said, as if reading his thoughts.

"Dunno," said Brian, surprised. "I would hardly think so. That's an odd question. Why?" He returned to the desk and sat down.

"I think it must be. You guys must get so frustrated with all this logical crap, you build up a head of steam. Look at you and Bill."

"What do you mean, me and Bill?"

He inspected the spreadsheets and reprogrammed the printer

"Well, look how he went on when I first came here. You'd think he'd never seen a woman before. He couldn't keep his hands off of me. And then there's you and Rita. The first time you've ever spoken to her and you're all over her, kissing her and feeling her tits and all, and in public too."

So that was it!

Brian looked at her levelly.

"That's the version that's going the rounds is it?"

"The kids are full of it. And you did kiss her didn't you?"

"No. She kissed me. To set the Deputy Rector's teeth on edge. It was nothing to do with me."

"She wouldn't have done it with just anybody, would she? You must have given her something to go on. What did you say?"

Brian decided it was not worth trying to explain.

"Look, why don't you ask Rita to tell you how it was? She's a friend of yours."

"I have."

"Oh." Brian was surprised. "And what did she say?"

"She said she enjoyed it. And you were giving her the business, the way you were looking at her. And telling her how good-looking she is and what a great actress and I don't know what all."

"Rita is hard to ignore. Any bloke's going to look."

"And touch if they get half a chance."

Brian became exasperated. He waved his arms and dragged his fingers through his hair. "Look, I've had enough of this. I'm going to tell you something. Rita is undoubtedly superb, yes, very attractive, but I will say to you here and now that in the sex stakes for me she cannot hold a candle to you. Ok? Is that what you wanted to hear? I've been keen on you since we met that evening in the entrance hall. So, now you're in the picture. Ok?"

"I knew that already. And you've no need to get aggressive about it," she said simply. "Christ, you're a real bunch of crazies, you Englishmen. You're just too romantic for your own good. You can look at women like Rita as easy game and don't mind getting randy but when you come across somebody you really go for, you put them on a pedestal and treat them as something so special you go all damp on us and turn yourselves into a bunch of dopey Romeos. It's all this public school crap. Women are either whores or angels. Don't you know that sort of stuff went out with Shakespeare? We're grown-up people now. If you want something why, for Christ sake, can't you ask?"

"Ok," said Brian, annoyed. "So, will you go to bed with me, 'for Christ's sake'? And I didn't go to public school, by the way."

"No," she said.

"Why not? Jesus, what is all this?" Brian paced around the chattering printer, picking up the spreadsheet and tearing it off angrily. "You're not a tease, are you? You like me, don't you?"

"Yes."

"Well then?"

"I like you a lot, as a matter of fact, you're a nice guy, but I don't want any complications in my life just now. Not with the run-up to finals. Ok? Better you should know now. Maybe we can get together after. It's just too important to me to do well for my dad's – well, never mind that. Anyway, if I'm going to go to bed with someone, I want it to be with the trimmings like a nice place, and good food and sun and wine and sea and all that. I come from California, remember. Not bloody Brindling! Now there really is a turn-off."

"Well, at least you've got the crappy air pollution here. Just like home."

"You know what I mean. A turn-off's a turn-off. I mean just look at this dopey yuk we're involved with here. Environmental Resources Committee yet! Jesus H. Christ! I can feel my drawers turning to concrete."

Brian laughed. "Yes, I know what you mean. Ok, fair enough. Until then we'll carry on playing silly begger Fartistas." In truth, Brian was quite surprised at how relieved he felt with Connie's attitude. Life was getting far too complicated for him too. God! how he longed for the summer vacation. He wondered if Connie's boat was seaworthy. A summer cruise would be just the setting to develop their relationship. "Of course," he said, smiling at her, "if it weren't for you, I'd never have been involved with this stuff in the first place."

"Serves you right for being so romantic. Let that be a lesson to you."

They smiled at each other and Brian turned once more to the computer which had now finished its print run.

"By the way," said Brian, "how is the painting in the gallery coming along? Will it be finished in time for your final show?"

"It's not part of my show. It's a sort of commission from Noel. It's going to be unveiled at the private view after the assessments."

"Oh. Are your parents coming? Will they have to fly over?" He carefully folded up the spreadsheets and began to pack them into his briefcase. "Don't want to leave the evidence showing too much."

"There's only my dad. Yes, he's coming."

"Why did you come to England to study? I've wondered about that."

"Because my dad said it's the best art education in the world. It's the only one where you get the freedom you need. And he was right."

"Is your dad an artist or something?"

"Yes." Connie picked up the paper with the passwords on it.

"Would I have heard of him?"

"What about this weird code here?" she said, changing the subject. Brian had already felt her increasing resistance to carrying on more personal discussion. "We haven't tried that one yet."

"Yes, we did, actually," said Brian, taking the paper from her. "Very early on but we got nothing, remember? And we didn't bother once we got into the Programme Development stuff. Yes, it's a real oddball that one, isn't it? It's completely different to the others. For one thing it hasn't got FRED in it, which means that there might be someone with a brain behind it. You can tell that anyway from the phrase: 'The right to search for truth implies a duty.' - it's way beyond your ordinary municipal tea-leaf like Huggett to think of a code like that. I thought a password would be buried in it, but no luck. It seems to work. It's kept us out. Maybe it isn't a code at all. But then why would he have such a phrase copied out? Really, really odd."

"Where's it from?"

"It's a quote from a statement by Einstein. I had a go in the library and tracked it down last night. But who would know about Einstein?

Certainly not Hugg..." As the answer came to him he became suddenly excited: of course, a physicist! And who was the most prominent physicist in Brindling? "Of course," he said out loud and began to tap in the code.

"Of course, what?" said Connie. "What? Tell me."

"Hold on," said Brian, when nothing happened, "there must be something missing. It didn't work last time on its own either. Let's see that list again." Connie handed him Rita's hastily scrawled sheet. "Aha," he said. To the phrase he had already entered he added a colon and the single letter 'h' which he had spotted in its isolated place on the paper and had assumed was a copying error by Rita.

"What's that?" asked Connie.

"That, my dear Watson, is the symbol for Max Planck's constant, on which the whole universe is built. Einstein never believed in it, you see. Quantum theory. You know?" Connie looked blank. "Never mind. Anyway, Einstein emphatically did not do his duty in relation to it, in other words. It's a sort of physicist's private joke. Still it shows the Rector isn't quite brain-dead yet."

"The Rector? You're kidding!"

"Who else. Only a physicist like him could find that remotely funny. Right, here we go." He entered the correct number of letters from the end of the phrase with the additional colon and letter and the screen was suddenly and satisfyingly filled.

"You've done it!" cried Connie, hugging him. "You're a genius."

He grinned as he turned to her and was about to follow up this sudden positive response towards him but realised Connie was now excitedly looking at the screen, apparently unaware of the effect her gesture had had on him. Disappointed, he turned to the screen himself.

In front of them was now displayed a menu of files titled: 'Notes AHPDWP.' Inputting the first file this became the 'Ad Hoc Polytechnic Development Working Party. Members: the Rector, the Deputy Rector, Councillor C. Huggett plus secretary, Amanda Donaldson. STRICTLY RESTRICTED ACCESS MEMBERS ONLY.'

"Now, let's see precisely what the three witches are brewing up between them," said Brian, settling down to read the first file.

An hour later it was two very sober people who looked at each other as the last of the files was printed and cleared.

"They don't care what they say, do they?" said Brian, rubbing his chin pensively.

"They've certainly got it in for you people," said Connie.

"So it would seem," said Brian. "You know, I don't think this stuff has been edited even." He picked up the print-out and began to look through it. "This Donaldson woman has simply taped it and inputted the lot. Christ! They've probably never got proper minutes from it, or even bothered to access it - too dangerous to put into print so they've been keeping it in their heads, assuming she would have the common sense to use her discretion when she wrote up the notes. That's the trouble with using local labour, they're far too naive for these kind of monkeyshines in Brindling. They probably chose her because they think she's too dim to see what's involved. That's how people like Huggett get away with it. In fact, I bet they have no idea what's in these files at all. They can't have, they're dynamite. Friend Amanda has really dropped them in it.

The material which had so shocked Brian and Connie was the plans for the transformation of the Brindling Polytechnic to the new University of Brindling. The elimination of Art and Design as an academic area and taking possession of its building they already knew about from what Rita had told Connie and the Fartistas, and the files fully confirmed it. But what shocked them were the terms which the Rector and Huggett applied to the process, the most graphic phrase being that of Huggett's: "flushing that arty --- down the pan". (The only deletions Ms Donaldson had made were of expletives. It occurred to Brian they had made the same mistake as Nixon; they hadn't bothered to check the record. If they had done so, they should have done what he failed to do: delete the text and keep the expletives.)

The Rector's contributions may have been less colourful than those of Huggett but he was much more explicit with " - getting rid of a lot of pretentious art claptrap and those layabouts with it. There's no place for that sort of stuff in Higher Education these days. Or anywhere else except infant school - that's about their mentality anyway. It's all old hat. Went out with the ark. Time's moved on. No academic respectability. Have you seen their submission? Good God! Practically illiterate - hardly understood a word of it. I'll see to it that CNAA does for them this time. It's got no relevance any longer. What is it anyway, art? I ask them and they can never tell me. Just a lot of historical gobbledeygook. That makes me very suspicious. I mean, what use is it? And they've got no structure to their courses. None at all - just do your own thing and it'll be alright. That's another thing that will be pointed out very firmly to CNAA. And those --- have the --- cheek to patronise us engineers. Waste of time and money, the whole thing. The sooner we're shot of it, the better."

As if this were not bad enough, the most recent discussions concerned expansion onto new sites, for student accommodation especially. Following the Rector and Deputy Rector's desire that any site should be as nearly contiguous as possible with the existing town centre location, Huggett came up with the idea that the 'Tofts' should be converted to a new student village. He assured the other two there would be no difficulty about getting the existing tenants out - where they were to go he didn't say - and that money for the conversion could be obtained from the urban programme. The estimate he put forward ran to one and a half millions! Creaming the top off that must be his biggest coup yet, especially with the bonus of the art college conversion, thought Brian. It made all the other extras shrink to insignificance. Perhaps Rita would get her trip to Scarborough at last.

Brian gathered up the sheets and packed them away quickly. He cleared the screen and switched off the terminal.

"Let's get out of here before we're rumbled. I don't know what the heck I can do with all this stuff but this 'Tofts' business is really nasty. I shouldn't think the Rector or Dr. Marshall know what's really going on over there. The people who live there hardly have the power of the press behind them. And look who their Councillor is. She's going to make a fuss on their behalf, I'm sure. What do you make of all this?"

Connie shrugged. "Compared to the graft at home, it's penny-ante stuff. Look at the Savings and Loan thing or the Iran-Contra scandal. That's how bad it can get with a zombie for president."

"Well, as they say, everything's bigger in the US of A," said Brian. "But this will do to be going on with. It's getting too hot for me."

"It gives me an idea for my painting, anyway," said Connie.

"For a painting? That seems unlikely. What on earth is it about that you can get an idea from this nonsense?" This remark of Connie's really intrigued Brian. "Nobody's ever seen it have they, your painting? Not even Noel de Vere."

"It's meant to be a surprise," said Connie nonchalantly, as they emerged into the main computer lab. But before Brian's imagination could get to work on what the nature of the surprise might be, they were brought up short by the approach of Bill Johnson and Dr. Marshall. Brian gave a mental gasp of relief they had not entered the room a few minutes earlier.

"All done?" said Bill.

"Yes, fine, fine," said Brian.

"How are the graphics coming?" he said to Connie.

"Oh, I don't think I'll be using them after all. Sorry, Bill. There really isn't the time to get anything coherent together before my show. But many thanks, all the same. You've been too kind to let me use the facilities like this. And I've learned a lot. About all sorts of things." She turned a devastating smile onto Bill. "And I'm still dreadfully sorry for that mix-up about my party time."

Bill was lost once more. "Oh, oh, that's Ok. No problem. It's a shame about the graphics though. Perhaps if I gave you my personal attention we could speed things up a ..."

"Oh look, there's your wife, Bill. Hi, Peggy," she called out across the lab and waved.

Bill recoiled from Connie as if from a dangerous spider.

"Oh, yes. So it is. Ah. Well, nice to see you again. Right, I'm just coming, darling," he said, and scuttled off so fast to his office Brian thought it was almost as though he'd left the impression of his anxious grimace behind him like the obverse of the Cheshire cat's smile. Peggy swept passed them without acknowledgement and Connie gave her a specially big beaming smile. After she had gone into Bill's office, Connie suddenly said:

"See you, Brian. I've got to run. We can get together on that other stuff and see what we do about it in the next few days. Ok?"

Before Brian had time to respond she was on her way. He watched her go, annoyed that after all his hard work he was not even going to have the pleasure of walking out with her. God, she was elusive, he thought, and had she really taken what happened with Rita on board? Marshall, who was also watching her, said:

"I've been very impressed in the short time I've been assigned to your Department, Dr. Mather, by the refreshing - informality, shall we say - of personal relationships you people in Art and Design manage to achieve in your roles as teachers. Both with the students - " (He paused and turned to look directly into Brian's eyes.) "and within the - er - body, shall we say of the staff itself. I suppose that comes from how - closely you have to work together to achieve results. Very - stimulating it must be for you and how different from the formality of lectures and tutorials and - the more usual arrangements the rest of us have to conform to conduct our relations with colleagues. Hardly like being a teacher at all, I expect."

The reference of Marshall's speech - Brian thought he detected an Oxbridge training in the parsing of his sentences and especially the over-emphatic use of the significant pause - was unmistakable but, as he held Brian's eye in a steady gaze, the direction was not clear.

"Most art schools are like that," said Brian cautiously.

"Are they indeed. One has heard such - bizarre stories about them. How interesting they must be for a student experience. Perhaps I should have developed my talents as an artist instead of as an engineer. I've been meaning to have a talk with you about the arrangements for research by the way. As you know, there is a meeting of the Committee shortly. I believe you are now your Faculty's nominee?" Brian nodded. "The Rector intends to have a rather - stringent review of the institution's research at that meeting, as the content of this year's 'Blue Skies' is going to be somewhat more significant than usual. I just thought you might like to have something on paper. It will make a big change for your Faculty, after all, if you could be included this year."

There was no mistaking Marshall's message here. Brian knew he was doing him a favour by warning him in good time. He wondered how they would take to the idea he had in mind that related to the dynamite in his briefcase. Perhaps Marshall's attitude and the Rector's were not as co-terminous as he had assumed. It dawned on Brian that Marshall had spoken hardly at all in the ad hoc meetings. And he certainly had not expressed any opinion as to the worth of Art and Design. Could he be an ally? His spell in the art college might be mellowing his views, although Brian still felt he was a man for all seasons.

"Sorry I couldn't alert you before but you really are such an elusive fellow, to be sure, Dr. Mather. Field visits and what not and down here with Miss Grey, is it?" He paused an even longer interval. "And, of course, in the life room."

"My first visit, the other day."

"Really?" Marshall's face became a taut mask. "From the - casualness of the whole thing I might have thought you were a frequent visitor."

"No."

Marshall finally got to the point.

"Fine figure of a woman, the model. Rita, is it?"

"Yes."

"She must be an - umm - inspiration to the students."

"I imagine so."

"I've not spoken to her myself."

"No? And yet you've been ..." Brian stopped himself in time.

"Yes?"

No point in making an enemy unnecessarily.

"She's very charming as far as I can tell from our short acquaintance."

"Short?"

"Yes, that was the first time I had ever met her the other day."

Marshall's mask dissolved and his expression displayed such a quick change of astonishment, disbelief and - yes - jealousy that Brian was tempted to burst out laughing. He decided to put him out of his agony.

"Of course, she's noticed you," he said.

"Has she?" Although his face had once again assumed its usual air, Marshall had a hard time disguising the eagerness he felt.

"Oh yes. I'm sure she'd be quite interested if you asked her to dine with you or something, you know. I gather she may be getting a bit tired of her current arrangements. Why don't you ask her out? You're not married or anything are you?"

"Not any more. Is she ....?"

"No. But perhaps I can give a word of advice."

"Thank you. I'd be grateful." There was no trace in his voice of its usual heavy irony.

"If she does agree to go out with you tell her you'll take her to Scarborough any time she wants. Tell her I said she might get there at last with you."

"How odd. Is it a *private* joke?"

"Sort of," said Brian. "And one more tip. I presume you were at public school?"

"Yes. Marlborough. Why?"

"Well, I should try and forget everything your old masters ever told you about women and how to treat them. 'Brief Encounter' was always a very bad model - apart from teaching a spot of ophthalmology on the female eye.

"Thank you." He looked at Brian thoughtfully. "We must have that game of squash sometime."

"Yes. Let's do that sometime," said Brian, as he left the lab.

Chapter Ten
Private Views

"I'll teach you to feel up my woman, you young bugger."

These words were growled menacingly from just below and behind, but directly into Brian's left ear. He recognised the voice immediately: Huggett. Brian hunched his shoulders and froze. Damn, he thought, that was careless.

"Er," he said tentatively, leaning away from the voice and towards one of Louie's beautiful framed etchings of a scene in Tuscany - already sporting a red spot - on the gallery wall in front of him, but there were no further private messages in reply. Brian cautiously turned his head. Huggett was now laughing and chatting a few yards away with a group of Governors and the Rector and Marshall. He swung his glass and plate of food around to point to one of the pictures. Without alerting the others in his party, he made a sweeping gesture with his plate across his throat and gave a venomous grimace to Brian as he did so. He then laughed heartily in chorus with the rest and moved off with them into another room in the crowded gallery to admire more of Louie's works. Brian stuck his finger into his ear and wiggled it about to stop the irritation Huggett's silly threat had caused.

"Grrrh," he said, as a strong nervous reaction set in, more from Huggett's gesture than his verbal menace. He shivered and regretted again that he had come to the opening knowing full well that Rita and Huggett were to be present - although not together. Since Rita had warned him, Brian had been very circumspect about his movements at night, but his colleagues' description of Elizabeth Bonetti's eats and the generous quantity of strong Italian wine that Louie supplied free were too strong a temptation and had overcome his caution. Very few private views these days supplied either without a payment. And his colleagues were right: this was the best food Brian had had for many months, and he was trying to do justice to it.

Like the students eking out their grants, Brian had attempted to keep his overdraft from skyrocketing while unemployed by economising on food. Even now, when he had had two monthly salary checks paid into his account, his bank manager saw to it that servicing and reducing his overdraft came before such gross self-indulgence as frequent meat-eating. He had found some very cheap workmen's caffs in the poorer parts of the town for his daily needs and one meal (in which egg, chips and baked beans were usually prominent) was all he allowed himself, plus bread, porridge oats - which he hated, but put up with for their cheapness - raw carrots, salad vegetables and fruit from the supermarket. At one stage in his unemployed days, this austere regime had meant he was constantly hungry, but not now. He found that, as his weight fell and he got quite used to it, it amazed him how little it was possible to keep fit on. He had even treated it as an experiment and had come down to the daily ration of a Briton in 1945 to see what it was like. No wonder they won the war, he thought - did they, that generation? - when people could exist on this and do a day's work.

Although tough on his will power, at least initially, his abstemious life style had yielded one significant - but also very dubious - advantage. He knew that his attraction for older women like Audrey Reaper, already at a fairly reasonable pitch, began to be so enhanced as to be almost irresistible. Few, especially those with sons, he was aware, could see his indrawn cheeks and soulful eyes within his pale face without immediately planning nourishing menus as a preliminary to becoming more intimately acquainted. He could almost list the à la carte from their expressions - especially the dessert. He found that resorting to sunglasses, like Noel de Vere, to remove his starveling provocation from their ken, kept them at bay and was glad that what passed for summer in Brindling had come at last and he could get a bit of peace. He only wished he'd been able to wear them in the lecture theatre that night. Nevertheless, Brian had enjoyed this effect his appearance caused for a while, but eventually it had become tiresome - it was not older women he was interested in, for God's sake. To most younger women, he thought it made him simply look poor and possibly ill.

Huggett and his party had now moved into another room in the gallery. The local Arts Centre, which housed the gallery, was, like many another up and down the country, converted from a large Victorian town house not unlike the one in which Brian rented his small flat, and hosted various aspects of the local art scene. In going through his print-outs in more detail, Brian had noted that the conversion of the Arts Centre was yet another of Huggett's 'extras' - price £350,000. The almost proprietorial air he adopted as he moved around the gallery had not been lost on Brian, who had been keeping an eye on his whereabouts to avoid him. Unfortunately, the combination of food, pictures and the drink had relaxed him so much that he had neglected to keep track of Huggett and his party sufficiently closely.

"Poor Brian, are you cold?" Brian jumped as the warm, breathy tones of Audrey Reaper were directed from just below, behind and into his right ear. He surreptitiously scratched that one as well. Between Huggett and Audrey, he was now thoroughly irritated.

"What? What?" he said. "Cold? No. Why?"

"You shivered. Perhaps you're in for something. You have to be very careful of these early summer nights. So deceptive. And, of course, you are so thin, Brian. You must have so little insulation."

Brian detected in Audrey's eyes the message that she, who was anything but slim, could protect him perfectly from the dank night air in the warm softness of her own generous cavity insulation.

"Just somebody walking over my grave," he said.

"It's a really weird expression, that, I always think," she said.

"Yes." He began to back away to mingle with the crowds. Audrey followed, holding him with her usual intense stare. Had she, as the cop suggested she might, forgotten all that had happened that night?

"You're building quite a reputation, you know," she said.

"Oh, yes," he said warily.

"Yes. Your fame has even spread to us benighted extra-murals."

"Oh." Condensed into this small syllable was the distilled essence of Brian's caution of all older women like Audrey. She went on without noticing it.

"Yes. For instance, no man at the college, as far as we know, has ever been - so close shall we say - to Rita as you seem to have got. How do you do it? We're all agog to know what it is that she finds so irresistible."

"Wonderful prints, aren't they?" said Brian, waving his glass desperately at the walls, but Audrey was not a woman to be put off by her quarry's change of subject: she had her own tactics.

"Did you know that Noel de Vere has decided that the extra-mural work we do is going to be assessed for a certificate?"

This sudden switch of focus foxed Brian completely. "What?" he said, distractedly. It was, in fact, complete news to him. With all his other preparations for CNAA, research and so on, he had not been keeping contact with detailed events in the Department. But he still could not see why she had so abruptly changed the subject.

"Yes. It will give us an automatic entry into Foundation - or even the degree course if they think we're good enough."

"How nice for you. Are you going ..."

"And as part of it we're to have personal tutors."

"Oh?" A rising inflection in the syllable this time betokened a sudden panic for escape on top of its caution, but he was too late: Audrey followed up her advantage.

"Yes. He's letting us choose our own from the full-time staff. Isn't that generous of him."

"I... " Oh no, the damned fool, thought Brian.

"I chose you. I hope you don't mind."

Brian took a deep gulp of his red wine.

"Er, er, do you think that's a good idea, really? I mean, I'm not an artist or anything so..."

"Oh, I know, but after your talk I just knew that my main interest was truly going to be in design. And even in design history - those beautiful Chinese pots and so on. Wonderful. You made it sound so exciting I knew it was something I could really get my teeth into at last, if you know what I mean." Her expression Brian told that the design she would like to get her teeth into was more an elemental product of nature than something raised on a potter's wheel.

"Er. How does your husband feel about that? I mean your possibly taking up degree work and so on? Won't it make for difficulties at home?"

Audrey moved in closer. "Shall I tell you something, Brian?"

Brian, recognising from long experience the female preliminaries to intimate but unwelcome revelations, opened his mouth to say "No" but Audrey could not wait.

"Since I started at the art college and contacted really sensitive, warm human beings - men, I mean - I've realised I married a first class prat. You know?" She waited for the effect of this to show in Brian but, apart from his eyes swivelling to find some route of escape, his haunted expression didn't change. She took a deep draught from her glass - a full tumbler, Brian noticed - tapped Brian's chest with it and ploughed on.

"Oh, we've got three grand kids, I grant you. I love them dearly and I'm grateful for that, I mean, there's nowt wrong with his genes just his brains - anyway, they've all left home now and I've got my own job, so bugger the tea on the table at six o'clock and hoovering round his beer gut because he's too idle to shift himself and take a bit of exercise instead of watching that idiot box and washing his stupid supporter's gear, and his boozing on a Friday night with all the other big guts in the Labour party club and getting his end away on a Saturday night - if they've won - God, do I dread the season they do well in the cup - Jesus, that titty woolly hat and that scarf. You've no idea - I could strangle him with it sometimes. Do you know, when they brought in coloured condoms he tried to get some in the town's colours - I tell you..."

"Yes, yes, oh dear. Sounds er..." Although he'd been warned about her capacity, he wondered how much Audrey had had to drink. Her revelations were going well beyond par even for Brian's sympathy course. Warm, sensitive men? Could she mean his colleagues? It would take a lot of alcohol - or a lot of desperation - to transform those frogs to princes.

"So I've got myself a little studio down near the docks and I spend a lot of my time there now," she continued, then stopped. She looked vague for a moment and Brian recognised a memory stirring fitfully. He breathed an inward sigh of relief as she went on without catching it. "And I've already sold some soft sculptures - sort of oversize soft toys - based on Winnie the Pooh characters - the Eeyore's dead popular. I do him nicely in a flowered print." (Audrey hesitated and frowned. Brian saw yet another glimmer of fitful memory flickering at the edge of her consciousness. He held his breath again.) "Yes, as I say, I could sell a million of them," she continued, and he swallowed a deep draught of wine himself in relief. "And I've got a show coming up next year, and Noel says I'm almost sure to get a place on the degree course, 'cos my work justifies it. I've got a real talent, he said. That's what he said! A real talent for 3-D design!"

She said this with a triumphant breathless flourish, challenging the slightly sceptical expression she thought she had detected on Brian's face. (It was not a sceptical frown but a headache which had suddenly struck him.)

"Yes, I'm sure you do have. That's if we manage to get the course through the quinquennial ok," said Brian.

"The what?" she said. Brian realised his remark meant nothing to her.

"Of course, Noel practically insists that if we're to do the degree course we've got to get ourselves a studio - there's no room in the college for us part-timers, so you see I'm half way there already. It's really cosy. You'll just love it, I know you will." The cop had been right! Thank God! "You and me'll be having quite a few tutorials there soon, in any case, as you know."

Brian was puzzled. "Do I?" he said vaguely.

"Won't that be nice?" she said, not catching his reply as she took a swig from her glass.

Brian felt his headache intensify.

"I suppose so," he said, hollowly. It seemed to have been said by someone in the next room.

"Oh, there's Louie. I must just go and congratulate him. These are smashing, aren't they? God, I think art's wonderful, don't you?" she said.

Audrey moved off in a blaze of enthusiasm to follow Louie whom she had glimpsed passing the door of the gallery room, certain in the knowledge that her 'tutor' was now safely potted and in the bag. Audrey's trouble, Brian thought, was that she had swallowed the bohemian myth of the artistic lifestyle, hook, line and sinker. It was the thought that they were at it like knives that pepped her up. Little did she realise that, these days, most of his colleagues were more concerned with whether they would cop a subsidy in the next regional arts council's grant distribution so they could afford a foreign holiday for their families, than putting their sex appeal over to students. Still, Brian thought, if art unlocked the door to her personal liberation, good luck to her. He only wished she'd picked on somebody else as the key. He thought of those "cosy" tutorials and the return wrestling bouts they might entail, and almost wished CNAA would put the course out of its agony. Why did they always latch on to him? He wondered if a little light plastic surgery could transform his expression sufficiently to keep them at bay. Nevertheless, Audrey's enthusiasm, although it might be touchingly naive, couldn't be denied as refreshing; she probably did get that big buzz from art that seemed essential to keep an artist producing. As the straight man of the college, he envied her the personal emancipation it seemed to be giving her. Although, after the episode with Rita, he wondered if that straight role was fully his any longer.

He rummaged in his pocket to find the aspirin he usually carried if he was to do any serious drinking. He swallowed two and washed them down with the remains of the wine. How many glasses was that, he wondered - five? six? - no matter. He felt dizzy, but his headache began to clear. He knew he was well out of practice with alcohol as well as food; this sort of quantity he had once seen as a mere aperitif. He moved to the door of the room and realised that the aspirins had made him slightly nauseous. More of Liz Bonetti's wonderful pizza to put a lining on his stomach was what he needed.

He cautiously looked out into the corridor. A few yards down, Louie was pinned to the wall getting the full treatment from Audrey. He hoped Liz Bonetti didn't see her. But at least she was right about "warm" and "sensitive" there. He could not see any of Huggett's party anywhere and so deemed it safe to go to the basement bar where the food and drink were being supplied. As he moved through the crowds towards the staircase, he was tapped on the shoulder. He turned.

"Now then, how're you getting on, sunshine? Right leg over, same as always?" This was followed by a raucous peel of laughter.

"Good God, it's Renee, isn't it? From the 'Tofts'."

"That's it, chaw. And you're the karate kid. Hey, I tell you this, like, this is a reet posh do, an' all. I've never been to owt like this before. And all this food and booze free. It's like a birthday party. I wish my lad was 'ere. Anyway, I've got my doggy bag filled up for him." She held up a bulging, shiny handbag. She herself was dressed in a party-style dress: no sleeves, deep plunge, very short, black with sequins. Left over from her disco dancing days, thought Brian but with her cropped hair and bristly halo, make-up, slightly flushed face from the drink and with her good musculature, she looked lively and not at all out of place among the mixture of dress of the other female guests, from student Oxfam to town council cocktail.

"The artist is providing it himself."

"Getaway. There must be money in it, then, like, eh? Have you seen what them pictures cost? 'Undreds of pounds some of 'em." She flourished her price list. "And he's sold some, an' all." She leaned towards him and lowered her voice. "Hey, they're a funny lot though, aren't they? 'Ave you seen them two fellas in dresses? One of 'em was with you lot when you came down our way, wasn't 'e?"

"That's right. He's a colleague of mine."

Renee looked at him leerily. "Eh? You don't wear a dress an' all, do you?"

Brian saw that she had misconstrued 'colleague'. "I mean he's on the staff of the college. That's Laurie Willoughby. He's in charge of photography and film. Very brilliant."

"Is he? Bloody 'ell."

"And the other one's not a man, by the way. He, or rather she's a woman. She's frocked-up tonight. She doesn't look like that normally. That's Zoe Tremaine - she's a potter."

"That's not what I'd call her, like." Another peal of laughter. Brian felt his headache hovering at the ready.

"Now, now, don't be so conventional," he said. "This is an arty crowd you're with now. When in Rome, you know. I like the outfit, by the way."

"Do yer?"

"Yes. You look very jolly."

"Just summat I chucked on, like - and that's nearer the truth than you think. I didn't know what to put on for a do like this but what with men in skirts and women the other way round, I don't think I need have worried, eh?" She gave her infectious guffaw.

Brian grinned. "How do you come to be here, by the way?"

Renee bridled.

"Why, do you think I'm too common for this lot?"

"No, no, not at all. Don't get me wrong, now. It's just that I didn't think you'd be on the Arts Centre's mailing list."

"You're right, I'm not. Ronnie brought me, like. Hey, 'ave you done anythingk about that Huggett bastard - I see 'e's 'ere an' all - no party wi'out Punch, is there. They'll do owt for free grub and booze, that lot. I stood right in front of 'im but 'e looked right though me, the twerp. I know 'e recognized me, like."

"Perhaps he prefers not to be reminded of that day."

"I'll remind 'im before the night's out. Or at least Ronnie will."

Brian did not like the sound of this. "What do you ..."

"Well?" said Renee aggressively. "'Ave yer done owt? Or are yer just one of them walkie-talkie warriors?"

"Yes, I have, " said Brian, "but it will take some time to get it under way."

"What?"

"I don't want to say owt - er - anything at present." He thought of the letter be had received that morning from a former student friend who was now in the Department of Environment, and the case he had put to him for spot-listing the 'Tofts.'

"Well," said Renee doubtfully, "I 'ope you are on the ball for your own sake 'cos these students think a lot of you just now, like."

"Do they?" Brian could not help feeling gratified by this piece of news. His threatened headache receded. "I see you're empty as well. Come on, let's you and me get a drink."

They started to make their way through the crowd but Renee stopped suddenly and gave a crow of recognition.

"Hey, well look who's 'ere. If it isn't the old grim Reaper 'erself."

If the appellation had been accurate, Brian thought, the look which Audrey gave Renee would have been enough to carry her off on the spot.

"Do you two know each other?" said Brian.

"No," said Audrey.

"Yes," said Renee.

"Ah," said Brian.

"About what we were discussing before, Brian," said Audrey, ignoring Renee and, as she was taller, speaking well over head. "You are happy with becoming my tutor, aren't you?"

Brian knew this was said entirely for Renee's benefit. He realised that he had been subliminally aware of Audrey watching Renee and himself when she had finished with Louie. She could not have missed how cheerful he had become in Renee's presence.

"Is she in your college?" said Renee incredulously.

"And why shouldn't I be? " said Audrey pugnaciously.

"What as? A cleaner, like?"

"A student, you cheeky...Not that it's any of your business."

"What? An art student?"

"Yes."

"Well, if you're there maybe I'll 'ave a do at it, an'all - I could always paint the knickers off you at school, even though you were a lot older."

"What are you talking about, woman? What school?" said Audrey haughtily.

"Santley Street. You were Audrey Lofthouse then. Don't try to make out you don't remember. And I got a grade one in 'O' level art which is more than you ever did. And don't you call me woman - I'll knock your block off, stuck up bit..."

"I don't know what the f... What you're talking about," she said, turning away towards Brian. Before she could speak and get him embroiled, Brian intervened. He could feel the drink gradually detaching him from reality.

"Ladies, ladies, please. Remember some of us have led very sheltered lives. We like to keep some illusions of feminine grace and delicacy intact. Like in the adverts. Have you noticed, the only happy people on the television are in the commercials? Everybody else gets kicked in the teeth and ends up facing the wall." He slipped into a cod Margaret Rutherford. "That is the meaning of fiction, dear Cecily. Christ, what artistry! What genius!" Spurred by the drink, Brian was in full flight. The temptation of the Wildean epigram, a danger when he was drunk and very rarely successful in its own right but often carried off if the audience was kettled enough, was too much. "The trouble with most modern drama, you see, is not that it is too realistic but that it is not realistic enough; it is still under the impression that drama is a conflict between good and evil without realising that evil triumphed years ago." He waited for the effect of this to sink in but was met by two blank faces. Ah well, at least it stopped them quarrelling. One day he'd get it right,

"So you paint as well?" he said to Renee.

"Aye. Well, I did. I do mostly drawerings now, like. There's bugger-all else to do if you don't want to go mad stuck wi' a kid and no money in a dump like the 'Tofts'."

"How ridiculous!" said Audrey, dismissing Renee's aspirations with contempt.

"Oh aye? No more daft than you hoity-toitying it in the Poly."

"Please," said Brian warningly. "Look, why don't you bring your stuff in and let the staff see it?"

"Maybe I will at that. Hey, maybe you can be my - what is it? - tutor, an' all, eh, Brian?"

This suggestion was more than Audrey could stomach. She ignored Renee and said, in a voice now harsh and forceful :

"I'll see you a week on Thursday, Brian. Noel de Vere told me you've to give me a tutorial on my portfolio as soon as possible. They're interviewing me in a few weeks time."

"Oh, I don't think I'll be able to do that on..."

"Then I shall have to speak to Noel about that. He wrote you a memo about it. He told me he had. I suppose you did read it?" She narrowed her eyes suspiciously.

Did he? "Oh. Oh, yes, of course." Brian's guilt must have been obvious; he had been ignoring de Vere's cascade of memos for some time as irrelevant.

"I'll see you at three o'clock, then. We can have a bit of tea and you can have some of my own bake cake. My seed cake has won prizes, you know." Brian knew that hysterical laughter was not far from him at this moment. "Oh, there's Peter," she said. "I have to see him as well. See you Thursday week." She did not speak to Renee as she wove through the crowd in pursuit of Peter Orrd.

"By, she's a cheeky cow, that one," said Renee. "You want to watch 'er. Owt in pants and she's sniffing round. And she 'its the bottle from time to time, an' all. I mean, real serious. You can tell she's 'ad a skinful tonight."

"Can you?" said Brian surprised.

"Oh aye. I can see the signs in 'er eyes and the way she talks - she likes to play the 'cut glarrss haccent' usually but it drops off when the booze gets at 'er. Then it's right back to Santley Street - I know 'er of old, see. I tell you she's been dried out more times than a dishclout, that one. I'd take a minder with you Thursday week, if I was you."

"Thanks," said Brian. "I'll remember." He was quite clear that no amount of tea nor the promised delight of Audrey's seed cake would tempt him near her 'studio' with or without a minder. De Vere could go and jump if she squawked about it.

"Of course, that tub of guts she's married to is a big pal of Huggett's, like. Labour Party mafia. That's 'ow he keeps his job on the Council. By 'eck, they've got it reet sewn up, them buggers."

Although Brian knew the population of Brindling to be over two hundred thousand, it seemed to him that the longer he was here the more like a village it became.

"Hey, let's see if we can unpick it for them a bit," she said suddenly, the bright light of combat in her eyes. "I'll see you later."

"Don't you want a drink?"

But she had hurried away.

Brian was now feeling very much in need of more wine. He moved once again towards the staircase, but was surprised to find himself more unsteady than he thought he should be; he really was out of practice. On the way, he passed Audrey deep in a one-sided conversation with Peter Orrd. Peter shot him a despairing look over her shoulder and mumbled his deepest growl. Audrey glanced round and caught Brian's eye before he could duck behind another guest. "Three o'clock, Thursday week," she mouthed, frowning. Brian nodded. Oops! Not a good idea.

Gathered in the hallway near the stairs when he reached them were a group of Noel de Vere's young staff - his 'real McCoys'. As they were mostly part-timers, Brian had met few of them. They were collected round Rita, who was looking utterly amazing in an outfit Brian recognized as modelled on one of Allen Jones Sixties sex icons - all black leather hot pants, elbow-length gloves, thigh boots and even a jewelled whip as a decorative motif. She had also donned an enormous black Afro fashion wig whose dimensions added to her already above-average height. In this outfit she completely dominated any part of the gallery she was in. Brian had seen the local press photographer having a great time taking her picture holding examples of Louie's work; Louie himself had not been photographed. She waved at Brian to join them.

The young artists, men and women mostly about his age or younger, made way for him and examined him with interest. He thought that some of them might be suspicious of him as he was an unknown quantity in an art college with his computing background. They probably knew plenty of artists using IT but would have to see him in a different category as a non-creative type. Brian assumed they had all heard of the life room business and wondered also what they made of that: not here five minutes and already knocking off the model. He doubted the feminists among them would approve. But he felt quite the lad, nevertheless, as Rita gave him a welcoming buss on his cheek and warmly squeezed his arm.

"Brian, darling, your glarrss is empty." She also had on a cut-glass mode, he noted. Brian liberally complimented her on her outfit.

One of the group flourished a nearly full bottle and filled him up and Rita introduced them all. Brian took a good deep drink and suddenly felt very cheerful as he sensed their open friendliness. Rita's acceptance was enough to guarantee his entrée and he knew that if Brindling art department survived he would never be short of congenial company. Recently, they had all had memos sent by him about including their exhibition CV's in 'Blue Skies' and their returns had been very impressive. De Vere had been quite right about their quality: they were coming men and women. In addition to breaching the 'Blue Skies' barrier, Brian was hoping that he could involve some of them in the research scheme which he was to present to the Research Committee and at the quinquennial.

Standing here at the foot of the stairs in a provincial art centre with talented, intelligent people he felt more determined than ever to hold on to his job by hook or, if that meant tangling with Huggett, by crook.

Prompted by Rita, Brian began to describe the episode in the 'Tofts' about which they had heard something already. He moved up a stair or two, carried by his actor's instinct to seek the limelight and was approaching the climax of the story to much hilarity from his audience, when Rita suddenly moved forward and pressed his arm to stop him. In telling the story his voice had risen a few decibels to project over the noise in the gallery. This enhancement drove his final words: " - and that daft begger, Huggett went arse over tip right into the hole with him - " with perfect clarity through one of those inexplicable hiatuses which often punctuate crowd noise. In his fuddled state, it seemed to him they hung in the air momentarily, to be caught by the official party he was suddenly aware of, descending the stairs behind him. He shifted aside to let them pass and Rita moved quickly away from him further into the hall. Amongst the party who passed him, the Rector and Noel de Vere stared at Brian in fury while Marshall suppressed his amusement behind them. Huggett simply looked menacing as he hissed at Brian:

"Don't say I didn't warn you."

The alcohol, which was now doubling its effect on him as it mixed with his intake of extra oxygen in the entrance hall, decided Brian that he had stood about as much of Huggett as he could stomach.

"Look here, you two-bit Don Colleoni, I'm getting damned shick - er - sick of this gangster movie crap of yours. I've only got one thing to say to you, Huggett."

"Oh. And what's that?" said Huggett, looking significantly at the Rector. Distanced from reality as he was, Brian was still aware that Huggett was expecting something that would give him an excuse to get the Rector to discipline or even fire him.

The crowd looked at Brian in trepidation at what possible challenge he could offer to the most powerful man in Brindling. Brian leaned towards Huggett and tapped out on his chest:

"Environmental - Resources - sub-Committee." The menace in his voice was quite a match for Huggett's.

The unexpectedness of this as an insult wiped away all previous expressions from the faces of most of the spectators and replaced them with looks of puzzlement. Brian looked round the group to see the effect of his challenge. He noticed that only Marshall and a large, plain, beefy female he'd never seen before, seemed not to share in the general bemusement. The Deputy Rector looked thoughtful and she looked grim. The rest looked at Huggett and were even more surprised to see the effect that Brian's riposte had had on him. He had gone white and subsided like a small, punctured football. He stared at Brian who now looked at him without any expression at all. Abruptly, he went down the last few steps, across the hall to a small office near the front door. They all watched him enter it then the Rector turned to Noel de Vere. From his expression, Brian concluded he was extremely disappointed that he could see nothing in Brian's remark to take satisfying disciplinary action over.

"I expect you to keep your staff in order, de Vere. I want to know how you deal with this. As for you, young man, my doubts at the time of your interview have been fully confirmed." He then moved off with most of the rest of the party, leaving Noel, Louie and Marshall.

De Vere made one of his strange, clawing gestures at Brian. "What the fuck do you think you're playing at?" he hissed. Brian had not seen him close to for some days, but was shocked at the change in his appearance. His handsome face now looked pale and drawn and his unshaded eyes were even more heavily dark-rimmed with bags, as though he were hitting the bottle. The anxious look which had been developing for some time as the pressures of the upcoming visit made themselves felt had developed into a look of permanent, incipient panic which Brian had heard from other members of staff frequently spilled over into a sort of hysterical, frantic activity as Noel constantly attempted to correct what he regarded as defects in which the CNNA might find grounds for criticism.

Louie had told Brian only the other day of one of these instances. Apparently, there had been trouble in the ceramics section between the students and a near fight had blown up. Louie had been called in as peacemaker. When he got to the root of the problem, it turned on one of the female students being informed by Zoe that she was a near genius and would definitely get a first. The student was Zoe's latest passion, so the other students naturally resented this and, even if it had been true that her pots were, as Zoe suggested, the greatest since Bernard Leach, it was completely unprofessional of her to predict the outcome of an exam not yet held. Consequent on Zoe allowing her feelings to distort her academic judgement, the other students had threatened to complain to CNAA in advance that the exam was not going to be objectively fair. This, naturally, would be disastrous for the course which would be sunk before even the quinquennial happened. Louie, at his most charmingly Italian, managed to head off the storm and calm it all down by a careful explanation of the marking system and how no one member of staff could guarantee anything. The students trusted Louie completely and were reassured. The situation calmed down. With Zoe he was as severe as he could muster, in spite of anger being only a tiny fraction of his personality. She was suitably chastened, never having seen Louie in this state before.

The effect of all this when he had related it to Noel de Vere was salutary as to their Head of Department's state of mind and Louie was glad he had had the foresight to keep Noel out of it. Louie described to Brian what had happened graphically as it had clearly shaken him:

"See, Brian, first, 'e putta 'is 'ead in 'is 'ands, like-a so." Louie thrust his face into his cupped hands. "And 'e make a sort-a noise like-a this." Louie gave the long, deep moan Brian remembered from his interview day. "Then 'e get up and 'e walk over to the door. Then 'e puts 'is 'ead down and 'e run - yes, Brian - 'e run atta the door with 'is 'ead like-a this. Boom!" Louie ran his head violently into his outstretched palm. "Then 'e stands atta the door and 'e goes-a boom, boom, boom with 'is 'ead. Then 'e walk-a back to 'is desk and sits-a down and 'e start-a writin' more memoses as if nothing 'ad 'appen. I tell-a you Brian, when the CNAA's is comin', it's-a gonna be foockin-a murder. 'E's a tutti-frutti nut-a case."

Brian focussed with interest now on Noel's forehead and he could indeed see welts across it.

"What are you staring at?" said de Vere. "Pay attention."

With some difficulty, Brian re-focussed his eyes on Noel's. The adrenaline, which had temporarily kept the alcohol at bay during his confrontation with Huggett was wearing off.

"What the hell was all that about? What committee? What's with you and Huggett, anyway? And stay away from the life room. I've heard all about you groping the model. If I hear you've been in there again, I'll fire you. Huggett was swinging round to our point of view before you interfered, you stupid sod. Don't you know that's his bit on the side? Now you've done it again. I'll have to start all over again buttering up the little shit. We'll give him another print, Louie. OK?"

"Give him the whole effing show," said Brian, "and a pound of best Shtork while you're at it but it'll not make a ha'porth of difference. I'm telling you - he's after a damn shight - sight bigger fish than that."

"What the hell do you know about it?"

Brian glanced round and placed his finger to his lips. "Shhh," he said. "Environmeltal - mental - Reshources - shub - Committee," he whispered stagily, winking and nodding.

Noel knew there must be more to Brian's behaviour than simply drunkeness; he had seen the effect it had on Huggett.

"What the hell are you babbling about? What is this committee and why is it so important?"

"Aah. Let shleeping croshes lie, man." Brian laid his finger along the side of his nose.

De Vere looked at him in baffled fury.

"Come on, Louie. This silly bastard"s pissed out of his gourd."

As Noel moved off, Louie looked at Brian and shook his head.

"Keep off-a the vino, eh, Brian. Is very strong - you notta use-a it." He clapped his shoulders sympathetically and followed de Vere.

Only Dr. Marshall now remained with Brian on the stairs. He looked at Brian thoughtfully.

Brian raised his glass.

"To the art of crime," he said.

"We might have a chat about that committee, some time, Dr. Mather," said Marshall. "Perhaps it might be useful for us to pool both our - resources."

Brian registered Marshall's careful emphasis. From his expression, he knew that the significance of his remark to Huggett had not been lost on him. Brian wondered how much he knew. He suspected that if he did know anything of what was going on, he did not share it with the Rector himself. Rita rejoined Brian.

"Looks like you shook him up a bit. He didn't even glance my way as he went over to the office."

"Could be, could be," said Brian. "Oh, Rita, do allow me to introduce you. Dr. Marshall, our distinguished Recuty Deptor - er - Deputy Rector. Sorry, I don't know your first name."

"Philip." said Marshall.

"Philip Marshall, Rita Shanderson - Sanderson. Sorry. Philip is a great admirer of yours, as you know."

Marshall and Rita formally shook hands and spoke their perfunctory greetings, both warily eyeing the other.

"There you are." said Brian. "Duty done. Suit meets beaut. At lasht. From now on, you're on your own, son. Oops, nearly gone," he said of his wine. "More of Louie's excellent vino is called for, I think."

"Keep out of dark alleys, Brian," said Rita, as he moved away. Her tone suggested more than a casual parting remark but Brian was too drunk to register it.

"Thank you," called Philip Marshall to Brian.

"Any time, old boy." said Brian with a wave as he crossed the hall to the basement staircase. He passed the main office of the Arts Centre on his way and saw Huggett still in there talking forcefully into the phone. He glanced up as Brian passed and caught his eye. His throat-cutting gesture this time was tinged with extra menace. Brian waved his empty glass at him but with somewhat less panache than he had felt on the stairs.

The descent to the basement was via the old servants' staircase at the rear of the hallway. It was quite badly lit and narrow, with a heavy fire door to the hall and another at the bottom to the bar, so it was isolated when both doors were shut as they were now. Brian reflected as he descended that this was probably one of the cost-cutting bits on which Huggett had drawn his extras. He had gone only a few stairs when he felt a sharp jab in the region of his right kidney. He jerked, then stumbled and fell to the middle landing, finishing in a heap against the wall. He looked up and tried to sort out lights, swirling walls, cornices and Victorian cherubs in the ceiling rose from what seemed to be a real female face looking down at him. In a few moments he had focussed sufficiently to recognise the beefy female who had been unamused by his remark to Huggett.

"Did you do ..."

"Listen you," said the face, in a menacing tone, "you just keep your trap shut if you know what's good for you." Somehow, the tone and the threat from this person seemed to Brian far more serious than that from Huggett.

"Who the hell are you?" he demanded from the floor. "And what's the idea of shoving me like that? I could have broken my neck." He tried to rise but she pushed him down with her foot.

"Pity I didn't shove harder then. And no witnesses either."

"Do you mind?" Brian said.

"Yes," she said shoving him down again. "You just lie there and listen to what I'm telling you. I am Mrs. Oswald Spiller."

"The devil you are," said Brian, a line from an old thriller role popping up from the drunken depths of his brain.

"As far as you are concerned, that's exactly who I am, sonny. I've got you by the short hairs, lad, and don't you forget it. If you want to keep your job, you'll say nowt about what you think you might know to anybody. Is that clear?"

"Why should ..."

I've got you by the short hairs, lad, and don't you forget it.

"I'll tell you for why. You like your job, don't you? Well, you've got a CNAA visit in a few weeks, right? What do you think would happen if I told that lot what my Oswald's been up to for the last four years, eh? That would put the cat among the pigeons, wouldn't it? Just think what Charlie and the Rector could make of that, never mind the press. 'The Invisible Lecturer'. 'Never spoke to a student for four years but got paid thousands and thousands for doing nowt.' Good stuff, eh?. That Noel de Vere thinks he's been so dead clever covering up for him all this time, well it's time for the chickens to come home to roost - and I'm the party who can call them in. So I imagine you've got the message now? Right? Right?" She kicked his ribs. She was a heavy woman.

"Oof."

"And another thing. Keep that fat slag away from him. Don't think I don't know about him and her."

The door to the bar below the landing opened and a noisy bunch of students erupted onto the stairs. Mrs. Spiller stood up. The students came across Brian on the landing still slumped against the wall. A cheer arose as they gathered round him and lots of comments were passed as to his state. They pulled him to his feet and he looked for his attacker. He saw that she had almost reached the top of the stairs again. She turned on the top landing and made the same threatening gesture as Huggett. This time he felt nervous enough unconsciously to rub his finger round the inside of his collar. His sympathies for Oswald Spiller knew no bounds; no wonder he had a few bolts missing. If she were his wife, Brian thought, he'd be living in the middle of Australia in a deep hole, never mind in a little tent.

The students brushed him down. From their laughing comments he felt his reputation as a bit of a dog rising. So Mrs. Spiller's idiotic threats had done him some good, at least. He noticed he had tipped what remained of his wine onto his suit, his only suit, in his fall. Damn! The students urged him to join them and not be late. Late for what? Never mind, he was more concerned with his suit and told them he would have to get cleaned up first. He went down to the bar as they went off up the stairs. He realised that, although he felt very shaky after his fall and his headache had come back, he did seem to be much more sober.

Brian was surprised to find the bar was now empty, apart from a very gloomy-looking Hermione standing by the table filling her glass from an orange-juice carafe and trying to find some palatable bits of pizza amongst the debris of Elizabeth Bonetti's feast. Their mutual greetings were very subdued.

"By the way, did you get my CV ok?" she said.

"Yes, indeed. Very impressive."

"Oh, yes. It's all there is to do in this dump. Write bloody papers."

Brian got the strong impression of a very deep frustration. He wondered briefly why she was alone. Was there a boy friend? Lover? Her outfit, a high-bodiced black cocktail dress, gold courts and discreet, very expensive-looking brooch and ear-rings was classically attractive. With high heels and her hair up she gave the impression of tall elegance, in complete contrast to her rather ordinary dress at college. Brian had the thought that her normal wear might be a cover for shyness

"Where is everybody?" he said. "Did somebody shout fire, or something?"

Hermione looked round. She seemed as surprised as Brian at the emptiness of the bar.

"I don't know," she said. "There were masses of people here a moment ago. I was talking to one of my students and when I'd finished they all seemed to be going off somewhere and then I talked to somebody else and she went off as well. They didn't invite me to join them. Story of my life, laughter in the next room. You know that?"

Brian nodded. "Sitwell. One of my favourites. That's a very nice outfit, by the way."

"Thank you. You're the first one who's noticed it. I'm afraid we're both the comic feeds of the college now, aren't we? The augustes of the art world." Brian was startled that she'd seen herself in the same role as himself. He felt an immediate close sympathy.

"You don't look too good yourself, by the way," she said, scrutinising him critically. "If you don't mind my saying so."

Brian was disarmed by her candour. He began to try and straighten up a bit.

"No I expect not. Do you know Mrs. Spiller, by the way?"

"Only by reputation."

"Which is?"

"Pretty horrendous. Why?"

"I've just had a short, pithy - not an easy word that in my state by the way - conversation with her. She is at least partially responsible for my dishevelled and offensive state for which I humbly apologize."

"Compared to the artists here, I can assure you you're Beau Brummel," she said drily. "It's a pity men have forgotten how to dress attractively - except Laurie Willoughby, of course. But then there's not much point with him. His only concern is to ask you "What are you wearing this evening, dear? We musn't clash, must we?"

Brian laughed at her imitation. He picked up a napkin and began to dab at the stain on his jacket.

"Hardly likely anyway," she said morosely. "No woman would be seen dead in all that taffeta he wraps himself in. Anyway it's all very discouraging to making the effort oneself."

She watched Brian's ineffectual efforts to remove the wine mark.

"That's no good," she said. "Here, slip your jacket off and I'll take it to the kitchen. There's bound to be something there for stains. I was pretty good at stains once over. I may even have a badge for it somewhere. I seemed to get one for everything else and a Duke of Edinburgh's."

Brian did as he was bid and handed her the jacket. She smiled at him. "I'll leave you to deal with the trousers." She moved off. "Remember, cold water only," she said.

Brian retired to the Gents and repaired the damage as best he might with his handkerchief and cold water. God, what a mess, he thought. A tentative glance in the mirror confirmed his impression. He washed his face, combed his hair and rubbed his teeth with the handkerchief. That would have to do. He joined Hermione waiting with his jacket.

"It should all dry out alright and this dark blue colour is good for disguising marks," she said. "By the way, a girl in there, in between being eaten alive by a young man, said that they've all gone up to the viewing room for some special presentation. Shall we join them?"

"What are we waiting for?" he said, but his heart sank when he thought what it might be.

While they made their way upstairs to the video and film viewing facility on the first floor - the diverted equipment discount from which was yet another little extra, Brian had discovered - Hermione said:

"You're finding it all pretty hectic settling in here, aren't you?" Her tone was sympathetic but objective, as though she were talking to a first year student.

"Just a bit out of practice, that's all."

"I must say, if you're new to art colleges, you must find it a tremendous culture shock."

"Did you find it like that?"

"Not really. You see, I was a painter originally."

"Good Lord, were you? I had you clocked as a straight up and down academic."

"I did a post-grad in Art History at Brighton."

"Why didn't you stick to it? The painting? These stairs seem to be getting steeper. Oooh." Brian stopped and bent over as the after-effects of Mrs. Spiller's jab caught up with him.

"What is it? Are you alright?"

"Just a pain in my side. It's nothing. It'll pass. Old ski wound. Gets at me when I've had a bit." Now why did he say that? Perhaps he was trying to impress her because she was relatively normal. Anyway, he could hardly tell her he'd been mugged by old mother Spiller.

"I do still do paint in my spare time - of which I seem to have rather a lot lately." she said. Brian wondered what the significance of this remark might be. He knew he was in for yet another female confessional - well, his jacket lapels were already soaked. "I was quite good, you know. I got a first at Central but that was in the days when everybody else did as well. I suppose I didn't carry on because I couldn't stand the permanent student life and all that awful hustling for gallery space. And the men were truly foul, some of them. Did you know there's a gallery couch like a casting couch? - well, more a chaise longue in the art world. And an invitation to a private view is often just that - very private indeed. It's funny."

"What is?"

"It seems almost impossible to be successful for a young artist these days without being permanently grubby and sordid. And, of course, there's far too much drug-taking among them as well. If you've got an instinct for the orderly life like me, nobody takes you seriously - it's our version of the pathetic fallacy. The rougher the cut, the more genuine the art. I suppose one could become a sort of female version of Margritte. Perhaps one already is."

"No, surely not."

"It makes it so difficult to relate to men in art as well. I mean, I'm not into drugs or alcohol or rock and roll." Brian noted she had omitted 'sex' from the litany. "The trouble is a good girl's school leaves its stamp, you know, just like the boy's public school. My nickname at college was 'Genteel'. I've never been able to live that down. I even get letters addressed to G. James."

"Tough," said Brian.

"So here I am washed up in Brindling. Oh dear, that does sound awfully gloomy, doesn't it? I don't intend it to be."

"Haven't you a boy friend or anything?" said Brian. "You're very attractive."

"I wonder what the anything could be," she said turning away slightly from the compliment. "A cat? A dog? A goldfish?"

Brian grinned.

"I had a chap but he had a boat. I hardly ever saw him. He works for ICI. I left a note on his car one day - it was either me or the boat. He never got the note apparently. He thought it was an advert for a car wash and tore it up."

"He chose the boat, then?"

"As he is at present sailing the Norwegian fjords without me, I imagine so." She shrugged. "Still if he couldn't distinguish between my best scented notepaper and a car-wash flyer it was probably doomed anyway. God, listen to that noise."

They had arrived at the first floor main corridor. Along it rolled gales of laughter from the viewing room at the end where a large crowd had spilled out into the corridor. Someone at the back saw them approaching.

"Here he is, the man himself."

A great cheer went up and Brian found himself hustled into the darkened room and thrust to the front of crowd where a large projection television set was playing. At the front were the Fartistas, Renee and Dorothea. He had half expected to see Connie with them. He had been looking for her at the show all evening - the prospect that she might be here was another thing that tempted him to come in the first place and risk a confrontation with Huggett - but he had spent so much time dodging the official party he hadn't been able to look properly. But she was not here, either. He had seen nothing of her since their last session in the computing labs and he had begun to wonder whether she really thought there were any prospects for their relationship after finals or whether she had later regretted saying there might be. The crowd parted in front of the screen and Brian knew that the inevitable was about to happen. Although the room was in semi-darkness, he was aware of the official party standing now just behind him. He almost could not bear to watch as the skilfully edited tape unwound to its inevitable climax. When this was reached a huge cheer went up from the spectators followed by a second cheer as Dorothea demonstrated her Superwoman prowess. The lights came up and Brian turned to face the noisy crowd.

The drunken cheering was still going on. In front of him, the frozen faces of Huggett, the Rector, Mrs. Spiller and Noel de Vere stared at him coldly. Brian felt that his goose might well be cooked so what the hell. He bowed low and elaborately. This was definitely not a good idea. As he bent forward, his head swam and his downward motion continued so that his forehead struck the carpet. He remained in this posture unable to rise or fall, his backside stuck in the air. People crowded forward and willing hands pulled him up straight once more. One pair belonged to Ronnie.

"Gee thanks, Ronnie," he said. "Great tape."

"No problem, wack," said Ronnie, grinning broadly.

Huggett stepped forward.

"I want that tape," he said angrily.

"Well, you can't have it," said Ronnie. "That's mine. I need it for my video installation for my degree show."

"You're not going to show that again," said Huggett.

"Oh yes, I am," said Ronnie. "Noel de Vere said I could. Isn't that right, Noel?"

The whinny of terror which escaped from de Vere was taken as assent by Ronnie.

"See," he said. "Anyway, I can make you a star - like Danny de Vito or Bob Hoskins."

"Bloody fool," said Huggett. "Give me that damned tape this instant, you cheeky young bugger." He stepped forward to the machine but Ronnie grabbed his arm. They struggled for a short while to the delighted cries of encouragement and laughter from the crowd until Ronnie, surprisingly strong, pressed the 'EJECT' button while holding Huggett at bay. Nothing happened. Ronnie pressed it again with the same result.

"Bloody hell, it's gone."

"What do you mean, it's gone," said Huggett released from Ronnie's grip. He pressed the button himself with as little result. Ronnie lifted the front flap and looked inside.

"It's gone alright. Some bastard's pinched it. Come on, you lot, who's got it? You rotten bastards. That's the only copy."

"Where's the original?" called Laurie Willoughby, moving forward.

Ronnie looked shamefaced.

"It got wiped accidentally," he said.

"Good God!" Laurie flounced off in a swirl of angry taffeta.

Brian felt very sorry for Ronnie who was almost in tears. He remembered his own finals when the typist he had given his unxeroxed dissertation to had had a nervous breakdown and burnt all her papers. However, he was glad whoever took it was not going to give it up; unlike his dissertation, Ronnie could not reconstruct a tape.

Ronnie swung round to the official party. "Right, you just wait. I'll give you bastards a final show to end all final shows. You just see if I don't."

Noel de Vere, knowing Ronnie's instability, stepped forward.

"Ronnie."

"Piss off," said Ronnie near to tears, and pushed his way out. The crowd cheered. They cheered again as Huggett said:

"You're for the high jump, the lot of you," and pushed his way through the crowd but with much more difficulty than Ronnie.

Brian could see the Rector in frowning conversation with Noel and gesturing in his direction. De Vere moved forward towards him but before he could reach him, the Fartistas, Renee and the younger members of staff crowded round him and he and Dorothea along with Marshall, Rita and Oswald Spiller swept off to begin a memorable crawl of the local pubs.

In a short time, the famous Brindling strong bitter ale had dissolved the embarrassments of the evening from Brian's mind. But he was aware of one glaring gap in the events of the last few hours, and although he enquired of all the Fartistas (now linked by Renee with the Tofters to form the Fartoffs) he could still get no answer to his question: where was Connie? Nobody had seen her for days, he was told. They thought she had finished her ceiling and she had not been into her work space, nor could anyone get any reply from her phone. The lack of satisfaction left him with a vague feeling of jealousy which he found difficult to shake off. He was still pondering her absence when he found himself swaying gently on the edge of the pavement in a badly lit street somewhere near the docks. It had begun to rain - Brindling seemed to have more than its fair share of rain uncharitably falling when he had no protection, he thought. The town was definitely trying to tell him something.

If he had been more aware of his surroundings he would have noticed a bulky shape carrying a cylindrical object moving slowly towards him in the shadows. It was about to step out when a car came round the corner. It drew up in front of Brian and its passenger door opened towards him. He was vaguely aware of an invitation to enter. Gratefully, he fell into the front seat, finishing up somewhere in the foot well. A female arm reached out and slammed the door behind him. The shadow drifted back into the darkness and moved off down the street. From an alcove on the other side of the street came a slight chink of empty bottles and a watching shadow moved away in the opposite direction.

Chapter Eleven
Grey Thoughts in a Blue Sky.

The vividly-coloured dreams which had plagued him all night - most of which involved flamingoes doing unspeakable things to the back of his skull - gradually came to a halt. The first coherent thought, or rather feeling, he was able to identify when most of the flamingoes had flown, was that he was very cold. He shivered and realised that he was stark naked. The second thought was, where was he lying so starkly naked: his bed or somebody else's? By dint of superhuman strength and will-power he cautiously opened one eye slightly. The light was filtered through curtains but he could make out, on the wall next to the bed, the familiar long-legged pink birds, now, apart from one which seemed to be roosting on his forehead, safely trapped once more in their frozen foraging. So, home sweet home then; there could only be one room in the universe decorated like this. He tentatively moved an arm and shivered again as it encountered a damp towel lying on the bed. There was no prospect of his raising his head from the pillow yet - pillow? There was no pillow. He explored further - there was also no bedding. He lay still, not bewildered, simply exhausted, his head pinned to the mattress, as he slipped back towards unconsciousness.

After a few minutes, in which sleep did not return, the roosting flamingo stood up - God! they were heavy birds - flexed its claws across his brow - oooh! - and hopped back onto the wallpaper. If he wanted to he felt he might now raise his head. Did he want to? May as well, he was young, he was fit, he could do anything if he really tried. The room lurched somewhat but settled down almost immediately. He looked round. The first thing he noticed was his clothes stacked neatly on a chair; of the bedding there was no sign. On the bed near him was his dressing gown which may once have covered him. His head fell back and he searched his mind but the events of last night following the first pub after the Arts Centre were a complete blank. He had a vague impression of Rita telling him something with Marshall looking on concernedly and he could recall Dorothea and Spiller making calf's-eyes at each other. He could also recall regaling the company with a solo stand-up routine he had once written about the advantages of being reincarnated as various animals. He gave an involuntary shudder of embarrassment and even blushed - one day he'd learn to control that - as he recalled the more obscene passages but the crowd seemed to have egged him on hilariously. And that was about the point at which his brain decided to say good night: all subsequently was in limbo file. How had he got home? Who had helped him? A man in drink does odd things but no way would he in his state have stacked up the clothes so neatly. And where was the bedding?

By moving carefully, he managed to sit up and get his legs over the edge of the bed. As the room wobbled to a stop, he glanced down at the small American mechanical alarm clock at his bedside table. (Amazing how they managed still to produce something so cheap and old-fashioned but so reliable with all that Far Eastern electronic competition, he thought. A real design classic. Amazing.) 12.45. Amazing. What? He looked again. No mistake. Oh God, he had a lecture at two. Then the Research Committee at 3.30. Oh, how deeply he regretted last night now. Or did he? No, damn it, he didn't. He hadn't had as wild a time for two years or more. Bless you, Louie. God knows what the consequences would be but most men understand the effects of alcohol: it excuses much.

He bathed, shaved, dressed and drank a half pint of milk with the jerkiness and lack of attention of an automaton. At the sink, when he swilled out the milk bottle, he noticed the plates stacked neatly, clean and gleaming with the tea towel carefully hung over the taps to dry. Even though his memory was blank, he knew that he hadn't done this - in fact, never in his life had he done this - so it must have been a woman who had performed the miracle of getting him home in one piece and into bed. Had she - who, for God's sake? - stayed for a sensual end to the evening? From the state he must have been in, it was unlikely, and there was definitely no physical evidence he felt himself. Also, the damp towel when he picked it up reeked of 'technicolour yawn' whose after-effects in his mouth still lingered. Christ, who could it have been? Well, he hoped they'd enjoyed the view if not the rest. But - oh God! No. Not Audrey Reaper. Please let it not be Mrs. Reaper. I'll be good. I'll be...

His panicky thoughts were interrupted by the sound of his door bell. He realised it must have been ringing for some time but his ears were buzzing so much he thought its muffled jangling was part of the hangover. Whoever it might be was determined to raise him and seemed to be leaning on the thing. He went down to the front door, the bell from his room sounding even louder in the thinly linoleumed, cavernous stairwell.

"Alright, alright. Knock it off." His head hurt abominably. He opened the door. On the step stood a tall, middle-aged man in a dark suit. He had a nearly white moustache and was wearing a trilby hat. He remembered Renee's categories of men with trilby hats. He knew instantly which of them this man fell into and swallowed hard.

"Dr. Brian Mather?" said the man.

"Yes."

"I am Detective Inspector Forsythe." (It was no consolation to know he had guessed correctly.) "Would you mind if I had a word with you, sir?"

"Er. Not at all. What about? Will it take long? I've a class at two and a committee meeting at three thirty. Will it take long? Er.." The unexpectedness of the man coming on top of his hangover threw him into near babbling. He needed a hair of the dog, definitely.

"Only a few minutes, I hope." said the detective. He had a cultivated Scottish accent. "May I come in?"

"Oh, sorry, yes, of course."

Brian led the way upstairs. "What's it about?" he said.

"All in good time, sir," said Forsythe.

"There's not much room to sit," said Brian, clearing some clothes from the only chair when they had entered the room. Forsythe settled himself on the chair, removed his hat to reveal a shock of wiry grey hair and took a notebook from his overcoat pocket as Brian sat on the bed. Brian thought the removal of the hat was significant recognition of his bourgeois status. It would not be something he did in the 'Tofts', he was sure. Forsythe went quickly through the preliminaries of who Brian was, what he did for a living, etc., ignoring Brian's questions about why he was there. Finally, he came to the point.

"I am investigating a rather serious matter, sir, and I believe you might be able to help me."

Whilst the Inspector had been following his policemanly rigmarole, Brian's forebodings grew: the hacking of the Civic Centre data bank he was quite certain must be the subject. Especially if they had put a policeman at senior level onto it. He braced himself. What does one say: a fair cop, guv? Or: can I go to the loo first? Something, as he sat immobile, he realised he had neglected to do in his semi-conscious state before the Inspector arrived. The subject was all the more unexpected then when it was finally revealed and was sufficiently startling to dispel his faecal urges.

"Last evening about two a.m. a colleague of yours was subject to a brutal attack near the docks by a number of assailants."

Brian swallowed hard. "Good God, who?"

"Dr. Marshall, Deputy Rector of the Polytechnic."

"What! Where? How is he?"

"Fortunately, sir, Dr. Marshall was not seriously injured, even though the assailants were employing baseball bats, we understand - he'll be back in harness in a day or so. He's a very fit man and as a former rugby blue gave a good account of himself. The young lady he was with - a Miss Rita Sanderson, the artists' model at your college, I believe - managed by her piercing screams - which by all accounts would have wakened the dead - to scare his attackers sufficiently to make them run. She also claims to have inflicted a number of injuries on them herself with a large whip she appeared to have about her person - something we have not got to the bottom of yet. She claims it belongs to a - " (He glanced at his notebook.) "a Mister Jones. Not a colleague of yours, is he, sir, by any chance?"

"No. You said assailants?"

"Yes, three apparently."

"I see. Well, how can I help you, Inspector?"

"You were with Dr. Marshall earlier at the Arts Centre, I believe and for some time afterwards."

"That's right, but I have to be honest with you, Inspector - er..?"

"Forsythe."

"Inspector Forsythe, After leaving the Arts Centre everything is virtually a blank."

"I see. So you wouldn't remember hearing any threats made to Dr. Marshall either then or earlier?"

"Threats? Good heavens, no."

"Any threats at all?" Here the Inspector paused and looked carefully at Brian. "To anybody?"

Brian hesitated, then shook his head. "No. No, I'm afraid not. As I say, I was so far gone as to be out of sight."

Forsythe looked at him levelly but said nothing.

Brian laughed nervously. "The wine was free, you see."

"Just so," said Forsythe, "just so."

"What sort of threats? And why would anybody do such a thing?"

"That is what I am trying to find out, Dr. Mather. Miss Sanderson has told us - well, what she wants us to know. We think she knew the attackers. She is, after all a stripper at the club down there in addition to her modelling duties - 'BoZo'Z', you've heard of it, no doubt, and its reputation - much exaggerated, I may say - and would certainly know most of the villains in this town even if it was dark, which indeed is how she no doubt mostly sees them. We do not think this is a random affair by the by. No, those men were waiting so we think it was quite premeditated but possibly - " (Here there was yet another very significant pause and look.) "a case of mistaken identity."

"Ah," said Brian.

"Just so."

He thought of Marshall. It had not struck him before but same colouring and height, much heavier, but in the dark? Both wearing suits. And with Rita to boot? Well, well. Poor old Marshall. Still, he no doubt got a bit of TLC from Rita. Very probably worth the odd clout from a baseball bat. As long as they didn't knacker the wedding tackle, that is.

"As you appear not to be able to recall the events of last night with any clarity, sir, would it interest you to know that you were observed within the vicinity of the attack some short time previous to it?"

"It certainly would. In fact, if anybody knows where I was, I'd be grateful. Who saw me and how did they know it was me?"

"Our informant encountered you on one occasion previously in the same area, also at night but has seen you a number of times since leading students through there during the day."

"I see. The eyes and ears of the world, then. It's a very interesting area of the town, you see - from the architectural/ historical viewpoint, that is," Brian added hastily. Brindling was a village, definitely a village.

"Just so, just so. You say then, you have no recollection of being in that area last night."

"None whatsoever. I really was blotted out, Inspector."

"I see. And you did not notice any person following you, therefore?"

"Following me? When? No."

"Tell me. Who was the lady driving the car you entered?" Brian was astonished at Forsythe's detailed information. He turned up his palms in a gesture of complete ignorance.

"If I got in a car, it's news to me, Inspector. A lady, you say. Well, it could have been a frog outrider on a pumpkin for all I was aware. It's all a blank. State dependent memory loss is the technical term, I believe."

"Is it, indeed?" Forsythe looked down at his notebook, and tugged at his moustache, thinking.

Two things puzzled Brian. He broached the first of them.

"Forgive me, Inspector," he said, "I don't know a lot about the ranking of policemen but aren't you a little - well, senior for this sort of routine enquiry?"

"Perhaps. But this is not exactly a routine enquiry, you see."

"Oh?"

"No. There are, shall we say, some associated ramifications and implications."

Forsythe's brogue rolled lovingly round these words, and he stroked his moustache again with satisfaction. (Brian suddenly had his answer to the second question that was troubling him. He'd seen this man before: outside Audrey Reaper's house in the patrol car and leading Charlie Huggett out of 'BoZo'Z'.) From under his bushy grey eyebrows - real Denis Healey's, those, thought Brian - his eyes suddenly made Brian flinch as they fixed him with a searching stare.

"For instance, last evening at the Arts Centre, it was reported to me that you mentioned a certain committee to a certain person." The last word was dragged out and heavily emphasised as 'pairrrson'. Brian sensed Forsythe's relish for melodramatic overacting; it made the significance of his statement seem slightly less threatening, at least momentarily.

"Ah. Did I?"

"So it is reliably reported."

"By whom?"

"A sober person. One of the few by all accounts. And did you?"

Brian made the same blank gesture. "Could be. As I say..."

Forsythe interrupted him. "Because if you did, and you do indeed have any information pertinent to the operation of such a committee, I would be very interested to see it, Dr. Mather, very interested indeed."

I'll bet, thought Brian. And how did you come by this pairrtinent information, Dr. Mather? Explain that away. Please, sir, I was so drunk I didn't know what I was doing. I just pressed a button and this stuff appeared on the screen.

"You see, Dr. Mather, what happened to poor Dr. Marshall last night may not be outwith certain ramifications of that committee's activities."

"Oh," said Brian. Jesus Christ, they were onto it. What the hell had he let himself get pulled into? Damn Connie Grey and her big blue eyes.

"They tell me you are a bit of an expert with the computer, Dr. Mather."

"Some rudimentary skill, yes."

"Very useful these days, no doubt. There's so much useful information washing about in them. If you can get access to it, of course. I myself am a little long in the tooth to grasp the game, although my children have been familiar from their junior school time. We in the force have our own experts, of course, but it can be like looking for the proverbial needle in a hay stack, do you see, without the right keys."

"It can indeed," said Brian. All the time he was speaking, Forsythe watched Brian carefully from under his thatched eyebrows. Brian turned away uncomfortably. "Well, if that's all, Inspector, I really must be going. I'm sorry I can't help you."

Forsythe stood and pocketed his notebook.

"You're a stranger to this town, are you not, Dr. Mather?"

"Yes."

"I should be careful of three things, if I were you. The ale, which is notoriously strong, the ladies, who are notoriously libidinous, and the dark streets, which can be notoriously dangerous, especially for persons trespassing into areas where they do not belong." The actor in Brian admired the technical drama of the Scottish "notooorrious" - real school of John Laurie. "Good day to you, sir. I'll see myself out and if anything is retrieved beyond the 'state dependent memory loss' - a useful phrase which I hope the villains in this town and their lawyers do not latch onto - I would be very grateful if you would contact me." He put down a card. "This number should reach me at most times. Oh, and should you wish to visit Dr. Marshall he will be in the General Infirmary at least until tomorrow.

"But he's definitely not badly hurt?"

"Just so. Just so."

Forsythe's visit left Brian, as he supposed it was meant to, speculating and worrying as to how much he knew about what had been going on. While Forsythe had been talking to him, lying on the table next to the bed was Brian's briefcase with all the evidence of municipal graft the man could want. And just who had told him about his mentioning the committee? Yes, and who pinched the video and why? And who had got him home? And where was the blasted bedding?

"Godammit!" he shouted aloud, as he got up and realised he had been sitting on the damp towel. He rushed to the lavatory.

By the time of the Research Committee meeting, Brian had worked through a complete catalogue of speculation. This soon dispersed as he focussed his attention on what he knew could be a severe test of his and the Department's credibility. He had chosen to sit next to the head of the table. Having been warned by Marshall that the Rector was likely to cut up rough about the Poly's research record - presumably as part of the preparations for applying for university status - Brian knew from long experience of acrimonious meetings in his previous college, that sitting away from an antagonistic chair gave the enemy the advantage. It allowed them to occupy a sort of horizontal belvedere from which to shower down buckets of molten verbal lead and judge their impact. Nearby, on the other hand, meant face to face slug it out on level ground; you might spot their weaknesses. Only if you carried your own camouflage like Peter Orrd, could you sit far away and be secure. Brian also felt confident that his acting technique was solid enough to control his own body language and there might be a chance of prompting some advantageous reactions in his opponent.

He was in the large, panelled Committee Room early. He nodded to and exchanged pleasantries with the other members as they arrived. These, the most senior members of the academic community of the Polytechnic, eyed him speculatively as they collected their tea and biscuits from the side table. They had all had a copy of his submission for 'Blue Skies' but none spoke to him or commented on it, not even Bill Johnson whose nod was markedly curt. (Brian surmised he had found the little message he left behind.) The language of art exhibitions and their legitimacy was out of their experience. They had also had a copy of his scheme for developing a research project using regional arts money and Poly funds combined. For them, the introduction of the new element of art promised to liven up the dull late afternoon meeting. Little did they know what Brian had been warned of, that the Rector was out for blood; there was never going to be anything dull about this show.

The Rector and the Polytechnic Chief Admin. Officer arrived and settled themselves at the head of the table. Brian stared at his papers but was aware that the Rector registered his presence nearby. From the little grunt which escaped him, Brian guessed he was none too pleased at his close proximity. He may also have been annoyed that a man of Brian's lowly status should attend this, the most academically prestigious committee in the institution, at   Brian had taken the precaution of buying a new white shirt and had added his college tie. He had changed into these and groomed himself carefully in the interval between his lecture and the meeting so that he looked once more like the sobersided straight man and not the debris of the night before. (Also, his trousers were now dry, thank God.) Besides, the lecture he had just given had gone particularly well and largely dispersed his hangover and the welcome tea and biscuits completed the process. So, as the meeting began, he was feeling in reasonable fettle.

He was given even more confidence by his surreptitious observation of a little vignette between Dr. Robson and his Admin. Officer just prior to calling the meeting to order. Brian saw the Rector lean over and whisper something to his assistant, who was sitting nearest to Brian. Brian's stage experience of actors conducting clandestine conversations on all kinds of topics whilst the play was in progress had made him an expert lip reader of even the most concealed lines and his ears were fine-tuned.

"Don't be too alarmed if it seems to get a bit lively," the Rector whispered. "Everything's under control." When he had finished his little aside, he looked up and his eye ranged round to table to see if any staff had picked it up, but they were too busy chatting, laughing and enjoying their tea and biscuits. Brian made great play of studying his papers and he felt the Rector's gaze pass him by. So we are to be treated to a performance, he thought. Thank you.

The first scene was enacted impromptu, the Rector taking the opportunity as a gift with which to signal the tone for the rest of the meeting.

Brian knew that if there was any part of the academic resource of the Polytechnic which the Rector hated more than Art and Design, it was Education. He had had occasion to visit the Education Faculty, in effect the old Brindling College of Education which like the art college had undergone a shotgun wedding with the Polytechnic. Its origin and buildings were of the same vintage as those of the Art Faculty and Brian was taking slides of their eccentric terra cotta detailing when he had had conversations with various members of the Faculty staff. Brian found them almost universally downcast. They were glad themselves to find in Brian somebody in the Polytechnic who, firstly, had had some experience of schools at least, and, secondly, appeared to have a modicum of culture beyond the classic formulae of engineering. On one occasion he had been taken into their common room to be met by that wave of over-hearty, near-hysterical laughter he recognised could be generated only by school teachers of both genders as a release from the fury they had constantly to suppress with their charges. He felt almost nostalgic for his former institution, unlucky enough to be too far from any Polytechnic to be saved from the humane killer. Almost, but not quite.

It was on this occasion that the depressed Education staff felt sufficiently safe with him to let him know what they were up against with the Rector, who, they assured him, would have loved to have administered the coup de grâce to them all himself with humane killer, shotgun, baseball bat, or anything else to hand, never mind being forced by the Department of Education to cohabit with them. He had already managed to denude the Faculty of most of its senior members through Faustian early retirement bargains and was busily pressuring even younger ones to jump ship as well. (Brian reflected that this particular spotlight was now being turned in a similar way onto Art and Design.) Consequently, the appearance at the Rector's side and the subject broached of the committee member for Education, was an opportunity not be missed.

"You want to do WHAT?" the Rector roared, in angry response to the innocuous question he had been asked.

The hapless lecturer recoiled as though he had stood on a snake. Around the table, a small shower of biscuit crumbs and spilled tea fell on papers spread in front of the committee members as they started at the Rector's bellow.

"Listen to THIS!" said the Rector. He swept his hand towards the open-mouthed member for Education dramatically and pointed an accusing finger at him. "Here's a man wants to leave this vital meeting at half past five to go off and DRINK SHERRY with his friends in some half-baked training college, instead of staying here and earning some of the VAST SALARY we pay him. What do you think of that?"

"But..But..I'm the external examiner. I'm to look over their dissertations. And the meeting is after hours."

"After hours? AFTER HOURS?" shouted the Rector, waving his arms in disbelief at the concept. "There's no such thing as after hours in this institution, man. You are a full-time lecturer in this Polytechnic, are you not? Then that means what it says - full time. Every hour God sends belongs to us! This college! It's us that pay your wages. Understand? Not some holiday camp for refugees from the classroom trying to pass itself off as Higher Education.".

This interpretation of what was meant by 'full-time' was startling in its novelty. Suddenly, the plight of the member for Education which had shocked them became even more directly relevant to the rest of the staff. One of their number, whom Brian had consulted briefly when digging out the plans of the art college and knew to be a mild-mannered, rather brilliant civil engineer spoke up. Unwisely, not yet catching the drift of the meeting fully, he tried to seek clarification of the Rector's definition of full-time. Did that include vacations as well? Brian winced as he anticipated the Rector's reply.

"I seem to remember last year we conferred on you the title of 'professor'. Correct me if I'm wrong."

As the bewildered man assented, Brian reflected how boring heavy irony was as a performance style. Still, it suited the Rector perfectly, especially combined with his finger banging the table and even the occasional fist to hammer home his points.

"For a man of your rank, THERE ARE NO VACATIONS! Vacations are the time when you do your real work, RESEARCH! When we've got rid of the damned students for you. You should be in your laboratory producing. That's what your future depends on, not lolling about the south of France in swimming trunks." Brian reflected that the Rector had probably never lolled anywhere in swimming trunks or anything else. He wondered briefly if the Rector's definition of full-time included your sex-life or sitting on the lavatory as well. Probably. Used condoms and bog paper could be produced as evidence of fulfilled contractual obligations. The man was clearly unhinged.

"This government wants results for its money and SO DO I! We're never going to get anywhere at the rate we've been going. And that goes for the rest of you." His head bent forward and his arm swept inclusively around the table as he emphasised his words. "The cleaners have vacations, the porters, the kitchen maids, the clerical staff, the drivers, NOT the academics and you can all tell your staffs that! And don't think you can go running to your union. From next year there are going to be new contracts and if you want to keep your jobs, you'd better get used to the idea. This is the 1990's and times have changed!" He leant back with a brief satisfied grin at the effect he had created.

By this time, the member for Education was surreptitiously trying to regain his seat at the lower end of the table. A mistake, thought Brian, as the Rector had not yet finished with him. God, he really was enjoying himself and he didn't even have the excuse of paranoia like de Vere. What a prick!

"The very idea, going off at all with a research report like THIS!" He held up the submission from the Education Faculty by the corner with two fingers as if it were contaminated. "Hardly an item here worth the paper it's written on. I looked through last year's 'Blue Skies' and the year before's and the year before that, and most of these members of staff have been working on the same topic without any result for years. What conclusion do you draw from that? Eh? I'll tell you what conclusion - that these are NON-PROJECTS!. Look at this one." He opened the document. "This man working for an M.Sc. on long-shore drift off the coast here. He's been returning that topic every year for NINE YEARS! NINE YEARS, for God's sake! Don't you think he could have found which way the waves are breaking by now? It's all my eye and Betty Martin, this stuff. RUBBISH!." With a snort of contempt he tossed the whole submission over his shoulder. It immediately came apart in a cascade of loose paper. The papers fell messily to the floor and it suddenly struck Brian that the Rector must have unstapled the papers prior to the meeting for them to fall that way. Just so. Just so.

"Should I minute this, Rector?" said the Admin. Officer.

"Minute it? MINUTE IT? I want it printed in letters of fire ten feet high! Sloppy politeness and taking a man's word for what he's doing are finished. From now on everybody in this institution turns out REAL RESEARCH if they want to keep their jobs. I want 'Blue Skies' to reflect that this Polytechnic is at the CUTTING EDGE of knowledge. So I've weeded out the dead wood in this submission. Here!" Expertly, he slid a single sheet of paper across the table. "That will be your submission this year. One sheet and when other people read it in other polytechnics they'll know just what that means." He held up the rest of the papers. "And that goes for quite a few entries in the rest of these as well. They all need a good culling and that is what we are here to do today."

The Rector looked round his senior staff on whom an appalled silence had fallen.

"Apologies for Absence," he said, with the same grim smile playing at the corner of his mouth Brian remembered from his lambasting of de Vere on his interview day. The Head of Humanities rose to replenish his tea, but caught the Rector's eye and quickly sat down again. If this was the preliminary to the meeting, thought Brian, what lay in store for the rest? He reflected that the Rector had chosen his blend of committee styles carefully: the compassion of Margaret Thatcher, the intellectual incisiveness of the Ayatolla Khomeini, the honest directness of Richard Nixon; quite a formidable weapon for our hard-nosed times.

For the next hour, as the Rector combed through submissions from the various departments and challenged the validity of many of them, there were no fireworks quite to match the opening salvo against Education. Brian observed that the poor rep. from that Faculty - himself one of the few members of it with a solid research record - sat comatose and shell-shocked, his head sunk into his shoulders, for the rest of the time. But it was the reaction of the rest of the staff that was really worrying. Like his colleagues in the Art Department when confronted by de Vere with all his new rules, Brian was dismayed at the feebleness of their response. Where research was of high quality, there was no argument, but anything slightly weak and the Rector was onto it. Brian realised that their own convictions about the legitimacy of some of the research they had submitted were not sufficiently strong to counter the Rector's arguments and defend their staffs; he had done his homework all too well and knew precisely where the loppable branches lay.

The time approached five o'clock and it became obvious to Brian that the Rector had worked through the Faculties, apart from Education, in alphabetical order with the glaring exception of Art and Design. It was clear he was saving this up for a grand finale. As Brian had had no comments on the material from the other Faculties and, as the time was fast approaching when his own material would be examined, he decided he must pre-empt the hostilities with a diversionary skirmish. This had to be chosen carefully and the voice register selected to outflank the opponent's expectations. (He mentally blessed all those extempore exercises he had had to go through in drama classes.) The timing had also to be chosen with precision. Brian waited until the penultimate item in the Faculty of Technology submission was about to be examined. Alphabetically, this was as near as he could gauge the time his own material would come up for scrutiny.

The floor of the Committee Room was polished wooden parquet on which no expense had been spared, but the cheeseparing of the local authority determined that the chairs were cheap. light wooden ones, notorious for the horrendous, teeth-tingling screeches they made when drawn awkwardly across it. (They had long ago lost their rubber feet which nobody had bothered to replace.) Staff were used to this and took care to move them carefully if they were shifting about in meetings. But Brian was a newcomer to the room and its chairs. If you can't have a

Reggie Perrin whoopee-cushion, use the weapon to hand, he thought. The secret of success in battle is improvisation over the terrain. He carefully gripped the arms of his chair and estimated the pressure it would need for maximum impact. He stood up, pushing his chair back ostentatiously. The result was most satisfactory. A noise like a dozen hard pieces of chalk being scraped across a polished blackboard pierced the room. All the staff winced, some groaned loudly and even the member for Education stirred briefly as the atrophied memory of whole classes of small boys squeaking in agony at a similar noise surfaced to speak to him of happier times.

"Good God!" said Brian in a loud, robust voice. "That's appalling. What a terrible design. And poor maintenance as usual." He clicked his tongue in disapproval. "I'm just going for a pee," he said, as there were no women on the committee. He then strode boldly round the table and out of the room.

What effect this had while he was out, he could have no idea, although, once in the empty corridor, he leaned against the door briefly and heard a muffled "Damned artists!" from the Rector. Brian then occupied himself for a few minutes in the lavatory. On returning to the room, he strode confidently round the table to resume his seat. He was aware of an ominous anticipation in the room and that all eyes were on him. "Broken hand dryer," said Brian. He shook his head. "Broken chairs, broken hand dryers, falling apart, the place. Lowest common denominator, cheapness. Always a mistake not to go for design quality. It's like trying to get a reliable stapler in this place. They fall out at the first bit of use, have you noticed?" Brian himself had quickly noticed as he was about to take his place that his submission, now at the top of the pile in front of the Rector, had been given a similar treatment to that of Education. Always a mistake as well, to go for a target twice with the same tactic, he thought. He made sure of an elaborately quieter reprise with the chair as he sat down, shaking his head and clicking his tongue.

"Are you quite comfortable now?" said the Rector with an attempt at silky irony. Not bad, thought Brian, not bad.

Brian burped loudly, a skill to order he'd learned at junior school. The Rector flinched away.

"That's better," he said. "Biscuits a bit off there, I think." (He knew that biscuits were notoriously never fresh in the Polytechnic as the domestic staff took it as a natural perk to select from new boxes and give the left-overs to the staff.)

"Carry on," he said breezily.

The Rector's face coloured crimson. He held up Brian's submission. Brian noticed that, as it was unstapled, he had to grip it carefully with both hands, which were shaking with anger.

"Can you seriously expect," he said menacingly, "that this Polytechnic would allow a submission like this into its Research Report, young man?"

Brian liked the "young man" touch. He reached down into his briefcase and pulled out a wad of printed documents. Like 'Blue Skies' they were all glossy prestige efforts. He banged them onto the table. Load!

"I don't know whether staff are aware of this," he said, "but I have here research reports from a wide selection of polytechnics, all with Art and Design faculties." Aim! "All - without exception - " (He emphasised this heavily in his seriously academic mode.) "have reports of the activities of their Art and Design staff. In fact, as far as my researches have taken me, I can only conclude that this is the only polytechnic in the country which does not report on the activities of its Art and Design staff." Fire! "I have already had comments on this from staff in other polytechnics."

A few days previously Brian had phoned the former Brindling staff member - now promoted to Head of Department at another polytechnic - whose lately vacated post Brian now occupied. He had asked him what he thought about how Art and Design was regarded in his new institution. It was very well-regarded, he had been told, and his Rector thought it generally aces and an all-round good thing. And at Brindling and how Dr. Robson saw it?

"And what did they say?" said the Rector, coldly. He had said: "That stupid bastard Robson wouldn't know a good artist if he was pissing down his leg," but Brian translated this as:

"That Brindling Polytechnic has no confidence in what colleagues elsewhere know to be a staff with an outstanding national and international record for exhibitions and academic publishing. It is one of the reasons why the Faculty attracts such able students. Our record of firsts and post-grad. places is one of the best in the country." Thanks to Peter Orrd, he thought.

"Well, perhaps it's time to call the bluff on these other places and take the pretensions of these so-called artists to task," said the Rector with relish. "Look at this." He slammed down Brian's submission harder than Brian had presented his collection of reports and yanked at the pages, forgetting that it was now loose-leafed. The sheets shot across the desk and onto the floor. The Admin. Officer and one or two other staff scurried round to retrieve them, their chairs screeching the while. Brian stayed put and said quietly:

"Staples again!" and shook his head. "I do have some extra copies here, Rector. I used my own personal stapler on these." He offered one across the table. The Rector ignored him.

The papers were now out of order when they were returned so Dr. Robson took some time to find his place.

"Page 8," he rapped out angrily at last. The staff dutifully - and with some care - turned the pages of Brian's submission.

"This man, here," said the Rector, poking the page hard a number of times with his finger. "What's his name? Ostrowski."

"It's pronounced Ostrovski," said Brian mildly.

"What is he?"

Brian was nonplussed. Better be careful here, it could be a flanker.

"He's English."

"No, no." said the Rector, "I mean what does the fellow do? He has nothing after his name. Where are his qualifications? Other people have at least something after their names though God knows what they mean. Most of them are nothing I recognise as degrees. What, for God's sake, is NDD? Or Dip.A,D. or Slade Dip.? Are they real degrees or like HND's or what? Or very likely some sort of Mickey Mouse letters got for a fee?"

Brian jumped in quickly to stem the attack.

"Ah, you mean like Oxbridge MA's?" he said. He felt a palpable hit with this.

"No, I do not mean like Oxbridge MA's," said the Rector testily. "Let's stick to the point. This chap's not the only one with no letters. Have they been left out through carelessness on your part or do they really have no academic status?"

"They have no what you call academic qualifications in the sense of degrees from universities, no - they don't need them." said Brian carefully.

The Rector was genuinely horrified at this statement.

"Forgive me if I've got it wrong, Dr. Mather," (By his exaggerated irony and emphasis on the Brian's doctoral title he managed to suggest that there might be some Mickey Mouse fraudulence about that as well.) "but I understood this was supposed to be an academic community. How can it possibly allow persons with no academic qualifications whatsoever to feature alongside staff with all the recognisable academic distinctions one could wish for?"

"Because they're artists," said Brian simply. The Rector gathered himself for a major snort of derision but Brian's timing slipped in ahead of it. "They create art. That is what they do and it is the recognition of other peer artists that counts in the creative world. That is where they find their credibility, not in bits of paper." Brian had carefully rehearsed a speech like this in preparation for the meeting and was not to be put off as the Rector opened his mouth to deliver his riposte. "And art is what they are paid to teach to students who want to be artists and designers. Would you if you had somebody in the English department who published poetry or novels or plays, say that they were not qualified to teach creative writing because they had no diploma for it? What would you say about that, Dr. Graville?" Dr. Graville, Head of the English School, squeaked aloud. "Er, er," he said.

Brian had swung the discussion towards him as he knew that the creative writing unit in the Humanities degree was Graville's crown of thorns. It was taught in the English Department by a well regarded but abrasively rough-diamond poet, an ex-merchant seaman who had left school at fifteen, who swore a good deal, was heavily tattooed and had multiple serial and parallel sexual liaisons among the female students, staff and general populace. Brian had met him in the Art Department where he gave a criticism class for an hour a week to students who aspired to be artist/poets. Brian knew little about poetry or poets, but thought he was probably the genuine article. Louie had told him also that this man's reputation was such that he only had to give his piercing whistle in the town centre for the business of the town to come to a dead stop as the offices were denuded of their typing staff. There was a story that he had brought the local hospital to the brink of disaster when he had injudiciously whistled outside it. He also made no secret of despising academic English studies and was therefore naturally very popular with the students.

"Well?" said the Rector. "Are you taken with this nonsensical argument, Graville?"

Brian could see the dilemma crossing Graville's face when he thought of losing a possible stick to beat his demon poet from the door but honesty prevailed.

"I think," he said carefully, "Dr. Mather may have a point."

"Dear God!" said the Rector. "We'll be filling the place up with people who haven't even got 'O' levels next."

"Oh, I think he has those," said Brian quickly, deciding to rub salt in the wound. "Or at least some CSE's.".

The Rector held his head in his hands. "That I, a former Cambridge don should be in charge of an institution brought to this."

"Didn't one or two of the Royals get to Cambridge on CSE's?" said Brian innocently.

The Rector looked up suddenly.

"Look, Mather, I know about art. I did an evening class at your place years ago, and my wife's never away from there." (This remark startled Brian. Nobody had ever mentioned her coming to art classes. Christ, he hoped she wasn't one of the extra-mural Poly wives.) "There's nothing mysterious or special about art, you take it from me. So it's surely not beyond their wits to get something respectable behind their names."

"But why should they need to?" said Brian.

"Because it might tell us something about whether they're any good or not, that's why. Look at this man here, Ostrowski."

"Ostrovski," said Brian.

"Do you speak Polish or Russian or whatever it is?"

"Polish - his father was a Battle of Britain type. No," said Brian.

"Then keep quiet. All we have here is 'Performances in -' then there's a list of places in Europe that looks like a Cook's Tour. What are these so-called 'performances'? I thought he was supposed to be an artist?"

"He is."

"Then what does he do? Tell us. Describe it. Let us all share in it if it's so wonderful."

Brian felt a pit open up with this question; he had not rehearsed this bit even though he knew vaguely what the performances were about from a garbled version Ronnie Oliver had told him. Damage limitation time, he thought.

"Putting a performance into words is not really going to do anything to convince you easily. It's like describing any stage performance or a painting or a poem. Those sort of things have to be experienced at first hand to carry conviction."

"Haha!" said the Rector triumphantly. "I thought so. Put any of this stuff under the microscope and it..."

"However, I'll try my best," Brian interrupted, sensing the Rector building a bridgehead. "Always remembering I'm having to rely on my own - and, of course, your - imaginations."

The Rector settled back to enjoy Brian's discomfiture.

"Oh, we all have vivid imaginations here, Dr. Mather," he said. "Although, no doubt, not as fertile at covering our tracks as you artists seem to have."

Crude but effective, thought Brian. He noted in passing that he was now thoroughly tarred with the same brush as his colleagues.

"Well, Ostrowski's theme - incidentally he does these performances usually in tandem with his wife - was a sort of post-feminist, deconstructionist one."

"What on earth does that mean?" said the Rector.

"Generally pro-male or at least anti gender-bias."

The Rector gave a sigh of exasperation. "Go on. Perhaps somebody else here understands what you're talking about," he said.

"It was based partly on his nickname with the students, Vlad the Impaler, and partly on the form of a fifteenth century painting by Antonello da Messina of the Martyrdom of Saint Sebastian."

"Who?"

"Saint Sebastian. You must know it. Very popular Italian Renaissance subject. The one who was filled with arrows. No? Derek Jarman made a very interesting film on the theme. No? There's a wonderfully gruesome one in the V and A."

"Is there? And what did he do with this Sebastian person?"

"Well, in the original picture while he is being filled with arrows, the saint is tied rather nonchalantly against his execution post as though he's waiting for a number 11 bus."

The staff laughed gratefully at this, the first light note of the afternoon. The Rector tapped irritably for silence.

"I suppose the artist wanted to suggest his indifference to suffer..."

"Yes, yes, never mind what some Eyetie dauber was after in fifteen hundred and something, get on with it."

"Fourteen hundred and something. He was of the Quattrocento not..."

"Will you get on with it."

"So Vlad..."

"Who?"

"Wladimir. That's his name. He set himself up in the same position but against a bus stop sign, and dressed as if he was going to the office with a brief case, suit and homburg hat. Then his wife, in her underwear, stood and shot arrows into him from a special crossbow he had made. Except the arrows were larger-than-life knives and forks made of light wood so he finished up looking like a porcupine. Of course, the suit and cutlery were special so they would stick. And there was a sound track of orgasmic noises and popular love songs à la Dennis Potter. Then a bus came along and he got into it. All the other men on the bus were also like porcupines as well - these were locals, extras, of course. Then he invited couples to borrow the suit and crossbow and have a go. It was very popular at the Karlovy Vary festival and others and most of the injuries proved not to be too serious. I believe there was a scheme to adapt it as an encounter therapy for marital problems at one place apparently, but they couldn't guarantee that something more lethal might not be substituted."

Brian sat back as he finished. At first there was a stunned silence then a slight chuckling began from well down the table away from the Rector, who was looking at Brian as though at a being from another planet. The chuckles swelled and soon the room was rocking with laughter. Even the Education rep, who had identified completely with Saint Sebastian throughout, managed the ghost of a smile.

The Rector tapped for silence but the laughter drowned it out. He rapped with his knuckles, also to no effect. Finally, there being no gavel to hand, he slipped off a shoe and hammered the table with it. Ah yes, of course - and the subtlety of Nikita Krushchev; he'd missed that.

When some semblance of decorum had finally been restored, the Rector looked at Brian and was about to speak.

"Shall I minute this as well, Rector?" asked the Admin. Officer mildly.

"Don't be ridiculous. The governors read this stuff. I have no desire to try explaining something like this to Huggett." He turned again to Brian. "And this is what you call modern art, is it?"

Brian shrugged. "It's a well-established genre for which Ostrowski has quite a reputation

"And people actually pay him to do this stuff?"

"Yes, indeed," said Brian. "Often handsomely. Wladimir has no difficulty gaining sponsorship. This one was supported by a well-known cider company, I believe. Although they wanted him to use a longbow - too inaccurate and not historically correct anyway."

The laughter at this was quelled by a single bang from the Rector's shoe. He stared round the table at them as he replaced it on his foot menacingly.

"And that's another thing," said the Rector, "money. I'm glad you brought that up."

Damn! thought Brian. Tactical error in a war of attrition.

The Rector suddenly lunged forward and pointed at Brian.

"I know what goes on at that art college, you can't fool me - people using the Polytechnic's time and equipment to produce stuff to make money. Look at that chap last night, what's his name, Bonetti - God, are they all foreigners? - look at those prices. Do we see any of that? Does he pay us for the use of our property? Not a penny piece."

"Mr. Bonetti has his own equipment and materials in his studio. And that's true of the other staff as well. The Faculty equipment is far too much in demand by students for it to be of any use to staff - some of it would not produce the quality they demand, in any case.

Here, the Rector's judgement slipped as his tactics in turn faltered. It had been a long meeting.

"But they still use our time, don't they? And that's money. Well, in future, the Polytechnic's going to get its share."

Brian seized on it immediately to open up a new front.

"Yes, Mr. de Vere has explained that to us. Incidentally, as I am in the process of writing a book, I suppose the rule of one half to the Polytechnic will apply to royalties as well? And, of course, there's consultancy fees to be considered."

No speech before Harfleur could have had a more electric effect. As one man, the staff sat up straight as their sinews stiffened; this was the first they had heard of the new ruling. "Could you explain that remark, Rector?" said the Head of Engineering, much less mildly than his wont. (His consultancy fees were legendary.)

For the first time, the Rector was flustered.

"It's - er - a proposal by the Governors." he said. (Lying hound, thought Brian.) "We'll leave discussion of that to some other occasion.

We're here to deal with 'Blue Skies', not that."

"Do I understand," said Bill Johnson, who had been enjoying Brian's own martyrdom more than most, "that we will be expected to pay a fat chunk of our fees to the Polytechnic in future? Will this be before or after taxation puts the bite on it?"

"I said we'll discuss it at some other time. Not now!"

So far the meeting had been indifferent as far as the fate of the Faculty of Art and Design was concerned. Many of the scientists and engineers shared the Rector's prejudice and had enjoyed his attack. But the thought that somebody should touch their hard-earned fees with which they supported their continental holidays, fuel-injected cars and, even more vitally, their mortgages produced a wholesale defection to Brian's side. The Rector sensed a new topic was called for quickly.

"I see you people have also applied to us for money to support some hare-brained community art scheme. What is it?" He turned to the two sheets Brian had circulated. "A 'Heritage Trail' - whatever that is."

"Yes indeed." Brian switched quickly to a young enthusiast mode. "It's based on a proposal I came across made by the local council a few years ago but not followed up for lack of funds. The idea would be to mark the trail with art works produced by us with the active participation of the local inhabitants and businesses - murals, sculptures and so on - emphasising those qualities which distinguish the various locations historically. Brindling has quite a few of these important sites, as you are probably aware - industrial firsts and so on. The regional arts organisation is keen to support it as part of their grass-roots initiative and could put up half the money if we can come up with a few thousand."

It was clear the Rector had dismissed this proposal without studying it, confident that the committee would not countenance any precious reserves being expended on it. Brian had included a map and, for the first time, the Rector noted where in detail the trail went.

"Hold on. This goes right through the 'Tofts.'"

"A very important location, the 'Tofts'. One of the few major works by Russell Brown, a seminal influence on the early modern movement between the wars and native to Brindling. He was part of the MARS group later, but was killed at Dunkirk before he really got into his stride, so this is one of the only major examples of his work. And almost entirely untouched - a real time capsule. Definitely significant. They've just been spot- listed Grade II, I believe."

"They've WHAT?" shouted the Rector. The staff stared at him in amazement. "When?"

"Oh, the other day," said Brian vaguely.

"How do you know this?" the Rector demanded.

"A friend of mine in the Department of Environment told me. Of course, they'll need sensitive revitalisation but that's no barrier to this proposal. I believe the local authority is already doing something of the kind." If you can call screwing the tenants and milking the Council that, he thought.

The Rector's fury could find no adequate means of expression. The silence in the room was broken only by his deep breathing as his face slowly reddened. He reached into a waistcoat pocket and took something from it. He put his hands below the table level and there was the pop of an opening pill container. Whatever he took out he put quickly into his mouth and washed it down with his now stone-cold tea. Before he had chance to recover fully, Brian pressed on.

"Incidentally," he said, "on the matter of funds. In making my trawl through the Departmental staff I calculated that external funding for their activity in the form of exhibition grants, commissions for public works and so on lies somewhere between 22 and 26 thousand for last year alone."

"Pounds?" said a voice incredulously.

"Pounds - although some foreign commissions do vary with exchange rates, naturally. I was very surprised to see that this was not incorporated into the Polytechnic submission to the national research funding body grossing its external funding for research and consultancy."

"How much?" said the Dean of Humanities disbelievingly. (He was embarrassingly hard-pressed to massage his total into the hundreds.)

"Well, that is a rough guide for the moment, of course, but between those figures 22 and 26K certainly. One contract alone for a sculpture garden at a major music college ran to 11K."

"What did they do that cost that much, for God's sake?" said another member.

"Er. I believe it was for the recreation of mediaeval minstrel figures based on some at Beverley Minster. Sort of musical garden gnomes."

"Jesus," said another voice, quietly.

"Of course, it couldn't be guaranteed to run at that level year on year but, as far as I can tell, it is usually pretty substantial. But perhaps this committee may have a policy I am not aware of in ignoring these monies. However, I would have thought it was something the Poly might like to swell its return. Still, if our research is not to be included in 'Blue Skies' perhaps it would be better if it were left out of future returns, after all." He thought he might have gone a bit far in his use of the subjunctive there but apparently not.

The Professor of Engineering spoke up, looking directly and very seriously at the Rector's face, now slowly returning to its normal colour.

"Well, speaking for myself, Rector, I think Dr. Mather has made out a reasonable - and if I may say so, entertaining - case for inclusion of the activities of the staff in his Faculty in this year's 'Blue Skies'. We don't want to be the odd one out in the national picture not doing it. And we should certainly take account of the external funds. Perhaps the awards sub-committee could consider the community art proposal which seems good for our own PR at least."

"And that is what you think, is it?" said the Rector pugnaciously.

"Yes," he said firmly, and equally determinedly went on: "And perhaps we might fix a date now for a future meeting when we could discuss this matter of sharing fees etc. with the Polytechnic - when we've had an actual sight of the Governors' minutes, of course." (The unloading of his own devices onto the Governors was by now a perfectly familiar Rectorial tactic to senior staff.)

The Admin. Officer opened his diary.

"June the tenth seems fairly free, Rector."

The Rector glared at him and he closed his diary hastily. He then glared at the stony faces of the staff. (Not a bad subject for one of those terrible, Russian, socialist-realist group portraits, thought Brian, looking round: 'The Deviationist is Unmasked in the Brindling Soviet.') The Rector could see no allies. He stood up. His chair shrieked.

"Fetch those papers with you," he said to the Admin. Officer curtly. He gave Brian a last venomous look but Brian's innocent expression betrayed nothing of what he was feeling. He watched the Rector's retreating figure and mentally registered that his backside-indignation quotient was off the top of the scale set so far by Noel de Vere. Without waiting for the Admin. Officer, Dr. Robson slammed the door after him, managing to translate all his frustration and anger into the noise. The sudden shock caused Brian's elation to plummet and he had a brief unpleasant vision of himself in twenty years time retreating similarly from a room followed by the silent contumely of his staff. Christ, he thought for the first time since he had taken the job, what was happening to him? Was Louie right? Was he becoming as big a prick himself? The nods and smiles of amused approval from some of the staff following the Rector simply made him depressed. He knew the taste of victory made ashes in the mouth.

Just so, just so.

Chapter Twelve
The Art of Survival

"Hey, Peter. Come in here and have a look at these."

Peter had been mooching along the top corridor past Brian's office in search of one of his students, now lost in the confusion of exhibition spaces being noisily erected by finalists for their 'Dip.Shows'. Brian had noted that in the Department, final shows were still called that by students and most staff, even though B.A. had replaced the Diploma long ago. He wondered whether this was just a sign of cussedness or possibly genuine moribund thinking. The CNAA might have had a real point about 'relevance' after all.

Brian, not involved himself in the marking of student studio work, marvelled at the levels of emotional fireworks he saw as the show preparations had progressed. Hysteria and tempers flared as students and staff fought a dogged trench war over the allocation of spaces. Here the emollient personality of Louie was invaluable. (Brian was relieved that de Vere was conspicuously elusive. Whenever spotted he seemed to be permanently immured behind his shades, conducting mumbled arguments with himself about the visit or making his peculiar hissing noise and clawing at anybody who approached him.) Students - and staff - who had forsworn excess alcohol, smoking or any other harmful solace, reneged. Sexual liaisons which had been stable, some formed from year one, broke apart under the pressure, especially where the partners suspected there might be a differential in the grading between them.

Brian realised, as the preparatory two weeks wore on, that he had gained a completely false impression of how the students actually viewed their degrees from their often-stated contempt for 'bits of paper'. Already, the unity of the Fartoff Solidarity Front had fallen apart under the pressure, and even the Fartistas themselves had lost their cohesion.

Ronnie had gone back to the 'cuckoo nest' for a spell, the loss of his tape having destabilised him again, making dire threats of what he would do at finals time. His space was empty so far. (Wladimir had given in to an atavistic East European gloom.) Patience and Alex were not speaking. Bridget openly went to Protestant church services wearing a Republican badge, although, as she told Brian when he suggested this might not be a good idea, her visits were largely to avoid the attentions of the Polytechnic nun, appointed by the diocese to oversee the morals of Catholic, especially Irish, women students. (This hell fire and brimstone zealot, whose piercing eye had already intimidated Brian into the purchase of several raffle tickets for a trip to Lourdes on three separate encounters with her, had become even more of a pest when she heard that a male model was to be employed in the life room, the home of sin in her eyes.) Brian guessed also that Bridget might be defiantly hedging her bets. If she were hauled in to the police station again, she had good grounds for appeal, although from Peter's comments she had no cause for anxiety. (And, in any case, the congregations of the local churches were so sympathetic and kind, there was no way they would ever shop her. Bridget's view of the English was thus under severe test.) Alex Uruski complained constantly to Louie about his ban from building sites and also threatened an immediate appeal if his degree was not up to scratch. Shaheen was embarrassingly plagued by her father, the hospital consultant, who had arrived unasked to help and was never out of Louie's office. The way Louie dealt with him, patiently but firmly not giving an inch but seeming to concede all, led Brian to think that in this stage of the year, Louie fully justified all his salary. (Brian himself, as well as other staff and students, tried to be on hand when these confrontations took place. The noisy combination of the fractured English of the pair - and their particular brands of ethnic semaphore - lightened everybody's burdens at this tense time. Shaheen herself was simply mortified.) With his staff almost as paranoid about the fate of their tutorial charges as about the imminent visit, Brian reflected that Louie could probably have run the UN if called on. And of Connie, there was still no sign.

Her space was finished first, although she must have prepared it out of hours as nobody saw her doing it: bare white walls in which nothing would be hung until the marking period. Brian had visited it often and made too-obviously casual enquiries of other students about her. They smiled to each other knowingly but could not help him. He had ventured into the docklands but she was never on her boat and, in any case, he had no wish to hang around in that area and he could get no response through the phone. Her gallery painting was long completed but heavily covered and still nobody knew its subject, not even de Vere whose defences, in one of his more lucid moments, Brian had penetrated to ask about her. The only clue he had came from Bernie Rodenstein who said vaguely that she might have gone to meet her father in London. In all this hubbub, Brian, having written up his new course proposal and research report for the visit - including the idea of a heritage trail, now fully approved by the Poly and endorsed by the Council - was at a bit of a loose end.

This was further compounded by Oswald Spiller, who had thoroughly wakened from his four-year slumber. He bustled round the place, whistling and humming cheerfully to himself and usually in the company of Dorothea and Ridley's dogs. As Brian had already found, his student records were impeccable and when it came to returning marks, grades and summaries of student qualities there was little for Brian to add. However, Spiller was not completely out of the wood yet, Brian guessed, in that not all his eccentricities had quite disappeared. He had installed three clocks in the office which he meticulously kept to time, and he retained his little tent at the ready, blowing it up in the park occasionally to test the repairs. Also, when Brian tentatively asked how his wife was keeping, he smirked - an almost permanent expression with him now and one which Brian found increasingly irritating; something would have to be done about housing him elsewhere - and said merely she had foregone some of her Council work, and was no longer Chair of the Environmental Resources sub-Committee. She had become active instead in the newly-formed residents' forum for the restoration of the 'Tofts'. Brian suspected immediately that this must be some new rip-off scheme devised by Huggett to compensate for the loss of the Poly expansion, but Spiller also let Brian know, with ill-concealed triumph, that he and Charlie Huggett had "come to an understanding" about certain matters in connection with his wife's former Council work. Brian was mystified as to how he had achieved these ends and when he enquired further all he got was a triumphant smirk and a "Tick, tock. Tick, tock," but he did add " - went the bomb.".

So it was that Brian, with time to spare, had been out plotting the detail of the Heritage Trail when he met Renee again and had invited her to bring in samples of the work she had made much of at Louie's private view. It was these, now piled on his desk, he wanted Peter to see. Peter recognised her without difficulty and grunted a greeting; Renee was not easy to forget. Her hair style alone was a challenge to experience. She was dressed today in what was very probably her best, Brian guessed, a bright pink model suit - courtesy of somebody's wedding via Brindling Social Services, no doubt - and shod in calf-length, surplus, German army field boots, much favoured lately over 'Doc Martens', Brian had noticed, by the students of both sexes.

"We'd be really glad of your opinion," said Brian, leading Peter Orrd over to the desk on which Renee's work was piled.

Peter slowly turned over the cartridge-size sheets - mostly cut from plain wallpaper rolls - while Renee and Brian watched him carefully. The sheets were "drawerings" in all kinds of medium: pencil, ink, charcoal, colour wash, pastels and poster paint of the life and people of the 'Tofts'. Each drawing occupied the full sheet, to the furthest corner of vision. Brian himself had been stunned at the maturity of the handling of space and form in the drawings but he had given nothing away to Renee until they had been seen by someone with more certain knowledge of quality than himself. The techniques used varied widely from drawing to drawing as though Renee had been setting herself difficult artistic problems to be solved. Some were done entirely in tone, some used line only, some were night scenes, some were on the edge of abstraction as the forms, such as those of people in action, were resolved only by colour values.

"How many are there?" said Brian to relieve the tension he could feel in Renee - and the excitement in himself as well - as Peter worked through the pile giving no sign of how he felt about them. Occasionally, he removed his glasses to look more closely at a drawing but they could get no clue as to how he rated them.

"I only fetched about thirty," she said. "There's about the same again at home, like."

"How on earth did you get them here? They must weigh a ton."

"'Morrisons' supermarket trolley," she said. "It's alright, I didn't pinch it, I put my fifty pee deposit in. Hey, I 'ope nobody else pinches it, though. I need that fifty pee for our kid's chips. I put a lock and chain on it to the front door and left a note that I was seeing you, like."

Brian said nothing further and Peter drew to the end of his inspection.

"Hmph," he said, as he straightened. They waited for more. "What artists have you looked at?" he said to Renee.

She was bewildered by the question and looked at Brian.

"I think Peter wants to know whether you've followed any other artists and how they used the same kind of medium or tackled similar subjects."

"Naw, I 'aven't got time to look at books and stuff, like. Them's just all mine. Mind you, we did look at masses of stuff when we did 'O' level, like. She was a real good teacher that one, but I've forgotten the names now of who did 'em. What I want to know is if they're any good. Not that I care much what you say if you don't think so," she said with a defiant sniff, "'cos I'll still go on doing 'em anyway.".

"Are they all on this scale?" said Peter.

"Eh?" she said.

"Are they all this size?"

"Naw, I do little 'uns as well, like," said Renee. "Thems the ones I give away, and I swop 'em sometimes with Archie at the pub, like, for the odd gin and tonic."

Brian suddenly recalled that, as he had stood in the pub in his terrifying trilby, behind the bar and pinned round the walls, the coloured ones framed, were numerous examples of what he now realised must be Renee's art work. He was in such a nervous state at the reaction he had caused that he had had no time to look at them properly. Archie must have his head screwed on, he thought.

"Well, if I were you," said Peter seriously, looking directly at her, "I wouldn't give any more away and they could be worth a lot more to you than the odd gin and tonic eventually."

Brian knew from the unaccustomed clarity of Peter's diction that he had been impressed. Renee rubbed her hand across her shaven head, her expression a mixture of pleasure and doubt.

"So you think they're ok, like?"

"Of course, they're a bit unrefined but..."

He was interrupted by the crashing open of the door. Noel de Vere stood dramatically in the doorway. His clothes were dishevelled and dusty, he had sticking plaster on both hands and one of the lenses of his prized shades was cracked.

"Is that fucking supermarket trolley anything to do with you, Mather?" he shouted. "I nearly broke my bloody neck on it."

"Naw, it's mine," said Renee pugnaciously. "Want to make owt of it? You should look where yer going. And mind yer effing language when there's ladies present."

Brian realised that Renee was shocked by de Vere's outburst; this was not what she expected of educated people. He also knew that in his present distracted state, de Vere rarely saw anything much of the world around him, especially not supermarket trolleys popping out of the college steps to snare him.

"I'm sorry," he said grudgingly. "But that trolley is outwith the Health and Safety arrangements we have here." Brian sighed when he thought of the polyspeak to come in two weeks time. "I'm surprised a member of the cleaning staff wouldn't know that."

Renee bridled.

"Yer cheeky bugger," she said. "Not that there's owt wrong wi' being a cleaner except yer get tret like dirt by people like you." She moved towards him clenching her fists.

De Vere backed away hastily from this booted pink apparition. A puzzled expression crossed his face as he took in her appearance. He prided himself on knowing every member of the student body, but he was sure Renee was not one of them. Anybody else, especially one who spoke like Renee he assumed was an employee and these he never distinguished. Brian reflected that outside the category of 'artist', Noel de Vere was at heart a snob.

"Look," he said, from a safe distance in the corridor, "who are you? Are you a student here or what?"

"No, I'm not," she said. "And if you're owt to go by not likely to be neither. Even the Social don't talk to you like that."

During all this, Peter has resumed his study of the drawings oblivious of de Vere. He looked up.

"Noel, here. Have a look at these."

Gingerly, Noel entered the room, taking care in its narrow confines to give Renee a wide berth. She watched him, her tiny fists still clenched tightly, but relaxed slightly as Brian briefly filled in the details of how Renee came to be there and how she had done the drawings at home. Peter picked out some sheets and they pored over them together. Noel removed his damaged shades the purpose so Brian guessed he was taking Renee's drawings seriously. Occasionally, he pointed to details and they looked at them closely making slight concurring noises and low-toned conversation. With their heads together over the sheets Brian caught only fragments, most of them technical, some of them mentioning artists' names, the German expressionists featuring in the bits he did catch.

Renee moved to Brian, nodding her head towards Noel.

"Who's that?" she mouthed.

"The boss," he mouthed back.

She grimaced and made two circles round her eyes. Brian nodded agreement that the state Noel's eyes had reached was indeed pretty awful. She then looked at Brian speculatively, her head on one side. She was probably wondering whether Noel's mode of address to his staff was habitually as rude, Brian thought. Perhaps she felt that this rarefied world of Higher Education was not so far removed from the 'Tofts' after all.

Eventually, Noel and Peter looked up. Noel's expression was now, like Peter's, professional and had some of the respect due to a fellow practitioner. And his eyes seemed to have lost some of their strain. Brian marvelled at how the artistic sensibilities of two such different people as Noel and Peter could dissolve their habitual antagonism so quickly when faced with the genuine creative article. They were real pros.

"Have you ever thought of pursuing a serious study of art?" Noel said.

"Not until I met the grim Reaper the other day, like. If she can do it anybody can."

They looked at Brian.

"Renee means Audrey Reaper. She met her at Louie's show."

"Ah. That reminds me," said de Vere. "Did you see her as I asked you to?"

Christ! he thought.

"Er." Before he could think of a reply, Renee broke in.

"And Brian asked me to fetch my stuff in, like, to see what you think. 'Ow much would it cost, like?"

"We can come to some arrangement about that later. But I think Peter would agree with me that you ought to do something with your talent. I think we both see that you've got a lot of potential. The degree course is not beyond you, you know. In fact, I could wish that some of those portfolios being set out now could have this level of intensity."

"Definitely the business, these," said Peter.

"Degree course?" said Renee. "I'm too old for that, like, I'd be with all them kids."

De Vere looked her up and down. "Oh, I think you'd fit in quite well - and we have mature students on our course much older than you. Some of them are actually pensioners, in fact. It would be a good idea to start with our new Certificate course in extra-mural first, though, to widen your horizons. You need a Foundation experience to develop your ideas and make progress."

Renee was cautious.

"You're not just saying this, like, are you?" she said suspiciously.

It was now de Vere's turn to be offended.

"If I say you've got potential, you've got potential! You've got decades of experience talking to you here."

Brian had a sudden idea.

"Look," he said, "I've been thinking." (He had to stop this massaging of reality; it was getting to be addictive.) "The 'Tofts' have just been listed and are going to go through major changes. Renee's drawings will be important as a record if nothing else. And from what you've said they're much better than just documentation and probably exhibitable to a wider public. How would it be if we organised a show for them. In the 'Tofts' or the Art Centre or the Civic Centre or better still our own gallery. We've got those movable screens. 'Renee's Tofts' or 'Farewell, the Tofts' or something. It could be the first shot in the Heritage Trail idea. There's loads of them in the pub there. We could include those as well. Wouldn't it be a bit of a coup? And if we got it set out by CNAA time it would show that relevance is our middle name. We could get Huggett to open it - or even the Rector. Or both of them. At the same time as Connie's ceiling. Good for PR." And good for nailing the lid down on the scheming of the Ad Hoc Poly Development Working Party as well! Brian still suspected that they had not finished with the 'Tofts' yet, in spite of Spiller's smirk of triumph.

De Vere looked at him thoughtfully. "What do you say, Peter?"

Good Lord, thought Brian, he was almost normal; he asked Peter's opinion.

"Why not. They're up to snuff. I bet some of the visiting party'll wish they could dig up students like this in their own back yard when they clock them. And it might give that bastard Evans something to stick in his pipe and smoke. He thinks the only artistic integrity left in the world is in Wales."

"We can't claim any credit for teaching her, though," said de Vere.

"No," said Brian, "but we can claim credit for encouraging her. How would you feel about that, Renee?"

"Has Audrey Reaper ever had owt like this, like?"

"No, of course not," said de Vere.

"Then it's ok by me. Can I sell stuff, like.?" Brian saw that Louie's prices still dazzled.

"They are yours," said Noel, shrugging.

"How much should I ask, like?"

"Well, we can discuss all that later, like..er.." (Brian suppressed a smile as Noel shook off Renee's cadences.) "Look, can we leave it to you to organise it, Brian? We'll select the pictures later. We're a bit busy at the moment - as you are no doubt aware." The remark, to Brian's surprise, let him know that Noel, in spite of his apparent distracted state had registered that Brian was much less vitally occupied than his colleagues at this critical stage of the year. "Perhaps you'd like to have a short chat before you go, Mrs. - er - sorry, I don't know your name."

"Renee Jewitt."

"Mrs. Jewitt."

"Ms," said Renee.

"If you'll bring your stuff along to my office we'll have a talk. It'll be your first tutorial. Perhaps I can suggest some things you could be getting on with before you start."

"Can't I 'ave Brian as my teacher like the grim Reaper?"

"This isn't Brian's field."

Brian could see that Noel was not about to let go somebody with Renee's talent, especially as there was the possibility of working a Pygmalion coup in the relevance stakes.

"Right, then," said Renee. She turned to Brian. Her face was shining with pleasure and she gave her raucous laugh. He saw Noel wince; that was something else he would have to get used to if he was taking her on. Renee was breathing deeply with pride in herself. It was obviously the best thing that had happened to her in a long time. Suddenly, she lunged at Brian, grabbed him round the neck and kissed him noisily.

"Thanks a bunch, Brian," she said. "I knew I could do it if I could only get here, like. If I see the grim Reaper, I'll be laughing teacakes now, eh?"

She turned to gather up her drawings with Peter's help.

Noel looked at Brian, who was trying to control the wince of pain from the effect of Renee's army boots on his toes, but he did catch Noel's speculative expression before the cracked shades were replaced.

"What is it with you, Mather?" he said in a fierce undertone. "The model, sniffing round Connie Grey, now this. And now I think of it, that Reaper woman had more than intellectual intercourse in her eye rabbiting on about having you for her tutor. You're the talk of the town, did you know that? You've only been here five minutes, for Christ's sake. You'll be going round the place with a permanent hard-on next, like that crazy poet. Are you training up for the dickathlon in the sexual Olympics or what?"

Brian made a gesture of perplexity.

"Hmm," said Noel. "Perhaps it's not such a good idea that you should tutor Mrs. Reaper after all. I'll think of somebody else. Laurie Willoughby should damp her fires a bit. Perhaps you would let them know as I'm - er - a bit busy at present."

Chicken, thought Brian, but he did feel considerably relieved nevertheless, especially as it got him off the hook of omitting to sample her seed cake. However, his elation was dashed as Noel continued: "And since you seem to have so much time on your hands and get on so well with the natives, you can take charge of administering the Extra-Mural Certificate. Get the stuff from Myra and get it written up properly for the visit. From now on you're Mr. Extra-Relevant-Mural."

Extra-Mural! The Siberia of Brindling! Thirty degrees below Foundation! The last stop of inadequate teachers before the exit sign! Was demotion staring him in the face? Blast! Another bit of instant micro-wave thinking; de Vere didn't so much work off the top of his head as the crack in his backside. He saw Peter, who had caught de Vere's edict, grinning broadly at him

"But I'm not an artist," he pleaded. "How can I run an art qualification? What credibility will it have if I'm in charge?"

"Credibility these days is in management, not creativity, kiddo. You, of all people, should know that by now. And you're the cleverclogs with the words and numbers, aren't you? Ok, use them. Develop the sodding thing. Blind the buggers with science. We want to build up our community links. Oh, and by the by, that performance of yours at the Research Committee the other day has got you talked about as well. And the Department. Everyone I meet in the Poly wants to tell me about it."

Oh Lord, thought Brian, who had been wondering for days what de Vere's attitude would be to what had happened. He could get no clue now from behind the shades; was this Extra-Mural sentence his punishment? Noel abruptly nodded at him. "If you can speak to those woodentops and convince them, you should have no problem. It worked this time but don't push it, that's all." He sniffed. "At least they gave us the money."

Brian realised that this, the first time he had mentioned it, was the nearest de Vere could get in his present paranoid state to handing out approval to him. Brian's unearthing of Renee had obviously cleared a few of the doubts his Head of Department had built up about his performance. His heart gave a leap of pleasure; Renee, you beauty, I love you. There might be a future with the artists for him after all. Mr. Extra-Relevant-Mural! You never know, it could be a sort of power base.

When they had all gone Brian went off to the office with a light step to write a note to Audrey Reaper. He still wondered if it had been she who had got him home that night. She had her own car, he knew, and lived not too far from there. Would she have had the bedding cleaned as well? (It had turned up from a laundry two days later.) It was this suspicion that it might have been her that had made him - he admitted it to himself now - avoid the tutorial. His speculations were interrupted as he reached the ground floor and met Dr. Marshall coming in. Brian still felt guilty about Marshall, and had been avoiding him since his discharge from hospital. He had glimpsed him in the distance occasionally, still sporting his head bandage for a while when he came to pick up Rita, and had blessed the nature of the building which had allowed him until now to escape a direct confrontation with him.

"Odd place for a trolley. Is the lock and chain an artistic statement about consumerism, do you think?" Marshall said by way of greeting.

Brian thought he might be catching the drift of life in an art college. "Could we have a quick word, Brian? I've been meaning to for a while."

Brian's heart sank. "Of course."

"In your room, perhaps," said Marshall. Damn, it was likely to be a serious quick word.

On the way, Brian expressed his sympathy at the attack and enquired if he was fully recovered. "Just so, just so," was Marshall's response. Brian added alarm to his forebodings. Marshall also said that he hoped to be out on the squash court again soon, although he seemed to have less time for that now. I'll bet you have, thought Brian, with Rita to see to. When they reached the second floor, Rita herself came along the corridor evidently on her way to meet Marshall. They greeted each other with warm smiles and squeezed hands. Brian was genuinely touched at the obvious affection they showed and he realised that he had got Marshall completely wrong; he might be a proper person and not a polycrat after all. Rita included Brian in her smile as well. Since Brian had persuaded Mike to employ a male model, Rita had fewer sessions in the life room and Brian had wondered how she might take to this. He had been ready to try and placate her, but with her new-found status as consort to the Deputy Rector, she had said she was glad to be out of it. And Philip wasn't too happy she should be doing it, anyway. She also no longer stripped at 'BoZo'Z'. Brian wondered what Huggett made of all this. To Brian's surprise, Marshall asked Rita to join them and they made their way with small talk to Brian's room.

Approaching along the top corridor, Brian was aware of a strange, high-pitched whining coming from his room. There seemed also to a low-pitched noise underlying it as well. Completely puzzled, he pushed open the door. As Ridley's two dogs switched their whining to delighted, aggressive barking, Brian pulled the door closed as they thumped against it. Not again, he thought. By opening the door suddenly, Brian had disturbed the dogs' hungry yearning at the scene being enacted in front of them by the two people in the office, Spiller and Dorothea, who were engaged in a passionate and noisily groaning embrace. He smiled uncertainly at Marshall and Rita and hoped - largely for Dorothea's sake - they had not seen what was going on. Marshall raised a quizzical eyebrow. Brian cleared his throat and laughed apologetically, but the dogs were silenced quickly at Spiller's command and in a few moments, the door opened.

"Sorry about that," said Spiller. "They're a bit excitable today." With good cause, thought Brian.

When they entered the room, Dorothea was seated demurely in front of the desk holding an essay - upside down, Brian observed. Her training in dodging matron for a quick embrace in the dispensary had stood her in good stead, evidently. The dogs sniffed the newcomers suspiciously, especially Brian, whose trousers they recognised as a bit of unfinished business.

"Could you excuse us?" said Marshall to Dorothea.

"Of course. I think we were nearly finished, weren't we, Dr. Spiller?" More like just getting going, thought Brian.

"Do you want the office?" said Spiller. "I'll leave you... "

"Could you stay as well, please," said Marshall firmly. "It's fortunate that I've caught you like this." Spiller looked terrified and Dorothea coughed nervously. "I needed to talk to you as I have, apparently, had no response to my notes to you."

Marshall's business-like tone reassured Dorothea but, when she looked for confirmation of safety from Spiller, Brian saw that the man seemed to have become even more terrified.

"Er, yes, yes, I suppose so," said Spiller. "Could you see to these chaps, my de...er, Miss Mullholland?"

She looked greatly troubled as he abruptly ushered the dogs and her from the room. The former gave a final, longing sniff at Brian's trousers before they were all bundled into the corridor.

Marshall went to the window, leaned on the sill and looked out. Rita seated herself on the chair vacated by Dorothea. Brian perched on the desk. Spiller sat behind it and began fiddling compulsively with his clocks. While they waited for Marshall to begin, Brian and Rita exchanged puzzled glances. Eventually, Marshall turned from the window.

"I would like to make it clear in all that I'm about to say to you, that my first and foremost aim is to protect the good name of the Polytechnic. Not out of any consideration for your reputations nor indeed any of the staff or any other persons in this town but for the sake of its students, who have come to Brindling in good faith to further their education and have the right to expect the best from us. Perhaps you might like to put that clock down for a moment, Dr. Spiller."

Brian looked at Spiller who was gripping the clock with both hands and staring at the back of it with a mad intensity. There was no response from him. It struck Brian he might be hoping the hands could suddenly start whizzing round, and it might sprout wings like the plates in 'Through the Looking Glass', and fly him straight out of the window.

"I think he may need to do that," said Brian. "Don't worry, he is with us." And at least he can't retreat into his tent, thank God.

"Very well. You know him better than I do," said Marshall. He looked at Brian pityingly. "First, I would like to reassure you all that Inspector Forsythe, on behalf of the Chief Constable, and myself, have come to a gentleman's agreement about the consequences of any irregularities which have so far, or might in future, come to light in connection with the activities of a certain person. Always provided some essential conditions are fulfilled, that is."

Brian heard Rita draw in a deep, intense breath and realised that he had involuntarily done the same himself at the mention of Forsythe. Marshall did not look directly at either of them but kept his eyes on Spiller.

"As you are no doubt aware, Dr. Spiller, that person has cast a wide net in which the Polytechnic was only one component. For instance, the new police headquarters itself was erected using, shall we say, an obscure local contractor, as were the hospital extensions and alterations to the fire station and many smaller schemes - or 'scams' perhaps might be a more accurate description."

There was a dead silence in the room. They all stared at Spiller. They watched as his grip relaxed slowly on his clock and his head gradually lowered towards the table. His shoulders began to shake. He was crying. Brian glanced at Marshall who had not at all altered his dispassionate expression.

"They used me," sobbed Spiller. He reached embarrassedly into his pocket for his handkerchief. It had some pink stains on it Brian noticed, in spite of his astonishment at Spiller's break-down. Spiller wiped his eyes still with his head down.

"I imagine 'they' refers to your wife and her brother?" said Marshall. "Or were there others?"

They waited for his reply. "No. Just a lot of fools like me," he said, looking up at last. Brian saw that his face, beyond its woebegone state, had experienced a subtle transformation. It was now that of a normal sane man expressing relief. He must have been carrying this burden for years. No wonder he'd gone doolalley. But he still did not see how Spiller was involved.

"As company secretary and a director for these sham contractors, I understand you prepared and signed most of the papers. The bids etc. Is that right?"

"Yes," he said.

"I must congratulate you on doing an excellent job. They were most convincing and meticulously done. Forsythe has shown me some of them. But tell me, something really puzzled us. Why on earth did you use copperplate handwriting of all things?"

"It was a clue," said Spiller simply.

"I beg your pardon?"

"I thought if I used something so ridiculous someone would pick it up and be suspicious that all these different companies should use something so daft. Of course, those two just thought it looked classy and let me go on using it. But in this town, that's a lot to ask."

"Ah. I see. I think. You actually wanted to be caught out?"

"I just wanted it all to stop. I didn't care."

Marshall looked at him with a hint of pity.

"What about the other directors? There are more names than your own on the documents."

"They're all dead."

"I beg your pardon?"

"They're all dead."

"But they signed the documents."

"That's right."

Marshall looked at Brian who was equally nonplussed.

"He didn't..."

"Of course not. This is Brindling, not Hollywood."

"They were all in the hospice when they signed them." said Rita. "The poor old baskets."

Spiller looked briefly at Rita and looked away, shamefaced. Marshall looked at her, thoughtfully. Brian speculated as to what else she might not have told him.

"They were old party cronies of his," Spiller said bitterly. "Or lodge members. Honest men turned into criminals in the last days of their lives. Most of them trusted the snake. Even if they were well enough to...But there aren't too many like that. Alzheimer cases can sign their own name often. It was always for the good of the party or the town. He was instrumental in getting the hospice set up in the days before...It was one of the first in the country. It may even have given him the idea. And I'm sure he made plenty out of the contract. He got them to give him powers of executor for their involvement as well, so nothing appeared in their wills, the cunning...He deserves to be dropped in it. It really stinks. God knows what he would have done if they'd recovered. I wouldn't mind going down with him either. It'd be a blessed release."

"I agree that it is pretty nasty, but it hasn't come to that yet. Why didn't you go to the authorities?"

"You're fairly new here, aren't you?" Spiller said, looking levelly at Marshall. "And so is this Forsythe man. You have no idea how deep it all went. And with my name on everything, I was the - what is it? - the patsy. And when they started to get their claws into the Polytechnic four years ago I just couldn't take any more. Anyway, I told them a fortnight ago it was finished. I was having no more to do with it and if they went on I'd shop them - somehow or other. They said they'd have me put away if I tried. They've threatened that before. I suppose my behaviour over the last four years might give them grounds, it has been a little odd but this time I stuck to my guns. I wasn't having it any more. They said alright, they'd leave me alone if I just kept mum. They thought it might not be a good idea to try anything else anyway until the 'Tofts' thing went through." (I knew it, thought Brian.) "And they'd find somebody else and that was going to be the last."

"How on earth could you get involved in the first place, for goodness sake?" said Marshall.

"I believe you've met my wife," he said. Brian recalled her kicking his ribs and shuddered: the Lady Macbeth of Brindling.

Marshall turned again and looked out of the window.

"Yes. She wrote to me the other day, actually."

"What?" said Spiller, startled.

"Yes. Some nonsense about an invisible lecturer she wanted CNAA to know about. I put it down to too much strain from her civic duties and binned it." Spiller looked immensely relieved. Brian knew that it was as much to protect the Polytechnic from awkward questions as to save Spiller from retribution.

Still looking out of the window, Marshall said quietly: "And the money?"

"I never took a red cent. I wouldn't, even though they wanted me to. To get me in deeper. They thought I was genuinely slightly cracked anyway. Or even very cracked." He thought for a moment. "Which I probably was. It was only in a place like this I could survive."

"Yes," said Marshall. "I'm beginning to see that art has to take all sorts under its wing to function properly."

"And your wife?" he said, turning from the window.

Spiller shrugged and rubbed his handkerchief around his face. "She will have to speak for herself. We don't have a joint account, even. I have no idea about the money. All they wanted was somebody at one remove. And the council passed everything, you know. Legally and properly. So it goes much further than those two."

"I realise that," said Marshall. He took his gold propelling pencil from his pocket and clicked the lead in and out while he thought. He then looked directly at Brian. "In a way, that's good. It should make it easier to trace it all. Once we know how to follow it through the council data..." He broke off and was suddenly very brusque with Spiller. "Look, I want you to go to Forsythe today and tell him all you know. Will you do that?"

Spiller nodded. "What will happen?" he asked dumbly, and took up his clock once more. "Not that I care much."

"Don't go slack on me now." Marshall said sharply, replacing his pencil. Spiller responded and put the clock down. Its alarm suddenly went off, jangling all their nerves.

"Tsk, a bit slow, that one," said Spiller, silencing it and preparing to adjust it. Marshall took it away from him and handed it to Brian.

Marshall said slowly and emphatically. "You will definitely do what I ask you to, won't you?"

"Yes, yes, I'll do it," said Spiller. "Sorry about that. After four years it's a bit habit-forming."

Marshall leaned on the desk in front of him so he could not be distracted again.

"Forsythe will ask you to sign various documents as director and company secretary for these so-called contractors. You can do that as there seems nobody else to consult. I may say that at the moment he is interviewing your wife and her brother. The documents will authorise repayments to the authority or any others who have suffered. The amounts will be calculated when we've got exact details. There will also be a demand for the setting up of a trust to absorb the gains. It might even have the Huggett name. I know that sounds awful after what he's done but it's politic. In any case, there will be no doubt it will be used for the benefit of the people of the town, whose rates and taxes the money came from in the first place. And to anybody who knows, it's a nice poetic justice."

"How about community arts?" said Brian suddenly. "Their budget's suffered more cuts than most."

"We'll see about that when the time comes," said Marshall. His expression suggested to Brian that Marshall thought he had already worked this out from some prior knowledge he might have. There was a hint of suspicion as to Brian's motives before he turned again to Spiller. "And we'll try to keep it out of the press for all our sakes, although in this overgrown village, it won't be easy. Fortunately, we are not blessed with doorstepping journalists here and Forsythe is a very close man. Even that raid on 'BoZo'Z' wasn't reported, you know, as, shall we say - certain young people not a million miles from this room, had made the police look foolish. And, in any case, the editor and some senior police officers were caught up in it. The editor's a great crony of Huggett's through the usual connections which operate in this town." He glanced at Brian who guessed from his expression that the Fartistas might now be uncovered - and probably his involvement with them. He began to feel very, very nervous. Marshall stood back from the desk. "I think your wife is going to be quite poor very soon, by the way, Dr. Spiller." Brian noticed that Marshall's tone had a striking effect on the man. He coughed slightly and began to compose himself to match it. "But she will not be in gaol, at least."

"Knowing her, I would not be surprised if she preferred that to being poor," he said. "We're parting, anyway."

"I'm no marriage counsellor but that seems to me it might be a sound idea. How on earth did you come to marry...Well,no matter. My marriage was no great model." He looked at Brian. "So what we are dealing with here today, stays here with us. Is that clear?"

Spiller looked at Brian and Rita. "What the hell have they got to do with it, anyway?" he said. He looked suddenly angry that they should have witnessed his humiliation. It was another sign of his return to normality, Brian thought.

"What indeed?" said Marshall. "Have you anything to tell me?"

Rita looked at Brian for help. He picked up his briefcase and took out the print-outs and list of codes. It felt as though a ton weight was being lifted from his shoulders, but he began to sweat slightly, nevertheless.

"I don't know whether Forsythe has cracked this lot yet but it may help," he said. The relief was exquisite. "Shall I tell you how it all fits together?"

"That's for Inspector Forsythe to work out. The less we know, the better."

"How did you know that I had the information?" he said.

"I told him," said Rita, looking down as Brian handed them over. Brian could see that this simple statement was costing her a lot. She was obviously deeply anxious that it would not affect Marshall's relations with her. At best, he thought, it would remind Philip Marshall of who had preceded him. He hoped Marshall never enquired as to the precise circumstances under which she had got hold of the codes. He wondered how much she had told him about the Fartistas, her friends. "At least, I told Philip I gave the codes to you," she said, looking up at him. Her expression, with her face turned away now from Marshall, pleaded with him not to say more. Possibly not too much then, he thought.

She had stopped and tensed as Marshall moved to her. He put his hand gently on her shoulder and gripped it. She let out a deep breath and subsided on the chair again.

Marshall said to Brian with his hand still on her shoulder: "We'll look upon this material simply as having been obtained accidentally in the course of your researches into Brindling's recent history." He looked at the codes. Brian saw him start as he recognised the Einstein quotation. He flipped through the print-outs and read some of the material it had guarded. He looked at Brian.

"That secretary will definitely have to be transferred," he said. "I suppose you can see now why I was so anxious that the Polytechnic should be protected."

Brian nodded. "And for my part why I was so anxious that the Faculty should be protected," he said, looking straight into Marshall's eyes. For the first time his composure slipped a little.

"I don't think it would have happened as it appears here," he said, looking away.

"I wasn't to know that," said Brian.

"No. I see why you were pushing the Heritage Trail so much to the Research Committee as well. The Rector found that very hard to swallow."

"I can imagine," said Brian. "Does he know about this stuff?"

"No. I'll tell him about it when it's all cleared up. How he'll take it I have no idea. He may be a dupe but he's not a crook. Incidentally, he's threatening great ructions at your validation event."

"May you live in interesting times, as the Chinese curse has it," said Brian, drily. At least we haven't got to the stage of self-validation yet, he thought; CNAA still represented an outside judgement. If University status was ever obtained, God help us. Brian saw Marshall rub his head as he studied the print-outs and a momentary look of pain crossed his face.

"How do you think Huggett will react?" Brian said. He was thinking that the man was probably vindictive enough to get the baseball bats out again and this time make sure they landed on the right target. He wondered if Marshall knew he had stood in for him that night.

"I don't think he'll cause any trouble," said Rita with relish. She was now confident enough to mention Huggett in Marshall's presence. "I've got that tape. If anything happens that I don't like, it goes straight to the press. And not the local press either. And the photographs. And other things. He got very careless with bits of paper when he thought he could get away with it all the time." Brian wondered what they were. "I've told him that. His little game's finito."

"Very well," said Marshall, looking at her admiringly. Brian wondered what his intentions were. Marriage? A potential Rector with an ex-stripper wife? He'd be lucky to have her. How would she fare as a hostess to visiting dignitaries? She was a good actress after all, and, as most of them would be male, she would more likely to stimulate their testosterone than their critical faculties. And she had the brains for it, anyway. Terrific! Do them all good! He almost wished he was a bit older himself.

"Perhaps if Dr. Spiller and I could have a word together?" said Marshall, bringing the business with them to a close but at the same time bringing a grateful smile to Rita's face as he gave her shoulder another reassuring squeeze. Definitely not just another polycrat, thought Brian.

They left quickly. Once in the corridor, they both released their tension through blowing out their cheeks noisily.

"Christ!" said Brian. "That was the hairiest thing I've ever been involved in. You were marvellous, by the way. I presume you haven't shopped the students."

"No. Forsythe tracked down the raid through Betty Flynn but he thinks it was just Ronnie's idea and the others did it for a lark. The same with the posters. And thank you for not saying anything. God, do I need some fresh air," she said. Their feelings of relief prevented both of them discussing what had happened and they avoided each other's eyes.

However, before she hurried off down the stairs, Rita gave Brian a very affectionate kiss on his cheek. Brian watched her departing figure. Quite a lady, he thought, wiping away any lipstick traces. He jumped as Noel de Vere's angry roar rang out along the corridor behind him.

"Mather! I'm going to have you neutered if you persist in carrying on like this!"

Chapter Thirteen
Validation - or Valediction?

"Wharrisit, do you think?" said the old lady, adjusting her glasses and peering at the tatty sheet of paper fly-posted on the side of the building.

"Nay, I've got no idea," said her companion. "Some sort of machine. I never know what nowt is these days, there's that many new gadgets. Our Vera's kitchen's got that many it's like a bloomin' factory. You daresn't touch nowt for fear of your fingers. And they never tell you owt on these posters, neither. Just funny pictures like in them TV ads. You've got to be a scientist to work them out."

"Maybe it's some kind of tin opener, this. But what's all that fuzzy stuff above it?"

"No idea. Leave it be, Sadie, or we'll be late for the coach again. You know how mad that soft article 'Opalong gets if yer even a minute late."

They moved off and passed Brian, who was approaching from the opposite direction and had caught their loud conversation.

"I do wish 'e wouldn't wear that daft cowboy 'at on these trips. It makes everybody stare at yer. My Jack would 'ave been disgusted at that. I tell yer, 'e'd 'ave pulled that stupid thing off of 'is 'ead and chucked it in t' river before 'e'd 'ave gone anywhere with somebody like 'im. Eeh, I don't 'alf miss 'im. Did yer ever know 'Opalong's wife?"

"Eeh, what a life she 'ad wi' 'im, poor soul. I can tell yer..."

She lowered her voice and was out of earshot.

Glancing at the poster, he recognised the left-over relic of Fartista handiwork that had puzzled them. The building wall it was stuck to, the rear of the Masonic Hall, formed one side of an alleyway. (Brian liked to vary his routes for exercise and had not passed this way before.) He stopped for a moment and looked at it. The 'signature' had been weathered off but had it been there, it would have still not made much sense to the two curious friends, he thought. They would be innocent of any need for this sort of device with husbands like the sorely missed "Jack", rather than "that soft article 'Opalong".

He studied it, and thought how disappointed the Fartistas would have been at the little disturbance it conveyed to the general public. It brought back the events of the term, now nearly ended, in a rush. He realised that his life before Brindling art college, even when he had had a job, had been utterly prosaic. The rules which governed the way everybody else lived on the whole, he had almost forgotten. When he met other people beyond the fault-line he was sometimes hard-pressed to talk to them 'normally'. He was not uncomfortable about this, he felt, as he noticed it developing through his short time at Brindling. Now he had become more and more integral to the set-up and especially in his front-running, straight Poly wordsmith role, he had achieved results. He sensed that his colleagues listened increasingly to what he had to say where they needed to. He suddenly felt a warmth from that sense of freedom he had craved all his life. But it was chilled immediately as he sensed that it might be snatched away again. CNAA had arrived!

"You don't want to stare at that too long, chaw. Yer'll go blind."

The bin-man laughed as he passed Brian, pushing his rattling trolley.

Brian took a last glance at the poster. He felt a pang of deep sexual frustration; it had been a long, long term.

Making his way to his room, Brian went by and through the final show exhibits, set out in spaces silent of the usual morning bustle and noise of the art college now the marking period was nearly finished. Yet, to him, the college did not feel empty. The scores of paintings, sculptures, ceramics, graphic designs, photographs, prints and sundry installations were resonant with the babel of youthful energy. Some gave off sheer exuberance in the materials and techniques mastered over their time at Brindling. Others expressed a sensuous re-shaping of the world to their own ideas of how it should be through colour and form. In many, in tune with their times, there was a striving for a cool ironic wit and detachment in their expressions which contrasted with the overt, angry commitment of a few others, not only Fartistas, to a different future. Altogether, as he had watched the shows assemble with such fervent conviction, Brian had had a growing sense of how important this form of education could be. But also how dangerous it could seem to the grey men and their young fogey hangers-on to have a body of the energetic young cleaving to their own ideas of the world.

He didn't know whether other colleges had shows like this but doubted it from what staff had told him. Elsewhere, apparently, retrenchment was the order of the day: play safe and keep your head down. Plenty of painting and drawing, formally time-tabled and any real dedication to a discipline massaged out by management techniques like 'modularisation' i.e. a bit of this and a bit of that. Even the dreaded conceptualist minimalism was to be preferred to adventurous exploration along the frontiers. As Peter told it to Brian, one head of department actually encouraged it because it was so "ridiculously cheap, old boy" with the added advantage of keeping the students' attention away from agitation. He'd never had such a peaceful time. They were the blue-eyed boys in their Poly because their 'resource management' was so impeccable. Another head had advised Peter to select students with plenty of good 'A' levels. Most of them were so knackered by the effort, they preferred thinking about the philosophy of the subject rather than testing any ideas that had not been cauterised through academic work. It did you no harm in a Poly either, and they had a better chance of jobs at the end of it with nice fat portfolios of stuff everybody could see was 'art'. Peter had speculated gloomily to Brian that Brindling might be the place that fulfilled another Chinese proverb: 'The nail that sticks up invites the hammer'.

Brian, with this in mind and being excited by the shows he saw, thought how miraculous it was that Brindling had escaped the creeping sclerosis of the Eighties. And how vulnerable it all looked now with ominous rumblings of 'the educational market', 'management-led innovative initiatives' (or cut-backs and rationalisation) and original thought dissolved by invented jargon. He recalled also what had happened to his former college and how easily a perfectly good system had been ripped out root and branch for no better reason than money - and on that nobody had really done the sums. Governments that had been in too long, he thought, simply became meddlers, especially like this one when it had buggered up the economy on the altar of a dim but stridently-proclaimed ideology. God help us all in whatever lunatic mischief they might devise if they got back again. Still there was little chance of that, at least, thank goodness, after the poll tax fiasco.

He tried to cheer himself up by making his usual diversion via Connie's space, now adorned with extremely impressive work. Goodness knows when she had put them up; Brian had not seen her and de Vere would tell him nothing. She was his star. He let Brian know in the usual forthright manner he employed with him since recognising that Brian was less of the Mr. Relevant than he had thought, that, under no circumstances, would he encourage Brian's interest. After she had secured her first, he could shag her to his heart's content, but personally, he would give strong odds against his chances of even getting her shoes off never mind her knickers. (Brian did wonder whether this statement was based on more than simply his understanding of her psychology.)

Brian walked round her space drinking the works in again. They were big, sumptuously realised portraits, some of groups, some of individuals. Many of them were of her Fartista friends and some staff members. (Peter Orrd, set in his habitual place in the public bar, came over as a cross between Augustus John and Methuselah.) De Vere had told him that the starting point of her work had been her admiration for an interwar French painter, Christian Bérard, not particularly well-known in Britain. (Brian saw the connection now with her Thirties retro beach outfit. One of his best known pictures was a double portrait on a beach.) She had tracked down works by him in New York and Houston as well as some in private collections in France to clock him properly. De Vere said proudly that Hermione, with the external assessor's concurrence, had given her a really outstanding mark for her dissertation on Bérard. (No surprise to him, of course; he had supervised it!) "A pleasure to read," was the external's comment. Brian reflected, but was sensible enough not to say that, as art students were often notoriously semi-literate, it would not take much to make it so. But that was just sour grapes. He thought Hermione would be as professional about this as anything else. She had the reputation that her marks were rarely altered and never overgenerous.

But, considering her radical tendencies and leadership of her group, Brian was surprised at the conventionality of Connie's paintings. De Vere, in telling Brian about them, was clearly relieved about that. The other Fartistas had been far less hidebound and showed Brian clearly when he asked about her that they thought it was a cop-out.

Brian saw that all of them had taken the chance to make some sort of personal political statement. Bridget for instance, had managed to work Republican and Orange colours into virtually every savage and witty print, most of them proclaiming a plague on both their houses. She had even collaged and manipulated images to produce a Republican Ian Paisley welcoming the true disciples of Christ to Ireland's shores. (She told Brian that his lot believed some nonsense of the sort.) She also had a recorded sermon of his which played on a doctored tape-loop in her space. As her show was near his room, this was driving Brian mad, and he had taken to slipping into her space and switching it off. Alex's exploited workers installation had made good use of his photographs set amongst a sculpture of scaffold poles, earth and bricks and there were two large figures of Degnan and Huggett in their hole together, clasped in a fond embrace. Shaheen, also on the same corridor as Brian, had a beautiful feminist installation of an Asian marriage of a child bride to a male figure derived from a pound sign. (Her father had been increasingly horrified as he had helped to build it and his voice had been turned on her rather than Louie. Their arguments in their native tongue had rung round the corridors for days and, clashing with the Reverend Paisley's foghorn version of English, had shredded tempers in the college until de Vere had made him leave eventually.) Julia Lee took the public into the overheated back rooms of her father's restaurant with drawings, prints and sculpture. Brian thought she had been clever in that the sense of exploitation here was implicit in the honesty of the images.

But the most radical show was, surprisingly, Bernie Rodenstein's. This was an array of blown-up photographs of men taken with a concealed camera in all sorts of locations, amongst crowds, in public lavatories, in church pulpits, in gay bars. They were mounted on two-dimensional, plywood cut-out models in appropriate settings, drawn and painted around and about them in the style of George Grosz. When Brian had first entered his space he had seen nothing at first to justify the furore they had caused amongst the staff. Only from the rear of the exhibits could the 'extras' be observed. The clothing of the models was carefully cut away on that side to reveal drawn private parts discreetly over-stamped with a large pink triangle with the name Huggett entwined in a swastika printed onto it. Brian had been greatly amused by the heart-searchings de Vere and the staff - apart from Laurie Willoughby - had had over the legitimacy of his show - especially as the college cleaners refused to enter it - and who the hell the men were, but to his admiration, they had allowed it, provided the faces were disguised. Bernie complied albeit reluctantly. (They had caused no problems to the external assessors.) Thus, amongst this radical exuberance, Connie's show seemed tame, however formally excellent it was. Brian wondered whom she was trying to please. He was also disappointed his own portrait was not there.

He was preparing to leave Connie's space when she suddenly came into it. Her face was turned away looking back into the corridor. His heart jumped but, as she turned and saw him, it plunged again as the smile she had been casting behind her disappeared abruptly.

"Oh," she said distantly. "Hi, Brian."

"Hello. Long time, no see," he said, giving her a big cheerful smile himself.

Her smile did not return as a tall, bearded man followed her into the space. "This is my father. Dad, this is Brian - you know the one with the computers," she said.

"Oh. How do you do?" said Brian, holding out his hand. The man shook it solemnly.

"Fine, just fine, thank you, young man," he said. There was an odd emphasis on the 'young man', not quite that of the Rector's usage of the phrase but emphatic nevertheless.

Her father had the same cultivated American accent as Connie. Brian was startled as he gripped the man's hand to feel that it was loose-skinned, bony and thin but strong. The man's clear blue eyes, startlingly like Connie's Brian noticed, took in his face and appearance in the brief interval of the handshake. Brian could see him quickly size-up his poor suit and well-worn shoes. He himself was expensively dressed in a seersucker jacket and summer slacks, impeccably pressed. His beard and crew-cut were both white and neatly trimmed and his nails, Brian noted, were probably manicured. He looked rich, confident, and successful, but it struck Brian, as their hands parted, that he was very much older than he would have expected Connie's father to be. Brian had almost no ability to judge the age of anybody over forty but his hands, and his face and neck now that he saw them more closely, suggested a man well on in his - seventies, could it be? Good Lord, he thought, she's done this all for him.

"Was there something you wanted?" said Connie to Brian. You know damned well what I want, he thought. But he said:

"No, no, just looking round. These are wonderful, aren't they, Mr.Grey? You must be very proud of her," he said, with a sweep of his hand.

"Oh, surely..." he began. Connie interjected, tight-lipped: "Perhaps, if he could get a proper look at them first. And his name isn't Grey."

Brian took the hint and left. By his presence he had clearly spoilt the dramatic revelation of her work she had planned for her father. He realised his hopes with Connie had just faded to zero. From the way she looked at him, he sensed she would find it difficult to match what she felt for her father with anybody under the age of seventy flaming five! Well, that was a - blank, blank - waste of time, he thought.

At this stage of the term, assessments for all groups apart from year three finalists had been completed. Brian gathered from staff that most students, apart from finalists, usually slipped away to summer jobs, or home or Glastonbury or inter-railing if they could afford it. This year was exceptional, however, in that de Vere had threatened dire consequences if they were not present during CNAA's visit. So the workshops and technical facilities were still operating and crowded for most of the day with slightly bored and resentful students, supervised by the less senior staff not required for meetings with the visiting panel.

The validation party had arrived the previous day and had held their first discussions with the staff in the cramped confines of the staff room. Everyone bore lapel badges with their names and status. Brian was surprised to find that his said: 'Acting Section Leader, Related Studies.' Marshall had a quiet word with him just as the meeting began, saying that he had directed Spiller to take sick leave. He told Brian that most of this was to be spent closeted with Forsythe in the police computer centre so the ball had dropped into his court for the visit. He also suggested that Spiller - with his particular experience - might be quite a useful addition to the Business Studies Department from next term. He did also wish Brian 'Good luck'. Gee, thanks, thought Brian. At this first session, the Rector had intervened almost immediately, to set a tone of confrontation.

"May I put the Polytechnic's point of view, Chairman?" he had said, interrupting the careful delivery of his introductory remarks by the leader of the panel, Charles Moffatt, a taciturn professor of painting and head of one of the Scottish art colleges, "I have another urgent meeting to attend." By his manner Brian surmised he was using the opportunity once more to put Art and Design in its place as low on the list of institutional and academic priorities. Without waiting for Moffatt's reply, he had gone on, glancing at a prompt paper he had taken from his inside jacket pocket:

"What the Polytechnic is after from you people is to tell us: a) what the quality of management and course delivery is like in the Department - as you will have seen from the submission, Chairman, there appears to be almost no formal structure anyone used to the accepted categories of Higher Education can grasp - b) is what happens here pertinent to our needs in the future as the Polytechnic evolves towards what will be an enhanced role in the national educational system, and is it relevant to what the perceived national requirements are likely to be? - c) is this course suitable for modularisation to which we are rapidly moving with all our non-science and engineering courses?" (There had been a stirring of shock at this as it was the first time the staff had heard the word. The Rector had known very well it would cause consternation and had smiled in grim satisfaction at its effect.) "and d) what is the legitimate definition you people understand by the term 'research'? We're having some problems with this."

At the end of his first three sub-clauses he had looked significantly at Noel and during the last at Brian. Brian had returned a blankly innocent stare. Noel, on the other hand, he had noticed was staring not at the Rector as he paused, but at the dreaded Welshman, Ivor Evans, grinning across the table wolfishly at him, and also Peter, for once fully alert. Brian had seen that Evans had picked up the implications of the Rector's tone and could not wait to get at the meat.

Louie had already filled in some of the background to this relationship for Brian. It seemed that Noel and Peter on a visit to another college in their capacity as CNAA panellists themselves, had steamrollered Evans' criticisms of the course because it was allowing students to stray outside the strict confines of what he, Evans, as a full-time practising sculptor not a college lecturer, considered to fall within his purview alone as the bearer of the pure soul of 'Fine Art'. Brian had thought of his own new course idea and what sort of a field day Evans might have with that. Louie had said, alarming him even more:

"'E's a bastard-a Methodicalist-a, Brian. All-a them Welsh preachers, you know? E"s-a gonna detest-a whatta you do. Keep outta 'is way. Ok? Don't-a for Christ's sake tell-a 'im about computers. 'E'll-a chew-a your ballses off."

As a final flourish to his demands to the panel, the Rector had leavened his remarks with what he considered a joke. Brian knew it was meant to be a joke from the little smirk which had accompanied it. The Rector had directed this sally at the only woman on the panel, the representative for Art History and Related Studies, Elspeth Finer, B.A.,M.A.,Ph.D.

"For instance, do we have to consider painting naked females as on a par with quantum physics?" he had said, archly.

The Chairman of the panel had put down his pipe slowly.

"It would be an interesting debate as to which has benefited mankind to the greater extent, Rector. But for another time, I think. We thank you for your attention in your busy schedule," he had responded. Christ, how does he keep from sticking a paint brush up his nose? Brian had thought; this Moffatt must be Mr. Cool himself.

Brian's immediate worry was not the nature of the Chairman's character, however, but the panellist to whom the Rector had directed his remark, Elspeth Finer. Since the meeting started, he had taken his eyes off her only when the Rector had referred to research. She was about his own age which surprised him as he had imagined her much older, power-dressed in a rather formal but elegant black suit with a sharply lapelled, white blouse, open at the neck and exposing a hint of cleavage. The jewellery on her jacket was a silver brooch, identified by Brian as deriving from a medallion in Botticelli's 'Primavera'. Hermione had told him that she had produced a well-known re-interpretation of the picture exploring its occult, feminist implications. Her hair was shiny and dark and shaped into an Eton crop, very Louise Brooks' 'Lulu' in style, Brian decided. To his designer's eye, it was a cut he had admired ever since he'd seen the film, but be didn't think it suited her strong and handsome rather than pretty features. He wondered what else she thought she had in common with that free spirit. 'Pandora's Box' and 'The Primevera'! Ye Gods! She wore no make-up as far as he could tell. At the Rector's remark, he had seen her bridle. She had then spoken out firmly to follow the Chairman's response.

"That's the sort of over-testosteronic remark that led to Nagasaki and Hiroshima," she had said, severely. At this, Brian swallowed loudly, attracting her attention. She had stared thoughtfully at him and checked the name on his lapel badge. Brian found himself to his considerable chagrin blushing under this scrutiny. The Rector's only comment was "Hmph," and he had left the meeting.

For the rest of the first day, to his relief, Brian had not been called on to discuss his section's work with this formidable figure, who, he confessed to himself, scared the tar out of him. He had glimpsed her striding boldly through the shows with what he thought from the droop of her shoulders, was a demoralised Hermione in her train. The loud comments he had heard from her echoing through the spaces, particularly concerned the number of pictures, both on the walls and in the portfolios, of naked females, especially Rita. She was not concerned about the implication of Rita's bum and tits for quantum physics, however. Brian heard the word 'testosteronic', of which she seemed fond as a pejorative, used frequently to describe the general tenor of many of the male student shows. As Brian himself could not get enough of Rita's torso, he fervently hoped she would keep off the subject with him when he had his formal meeting with her at ten a.m. in Hermione's office. To ease himself into the mood, he arrived well before the Poly minibus had delivered the visitors from their hotel.

"How's it going?" he said to Hermione, who was sitting behind her desk when he entered. He tried to say it as with as much cheer as he could muster for her sake; she looked tense even beyond the gloom he'd seen her display at Louie's show.

"I'm being radicalised," she said wearily.

"Sounds painful," he said, sitting on the chair in front of the desk and leaning his elbows on it. As he looked at her, Brian guessed she was trying to establish a contrast with her tormentor by wearing a full but simple floral-pattern dress without adornment and had done her hair overnight so it now fell to her shoulders in soft waves. He thought also she might have used a rinse as it seemed a lighter shade of blonde. The contrast with Dr. Finer should be effective, he thought; she was clearly trying to fight back. In fact, she struck him as very attractive and feminine in spite of her downcast mood. She was a really bonny woman. "Hey, can I make us a coffee? You look knackered," he said.

"Thank you. I've already had one but I'll have another. It creates a legitimate excuse to escape to the loo. The kettle's probably still hot. Don't use the decent mug though, she likes that one herself. Of course, it's my favourite, as well." She leaned back in her chair and relaxed slightly. "When you knocked I thought it was her. It damned well is painful, I can tell you."

"Is she trying to graft a set of 'ballses', as Louie calls them, onto you?"

She laughed a little and her mood lifted slightly. "Sort of. The trouble is she's a proselytiser. And I'm cast as the dim female academic meekly accepting the male interpretation of Art History. And, of course her track record in publishing leaves mine at the post. She wants the syllabus changed to reflect the discoveries - if that's what they are - of the feminists in the last few years, and much more emphasis on the role of women in art. She implies - and perhaps she's right - that I'm behind the times. Not relevant to the needs of the women students today in my courses. And only a handful of feminist dissertations to prove the point."

"Milk and sugar? And what about the men students?" he said

"Just milk, thanks. The 'testosterone brigade'? She thinks it's all been a big con, art, that is, by men to extend their control over the feminine in their natures so they can use it as a put down on women. Only a thorough overhaul of art history can demonstrate this properly. And bring out those male artists like Botticelli who understood gender "

"I gather you're not convinced?"

"Not really. I've read a lot of their stuff and where I think it's valid, I include it, but the clitoral shock-troops stick in my throat, they're too shrill for me - although she is much better than that, I'll admit. Trouble is, I rather like men, you see. She doesn't. At least not the ones here. You should hear her on Mike Brierley. The only one she approves of is Wladimir and maybe Laurie. Pity about poor Ronnie, by the way. He did a rather a good dissertation on performance art in the Seventies. Thanks," she said, as he handed her a mug.

"They'll probably give him an unclassified pass on his course work."

"I hope so."

"Heard anything about how the rest of it's going?" he said, as he sat down again. He put his feet up on the coffee table between the institutional easy chairs and Hermione's desk.

"Do you mind?" he asked.

"Carry on," she said. "We need all the relaxation we can get. How's it going? From what I gleaned yesterday, not good. That fellow Evans is finding fault with everything. All the rest of the panel are scared stiff of offending him. They know he might be on their next visit - he does umpteen of them. He's a sort of Rottweiller for CNAA these days. Everybody remembers Ipswich. He's into everything - records - he had a whale of a time with them - teaching methods, equipment, even the quality of the technicians. And above all the philosophy. He's already had a go with de Vere and Louie about your new course idea. Poor Louie was reduced to trying to explain things in Italian he got so apoplectic with him. And Peter simply told him to piss off. It looks like we've had it this time. Well, it was nice while it lasted."

"Damn," said Brian morosely. "I was really beginning to like it here. Oh, well, back to the merry old dole queue till the next turn of the educational rack."

She shrugged. "I may be wrong but be prepared for the worst tomorrow when they give their verdict. They're sitting in on our finals grading session in the morning, then we go straight into dealing with their beefs in the afternoon. What a palaver all that's going to be."

"Yes, I'm not involved in the morning, except to be available for possible queries. What about the Chairman, Moffatt? Can't he handle him?"

"He's said hardly a word to anybody much but de Vere. Oh, and that chap with the white hair he's been going round with. Who is he, by the way? He's not a panellist, is he? He seems familiar but I just can't place him."

"What? Tall chap, quite old. White hair and beard. Very well dressed."

"That's hi..." There was a knock at the door and Elspeth Finer entered abruptly. Hermione jumped and spilled a bit of her coffee on her dress.

"Damn!"

"Oh, sorry." said Finer. "The door was open slightly and I heard your voices. I didn't mean to startle you. Good morning, Hermione." She held out her hand to Brian as he removed his feet from the table and stood up. "How do you do, Dr. Mather? I'm Elspeth Finer." They shook hands.

"Would you mind if I went and sponged this off?" said Hermione, tartly.

"Of course not. As you know it's really Brian's section I'm concentrating on at present." She turned and smiled at him. "Take as long as you like," she said over her shoulder to a jaw-clamping Hermione leaving the room. "Oh dear, I'm not too popular there, I think."

Brian took in her appearance, now strikingly different to the previous day, and thought it was not only the soiled dress that had caused Hermione's teeth-grinding, but the whole outfit Elspeth Finer was wearing. Gone was the power-dressed academic; in was the soft-centred woman beneath. She had also adopted a flowered print but of a startlingly bold pattern obviously more expensive than Hermione's and shorter, almost mini-skirt length. She had had her hair re-done, and although it could not match Hermione's in luxuriance, nevertheless it framed her face in soft curls. She was also wearing make-up. He began to wonder what quirks Elspeth Finer's particular interpretation of 'feminism' might encompass. He could not either be other than impressed by her bosom, emphasised by the high-waisted cut of the dress, particularly as she pumped it up and down once or twice ostensibly to get her breath. Brian ran up the storm signals again. His instincts were usually unerring: he was as long on experience as he was short on commitment.

"Oh, what a lot of stairs in this building. It's rather good, though, isn't it for its time? I understand you're an architectural historian among your many other claims to fame. Would you agree?"

"Definitely." She was smiling rather too much for his peace of mind.

"Shall we sit down?" she said. She sat in one of the low easy chairs and crossed her legs. They were bare, very smooth and came a long way out of her skirt.

"Can I get you a coffee?" he said.

"Why not? Thank you. Black, no sugar."

As Brian busied himself with the coffee-making, she said:

"I've been hearing quite a lot about you yesterday and at our meeting last night."

"Oh," said Brian. "None of it complimentary, I hope. That would be too boring for you." He had no idea why he said this. Another remnant from some drawing room comedy, probably.

She laughed. It was perfectly produced but Brian detected that it was quite practised.

"Yes," she said. "Much of it from the students." The women students, no doubt, he guessed. "I've also heard one of your lectures on a tape the students lent me.""

"Oh dear," he said involuntarily.

"Why "Oh dear"? I enjoyed it. Lots of good ideas. Very lively and challenging. Not a lot I could quarrel with. I fully agreed with your analysis of the - what was it? - 'branch-line' role of art as entertainment for the power brokers, and I agree it is much more important than that." She paused. "The staff here seem fond of taping their lectures. I understand Dr. Spiller uses it a lot."

"Er, yes," said Brian. "He's been absent rather frequently of late."

She laughed again. "So much so that the students christened him 'The Invisible Lecturer', I understand.

"I believe so," he said. Trust this lady to dig that out, he thought. Damn Spiller! However, his fears were relieved as she continued:

"Still, his results are good in spite of that. And we can't penalise people for their afflictions and he took good care to keep the course going, his marking and so on." She grinned at him. "I believe your own course has attracted an amusing soubriquet, as well."

"Has it? Oh," he said, as the kettle began to boil. "Ouch!" The steam caught his wrist when he picked it up. He was more nervous than he had thought.

"Yes. I won't embarrass you by repeating it. The student who told me said you might blush. She seemed to think you took her teasing in good part, nevertheless."

"It wasn't that bi - er - woman in a uniform was it?"

"As a matter of fact it was." Brian could tell that she was not the only one who enjoyed teasing him.

"Yes, I listened to your lecture in bed last night."

"Much better than sleeping pills, I expect," he said. "Your coffee." He handed her the favourite mug. An ominously early mention of her night-time arrangements there, he thought; he'd not heard of a taped lecture as a turn-on before. "I understand you prefer your coffee in this one," he said.

"How very thoughtful. Thank you," she said. Brian sat down, keeping out of range by a chair's distance.

"And I understand that you were the one who discovered that wonderful natural feminist artist whose drawings are in the entrance hall?"

"Ah. Renee. Yes."

"I'd love to meet her."

"You probably will. She'll be at the formal opening of the third year shows tomorrow night. I'll introduce you. You are coming to that, aren't you?"

"Of course."

He laughed. "She's a real character. You'll like her."

Whether Renee would reciprocate was another matter.

"I did talk to one student with whom you weren't too popular, though."

Good Lord, thought Brian. "Oh? Who was that?"

"A Mrs. Reaper, the extra-mural rep. on the Course Board."

Blast the woman! Still, she was entitled to her revenge, he supposed.

"Yes. I'm afraid Noel de Vere decided I wouldn't be suitable as her tutor."

"I wonder why?" she said, looking at him over her coffee mug.

Brian shrugged. What the heck had she told her?

"Still, the Certificate idea is a real inspiration. It should benefit many of the women of the town especially, by providing a challenge for their creativity at a more than leisure hobby level. And, of course, there's much more personal contact than with the OU. Womens' natures need that so much more than men, don't you find?"

"Er. Oh, certainly," he said.

She put down her cup on the coffee table and, picked up her expensive-looking briefcase from it. She took out the sections of the submission which set out the aims etc. of Related Studies.

"I understand Dr. Spiller prepared these before you arrived?"

"That's right," he said.

"They seem innocuous enough," she said. Brian tried to make his relief invisible and mentally patted Spiller on his deranged pate. Working in a little tent maybe wasn't such a bad idea, after all.

She selected Brian's new course paper. "But this new course idea is yours alone, is that right?"

"Yes."

She examined it. A doubtful frown and pursed lips replaced her smile, dispelling Brian's relief.

"My computing skills are only rudimentary, I'm afraid, but from what I've seen of the people who do this sort of thing, it tends to be highly gender specific. I've come across many men in this field who seem to use it as an escape into a world without real people, especially women. And, of course, all these dreadful games, zapping monsters and so on, merely encourage an excessive testosteronic morbidity in the young male. They're quite awful. I have seen a good deal, as a matter of fact, as I'm preparing a paper on it now dealing with the semiotics of the imagery used. Of course, there are some female animators and artists who do use computers imaginatively and with an awareness of gender, but they are few. Do you not think this course will simply reinforce the male orientation in this place which I feel is already present to an excessive extent? What are your views on the subject?" She looked directly at him and raised an eyebrow. Brian imagined the terror that simple movement would engender in many a student confronted by it. He realised that this question was going to be as important as any he had answered in his whole career. The viva for his own Ph.D seemed like a doddle now compared to being quizzed by Elspeth Finer; his job didn't depend on it then. And this lady was a real pro. player.

He decided to swing in from an angle he was aware of but he thought she may not have clocked, because he was quite sure the obvious ones she would have very well covered, rudimentary computing skills or no, if she was writing a paper on it.

"Well," he said, "I don't think I'd disagree with you as it appears from how most software design must look - because it is software design the course will be about mainly - in its western context, but I think that's largely an accident of its historical development in our gender-polarised educational system. In other cultures, without that hangover, the particular qualities which women can bring - attention to detail, a gift for contextualisation and so on - are ideally suited to the design of software. For instance, in India, software design is becoming almost a female art. Indian women are highly valued in Silicon Valley."

She looked thoughtfully at him. "Is that so?" This had thrown her slightly but he saw her squirrelling away what he had said, probably for her new paper.

"Oh yes," he said firmly. For once he had no need to massage the truth. "Undoubtedly. By the end of the century, they'll probably lead the world and be in demand everywhere. It will be quite a revolution."

"That's most interesting. I am not aware of this. I'd like to know more. But, surely, it's going to be a mountainous task to overcome the prejudice of most women students here - especially art students - towards what they see as a male preserve and general exclusion zone? Oh, that life room!" She shuddered. "The methodology of the course will be tricky. I'd like to hear your views on that. Perhaps we might discuss this further out of hours - at my hotel, say this evening?"

Brian was saved from answering this question which he knew was going to be an even more difficult one to respond to, by the return of Hermione.

When they had settled down again, Finer explained briefly what they had been discussing. Her remark about the life room suddenly inspired him to see a chance for diversion. He was finding Dr. Elspeth Finer increasingly hard to handle.

"Have you read the Faculty research report, by the way?" he said.

"Yes, I have."

"How did the idea of a comparative attitude survey to gender in the life room strike you?" He thought this bait would draw her fire. "Hermione, Mike and I thought we might all work together on it. A bit of applied social anthropology in a historical context."

He caught the startled look on Hermione's face.

"Oh, I approve entirely." she said enthusiastically.

"I gather you've experienced our life room already?" he said lightly.

"Yes, Hermione took me there yesterday." Brian knew that it had been Rita's turn the previous day. "Moribund, I'm afraid it struck me. Entirely traditional and mostly irrelevant to women. And that model! Oh dear. You can hardly see her musculature at all beneath all that - fat. And her skeletal articulation is entirely invisible." She snapped her document case decisively. "I would have thought it might be very difficult to get a full, unbiased sample with an atmosphere so hidebound."

"Ah. Then you haven't been when the male model was present?"

"No."

"Let's pop along now, shall we? You may be surprised."

When Brian attempted to open the door of the life room, he found it difficult. There was much scraping of chairs on the other side. The three of them squeezed into the room which was closely packed with women students sitting in silent concentration on the male figure, entirely nude on the dais.

Brian heard Hermione catch her breath. "Good Lord!" she said. She had not visited the room before herself with the male model present. Elspeth Finer said nothing but seemed transfixed. The sailor's friend's description of the model's appurtenance had been, if anything, too modest, Brian thought. The life room was now the most popular room in the college - at least with the women - although Brian did catch Bernie Rodenstein dodging quickly out of sight behind his easel.

Elspeth Finer spoke at last. "Perhaps this would be a good chance to test out gender attitudes for myself in the college." She stuck out her hand. "It's been most interesting, Dr. Mather. I think I've got a clear picture. If I need to talk to you again, you will be available no doubt. I'll see you later in the day Hermione."

Brian and Hermione left her to it.

Out in the corridor Hermione looked solemnly at him. "Thank you for including me in the survey. Even though I know nothing about it. It makes me seem slightly less of a feminine wimp, at least. And thank you for diverting her for a bit."

Brian grinned at her. "Don't thank me, thank the dong with the numinous pose," he said.

Chapter Fourteen
The Show Must Go On

As the visit wore on to the final meeting the following day, Brian kept out of the limelight as much as possible. He took to circulating slowly round the building and removing himself for a rest to the furthest corner of the library stacks and reading through back copies of obscure, ephemeral continental journals of the avant-garde, mostly donated by Wladislaw. Where on earth did they get all the money for this sort of junk? he wondered. Perhaps if this job folded he should be looking abroad himself; with his acting skills he might be in with a chance. From what little contact he did have with his colleagues, it seemed that the visit had gone from bad to worse. They were uniformly gloomy.

He did take one major diversion out of the building on the morning of the last day of the visit. Looking for a legitimate excuse to be out of the oppressive range of CNAA, he visited a student show he had not seen, housed in the old municipal baths building which shared the park site with the college. The staff had talked a lot about it but the student, Jenny Barnaby, was not known to Brian, so he had not paid much attention. However, he had registered that when Peter spoke about her his words were touched with awe. To him she was obviously in the same category as Connie was to de Vere.

He understood that her construction was on a massive scale and used one of the two empty swimming baths. When he entered the building and saw it he was amazed at the size of the structure which had been erected. At the shallow end of the swimming bath was an enormous container made of very thick, flexible, black plastic supported by scaffolding built over the bath and reaching to the roof. The base of the container filled the whole of the floor of the bath at that end and was swollen like a huge inverted hot-air balloon; there was nothing minimalist about this. But where was the art in a gigantic bin-liner? It reminded him of the continental rubbish he had just had his fill of.

"But is it art, Watson? That's the real question we must ask ourselves. Is it art?" he said aloud. His words echoed in the cavernous space.

"What? Hello, who's there?" said a female voice. "The show isn't open until tomorrow."

Dwarfed by the structure, he saw the figure who had spoken, a student he vaguely recognised dressed in check shirt and jeans, standing by a tripod and camera near it. He hoped she hadn't caught the implication of the bit of monologue he had amused himself with.

"Oh, you're on the staff, aren't you?" she said.

"Yes. Is this yours?"

"Yes. Come down and I'll switch the lights on for you. You won't try any of your karate chops on it, though, will you? Not that it's delicate but I don't want to take any chances."

The bath still had its well-worn, gritty stone steps leading down into it and Brian descended these.

"Gosh," he said, "this must have cost you a fortune."

"Not really," she said. "Supplied by ICI for publicity, and a local builder did the scaffolding."

You'll go far, he thought, with or without art.

"Could you just stand there for scale?" She smiled at him. Close to, she actually was quite small, not especially pretty, but intelligent-looking and fresh-faced.

"Of course," he said; he didn't mind at all. She took flash photographs from various angles and directed him around to different positions.

"Now," she said, "Watch." She went up the steps to a switch-board she had rigged on the wall and flipped a lot of switches. Brian was expecting something dramatic but nothing seemed to happen. Then he noticed in the side of the plastic 'balloon', a tiny pin-point of light had appeared.

"Have a look inside," she said.

He stepped over to it and put his eye to a small lens welded into the material. He caught his breath in astonishment. The interior, now brilliantly lit from concealed lights above, was filled by a mass of greenery and exotic-looking flowers, a realistic jungle scene. It took him some time to register that they were artificial. Amongst them he glimpsed faces and half-hidden figures of brown-skinned, semi-naked men and women with South American Indian decoration. In front, nearest the peep-hole was a white sculptured female figure, naked and stretching her arms upwards to the light. Brian thought it looked like a body-cast of the artist. He turned to look at her. So? he thought.

"Keep looking," she said, coming back down the steps.

He turned back and peered in again. Then he saw it. Darting amongst the greenery and then circulating above it as it got used to the light, was a single, beautiful, golden carp, about eight inches long, looking for all the world like a flying fish/ bird. Of course, the whole thing was filled with water which was invisible in the powerful light. Now this was avant-garde, he thought, and it was also, most definitely, art, Watson, old son. In fact, it was one of the most stunning visual experiences he had ever had, and then he remembered:

"Ravenna!" he said suddenly. "Right?"

She was enormously pleased. "Right," she said. "You know it then, the flooded crypt? Where you put your coin in and the lights come on and the goldfish is flying round. You're the first one who's spotted it."

"It's the four elements isn't it? Earth, air, fire and water. I get the others but where's the fire? Don't tell me," He held up his hand. "The light. Of course. How dense of me." He looked into the peep-hole again.

"Yes. And Marcel Duchamp, as well."

"Oh?" It seemed nothing like anything that seminal figure was known for to Brian.

"You don't know his last work, then, the gallery installation in the States?" she said.

"No. I've never seen a picture of that. Why isn't it in the books?" he said, turning to her again. He was loth to give up the pleasure of looking.

"There aren't any. You can only see it through a peep-hole like this. I went to see it last summer after my stint with Camp America"

"I must get to see that some time." Typical of old Duchamp, he thought; to checkmate the moneychangers at last when he couldn't do it with sweeping brushes, old bicycle wheels or urinals. What a man! What an artist! "It will have to be good to stand up to this," he said, turning again to the peep-hole; the fish shimmered past again. "This will simply freak them out at the opening tonight. It knocks that Ravenna thing into a cocked hat."

"So we understand," said a Scots brogue from above them.

They looked up to see Moffatt and Connie's father standing at the side of the bath.

"May we join you and have look too, lassie?" he said.

"Come on down."

"I've been looking forward to this," he said, as they came down the steps. "Jenny Barnaby, is it?"

"That's me for my sins."

"Whoops," said Moffatt, as he nearly slipped on the shiny white tiles of the bath floor. "Be careful there, Winslow," he said to his companion. "The tiles are a wee bit slippery for geriatrics like us. They are dry aren't they?" he said, doubtfully."

"Bone dry," she said. "These baths haven't been used for years. Fortunately, they still have the water supply in case of fire. It was the fire brigade testing the supply that filled this up for me."

She will not only go far she will go a very long way, Brian thought. He wondered if she had any artwork for sale. Might be a good investment opportunity. Moffatt steadied himself and shook hands. He did not introduce Connie's father, who had followed him down, to either of them. Brian had no way of telling whether Winslow was his first or last name, but the name had struck a bell with him nevertheless. Before Brian could search his mind to track down the context in which he'd heard the name before, Moffatt said:

"You're Dr. Mather, right? The whizz-kid computer laddie?"

"Yes," said Brian. Oh dear, he thought, not only a panel member but the Chairman himself.

"We must have a talk some time." He began to fill his pipe.

"Would you mind not doing that?" said Jenny, firmly. "It is thick material and ICI said it would be quite safe, but you never know - with the sparks, I mean."

"Oh, of course," he said. "Thoughtless of me, lassie. I apologise. We slaves to the weed hardly know we do it. The Benn/Wilson syndrome, you know." She looked blank. "Never mind, you're far too young." He indicated Connie's father but, again, did not introduce him. "My friend here has been told a lot about you by his daughter."

"I beg your pardon?" she said.

"Look, I must be going," said Brian. This close to the Chairman of the panel was too close for comfort.

"Of course," said Moffatt. "Incidentally your finalists' assessment meeting has just finished. Very straightforward. Rigorous argument. No student left unturned. We'll see you anon at lunch, no doubt." Brian began to move towards the steps but Moffatt laid a hand on his arm and detained him. Oh Christ! thought Brian. Now what? "In case we don't, by the by, I'd just like to say I found the ideas in your new course interesting. Most interesting. And Connie has told me how much of a chance you took to help her and her friends." He chuckled. "I like the name they gave themselves. Droll, very droll." Brian was relieved and surprised; Connie must trust this man. And she had talked about him; at least he'd had some effect. "Good to see a bit of spirit about these days, eh? Ah, to be a student again. You know, you might like to make us a visit next year. Would that be alright with you?"

Brian gulped and nodded. "Er. Yes. That would be..."

"You could have some interesting stories and ideas for us."

Brian recovered. "Er. Yes, yes. I'd be glad to." Very interesting stories, he thought. If there is a next year for Brindling.

"I'll write to you. In a few weeks. We're in the throes of organising our programme just now." he said.

"Thank you."

Brian went quickly along the side of the swimming bath towards the exit and he heard cries of delight from the two men as they peered into the watery world. He looked back and saw Connie's father begin an animated discussion with the student. She, in turn, gave a cry of astonishment and pleasure and shook his hand fervently before rushing off to get her camera to take his picture beside her structure. Brian wondered what all that was about, but the inward delight which suddenly gripped him at Moffatt's invitation and its implications soon took all his attention not to let out an ecstatic shout of "Whacko the diddley-oh, yer bugger." Emerging into the summer sunlight of the park, he did allow himself a single, energetic, high, heel-click leap in the air. Ridley's dogs, exercising on lead in the park with their master, gave out a cacophany of barks.

"Stupid - mutts," he shouted, from a safe distance.

"You shouldn't - provoke them," Ridley shouted back as Brian's heedless figure walked briskly away towards the main Poly building and lunch. "They're - sensitive animals, these buggers.""

Brian had not attended a Poly lunch for visiting CNAA panels before and was surprised at its lavishness, especially in the amount of wine available - all of it east European, he noticed. He presumed the idea was to fray the edge of the panel's critical faculties and create an atmosphere favourable to whatever course was under scrutiny. If this was the idea, he thought, they had reckoned without the capacity of a bunch of artists to sink alcohol in quantities which would burn holes in the critical faculties of representatives from more academic disciplines, and with almost no detectable effects. He did spot, however, that the despondent mood of his colleagues seemed to deepen the more they drank. (Their mood was matched by that of the domestic staff, who watched with dismay as bottle after bottle was emptied. It was another of their perks to decant the part-used bottles - whose number they made sure was always greater than actually needed - for their own consumption later.) Brian, after his lesson at Louie's show had demonstrated his capacity to be seriously deficient, knew better than to match his colleagues and slowed his intake as theirs speeded up. He needed to keep a clear head, in any case, to keep out of range of Elspeth Finer, who appeared to be of the artistic tendency herself. She kept giving him beaming smiles when he did catch her eye and raising her glass to him but, to his relief, was diverted eventually by beginning an argument with the Rector and the Poly's tame HMI who was to sit in on the meeting, over their attitude to life-painting.

By the time lunch was over and they had assembled in the Committee Room of the Poly, the alcohol had given de Vere a strong shot of Dutch courage.

"I'm really going to tell these bastards what I think, this time. Especially that cunt, Evans," he said, in an aside to Brian as they went into the Committee Room together. "If we're going out, we're going out with a bang not a fuck - " burp! "- fucking whimper."

Brian prayed silently that Noel might keel over and pass out before that happened. Particularly when he spotted that the Rector had registered de Vere's loud burp and had smiled grimly at the prospect of this arrogant Head of Department finally getting his come-uppance. He had been talking a lot with Evans at lunch and, from his expression, Brian guessed he was already choosing the décor for his new posh office in the art college building.

"What the hell's he doing here? And who the hell is he anyway?" said de Vere, as he reacted to the sight of Connie's father sitting with Moffatt at the head of the table. They made their way round the sides of the room along with the others, towards their allotted chairs, Brian's at far remove from the VIP's.

Brian was astonished. He stayed at de Vere's side as the latter dumped the papers he was carrying heavily on the table behind his name-plate.

"It's Connie's father," whispered Brian.

"I know that, you fool," he snarled under his breath. Brian saw that the drink had given him a foul temper on top of his dyspepsia, "but exactly who is he? What's he been hanging round for?"

"You mean - you've not been introduced?" he said, unable to keep the incredulity out of his voice.

De Vere was both angry and embarrassed. "That Scotch bastard hasn't seen fit to introduce us properly. All he said was did I mind if this man hung around for a bit. Damned cheek." He sat down. "He's another one I'm going to blast. He's hardly spoken to me in three days. He's let that twat, Evans, do it all for him. I only let this man Grey stay because Connie asked me if he could. I'll chuck him out if he's still here when the meeting starts, Connie's father or no father. She's got her first now, so to hell with the pair of them."

"His name isn't Grey, it's Winslow, but what Winslow or Winslow what, I have no idea."

"How the hell..." Then he stopped. "Are you sure?"

"I heard Moffatt use that name, yes."

"Good Lord," said de Vere.

The Rector coughed loudly. Brian looked up from de Vere's now thoughtful face and realised that everyone was seated and waiting for him to take his place. He hurried to the foot of the table, glancing across at the expressions of the Rector and Evans as he did so. He remembered one of his pigeon Siamese lines from a seaside summer production of the 'King and I': 'It will be very interesting meeting.'

"Before we begin our deliberations, I have a very pleasant task to perform," said Moffatt, tapping for attention on the table with his pipe bowl.

"Mr. Chairman," said the Rector cutting in to establish his rights, "has your companion, to whom nobody has seen fit to introduce me, got any reason to be here?"

"Yes. Who is this chap?" said Evans, rudely

"Good afternoon," Winslow said to the assembled company, ignoring both the Rector and Evans. "I hope you don't mind if I intrude for a few moments before you begin your deliberations formally. Allow me to introduce myself. My name is Winslow Grish."

Along with the rest of the artists around the table, Brian gave a gasp. Of course! Now he knew it - Winslow Grish! The one that got away! About the only one of the founders of American modernism not dead from drink or drugs. His early abstract expressionist paintings sold now for London telephone number figures. Here in the same room - at Brindling Poly! If you couldn't have Jackson Pollock, Winslow Grish would do. And Connie was his daughter! And had just been given a first! Brian looked quickly round the table. Mouths were still ajar, except for the Rector, Deputy Rector, the HMI and Evans. The first three were puzzled and the last furious.

"Do I gather that is supposed to mean something?" said the Rector, acidly.

"My dear," said Laurie Willoughby, "to meet someone of Mr. Grish's stature would require a whole wardrobe of new frocks and probably new undies as well."

This infuriated the Rector. Elspeth Finer laughed out loud. Brian suppressed a smile. De Vere's warning look at Laurie was apoplectic. Brian saw Laurie respond with a slight, defiant moue. He also registered that the Rector suddenly recognized him, even without the outfit he'd worn at Louie's opening.

"I don't know why your sort of..." (He suddenly altered his sweeping pugnacity and Brian guessed he had the suspicion that there might be members of the visiting panel of similar tendencies; they were artists as well.) "why you stay in Brindling," he continued, a mite less harshly but still glaring across the table at Laurie.

"It is a port, after all, darling," said Laurie, simply.

The Rector crimsoned and was about to respond, but Winslow Grish cut in with a placatory tone. "Let me explain," he said. "As some of you already know, my daughter has been a student here for three years. Connie Grey - we thought the real name would be a bit obvious. It's not very common, after all. When you have need to find your way as an artist, you must do it on your own. I'm afraid my reputation for good or ill, would have weighed rather heavily on her. My own name, which my artistic parents saddled me with, was a bit unfortunate, even when I was a student - people expected seascapes from me." The artists in the room got the reference and laughed politely. The Rector looked at the ceiling in impatience. Brian turned to Hermione next to him and raised his eyebrows questioningly. As Grish continued, she wrote down 'Winslow Homer'. Brian recognised it as the name of a nineteenth century American landscape and marine artist. "So three years ago I asked my friend, Professor Moffatt here, what he thought would be the best place for her to study over here. In the States, you see, she would never have escaped and art is so much in the grip of the money men now that any student with talent, especially with a name, could be so easily diverted from what was best for their future development. He suggested she come here."

"Why?" said de Vere, jumping in quickly. From his tone Brian concluded that he had spotted what advantages the explanation might have for the forthcoming post-mortem on the visit.

"Perhaps Professor Moffatt might like to answer that. He knows your course better than I do. Although I will say that the last few days have fully vindicated my faith in his judgement. And I must apologise to you personally, Mr. de Vere, for not introducing myself to you earlier but I felt it was best you should not know who I was until after your grade meeting. For obvious reasons. I do hope you'll forgive me?" said Grish.

Noel waved his hand magnanimously.

Moffatt leaned forward on the table.

"I suggested Brindling to Winslow because I thought it was one of the few colleges in England - " (He paused to emphasise this heavily and looked at the Rector and the HMI.) "where there was still some spirit of art education as an adventure remaining. From my experience of visiting with CNAA across the border, I have found that even colleges with once great reputations for encouraging students to test the boundaries of art were playing safe to survive. In many of them staff were more and more devoting their time to tiresome 'management' considerations and losing sight of why we have this form of education for the talented young in the first place. They were becoming 'afeared of the boggarts' of polytechnic power. And although they were 'efficient', and produced results they were becoming artistically constipated. Of course, I could have suggested my own college for Connie, but I think that would have had too high a profile and been personally awkward. Also we expect four years, as you know, and Connie was anxious to get going. And finally, I suggested Brindling because it was small, and had no house style, had admirable teachers with a reputation for looking after their charges and was far enough from the metropolis not to be bound by the latest gallery fashions."

He leaned back, picked up his pipe, and watched from behind the cloud of smoke he generated, the effect of his words. Apart from Elspeth Finer coughing loudly and waving her arms around, there was no visible reaction as the staff and panel waited on events.

"So," said Grish, "I am extremely grateful for the education my daughter has had here. I think Professor Moffatt chose very wisely. It has been exactly what I think art education should be. I only wish I'd had it myself - it would have saved a lot of time in my twenties. And for that reason, with your agreement of course, I would like to set up a scholarship scheme here for student exchange with the States and linked to Professor Moffatt's college. I hope you don't mind, but I've already selected one student for next year from your finalists, the girl with the swimming bath installation. I was thinking of a sum around one hundred thousand dollars for the purpose - initially that is."

While Grish paused to let this sink in, Brian saw that the Brindling staff were trying to keep the delight out of their expressions, but the visiting panel members were trying not to look envious. Neither was doing it very well. Across the Rector's face there paraded in quick succession, incredulity, annoyance, uncertainty and finally sheer greed. It was probably the "initially" that swung it.

Grish continued: "As you know my pictures sell for quite ridiculous sums these days - nobody deplores that more than me, but that's business, as they say - however, they are not all on the market yet. I no longer produce for the galleries myself, only my own pleasure, drawings mostly - I made all the painterly statements I want to long ago - but I have kept some early works under my own control so the money is not a problem. Of course, a sum of that amount may seem too large for the purpose." He looked very puzzled at the lack of response. "Perhaps, you might have something more modest in mind?" he said.

The Rector and de Vere spoke simultaneously, vying with each other to assure Winslow Grish that to "a mature art college" and "a mature Polytechnic" such a sum would cause no problems. When they had finished, Grish said:

"And, of course, your redesignation as a University would give added credibility Stateside."

The assembled company looked at the Rector. Oops, thought Brian, Connie had been talking.

"Er. Well, that's not certain yet, of course," said the embarrassed Rector. "We still have to make a formal application."

The HMI spoke up.

"May I just interject a note here, Rector, on that point?"

"Of course."

"I don't think there'll be any difficulty about that." The Rector smiled delightedly, and beamed round the table. It was the first time Brian had seen an expression like that from him. It was the expression of a man whose life's dream was about to come true. He sat back and prepared to speak when the HMI went on :

"No. You see HMG thinks that the Polytechnics are now mature enough to take on self-validating responsibilities and the intention is to redesignate all of them as Universities. Probably after the next election - when the current HMG is in a position to do so." Oh God, no, thought Brian, not again. He groaned out loud and put his head in his hands. Everyone looked at him.

"Are you ill, Dr. Mather?" said Moffatt, solicitously.

"Not as ill as I suspect we're all going to be after the next election." he said, slowly looking up. De Vere made his hysterical grimace at him to shut it, but without the hiss and clawing movement.

The HMI sensed the effects his words might have had on the company as a whole. "In any case," he continued, looking away from Brian with a hint of a smile, "there is currently quite a broad cross-floor agreement between the parties on this as the general confusion in the punters' - er - public's mind on the meaning of the tripartite Higher Education system is becoming, frankly, an embarrassment."

The Rector looked horrified. "What? All of them? All the Polys?"

"Oh yes. Nem con. And some of the more mature Higher Education colleges as well and possibly some FE...""

"What? You mean places like Basingstoke and Darlington?" the Rector interrupted.

"Well, that's not fully decided but the development of some F.E. colleges has been most impressive, you know. Of course, the chartered universities will try hard to maintain some differential, probably, especially in funding and research but...Sorry, I digress. Not germane. However, what is germane is that HMG is fully aware that one of the most distinctive sections the Polys have to their credit is art and design and sees courses like your own as contributing greatly in future to the regeneration of our industrial base. For example, your new initiative on the art/computing interface was most interesting to us in your submission. It's that kind of sensitivity to the relevance of present-day requirements in national educational needs we like to see."

The Rector's dismay at almost every aspect of the HMI's statement was total. As the man was speaking, he began to go red in the face. Brian saw him reach into his waistcoat pocket for his pills. They were not there. The meeting watched fascinated as he frantically tried his other pockets without success. At the end of the HMI's statement, the Rector suddenly leaped from his chair, which screeched in protest, and rushed over to the coat stand. (Along with some other members he had brought a light rain-coat as it had the sky had clouded over earlier.) He banged the raincoat pockets listening for the rattle of pills. There was no response. He resumed his seat, poured himself a drink from the water carafe in front of him and subsided into a deep-breathing, crimson-faced silence. The meeting relaxed again. In the silence Brian heard de Vere whisper to himself in a satisfied way: "Tick, tock." The Rector was past either hearing or responding.

"So, can I gather from all this that you think my idea is a reasonable one?" said Grish, breaking the tension.

The meeting agreed it was and, with the details to be settled later, Winslow Grish left them to it.

The rest of the affair was a formality. Brian saw the panel members quietly tearing up their criticisms which now looked carping and minor after the accolades the course had been given by Grish, the Chairman and the HMI. Evans looked darkly furious and contributed almost nothing. Elspeth Finer did maintain her academic function, however, but to Hermione's relief, which she shared by her expressions with Brian, it was only to note the pleasing new sensitivity she had detected in the area of her own responsibilities, of the special needs of women. With this she gave Brian a look which he could only describe as arch - on somebody like her it sat very oddly, he thought.

When the meeting had reached the stage of summing-up, Marshall spoke as the Rector was still red-faced and silent. (Brian wondered if he was dead and propped up like El Cid.) He thanked the Chairman and panel for their admirable efforts and looked forward to the next five years of equal success. He had one note, however, which cheered both the panel and the staff - apart from Brian.

"This will be the last function CNAA will carry out for us in this area," he said. "In future the Poly - or should I say University - will be maintaining validation procedures for its own degrees. We hope we can carry them out as well as has been done for us in the past by CNAA. Thank you all."

And good night, thought Brian.

Chapter Fifteen
What a Performance!

The opening of the student shows at Brindling was an annual social event of some note in the town. Brian, still not able to afford clothing suitable to an occasion attended by parents, friends, and lovers of the students as well as the great and good of the locality, was in two minds whether to go along at all.

He felt depressed after the validation meeting, unlike his euphoric colleagues, delighted that it was the last they would see of their ordeal by CNAA. He was sure their optimism was misplaced. Self-validation meant explanation to engineers and so on led, no doubt, by a Rector - not an El Cid to Brian's disappointment - who had raised Philistinism to an art form. At least there was a shared culture with CNAA panel members. And knowing the way politicians loved power, the HMI's speech cut no ice with him either. His little slip of the tongue had given him away for all his urbanity. He suspected that what they were really after was cynically taking back into their own hands the say-so on courses and spending to keep it as far away from the 'punters' as possible. In their eyes, CNAA were just that, and much too interested in education to be allowed free rein. Those palmy days were over. They actually validate courses which need extra money, for God's sake! And in all sorts of ridiculous subjects we never had at Oxbridge in our day. We can't have that, you know. No, give the power to the college directors, and make them all universities. They'll soon cut that nonsense down to size when they've got to balance the books themselves.

These black thoughts were prompted as well by the suspicion that this same HMI was amongst the shadowy figures you could never get at, directing the crew that sank his former college. A useful 'teeth-cutting exercise' before he tackled less vulnerable institutions, no doubt. However, in spite of his shabby suit and how he felt, what the heck; he still had a job. Make hay while the sun shines. Which it was: a perfect June evening, the threat of rain now gone.

The entrance hall and gallery were crowded when he got there and he was glad he had come slightly late so that he could mingle anonymously amongst the guests, talking and laughing and balancing their paper plates of food and glasses of wine. He noted that Renee's drawings were attracting lots of admiration and she waved a piece of red sticky paper at Brian when she spotted him at the edges of the crowd, and poked a finger through some large round holes cut from it. She gave her delighted raucous laugh and caused some of her admirers to spill their drink. He waved back and gave her a thumbs up sign, wondering at the same time what the 'Social' would make of her new source of income. He noticed also she had her little boy at her side this time - many of the pictures were of him in his usual street garb, or eating, watching telly or sans clothes in the bath - now scrubbed, polished and looking utterly mystified at the sudden translation of his mother to stardom. He saw Brian and looked daggers at him; he knew who was the cause of his downfall. Brian thought how fortunate he was that none of his Tofter pals could see his mortification as the ladies patted him on the head and said how sweet he looked. Brian's sympathy went out to him; to be drawn fully clothed and then exhibited was bad enough, but in the bath! Starkers and your dick showing! Something a lad of parts could never live down. As he mounted the stairs he thought maybe Renee's next few years could get a mite more difficult than she imagined.

Brian circulated quickly through the noisy bustle of student exhibitions on the upper floors looking for a friendly face. What he found instead were young people he took to be strangers to the college, who greeted him by name and introduced him to their parents and friends. Time and again, he had to look to identify those performing the introductions definitely as Brindling students. Female faces and hair that had scorned make-up and grooming were now shiny and colourful, and bodies of both sexes which had pupated in the leftovers of society for three years, had now emerged as often stunningly fashionable butterflies, looking once more like the young hopefuls their parents had sent off to college. Some of the men, Alex, Gerry and Bernie even, were actually wearing dinner suits! He felt shabbier than ever. Most of them, he was sure, had never looked so attractive and 'normal' since their interviews. He visited Connie's space, but of her and the staff he could find not a sign. Perhaps he was first on the scene, after all. Not very likely, he thought; Louie had specifically told him to get there early as the students were 'like-a fooking-a gannets' to get at the food and drink, although many of the student spaces actually held ample private supplies provided mostly by indulgent parents. With these they liberally plied Brian, at the same time asking him awkward questions about "What sort of jobs do people with this kind of degree get, old boy?" He was thoroughly mystified as to where his colleagues had got to. He was certain there must be a source of free alcohol somewhere he knew nothing about.

It was only when he reached the entrance hall again, that he found the answer. Coming into it, as he descended the stairs, was the official party of staff and guests, amongst them Connie and her father. Noel de Vere, who looked jocular after the day's events, Brian observed, greeted him at the foot of the stairs.

"Where the fuck have you been?" he hissed, keeping his good cheer strictly for public display. "Why weren't you at the reception? Winslow here wanted to talk to you."

"What reception? "

"In the marquee on the back lawn."

"Nobody told me."

De Vere snorted. "Bloody fool! Anyway, you're here now. In time to see Connie's ceiling unveiled, at least. This is the high point of the evening."

The Rector came up with his wife.

"Will the rest be here soon, de Vere?" he said.

"I've sent Ridley to pass the message," said Noel. "He's slow but sure." The Rector moved off and de Vere made to follow him, but first he gave a quick aside to Brian:

"We're the blue-eyed boys for the moment with a hundred grand coming our way. So don't do anything or say anything to spoil it. No insulting the Chairman of the Governors or groping his bird. Ok?"

"That's old hat," said Brian.

"What is?"

"Rita and Huggett. She's Marshall's bird now."

De Vere looked at him with disbelief.

"How do you know?"

Brian sniffed. "Common knowledge," he said, and went on: "A pity you won't be able to enjoy the prestige from Grish's benefaction," he added casually.

"What?" De Vere looked alarmed. "What do you mean? Who've you been talking to?"

"Early retirement," he said.

"What? Who?" He saw de Vere look puzzled for an instant, then he said firmly:

"That was never on the cards and don't ever mention it to me again."

Brian reflected that de Vere, like most creative people, had much in common with many successful politicians: they automatically edited the past to fit whatever fantasy fulfilled their needs of the moment.

While the Rector, de Vere, Winslow and Moffatt fell into conversation, Connie moved to Brian's side accompanied by the Rector's wife. De Vere had told him she was much younger than the Rector but not as young or as pretty as this and he certainly had no recollection of seeing her at his extra-mural lecture, although he did have a vague feeling that he'd met her before. He wondered briefly what she could possibly have in common with the Rector. He had heard that she had formerly been his student at Cambridge. Certainly, she seemed barely as old as Brian himself. He asked her if they had met previously. She shook her head decisively and said she thought not, and moved away as some other staff wives took her attention.

"I want to apologize for being so short with you the other day. It was real dumb of me," said Connie.

"No problem," said Brian. "It's not every day you can show the results of three years work not just to your father but to a major artist. I was intruding. You look great, by the way."

Brian had had the same feeling when she approached him as with the other transformed students: here was a new person. She was dressed in a simple, white muslin dress, very demure, her decolletage strictly out of sight and had had her hair set in a fashionable tempest of curls. Her make-up was understated to emphasise her natural good colouring. Her shoes were low-heeled, cream suede with simple gold and red buckles. She gave the impression of being very young, almost a teenager, and very vulnerable. Perhaps that was the idea.

"What happens now? Where do you go from here?" he asked.

Connie did not catch the true drift of Brian's question.

"Well, I'm selling the boat, then Dad and I are going to Italy - he has a place there near Florence - then it's back to the States."

"I see."

Suddenly she put her hand on his arm. His mind went back immediately to the night outside 'BoZo'Z' where a similar move had given him such hope. It almost felt like that again.

"Look," she said, "why don't you come with us? I'm sure Dad wouldn't mind and there's plenty of room."

Brian's heart lurched as she moved closer and looked up at him. He was on the point of saying - shouting out even - yes, of course I'll come. Then he hesitated. Finally, he shrugged. With her father there as well? he thought.

"Sorry," he said. "No money. I'm up to my ears in debt. Also..." He stopped as his embarrassed glance away from her had taken in that her father was looking beyond the little knot of people directly at him and his daughter. Brian had a quick frisson of insight that he was so watchful of her that even her small gesture towards his arm had attracted his attention. He had been right in his instinct for caution; it would be hell. And...There was another thing.

"Don't be shy about it. I am my own mistress, you know. Dad's quite used to my having adult relationships. And the money would be no problem."

"Not for you, perhaps."

He suddenly decided he had to say something for her own good, not as a suitor for her favours but as a tutor; somebody who'd been given the trust to do that for her. The youthfulness of her dress had opened a gap between them, not simply one of age, but function; it had reminded him of what he was actually paid for. It had undone him.

"If I were you, I wouldn't go to Italy with your father or anywhere with him for a good long time yet."

She quickly withdrew her hand. "That's a very personal thing to say to me, for Christ's sake. Whyever not?"

"Don't get me wrong. It's just - well, if I were you and I had your talent, I'd go to London, get a room or live on the boat, and work like the devil to make it on my own. If you're really serious about being an artist, you need to hustle. You've had three good years building for yourself and Moffatt was right, you were lucky to come to Brindling, but don't let what you've got slide now. Because it will if you don't catch it on the upswing. And don't, for God's sake, go back to the States. You'll never stay anonymous and the galleries will eat you alive, just to cash in on your father. Remember how you're father did it? He's given you this chance to make it on your own as well. At your age nobody gave a tinker's cuss about him."

She looked so confused and vulnerable that he had to clench his fists not to apologise and say take no notice of me, what do I know about it. But he simply looked at her with an even expression.

By this time, the crowds were surging into the entrance hall and gallery and de Vere and the others were moving on as well. Grish left them and moved to Connie and Brian.

"Ok, sweetness," he said, "this is it. Your big moment in pictures." He nodded to Brian and swept her off with an arm. She glanced back at him over her shoulder, looking nervous and uncertain. The End. Roll the credits, thought Brian.

The crowd had gathered and the mercifully short VIP speeches were all done. The Rector invited Huggett to step forward and pull the tasselled cord that hung from the drapes covering the ceiling. Because the gallery had been closed off and the lower part of the windows covered while

Connie had been painting, it was the first time Brian had seen inside. It was an excellent design, oval in shape with a curve of long windows facing north towards the park. It had a false ceiling, slightly dome-shaped, edged by a simple frieze supported by classical pilasters along the wall and between the windows. The drapes covering the painting were triangular, white strips of light material stretched from the frieze to the centre where they were tied with a maroon cord whose ends hung down to head height above a small podium from which the VIP's had spoken. Huggett stepped forward onto the podium, reached up and gripped the cords.

"I name this ship..." (The company laughed.) "No, but it gives me great pleasure as Chairman of the Governors of the Poly" (How could he stand here, smiling away as if nothing had happened after being caught with his hand in the till? Brian thought. Politicians! They must all have a gene for brass neck.) "to reveal this wonderful piece of art - we hope - " (More laughter.) "which this clever young lady here has painted for us. I'm sure that it will be a credit to her and a pleasure for us all. And here's to the next hundred years of art in Brindling. Thank you." (Clapping.) "So here goes!"

He gave a yank at the cords and the drapes fell away and swung down to the crowd who reached up and pulled them towards the walls revealing the picture. There was a hubbub of delight at what had been done.

The picture was a version of a roccoco trompe-l'oeuil heaven, richly coloured in pinks and blues with swirling cloudscapes around an imposing central Madonna and Child seated on a throne of golden light. The manner in which it was painted was a step on from the pictures in Connie's exhibition space, and owed a lot to the ceilings of southern Germany. But the modernity of the figures and their familiar everyday dress, freed from gravity and flying amongst the clouds, gave a strange surreal cast to the work. Also, strikingly breaking with the tradition of classical painting, both the central figures were completely naked, the child being breast-fed and held by the woman's left arm, while her right arm was raised in a gesture of command. Around this centrepiece and smaller in scale were figures clambering over the clouds or flying towards it and, falling down towards the spectator out of the heavenly light, were several other figures. These, like the central figures, were naked but were painted with a much darker, even sinister, cast than the others and illuminated from below by a red glow.

Brian thought it was certainly a stunning piece of work but what was it...? He looked at de Vere, standing with the rest of the delighted party around the podium, prominent amongst them being Elspeth Finer, embracing Connie warmly. Brian could hear her voice loudly commending Connie on the picture's feminist power. But Noel was oblivious to all this. His face was frozen in horror as he looked up at the picture. Brian examined it again. Oops! The figure in the middle, although her hair was now arranged differently, was unmistakably Dr. Robson's wife and - of course - she was the woman with the baby who had been greeted by Connie when he was chasing Spiller. That's torn it, he thought. He had soon identified the other figures as well: those climbing towards the light were the staff and Connnie's friends and those being cast out of heaven were unmistakably the Rector, Huggett, Ridley and various other of the damned he did not know.

"That one on the left with the big gut falling down looks just like my...Oh, bloody 'ell!" said a voice from the party he recognised as Audrey Reaper's. It was followed by a peal of laughter almost as raucous and nerve-jangling as Renee's.

By this time many of the spectators who knew the people in the picture had spotted its intention and Brian detected below the sounds of pleasure which still dominated, an ominous undertone of concern. He glanced round to pick up the rest of the staff's reactions amongst the crowd, and saw the nervous anxiety amongst them as they looked towards the VIP's and muttered to each other. Only Peter looked cheerful. Brian moved towards the podium. The Rector and Huggett were together still looking up at the picture. De Vere and Louie were conversing in rapid whispers out of the side of their mouths, and had moved away towards the rear of the podium. Brian tried to sidle inconspicuously past the Rector and Huggett to join them, but the Rector turned suddenly and saw him.

"Now that's what I call art," he said, flourishing a hand aloft.

"Oh," said Brian.

"Most definitely," said the Rector. "You can really see what that's about."

"Er. Yes, indeed," said Brian. From the corner of his eye, he saw De Vere's grimacing at him to get away. This time he was hissing and clawing the air.

"None of your daft performances about this - sticking arrows in people and such-like. Saw something like it at a conference in Germany once. Wurzburg."

"Ah. The Residenz. The famous ceiling. How clever of you to spot it." A bit of oil judiciously applied might keep his attention away from it. "Yes. I imagine its based on something like that," said Brian. He glanced up. "But its style is much more contemporary than Tiepolo, of course." A bit of academic sand in the eyes did no harm either.

Huggett joined in. "Plays the old Harry with a touch of arthritis in your neck, though, looking at it," he said rubbing it vigorously. "Don't I know you?" he said to Brian, aggresively.

"No," Brian replied quickly.

Huggett subsided and went on to the Rector: "Fine-looking lass that one, eh? With the baby. Who is she? One of the students?"

"I don't know. I believe she volunteered for it," said Brian, evenly. Jesus Christ, were they blind?

The Rector's wife joined them. She looked at Brian with a challenge in her eye. He knew now that she had recognised him earlier. Beyond her he could see de Vere, by this time making grimaces and clawing gestures of such vigour that Brian noticed the spectators near him were beginning to look at each other with concern. They probably thought he was having a seizure. In fact, even as he watched, one of them, Shaheen's consultant father, stepped forward and asked him if he was alright. De Vere almost gave him the hissing claw treatment but restrained it just in time. Near to de Vere and Louie, Brian saw that Connie was being congratulated by her

Brian detected below the sounds of pleasure, an ominous undertone of concern.

Fartista friends. He was glad about that for her; it would have been a pity to end her time at Brindling seen by them all as a cop-out aesthete.

"What do you think of it, dear?" said the Rector's wife to her husband. Her tone gave nothing away.

"Oh, an excellent piece of work. Excellent. A credit to the Polyechnic."

She smiled, more to herself than to him.

"Perhaps you should come back and take a longer look when it's quieter - with your glasses on." she said. The Rector looked embarrassed. Brian had the sudden insight that he was so vain, he refused to wear his glasses in public. Mentally, he breathed a sigh of relief in spite of the Rector's tetchy:

"I can see perfectly in a good light like this, as you know very well."

Brian looked up at the picture again. Not so well, he thought, that he could spot a very distinguishing pattern of moles included on the figure's lower belly. He would have to take a longer look himself to get all the detail and fun that Connie had put in. He laughed aloud as he saw two bearded figures, hand-in-hand, flying free of the clouds. One, ecstatically brandishing a memo in his free hand, was leading the other, who was asleep and cradled a pint of beer on his arm. He spotted a fond rendition of Louie, who had been given a halo, the only one in the picture, blessing a small assembly of kneeling students, but before he could pick out further detail, de Vere leapt onto the podium; he had obviously decided diversion was the best plan before the unveiling grew into a scandal. He flinched as a powerful camera flash went off in his face. It was the local press photographer.

"Oh Christ!" he shouted out.

This had, at least, the effect of diverting the crowd's attention away from the picture.

"I apologise. Sudden shock." He cleared his throat which Brian thought must have become almost completely congested by all that grimacing. "Ladies and gentlemen, we would like you all to come back later and enjoy our new ceiling when conditions are more - er - conducive to taking in its detail. Say, the day after tomorrow when we've had time to clear up a bit." Oh, you naughty fibber, thought Brian. You'll be up the ladder tomorrow, painting for all you're worth to bury the bodies, I'll bet. Nothing, not even Connie's work, was sacred enough to spoil the triumph of his Department. At least this will wake the 'sleeping beauty' of de Vere's painting talent at last. "For the moment we would like you all to accompany us to another spectacular show by one of our final year students - the first holder of our new Winslow Grish exchange scholarships with the USA, most generously funded by that distinguished artist who, I am happy to say, has graced us with his presence this evening." He led a round of applause as Winslow Grish, looking at his daughter and shaking his head with suppressed mirth, raised a deprecatory hand. "If you'll just follow me..."

He jumped down and strode vigorously through the crowd towards the exit. Bien joué, thought Brian, as the crowd began to stream after him. Brian hung on until only he, Marshall and Rita were left in the gallery.

"Aren't you going, Brian? " said Rita.

"I've already seen it," he said. He was studying the picture again, trying to fix the detail in his mind before it was altered, as he was sure it was going to be. (De Vere had always told him that whatever students did on the course actually belonged to the college and not to them, although this rule was rarely applied. This was going to be one of those times when it was.) He was also looking for something.

"I am right," said Marshall, "in what I think I'm seeing in this picture, aren't I?"

Brian looked at him cautiously. "Probably." he said. "Will you say anything to...?"

Marshall shrugged. "Not my business. I'm not there, am I? Truth to tell, I'm a bit disappointed about that.""

"Even if you were, I don't think you'd be there too long," Brian said.

"Who is that in the middle? She looks familiar," said Rita.

"Just a friend of Connie's," said Brian.

"Body's not bad," said Rita, implying it would just about do for an amateur. "Oh, here." She handed him a large stiff envelope. Brian opened it and took out an invitation to a wedding in a month's time.

He warmly congratulated both of them. "So you are going to Scarborough at last?" he said to her, eventually.

"No, the honeymoon's in the Seychelles." she said with a puzzled expression.

Brian thought this editing of the past must be catching.

He assured them that the show in the baths was worth seeing and decided to go with them. Leaving the gallery, he glanced for the last time at the painting. From this angle he finally saw what he was looking for. On a small cloud, standing alone next to a little tent, was a figure in a shabby suit, looking a bit like Montgomery Clift. It was facing away from the central figure holding a map in one hand and scratching its head in bewilderment with the other. Maybe he was the one who was shortsighted, he thought.

When they reached the swimming baths, most of the company had descended the steps and were queuing to get a glimpse through the peephole. Jenny was there talking with Grish and Moffatt to the local reporter and being photographed. The crowd was excited and admiring. Marshall and Rita decided that they would see it later. From the look they gave each other, Brian thought enviously, they had better ways of occupying their time, and they left. He was about to go down the steps when the journalists came up.

"Bloody good idea, that," said the photographer as he stood aside for them. "Pity I can't get a good shot of it." De Vere hurried over to Brian as he made to join the queue.

"What did he say?" he said

"Who? The reporter? Bloody good idea, he thought."

"Not him, you fool, the fu... The Rector, man."

"Nothing. He thinks it's wonderful."

"Are you sure?"

"Perfectly."

"Thank Christ for that," he said. "We can bless our lucky stars that they're all born in this town with total aesthetic anesthesia. I've told Ridley to lock up the gallery and bring me the key. You are sure, aren't you?"

"Yes. Although Marshall twigged it."

"Oh God."

"But he says it's none of his affair."

De Vere was joined by Peter.

"Another triumph for the sculpture section," he said.

"Don't you start," said de Vere pugnaciously. "I'm trying to get into a good mood again. You..."

But he was interrupted by a booming amplified voice which drowned all the noise.

"Hello folks!" it said in the manner of a game show host. "Are we all happy?" The crowd, thinking it was part of the show responded with a ragged "Yes", looking about at the same time to locate the voice.

"Can't hear you," boomed the voice. "ARE WE ALL HAPPY?"

"YES!" shouted the crowd.

"Oh Jesus, what the fuck now?" said de Vere.

"Well, you soon won't be," said the voice. The crowd laughed.

Julia Lee suddenly shouted and pointed:

"He up there. It's Ronnie!"

High up on the scaffolding above the installation, Ronnie could be seen outlined by the floodlights from below. He had the shouter in his hand and moved along the narrow planking catwalk to the edge of the scaffolding above the swimming bath. He seemed to be dressed in a long white robe. It had the word 'ART' painted on its front.

"Welcome to the most spectacular show of them all," he called through his megaphone. "THE HANGING OF ART' or 'THE TRIUMPH OF THE MANAGERS.'

"What's he doing? What's he doing?" said de Vere. "Where's Wladimir? Get him down from..."

"You all know that one of the most important parts of an art show is how its hung. Well, that's what this is all about. No pictures, just the hanging. See?"

He reached up and pulled a thick cord up from his neck.

"Oh my God!" said de Vere. "Ronnie, Ronnie, don't be a fool. Come down!" he called to him. "Come down, for God's sake!"

"I'll be down in a jiffy, wack. No problem."

Up to this point the crowd had not known how to take what Ronnie was up to, but the panic and alarm in de Vere's voice cued them. They set up a cry as the men shouted at him.

"Stop him! Stop him!"

"Too late!" shouted Ronnie. "And to all those who've said art is a waste of time, remember this is what the bastard grey men would like to do to us all and just remember it was me, Ronnie Oliver, that showed you what it means." He threw the megaphone into the water in the installation where it crackled as it shorted, and stepped to the edge of the catwalk. "The ultimate performance. All together now; one, two, three and 'ERE WE GO!'" he called out, and stepped off. Many of the women screamed and some fainted.

He fell, calling out the other two 'Ere we go's', and the two or three seconds seemed an eternity to Brian. The crowd held its breath as the rope followed him and tautened towards its end. But the sudden sickening jerk and crack when it had reached its limit, for which the crowd was waiting, were unfulfilled. Instead it simply stretched and, when Ronnie had nearly reached the floor of the bath, he was pulled up again. It was a bungee rope. Nor was it attached to his neck; that was another short rope Brian saw dangling from him. The bungee rope was attached to a harness under his shroud.

Suddenly Ronnie's apparently lifeless body moved and his head came up and he shouted:

"ILLUSION IS THE MOST IMPORTANT PART OF ART."

Wladimir started a little war dance beneath the rebounding Ronnie.

"That's my boy, that's my boy!" he shouted, and whirled round and round. The crowd began to laugh and the women revived. De Vere was beside himself with rage.

"Get him down, get him down! I'll really hang the silly young bugger! He's as sane as I am."

"Here, Brian." said Louie. "Jump-a up and catch-a him and cut-a the daft-a booger down." He handed Brian a retractable Stanley knife from one of his voluminous pockets. Brian took it and ran across the bath towards the gesticulating, bouncing figure, now laughing maniacally. At that moment, Ridley came into the building to hand de Vere the keys. He had his two dogs with him. The sight of Brian, jumping up and down trying to catch hold of Ronnie's feet, was too much for them. They gave a single joyful bark, pulled Ridley over the edge of the bath and broke away. Both dogs hit Brian square in the back. He shot forward and the Stanley knife plunged into the plastic of the installation and ripped it wide open. There was a moment before the water hit him in which Brian thought: Oh shit! Then a wall of water surged out as the rip was extended to the full length of the side by the pressure, and swept all before it to the deep end of the pool.

The water sloshed back and forth a few times carrying people, artificial flowers and luridly painted figures with it. When it finally allowed the people to regain their feet it was not very deep, fortunately, but it was still deep enough to swim in. Brian waded to the edge of the water with the guests, and students, their clothes now a sodden mass of finery. Here he was joined by Ronnie, who had freed himself from the harness and surveyed the scene with satisfaction.

"Après moi, le déluge, eh wack?" he said. "Hey, what say, you lot?" he shouted suddenly. "Let's all have a starkers swimming party before it drains out. 'Ere we go. 'Ere we go. 'Ere we go." And with this, he stripped off and plunged into the water.

In vain did the parents try to stop their offspring from joining him and soon the water was a seething mass of naked bodies, artificial plants and fibreglass South American Indians. The two dogs joined them barking excitedly and attacking the limbs of the dummies. Brian also saw Renee's little boy in with them as well. He shouted to his mother:

"Hey, our mam. I wanna be a artist an' all when I grow up!"

Renee plunged in to catch him. "Come outa there, yer little tyke," she said, grabbing him and clouting his bare backside.

Brian looked for de Vere. He saw him at the edge of the pool. He hadn't bothered to wade to the shallow part. He was still in the water but slumped against the side so that it came up to his neck, his hands covering his face and the back of his head gently banging against the tiles. The Rector had climbed out of the bath and stood above him on the side noisily getting his breath ready to begin his harangue when his blood pressure returned to normal. Brian waded towards him as the Rector gathered his strength but he was joined by wife before he got there. Her dark hair was now down onto her shoulders. He saw the Rector suddenly start as his wife's appearance struck a chord of recognition. He heard him say :

"You. In that picture. It was..."

But he heard no more; the splashing, laughing students covered his wife's remarks as she gently led him away.

Winslow Grish waded over to join Brian when he had reached de Vere.

"I don't suppose you'd consider putting that young man in for a scholarship as well, would you, Noel?"

De Vere uncovered his face; his eyes were glazed. "Take the silly fucker as far away from me and mine as possible," he said, and resumed his gentle head banging. Grish turned to Brian.

"Is he alright?"

Brian turned to de Vere.

"Are you alright, Noel?"

"Piss off and leave me alone," he said, from behind his hands.

"Yes. He's alright," said Brian.

Noel emerged from behind his hands again and spoke:

"And you can tell that silly sod from me that some kid at Leeds did the same thing back in the Sixties - only for real, before they cut him down in time. And you can also tell him as well that the most important part of art is truth and to fuck with illusion." With this, he replaced his hands once more and gently submerged until his long, dark hair was wafting to and fro in the ripples.

"My daughter thinks a lot of you, you know," said Grish, ignoring Noel's melodramatic exit. "I think it's probably you I've got to thank for depriving me of her."

"Sorry?" said Brian, who had been fascinatedly watching the bubbles Noel was producing.

"She thinks now that she might stay in Britain for a while," he said. "I think it's maybe not a bad idea, for her sake. But I'm certainly going to miss her."

Brian looked for her in the receding water. He knew that to see her like this was something he had longed for all term and now it was too late. Naked and leaping to catch one of the dummies' heads, a shaft of light spilling from the shredded installation caught her body which glowed momentarily. He gave a final regretful farewell to this vision and swallowed hard. It was just too bad but he was a teacher at heart. Louie would have been proud of him.

"Me too," he said.

"Well, it's been a pleasure to meet you, young man," Grish said, and stuck out his hand. Brian shook it. "If you're ever in the States, come and see me."

"Thank you."

Grish shook his head and grinned. "All this. It's too much, too much. Thank you."

Brian waded to the edge of the water and decided that it was probably time to slip away, either before Noel came to and remembered who had ripped the installation or actually did drown himself. He looked at the now limp plastic hanging down into the pool and caught sight of a movement inside. He pulled the rip apart and stepped in. It was Hermione. There was no water left inside and she was pulling up the debris and seemed to be searching for something.

"Have you lost anything?" he asked.

"Oh hello, Brian. Not exactly," she said.

"Can I help?"

"Ah!" she said. She bent down and picked something up from beneath an artificial palm leaf. As she did so her thin, soaked summer frock stretched and became see-through. Brian caught his breath; he always knew that susceptibility was his middle name but she really was a bonny woman.

"What is it?"

"The poor thing," she said. In her hand was the gaping and feebly flapping goldfish.

"Hold on," said Brian. He picked up one of the buckets filled with gravel which had held the artificial plants and emptied out its contents. He went to the water's edge to scoop some in. While he was bent down, Elspeth Finer came over to him and said:

"Wonderful evening. It will go down in the annals of art history. I shall write it up. It was a real privilege to be part of it. Thank you."

"You're welcome," said Brian. "Have a nice day."

"Now where is that man? Ah."

Carrying the bucket back to Hermione, he saw Elspeth wade into the water and pull the male model back in with her when he tried to climb out of the bath. She playfully dunked him. He also noticed a small crowd gathered round someone at the side of the bath. Shaheeen's father was amongst them, bending down and apparently administering the kiss of life to someone. Brian returned to the wrecked installation and Hermione popped the fish into the bucket. It began to swim vigorously.

"I'll take it home with me," she said.

"That was kind," said Brian. "To bother about the fish."

She shrugged. "I rather like fish," she said. "They don't make a lot of fuss about it."

"Look," said Brian suddenly, "what are your plans for this summer?"

"Well," she said, without looking up from the fish now settled down to its normal unfussy pace, "I was going to Italy with a friend but he... Never mind that, no plans now, really."

"You wouldn't like to come away with me, would you?"

"Oh, I don't..."

"You see," he went on quickly, "I seem to have won this daft raffle for two to go to Lourdes. I mean we needn't stay in Lourdes - unless you want to, of course. You might have something you'd like cured. But it is France, isn't it, even though Lourdes is the naffest place in the universe. Well, nearly. Oh, France! France! You beauty."

"Well..." she said doubtfully.

"Do say you'll come. Please."

"Look," she said, "why don't you give those Lourdes tickets to somebody who'd really appreciate them and we'll go under our own steam."

"Oh," he said. "That's a bit awkward, I'm afraid. You see I'm flat broke. Well, all but."

She smiled at him. It was a very good smile, wide and generous.

"I know. But we can go in my car - I'll get it across the Channel and you can pay what you can."

"Well..." It was his turn to sound doubtful.

"After all," she said lightly, "we might be sharing all sorts of things in future, mightn't we? You never know. Let's just try it and see how it goes, shall we?"

Brian matched her smile with a broad grin.

"Ok," he said, "you're on, mate. Look, would you like to come back to my place now and clean up?"

"No," she said, surprisingly firmly. "Can I say something quite personal to you?" she continued seriously.

Brian was surprised. Oh damn, he thought, perhaps she doesn't believe in sex before marriage or something. "Er. Of course. Yes. What is it?"

"There is no way I will ever come to your place - " Oh, God! thought Brian, deciding he had completely misread her smile. " - until you get rid of that dreadful wallpaper with those awful flamingoes on it."

She smiled at him again, and he at her as a little mystery cleared itself.

They looked down fondly at the goldfish. The bright lights flashed iridescent on its scales as it contentedly explored its new home.